Will these hou
happily-ever-aft
Prince Char
handso

AT HIS SERVICE:
CINDERELLA
HOUSEKEEPER

Three fabulous romances from favourite
authors: Fiona Harper, Melissa James
and Jennie Adams

Available in
July 2012

Available in
August 2012

Available in
September 2012

Available in
October 2012

Available in
November 2012

Available in
December 2012

AT HIS SERVICE:
CINDERELLA HOUSEKEEPER

FIONA
HARPER

MELISSA
JAMES

JENNIE
ADAMS

MILLS & BOON

Mills & Boon, an imprint of Harlequin (UK) Limited, Eton House, 18-24 Paradise Road, Richmond, Surrey TW9 1SR

AT HIS SERVICE: CINDERELLA HOUSEKEEPER
© Harlequin Enterprises II B.V./S.à.r.l. 2012

Housekeeper's Happy-Ever-After © Fiona Harper 2010
His Housekeeper Bride © Melissa James 2009
What's a Housekeeper To Do? © Jennie Adams 2010

ISBN: 978 0 263 90180 1

027-0712

Harlequin (UK) policy is to use papers that are natural, renewable and recyclable products and made from wood grown in sustainable forests. The logging and manufacturing processes conform to the legal environmental regulations of the country of origin.

Printed and bound in Spain
by Blackprint CPI, Barcelona

Housekeeper's Happy-Ever-After

FIONA
HARPER

As a child, **Fiona Harper** was constantly teased for either having her nose in a book or living in a dream world. Things haven't changed much since then, but at least in writing she's found a use for her runaway imagination. After studying dance at university, Fiona worked as a dancer, teacher and choreographer, before trading in that career for video-editing and production. When she became a mother she cut back on her working hours to spend time with her children, and when her littlest one started pre-school she found a few spare moments to rediscover an old but not forgotten love—writing.

Fiona lives in London, but her other favourite places to be are the Highlands of Scotland and the Kent countryside on a summer's afternoon. She loves cooking good food and anything cinnamon-flavoured. Of course she still can't keep away from a good book, or a good movie—especially romances—but only if she's stocked up with tissues, because she knows she will need them by the end, be it happy or sad. Her favourite things in the world are her wonderful husband, who has learned to decipher her incoherent ramblings, and her two daughters.

For Sian and Rose,
my darling girls, who I could never, ever forget.

CHAPTER ONE

ELLIE gave in to the insistent nagging at the fringes of her sleep and woke up. She focused on the display from the digital clock next to the bed.

Two-sixteen—and she needed to go to the bathroom. But it was her first night in an unfamiliar house and she didn't really want to be crashing around in the dark, even if she was the sole occupant.

She punched her pillow and flopped onto her other side, burying her head under the duvet. She could last. Clamping her eyes shut, she shifted position again, wriggling into the mattress. The seconds sloped by in the thick silence. She lay completely still, counting her heartbeats.

Apparently she couldn't last. Bother.

She blinked and tried to see where the outline of the door was in the blackness of the bedroom. The dull green glow from the alarm clock lit the duvet but not much more. The edge of the bed was about as inviting as the edge of a cliff.

Ellie Bond, get hold of yourself! A grown woman has no business being scared of the dark. Even in the kind of huge old house that looked as if it might have ghosts or bats in the attic.

She flung the duvet off and planted her feet firmly on the carpet, but hesitated for a couple of seconds before she stood up and inched towards the wall.

Ouch! Closer than she'd guessed.

Maybe she should have paid more attention when she'd dumped her cases in here, but she'd been so exhausted she'd only managed half her unpacking before she'd fallen into the large, squashy bed.

She rubbed her shoulder and felt along the wall for the door. It was a couple of steps to the left from her point of impact. The antique handle complained as she twisted it millimetre by millimetre. She winced and opened the door slowly and carefully. Why, she didn't know. It just seemed wrong to be too noisy in someone else's house late at night, even if they were away from home.

Ellie leant out of the doorway and slid the flat of her hand along the wall in search of the light switch.

Where was the stupid thing?

Certainly not within easy reach. But as she crept along the hallway the clouds parted and sent a sliver of moonlight through the half-open curtains at the end of the landing. Bingo! She could see the bathroom door, right next to the window. She padded more speedily along the wooden floor, her bare feet sticking to the layers of old varnish.

Relief swirled through her as she scrambled inside the bathroom and yanked the light cord. A few minutes later she opened the door and froze. The moonlight had evaporated and she was left standing in the pitch-dark.

Don't panic, Ellie. Think!

There had to be logical way to deal with this.

'Okay,' she whispered out loud, 'my room is the—' she counted on her fingers '—third on the left…I think.' All she had to do was feel for the doors and she would be back in that wonderfully comfortable bed in no time.

She tiptoed close to the wood panelling, letting her left fingers walk along the surface in search of door fames.

One…

Two…

She meant to creep slowly, but with each step her pulse increased, adding speed to her steps.

Three...

She opened the door and made a quick dash for the bed. Ever since she was a child she'd had an irrational fear that some shadowy figure underneath would grab her ankles when she got close. She'd even perfected a sprint and dive manoeuvre in her teenage years. She decided to resurrect it now.

Big mistake.

She tripped over a discarded shoe and stumbled into a solid wall of...something.

It was warm. And breathing.

Oh, heck.

There was somebody in the house! A burglar, or an axe-wielding maniac...

Her brain short-circuited. Too much information at once. Too much to process. Thankfully, more primal instincts took over. She backed away, hoping she hadn't got muddled and that the door was still directly behind her. But she hadn't made more than two steps when a large, strong hand grabbed her wrist.

Ellie's stomach somersaulted and she froze. Without even thinking about why or how, she lunged at him, whoever he was, and shoved the heel of her hand under his chin, causing him to grunt and stumble backwards.

Mother, I will never moan about the self-defence classes you made me go to in the village hall again!

In the surreal slow-motion moment that followed, she wondered why a burglar would be bare-chested in March, but before the thought was fully formed in her head his other arm grabbed her and he fell, taking her with him. She came crashing down on top of him, and then they lay winded in a tangle of arms and legs on the floor.

Here, he had the advantage. She didn't know how, but she could sense he was taller than her, and if the chest she'd just landed on was anything to go by he had five times as many muscles. Somehow as they'd fallen they'd twisted, and she was now partly pinned underneath him, her legs trapped. She started to wriggle.

I should have paid more attention at those classes, instead of gossiping at the back with Janice Bradford.

Because the man obviously had no intention of letting her loose. In one swift movement he flipped her onto her back, his hands clamping both her wrists and digging them into the scratchy wool rug while his knees clamped her thighs together. The air left Ellie's body with an 'oof' noise.

She flailed and struggled, but it was like trying to dislodge a lump of granite. Eventually she lay still beneath him, every muscle rigid. His toothpaste-scented breath came in short puffs, warming the skin of her neck. Panic fluttered in her chest.

It dawned on her that her original assumption that he was a burglar might be a tad optimistic. Things could be about to get a lot worse.

She had to act now—before he made his next move.

In a moment of pure instinct, she lifted her head and sank her teeth into the smooth skin of his shoulder. Then, while he was yelping in pain, she used every bit of strength in her five-foot-five frame to rock him to her left, getting him off-balance and thereby gaining enough momentum to swing him back in the other direction. The plan was to fling him off her so she could escape.

The plan was flawed.

He tumbled over, all right, but as she tried to crawl away he got hold of her right foot and dragged her back towards him. Ellie tried to stop herself by twisting over and clawing at the rug, but large tufts just came away in her fingers. And then she realised she was travelling further than she'd scurried away. She was being dragged back towards the bed.

That was when she started shouting. A wave of white-hot anger swept up her body.

How dared he?

'Get out of my bedroom!' she screamed. 'Or I'll—'
'*What?*'

He was angry, but there was something more in his voice—confusion?

Harsh light flooded the room, accompanied by the click of a switch. Ellie peeled her face off the carpet and blinked a few times, desperate to focus on anything that might give her a clue as to where the door was. Her eyes began to adjust, and she made out a tall figure against the pale blue of the wall.

Pale blue? Oh, help! My room is a kind of heritage yellow colour.

She crinkled her eyelids until they were almost shut, and swivelled her head to face her attacker. Through the blur of her eyelashes she saw a pair of deep brown eyes staring at her. There was something about them... Had she dreamt about a pair of eyes just like that before she'd woken up? Half a memory was lodged somewhere, refusing to make sense.

Ellie's chest reverberated with the pounding of her heart and she felt the fire wash up her face and settle in the tips of her ears. He looked as astonished as she felt.

She *had* seen those eyes before, but not in her dreams. They hadn't been scowling then, but laughing, *twinkling*...

Ellie let out a noise that was part groan, part whimper as the memory clunked into place. She started to collect her limbs together and move away.

'I'm...I'm...so sorry! I got lost in the dark...' She shot a glance at him, but his face was still etched with confusion. 'I mean, I thought you were a—a maniac.'

He blinked. Something told her his assessment of her hadn't been dissimilar.

'Mr Wilder... I...'

'I know who I am. Who on earth are *you*?'

She licked her lips—they seemed to have dried out completely—and cleared her throat. 'I'm Ellie Bond, your new housekeeper.'

One month earlier

Ellie's limbs stopped working the moment she crossed the threshold of the coffee shop. The woman in the red coat was early. She wasn't supposed to be here yet, but there she was, sitting at a table and reading a newspaper. After a few seconds the door swung closed behind Ellie, hitting her on the bottom. She didn't even flinch, mainly because she felt as if she'd swallowed a thousand ice cubes and they were now all jostling for position as they slowly melted, spreading outwards through her body.

The woman's long dark hair almost touched the tabletop as she bent over an absorbing story. Chunky silver earrings glinted in her ears when she flicked her hair out of the way so she could turn the page. Earrings that Ellie had given her for her last birthday.

The woman hadn't noticed Ellie yet, and she was glad about that. She stared harder. Perhaps if she just stood here for a moment, took her time, it would come to her.

Something the woman was reading must have bothered her, because she stiffened and, even though her head was bowed, Ellie knew that three vertical lines had just appeared above the bridge of the woman's nose. That always happened when she frowned. When people had been friends for more than a decade, they tended to notice little things like that about each other without even realising it. The brain collected a scrapbook about a person, made up of assorted images, sensations, sounds and aromas, all of which could be called up at a moment's notice. And Ellie had plenty of those memories flooding into the front of her consciousness right now—untidy college bedrooms, the smell of dusty books in the library, the giggles of late-night gossip sessions…

A fact that only made the current situation more galling.

Ellie couldn't remember her name.

Since the accident, finding the right name or word had

become like rummaging around in the cupboard under the stairs without a torch. She knew the information she wanted was in her brain somewhere, but she was fumbling in the dark, not really knowing what she was looking for and just hoping she'd recognise it when she finally laid hold of it.

A waitress bustled past her, and the movement must have alerted her friend to the person standing at the edge of her peripheral vision, because she looked up from her newspaper and smiled at Ellie.

Ellie waved back, but behind her answering smile she was running through the letters of the alphabet, just as she'd been taught at the support group, to see if any of them jogged her memory.

Anna? Alice? Amy?

The woman stood up, beaming now, and Ellie had no choice but to start walking towards her.

Belinda? No.

Brenda?

The chunky earrings bobbed as her friend stood and drew her into a hug. Ellie just stood there for a moment like a rag doll, and then she made a conscious decision to contract her arm muscles and squeeze back. Not that she was opposed to hugging; it was just that her brain was far too busy ferreting around for the right letter, the right syllable, to get her started.

Christine…Caroline…Carly?

Carly. It seemed right and not right at the same time.

A whisper tickled her ear. 'It's so good to see you, Ellie!'

Ellie knew her friend would understand if she just admitted her memory blank. But Ellie was fed up with being *understood*. She just wanted to *be*—to live her life the way everyone else did, without the sympathetic glances. That was why she'd arranged this meeting in the first place.

A familiar sensation washed over her. She imagined it to be what it might feel like if portions of her memory were buoys, chained to a deep and murky ocean floor, and then all of a sudden one freed itself and floated upwards, arriving on the surface with a plop.

Charlotte Maxwell.

'Hi, Charlie,' she said, and finally relaxed into the hug. 'It's good to see you too.'

She tried not to, but as she pulled away and sat down Ellie sighed, deep and hard. Charlie tilted her head and looked at her.

'How are you?'

Ah. How innocent that phrase sounded. How kind and well-meaning.

Ellie had come to hate it. People were always asking her that, normally wearing a concerned expression. Oh, she wasn't fooled a bit. It wasn't small talk. Chit-chat. What people wanted from her when they asked that question was a full psychological and medical rundown.

She smiled, but her lips remained firmly pressed together. 'I'm great. Really.'

Charlie kept staring at her. 'Still getting the headaches?'

'Only occasionally,' she replied, shrugging the observation away.

The wicked twinkle returned to Charlie's eyes as she stood back and looked Ellie up and down. 'You've had your hair cut,' she said.

Ellie automatically raised a hand to feel the blunt ends of her tousled blonde curls. She'd only had it done a few days ago, and she still wasn't used to finding fresh air where there had once been heavy ringlets that reached halfway down her back. The ends now just brushed the tops of her shoulders. It was shorter, maybe a bit younger, and a heck of a lot more manageable.

'I was ready for a change,' she said.

Change.

That was why she was here. She might as well get down to business and ask Charlie the question that had been burning her tongue all morning. If she didn't do it soon she was likely to get distracted and end up going home without mentioning it at all. She opened her mouth to speak.

'I don't know about you,' Charlie said in a grave voice, 'but I can't be expected to indulge in a month's worth of gossip without a side order of caffeine—and possibly a muffin or three. It's just not done.'

Ellie glanced over at the counter then stood up.

'I'll have a…'

Oh, flip. What was the word? She knew she knew it, but it seemed to be speeding away from her, like a dream that was fast evaporating with the last traces of sleep.

'You know…the fluffy, milky drink with powder on top.'

Charlie didn't bat an eyelid, bless her. 'Two cappuccinos, please,' she said to the barista.

Ellie leaned forward and looked at the girl over Charlie's shoulder. 'And a chocolate muffin, please.'

'Make that two.' Charlie turned and smirked at her while the barista rang up the sale. 'That's my girl. Couldn't forget chocolate if you tried.'

If her mother or her sister had said something like that Ellie would have snapped at them, but she found herself laughing at Charlie's sideways comment. Maybe she was too sensitive these days. And she'd wound herself up into a state about meeting Charlie before she'd even got here. No wonder her memory was malfunctioning. It always got worse when she was stressed or nervous.

Charlie understood. She made Ellie's 'condition' seem like no big deal. That one positive thought gave her confidence. She was going to ask her. She was ready.

But the first cappuccinos had been drained and the second round ordered before Ellie finally worked up her nerve. She twiddled the silver locket she always wore between her thumb and forefinger.

'Actually, Charlie, there was a reason I suggested getting together this morning. I need a favour.'

'Anything. You know that.' Charlie leaned forward and rubbed her forearm. 'I'll do anything I can to help.'

Ellie took at deep breath. She was asking for a lot more than the usual sympathetic ear or moral support at social functions. A lot more.

'I need a job.'

Charlie just seemed to freeze. She blinked a couple of times. 'A job?'

Ellie squeezed her bottom lip between her teeth and gave a little nod, but Charlie broke eye contact and took her time while she folded a corner of the newspaper page into a neat triangle. She glanced up once she'd scored it with a long, red fingernail.

'I'm sorry, Ellie. I only need a couple of people in the office, and I've got all the staff I require at the moment.'

Oh, fab. Charlie thought she was asking her for a pity job—one with minimum responsibilities and no challenges. But Ellie couldn't give up now. She was desperate. She stopped fiddling with her locket and folded her hands in her lap.

'No. I mean I want you to put me on your agency's books, preferably for a job where I can live in. I need to…get away from Barkleigh for a while. You must have something I could do? Something that uses my skills? You know I'm a fantastic cook.'

Charlie nodded and said nothing, but Ellie could see her mind working. She made a rather nice living running an exclusive little agency providing the well-off with domestic staff—from butlers and chauffeurs to cooks and nannies.

'But are you…? Can you…?' Charlie wrinkled her nose and paused.

Ellie knew what she was trying to ask, what she really didn't want to put into words. Was the patched-up and rehabilitated Ellie capable of holding down a full-time job? The truth was, Ellie wasn't even sure herself. She thought she was. She'd worked hard to put strategies and coping mechanisms in place to help with the memory and concentration problems that were so common after a serious head injury, but she was shaking in her boots at the idea of moving away from everything familiar and starting again somewhere new.

'I just have to work a little bit harder than everyone else at keeping myself organised nowadays. But I can do this, Charlie. I know I can. I just need someone to believe in me and give me a chance, and you said you'd do anything you can to help.'

Okay, that was playing dirty, but she was desperate. The pained look on Charlie's face was almost too much to bear. She wasn't convinced. And if Ellie had been in her shoes maybe she wouldn't have been either.

For a long time Charlie said nothing, and Ellie thought she might be creating brand-new wrinkles on her forehead with all the mental wrestling she was doing. Then, slowly, the lines faded.

'Okay,' she said, staring out of the window. 'I just might have something. I'll let you know.'

The cottage door slammed. There was something very final about the sound of the old door hitting the door frame. Ellie tried to remove the key from the worn Victorian lock, but it refused to budge.

Today was not going well. Lost keys, a case that wouldn't shut and a pigeon stuck in the roof had already plagued her this morning. If she had been one to believe in bad omens she'd have run upstairs and hidden under her duvet a few hours ago. But the duvet was freshly laundered, waiting for someone else, and the rest of her life had been divided into packing boxes and suitcases. The cottage was now bare of all personal possessions, ready to be rented out by the week. The holiday lettings company had jumped at the chance of a child-friendly property in the picturesque little village of Barkleigh. Other families would build memories here now.

She caught the tip of her tongue between her teeth and resumed her negotiations with the lock. The choreographed sequence of turns, pulls and twists had long ago become a matter of muscle memory rather than conscious thought, and finally the key jerked free. It always did in the end. It just needed a little gentle persuasion.

It was time to leave. Ellie shoved her keys in the back pocket of her jeans and stared through the stained glass panels that filled the top half of the heavy old door. Once, the hallway had been warm and inviting, filled with discarded shoes, coats hanging haphazardly on a row of hooks. Now it was cold and empty, distorted through the rippling glass.

A large drop of rain splashed onto the top of her head. She shuddered, picked up the last piece of luggage, then turned and walked down the path towards her waiting car.

Ellie looked out across the fields. An overstuffed dark grey cloud was devouring the sunshine, heading straight towards her. Another plop of rain dropped on the back of her neck and ran down between her shoulder blades. She increased her speed. The boot of her old hatchback stood gaping and she slung the holdall in the back, slammed the door shut and hurried round to the driver's door. The tempo of the rain increased. By the time she was inside it was drumming an unpromising rhythm on the roof of the car. Warm, earthy smells drifted through the ventilation system.

She glanced at the handbag sitting on the passenger seat. Poking out of the top was a worn blue teddy bear with one eye and bald ears where the fluff had been loved off. The backs of her eyes burned, but she refused to blink, knowing that any moisture leaking over her lashes would feel like acid. The pummelling on the roof of the car magnified, filling her ears and pulling the world away from her down a long, invisible tunnel.

Not now. Today of all days I need to keep it together.

She forced herself to sit upright in the driver's seat and stared blindly into the blurry grey scenery beyond the windscreen, then turned the key in the ignition. The car rumbled grudgingly to life, coughed once, and promptly stalled.

Still she didn't blink, just held her breath for a few seconds, then reached out to stroke the dashboard.

Come on, girl! Don't let me down now.

She pumped the gas a few times and tried again, and when the engine rewarded her with an uneven purr, she released her breath and put the car into gear. She pulled away slowly, rumbling down the country lane, and didn't allow herself the luxury of looking back.

An hour later she was sitting behind a caravan on the motorway. It was only going at about fifty, but she made no attempt to pass it. This speed was fine, thank you very much. Driving wasn't her favourite occupation these days, and she hadn't been on a motorway in a long time. She distracted herself from the haulage trucks passing her at insane speeds with thoughts of fresh starts and new jobs.

Everyone had been so happy when she'd come out of hospital after the accident, sure she was going to be 'back to normal' in no time. And after a year, when she'd finally moved out of her parents' house and back into the cottage, her family and friends had breathed a collective sigh of relief.

That was it. Everything done and dusted. Ellie is all better and we can stop worrying now.

But Ellie wasn't all better. Her hair might have grown again and covered the uneven scars on her skull, she might even talk and walk the same, but nothing, *nothing*, would ever be the same again. Underneath the 'normal' surface she was fundamentally different and always would be.

She focused on the droplets of rain collecting on the windscreen.

Water. That was all those tiny splashes were. Almost nothing, really. So how could something so inconsequential alter the course of three lives so totally, so drastically? She nudged the lever next to the steering wheel again and the specks of water vanished in a flurry of motion.

Thankfully, within a few minutes the rain had stopped

completely and she was able to slow the squeaking wipers to a halt. Warm afternoon light cut clean paths through the clouds. Her shoulder blades eased back into their normal position and she realised she'd been clenching her teeth from the moment she'd put her foot on the accelerator. She made a conscious effort to relax her jaw and stretched her fingers. The knuckles creaked, stiff from gripping the steering wheel just a little too tightly.

A big blue sign was up ahead and she read it carefully.

Junction Eight. Two more to go.

She'd promised herself that she would not zone out and sail past the turn-off. Getting lost was not an option today.

The caravan in front slowed until it was practically crawling along. Ellie glanced in her wing mirror. She could overtake it if she wanted to. The adjacent lane was almost clear. Still, it took her five minutes and a stiff lecture before she signalled and pulled out.

She was still concentrating on remembering to exit at Junction Ten, visualising the number, burning it onto her short-term memory, when a prolonged horn blast startled her. A car loomed large in her rear-view mirror. It inched closer, until their bumpers were almost touching, its engine snarling. Ellie was almost frightened enough to speed up to give herself breathing room. Almost.

Flustered, she grabbed at the levers round the steering wheel for the indicator, only to discover she'd turned the fog light on instead. She fought to keep her breathing calm, yanked at the correct lever and pulled into the inside lane. What she now realised was a sleek Porsche zoomed past in a bright red blur.

A sigh of relief was halfway across her lips when the same car swerved in front of her. She stamped on the brake and glared at the disappearing number plate, retaliating by pressing her thumb on the horn for a good five seconds, even though the lunatic driver was now a speck in the distance, too far away to hear—or care.

It had to be a man. Too caught up in his own ego to think about anyone else. Pathetic. She had made a policy to keep her distance from that type of person, whether he was inside a low-slung car or out of it.

She shook her head and returned her concentration to the road, relieved to see she was only two miles from the next service station. An impromptu caffeine break was in order.

It wasn't long before she was out of the car and sitting in an uncomfortable plastic seat with a grimy mug of coffee on the table in front of her. She cupped her hands round it and let the heat warm her palms.

The crazy Porsche driver had flustered her, brought back feelings and memories she had long tried to evade. Which on the surface seemed odd, because she couldn't even remember the accident itself.

But perhaps it was better not to have been conscious as they'd cut her from the wreckage of the family car, the bodies of her husband and daughter beside her. Not that her battered memory didn't invent images and torture her with them in the depths of the night.

She had no clear memories of the beginning of her hospital stay either. The doctors had told her this was normal. Post-traumatic amnesia. When she tried to think back to that time it was as if a cloud had settled over it, thick and impenetrable.

Sometimes she thought it would be nice to lose herself in that fog again, because emerging from it, scarred and confused, to find her lovely Sam and her darling eight-year-old Chloe were gone for ever had been the single worst moment of her existence.

All because it had rained. And because two boys in a fast car hadn't thought that important. They'd been arrogant, thinking those little drops of *almost nothing* couldn't stop them, couldn't spoil their fun.

She looked down at her coffee. The cup was empty, but she didn't remember drinking it.

Just as well.

Brown scum had settled at the bottom of the cup. Ellie shook off a shudder and patted down her unruly blonde curls, tucking the ends of the long fringe behind her ears. She couldn't sit here all day nursing an empty cup of coffee. But moving meant getting back in the car and rejoining the motorway. Something she wanted to do even less now than she had when she'd left home this morning. She closed her eyes and slowly inflated her lungs.

Come on, Ellie. The only other option is admitting defeat and going back home to hibernate for ever. You can do this. You have to. Staying at the cottage is eating you alive from the inside out. You're stagnating.

She opened her eyelids, smoothed her T-shirt down over her jeans, swung her handbag out from underneath the table and made a straight line for the exit.

Back on the road, her geriatric car protested as she reached the speed limit. She filtered out the rattling and let the solitude of the motorway envelop her. She wasn't thinking of anything in particular, but she wasn't giving her attention to the road either. Her mind was in limbo—and it was wonderful.

The sun emerged from the melting clouds and flickered through the tops of the trees. She flipped the visor down to shield her eyes. The slanting light reflected off the sodden carriageway and she peered hard at the road, struggling to see the white lines marking the lanes.

In fact, she was concentrating so hard she failed to notice the motorway sign on the grassy verge to her left.

Junction Ten.

CHAPTER TWO

WHEN she finally arrived, her new workplace was a bit of a surprise. Big shots like her new boss normally wanted their homes to shout out loud how rich and grand their owners were. Yet as she drove up the sweeping gravel drive and the woodland parted to reveal Larkford Place, she discovered a small but charming sixteenth-century manor house surrounded by rhododendrons and twisting oaks. The mellow red bricks were tinted gold by the rays of the setting sun, and the scent of lavender was thick in the air after the rain. The house was so much a part of its surroundings she could almost imagine it had grown up together with the ancient wisteria that clung to its walls.

For the first time since she'd decided to escape from her life she felt something other than fear or desperation. It was beautiful here. So serene. Hope surged through her—an emotion she hadn't experienced in such a long time that she'd assumed it must have been wiped clear of her damaged memory banks with everything else.

The drive swelled and widened in front of the house, a perfect place to park cars. But this wasn't where she was stopping—oh, no. It was the lowly tradesmen's entrance for her. She changed gear and followed a narrower branch of the drive round the side of the house and into a cobbled courtyard. The old stables still had large glossy black doors, and

Ellie admired the wrought-iron saddle rest that was bolted to the wall as she got out of her car and gave her legs a stretch.

Once out of the car, she stood motionless in the courtyard and stared at the ivy framing the back door. Wind rippled through it, making it shiver. With measured steps she approached it, pulling the key she'd picked up from the previous housekeeper out of her pocket, then sliding it into the old iron lock. She pushed the wooden door open and peered down a dark corridor.

The excitement she'd felt only moments ago drained away rapidly, gurgling in her stomach as it went. This threshold was where yesterday and tomorrow intersected. Crossing it felt final, as if by taking that step other doors in her life would slam shut and there would be no return.

But that was what she wanted, wasn't it? To move forward? To leave the past behind?

She willed her right leg to swing forward and make the first step, and once she'd got that over with she marched herself down the corridor, her footsteps loud and squeaky on the flagstones, announcing her decision and scaring any ghosts away.

A door led to a bright spacious kitchen, with a pretty view of the garden through pair of French windows on the opposite side of the room.

Ellie turned on her heels and took a better look at the place that would be her domain from now on. It was a cook's dream. The house had been newly renovated, and she'd been told the kitchen fitters had only finished last week. The appliances looked as if they'd walked straight out of a high-end catalogue. They even smelled new.

A long shelf along one wall held a row of pristine cookery books. She wandered over to them as if suddenly magnetised. *Ooh.* She'd been eyeing this one in her local bookshop only last week…

Without checking her impulse, she hooked a finger on the top of the binding and eased it off the shelf. She had plenty of time to explore the house—almost a whole week—before her new boss arrived home from his overseas trip. The wall planner and the sticky notes could come out tomorrow, when her brain was in better shape to make sense of all these unfamiliar sights and sounds. Right now she needed to rest. It had been a long and tiring day and she deserved a cup of tea and a sit-down. She opened the book and flicked a few pages. It was legitimate research, after all…

It didn't take long to locate the kettle, the teabags and even a packet of chocolate digestives. While she waited for the water to boil she wandered round the kitchen, inspecting it more closely. What was that under the wall cabinet? It looked like a…

Oh, cool. A little flatscreen TV that flipped down and swivelled in any direction you wanted. She pressed the button on the side and a crisp, bright picture filled the screen—a teatime quiz show. She'd work out how to change channels later. For now it was just nice to have some colourful company in the empty house, even if the acid-voiced presenter was getting rather personal about a contestant who wasn't doing very well.

She made her tea and hoisted herself onto one of the stools at the breakfast bar, the cookery book laid flat in front of her, and started dunking biscuits into her mug before sucking the chocolate off. Nobody was here to catch her, were they?

Now, what could she cook Mr Big Shot for dinner on his first night back? It had to be something impressive, something to make him want to hire her permanently when the three-month trial period was up.

Ellie suspected she wouldn't have been offered the job if the man in question hadn't been a) Charlie's cousin and b) desperate for someone to start as soon as possible. Her new boss was something big in the music industry, apparently. She thought the name had sounded vaguely familiar, but she really didn't keep up to date with that sort of thing any more.

Her oldest friend, Ginny, had actually seemed impressed

when Ellie had made the announcement about her new job. She'd gushed and twittered and gone on about how lucky Ellie was. Ellie hadn't stopped her, glad that Ginny had been too distracted to ask any difficult questions about the *real* reason for Ellie's sudden need to uproot herself from her comfortable little life and flee.

But she wasn't going to think about that at the moment. For once she was grateful for her brain's tendency to flit onto a new subject without a backward glance, and turned her whole attention to the colourful book on the counter in front of her.

Now, was squid-ink pasta really as stupendous as those TV chefs made out? Or did they just use it because it made the pictures in their glossy cookbooks look good?

The cooking part of the job would be fun. She'd always enjoyed it, and had even taken a few courses at the local adult education college to hone her techniques before Chloe had been born. In the last couple of years it had become almost an obsession. But obsessions were something she could excel in these days, and since she'd been out of the workforce and had a lot of time on her hands it had been a perfect way to keep herself occupied. Funnily, it was the one skill she seemed to have clung on to without any deficit since the accident. She didn't know why. Perhaps that knack of combining flavours and textures was held in a different part of the brain—one that hadn't been shaken and swollen and bruised as the car had rolled and crumpled around her.

There it was again, that feeling that the world was retreating, leaving her in an echoey bubble all on her own. Her fingers automatically found her locket while she tried to distract herself with the book. Initially the print blurred and the pictures refused to stay in focus, but she blinked twice and forced her eyes to work in unison, and eventually everything slid back to normal.

The television was still on low in the background and Ellie glanced at it. The quiz show she'd had half an ear on was over and something else had started. It looked like some red carpet thing that was obviously going to clog up the TV schedule for the rest of the evening. An eager reporter in a low-cut top clutched her microphone and tried not to let on she was shivering in the brisk March wind.

Just then a graphic flashed up at the bottom of the screen. Ellie did a double-take, then lurched forward in an effort to get closer to the television—anything to help her unscramble the images swarming up her optic nerve and into her brain.

'That's—that's him!'

The book lay on the counter, forgotten, and her finger, which had been scanning a list of ingredients, now hovered uselessly in mid-air. She jumped off the stool, walked over to the little TV and used that very same finger to drum on the volume button.

'*Mark Wilder*', the caption at the bottom of the screen said.

Her new boss.

Crumbs, she could see why Ginny had gone all twittery now. He certainly was very good-looking, all ruffled dark hair and perfect teeth. Not that those things really mattered when it came down to forging a long-lasting relationship. Nice dental work amounted to nothing if the man in question turned out to be a shallow, self-centred waste of space. She was much more interested in what a man was like on the inside.

She looked at Mark Wilder again, *really* looked at him. He was about the same age as her. Mid-thirties? Possibly older if he was aging well—and, let's face it, his sort usually did. But who was he beneath the crisp white shirt and the designer suit? More importantly, what would he be like to work for? She stood, hands on hips, and frowned a little. When Charlie had phoned to offer this position she'd been too excited that her plan was coming to fruition to think much about her future employer. He'd been more of an escape route than a person, really.

Suddenly a woman slid into shot beside him—early twenties, gravity-defying bust and attire that, if it stretched in the wash, might *just* qualify as a dress.

Ellie sighed.

Oh, he was *that* kind of man. How disappointing.

The reporter in the cleavage-revealing top didn't seem to be bothered, though. She lurched at him from behind the metal barrier. 'Mr Wilder! Melissa Morgan from Channel Six!'

Oh, yes. That was her name.

This should be interesting. From what Ellie remembered, this woman had a reputation for asking awkward questions, being a little bit sassy with her interviewees. It made for great celebrity soundbites. You never knew what juicy little secrets she might get her victims to accidentally reveal.

Wilder spotted the reporter and strode over to her, his movements lean and easy. In the crowd, a couple of hundred pairs of female eyes swivelled to track his progress. Except, ironically, those of his girlfriend. She was looking straight at the camera lens.

Even the normally cool reporter was fawning all over him. Not that Wilder seemed to mind. His eyes held a mischievous twinkle as he waited for her to ask her question.

'Pull yourself together, woman!' Ellie mumbled as she brushed biscuit crumbs off the cookery book with the side of her hand.

Melissa Morgan blushed and asked her question in a husky voice. 'Are you confident your newest client, Kat De Souza, will be picking up the award for best female newcomer this evening?'

Go on, Ellie silently urged. Prove me wrong. Be charming and gracious and modest.

He increased the wattage on his smile. The reporter looked as if she was about to melt into a puddle of pure hormones.

'I have every confidence in Kat,' he said in a warm, deep voice, appearing desperately serious. But then his eyes did that twinkly thing again. 'Of course, having superior management doesn't hurt.'

How did he do that? Special eye drops?

Of course the reporter fell for it. She practically tripped over her own tongue as she asked the next question. Wilder, in turn, lapped up the attention, deliberately flirting with her—well, maybe not flirting, exactly, but he had to be doing *something* to make her go all giggly like that.

Ellie reached for another digestive without taking her eyes off the television, and knocked the packet onto the floor. The man seemed to be enjoying the fact that a couple of million viewers were catching every second of his very public ego massage. And what was even more annoying was that he batted each of the reporter's questions away with effortless charm, never losing his cool for an instant.

There was no end to the reporter's gushing. 'I'm sure you are not surprised to discover that, due to your success as one of the top managers in the recording industry today, *Gloss!* magazine has named you their most eligible bachelor in their annual list.'

He clasped his hand to his chest in mock surprise. 'What? *Again!*'

Oh, great. Self-deprecating as well as shy and retiring. This guy was going to be a blast to work for. Just as well Charlie had said he spent the greater part of the year travelling or in endless meetings.

He stopped smiling and looked deep into the reporter's eyes. 'Well, somebody had better just hurry up and marry me, then.' He looked around the crowd. The grin made an encore. 'Anyone interested?'

The reporter blushed and stuttered. Was it just Ellie's imagination, or was she actually considering vaulting the barrier? And Ellie didn't think she was the only one. Something about the scene reminded her of a Sunday night nature programme she'd seen recently—one about wildebeest. A stampede at this moment was almost inevitable.

She flapped her book closed, ignoring the puff of crumbs that flew into the air, and let out a snort.

The reporter stopped simpering and suddenly smoothed her hair down with her free hand. Her spine straightened. About time too, Ellie thought. This woman was supposed to be a professional. How embarrassing to catch yourself acting like that on national television.

This time when she fired her question, the reporter's voice was cool and slow. 'Was it hard to rebuild your career after such…*difficult* beginnings, both in your professional and personal life?'

Her face was a picture of sympathy, but the eyes glittered with a hint of ice. Ellie almost felt a tremor of sympathy for him. But not quite.

Something other than lazy good humour flashed in Mark Wilder's eyes.

'Thanks for the good wishes.' He paused as his stare hardened and turned to granite. 'Good evening, Ms Morgan.' And then he just turned and walked away.

The reporter's jaw slackened. It was as if she'd been freeze-framed by her own personal remote control and all she could do was watch him stride away. The camera shook a little, then panned to include Mr Wilder's companion. Miss Silicone pouted a smile and trotted after her man, leaving the floundering reporter to find another celebrity to fill the gaping space in front of her microphone. She turned back to the cameraman, looking more than a little desperate, and then the picture cut to a long shot of the red carpet.

Ellie shook her head, punched the button on the side of the TV and flapped it back into place under the cabinet. She was starting to fear that this whole new job idea was one of the random impulses that had plagued her since the accident— just another one of her brain's little jokes.

She tucked the cookery book under her arm and tossed the empty biscuit packet in the direction of the bin. It missed.

With a few long strides Mark put as much distance as he could between himself and the trouble his smart mouth had caused him. Flashguns zapped at him from every direction. Suddenly his expensive suit seemed really flimsy. No protection at all, really.

He'd been bored enough to welcome the devilish urge to tease Melissa Morgan, but he'd forgotten that behind the batting eyelashes was an intelligent reporter—one who didn't hesitate to go for the jugular where a morsel of celebrity gossip was concerned. She'd done a number on quite a few of his firm's clients in recent years, and the opportunity for a little payback had just been too tempting. But it had backfired on him, hadn't it? The story he'd wanted her to focus on tonight was Kat and her award nomination, not his own less-than-glorious past.

He glanced at the crowd bulging against the barriers as he overtook an up-and-coming British actress in a long, flowing gown. He should be loving every second of this. It was the life he'd always worked for. What most people sitting in front of their TVs with their dinners on their laps dreamed of—red carpets, beautiful women, fast cars, exotic locations, more cash than they knew what to do with…

So what was wrong with him?

He shook his head to clear the baying of the photographers, the screaming of the crowd, and became aware of determined footsteps behind him.

Oh, heck. Melodie. Ms Morgan must have got him more rattled than he'd thought. He gave himself a mental slap for his lack of chivalry and turned and waited for her. She was only a few paces behind him, and as she came level with him he placed a guiding hand on her elbow.

Melodie's agent had called his PA a couple of weeks ago and asked if he would like to meet her. This was what the love lives of the rich and famous had come to. Relationships were practically conducted in the third person. *My people will call your people…*

He didn't normally respond to requests like this, but he'd

needed a date tonight at short notice, and Melodie was young, sexy and stunning—just the sort of woman he was expected to have on his arm at a bash like this. It didn't matter that he suspected she didn't have any romantic yearnings for him when he'd called to ask her out. And that the industry grapevine had confirmed that a certain C-list model was looking to kick-start a pop career.

It was all very predictable. But predictable was good. At least he knew what to expect from this self-serving approach, even if his choice in female companions only inflamed the tabloid gossip about his private life. He hadn't even met half the women the papers had paired him with. And the ones he did date were just like the woman walking next to him: happy to use him for their own ends.

Good for them. It was a dog-eat-dog world and he'd learned one vital piece of wisdom early on: the woman who talked of love and commitment was the one who turned and bit you on the butt when you were least expecting it. He had the scars to prove it.

They moved inside the old theatre. Had they redone the décor in here? It had seemed opulent and elegant last time he was here, but now the crimson walls screamed at him, and the gold leaf everywhere just hurt his eyes.

He hadn't planned on coming to the awards this evening, but duty had called. Or, to be more accurate, duty had cried and pleaded down the phone in the shape of his newest and youngest signing, Kat De Souza.

They reached a flight of stairs and he held back and let Melodie walk up the sweeping staircase in front of him. Her dress was shimmering silver, backless, with a neckline slashed almost to her navel. It clung in all the right places. And Melodie certainly had *places*. Mark did his best to appreciate the view, but his pulse was alarmingly regular. Just another indicator that he was out of sorts tonight. Must be the jet lag.

An usher led them to their table at the front of the audi-

torium. Kat was already there, with her boyfriend *du jour*.
This one was a drummer, or something like that. Mark pulled
out Melodie's chair for her and made the introductions, then
leaned across to Kat.

'Nervous?'

Her head bobbed in small, rapid movements.

'Sorry I woke you up and snivelled down the phone at you
the other day.' She paused to twirl one of her long dark ringlets
around a finger with a bitten-down nail before looking up at
him again. 'The time differences are so confusing, and I was
in a bit of a state.'

He remembered. Technically, although he'd been the one
to 'discover' Kat, after he'd walked past her busking on the
Underground, he wasn't her personal manager. He was careful
not to get too close to his clients nowadays, normally leaving
the legwork to his junior associates. He'd been in the business
long enough to pay his dues, and had ridden more tour buses
and slept on more recording studio floors during all-night recording sessions than he cared to remember. He'd paired Kat
up with Sasha, a hip, energetic young woman at his firm who
had the potential to go far. But where he'd hoped there would
be female bonding, there had only been friction.

In the end he'd decided to step in and take an active interest
for a few months—ease the teething process, if you like. Kat was
only seventeen, and a bit overwhelmed at her sudden shove into
the spotlight. She needed stability at the moment, not constant
bickering. A happy client was a productive client, after all.

Mark smiled back at Kat and waited for her to finish fidg-
eting with her hair. 'Who needs sleep, anyway?' he said,
giving her a little wink.

'I'm so grateful you changed your plans and flew in at the
last minute. I'm frantic! I don't know whether I'm more
scared of winning or not winning. How crazy is that? And I
reckon I need all the support I can get.'

The scruffy excuse for a musician sitting next to her

swigged a mouthful of champagne out of the bottle and produced a proud burp. Mark shifted position and tried to block his view of him with the avant-garde floral arrangement exploding from the centre of the table.

Great choice of support, Kat. First class.

Proof, yet again, that his client was young and naive and definitely needed a guiding hand.

With the uncanny knack females had of confirming his opinions of them, Kat reached for the glass of champagne in front of her and swung it towards her lips. Mark's arm shot out in a reflex action that stopped the flute reaching its destination.

'Hey!'

He prised the glass from her fingers. 'No, you don't, young lady! You're underage.'

Kat's chin jutted forward as she had one of her teenage Jekyll and Hyde moments, switching from sweet and grateful to sour and belligerent in the snap of a finger. 'Chill out, Mark! You can't tell me what to do, anyway. You only manage my career, not my personal life.'

Okay, technically she was right. And if it had been anyone else on his agency's books he would have minded his own business. But it just didn't seem right to sit there and do nothing.

'No, you're right. I can't tell you what to do, but I can *advise* you. It's my job to look after your best interests. It's what I take my fifteen percent for, after all.' He placed the glass out of reach behind the spiky centrepiece. 'Anyway, you don't want to be tipsy when you collect the award later. And I mean *when*, not *if*.'

When in doubt, flatter. It always worked. He raised his eyebrows and waited for the thaw.

Kat's blistering stare softened a fraction. Girls of her age could be fiendishly stubborn. It was just as well he seemed to have the knack of charming each and every female he met, whether they were nine or ninety. Kat continued to glower at him, but he knew he'd won. He would let her back down gracefully without pressing the point further.

'Water is better for my voice, anyway,' she said, lounging back on her revolting boyfriend to give him a defiant kiss.

Mark beckoned a waiter and smiled to himself while his face was hidden.

Six months ago no one had heard of Kat De Souza. Despite her youth, she had a wonderfully mature soulful voice. Not only that, but she wrote the most amazing love songs and played the acoustic guitar to accompany herself. Her pared-down debut single had been a smash hit, catapulting her to overnight fame. His firm's expertise and connections had helped, of course, but she had ten times the talent of some of his other clients. Securing a recording deal had been a breeze. Now he just had to make sure that the pressure and the insanity of the music industry didn't derail her before she got to where she was destined to go.

He watched Kat bite her thumbnail down to a level that surely had to be painful. Mature talent, sure, but she was still just a scared schoolgirl underneath all the bluster. He was glad he'd shuffled his life around to be here tonight.

At that moment a wave of unexpected tiredness rolled over him. He hid a yawn and ignored the jet lag pulling at his eyelids.

It was going to be a long night.

Once Ellie had rustled herself up something more filling than biscuits to eat from the well-stocked larder, she decided to give herself a tour of Larkford Place. Tomorrow she'd get her Post-it notes out and label every door in the house—which was saying something. It seemed as if there were hundreds of them, all leading to rooms and corridors you wouldn't expect them to.

The scraps of coloured paper would be gone again by the time her boss returned, of course. It wasn't everybody's taste in décor. But in the meantime they'd help her to create some new neural pathways, remember the layout of the house. So, hopefully, when she wanted to cook something she'd end up in the kitchen and not the broom cupboard. She'd had to resort to this technique when she'd returned to the cottage after the accident, which had seemed utterly ridiculous. How could she have lived in a house for almost a decade and not remember where her bedroom was?

But it had all sunk in again eventually. And it would happen here at Larkford too, if she had time and a little bit of peace and quiet so she could concentrate. She mentally thanked Charlie again for organising things so she could have a week here on her own before her boss arrived back from wherever that red carpet was. Had Charlie mentioned New York…?

As she wandered round, she was pleased to find that the inside of Larkford Place was as lovely as its exterior. It oozed character. No steel and glass ground-breaking interior design here, thank goodness. Just ornate fireplaces and plasterwork, high ceilings and ancient leaded windows.

Ellie's jaw clicked as she let out a giant yawn. Fatigue was a normal part of her condition—due to the fact she had to concentrate on things most people did automatically. And today had been a day that had required an awful lot of mental and emotional energy. No wonder she was ready to drop. It was time to check out the housekeeper's apartment above the old stables, so she could crash into bed and become blissfully unconscious.

She pulled a couple of bags out of the boot of her car as she passed it, and made her way up the stairs to her new home. But when she opened the door, the smell of damp carpet clogged her nostrils. And it wasn't hard to see why. Water was dripping through a sagging bulge in the ceiling, and the living room floor was on its way to becoming a decent-sized duck pond. There was no way she could sleep in here tonight.

So she dragged her bags back to the main house, up the stairs and into one of the guest rooms on the first floor. By the time she'd left a message with a local plumber and placed some kitchen pans underneath the damaged ceiling to catch the worst of the dripping water, the yawns were coming every five seconds. She only made it through half of her unpacking before she decided it was time to stop what she was doing and tootle down the hallway to the bathroom she'd spotted earlier before falling into bed.

But as she lay there in the dark, with only the creakings of the old house for company, she found she could close her eyelids but sleep was playing hide-and-seek. Running away from home had seemed such a good idea a few weeks ago, but now she was second-guessing her impulse.

What if she proved Charlie's unspoken fears to be right? What if she wasn't up to the job?

And she *needed* to be up to this job, she really did—for so many reasons.

She'd just about come to terms with the fact that the accident had not only destroyed her perfect family, it had also altered her brain permanently. She would never be the same person she'd been before that day, never be the Ellie she knew herself to be.

Sometimes it felt as if she were inhabiting the body of a stranger, and she could feel her old self staring over her shoulder, noticing the things she couldn't do any more, raising her eyebrows at the mood swings and the clumsiness.

She rolled over and tried another position. Was it possible to haunt yourself? She certainly hoped not. She had enough ghosts to outrun as it was.

She sighed and clutched the duvet a little closer to her chest.

Maybe she'd never be that person again, but this job was her lifeline, her chance to prove to herself and everyone else that she wasn't a waste of space. This was her chance to be *normal* again, away from the judging eyes and the sympathetic glances. She was just going to have to be the best darn housekeeper that Mr Mark Wilder had ever had.

As the awards ceremony dragged on Mark was proved right. It had been an *incredibly* long night.

Melodie was irritating him. The package was pretty, but

there wasn't much inside to interest him. He had tried to engage her in talk about the music industry, but even though she was trying to veer her career in that direction she seemed superbly uninformed about the business.

The show was good, but he had the feeling he'd seen it all before—the pseudo-feuds between cool, young indie bands, the grandpa rockers behaving badly as they presented awards and the hip-grinding dance routines by girls wearing little more than scarves. Well, maybe he didn't object to the skimpy dresses that much, he thought with a chuckle. He was tired, not *dead*.

The only highlight of the evening had been Kat's victory in the 'Best Newcomer' category. Nobody else might have noticed the way her hands shook as she held the supposedly funky-looking trophy, but Mark had. She'd accepted her award with simple thanks, then performed her latest single, sitting alone on the stage except for her guitar and a spotlight. The whole audience had been silent as her husky voice had permeated the sweaty atmosphere. When she'd finished, even the most jaded in the crowd of musicians and industry professionals had given her an ovation.

The remainder of the ceremony was a blur as Mark tried to keep his eyes open. He began to regret the two glasses of champagne he'd drunk. He hadn't eaten since the flight this morning, and the alcohol was having a less than pleasant effect on him. Instead of mellowing him out, everything jarred. All he wanted to do was get home and sleep for a week solid.

The ceremony drew to a close and Kat leaned over to Mark. 'Are you coming to the after-show party?'

Melodie, who was eavesdropping, looked hopeful.

Mark shook his head. 'I'm tired and jet-lagged. I'm going home to bed.'

Melodie looked even more hopeful.

Erm…I don't think so, sweetheart.

It was time to ease himself out of the situation. Melodie would probably be happier at the party, mixing with the boy bands, anyway. He gave her a non-commital, nice-to-have-met-you kiss on the cheek. 'I know I'm being boring, but why don't you join the others at the party? I'm sure Kat and…er…'

'Razor,' said Kat helpfully.

'*Razor* will look after you.'

Melodie weighed her options up for a second, and decided the offer wasn't too shabby after all. 'That's cool,' she said in her little-girl voice and flicked her hair extensions.

Mark slipped away, leaving the theatre by the back exit, happy to distance himself from the muffled roar of the paparazzi as the stars emerged onto the red carpet out front. He fished his mobile phone out of his jacket pocket and called a cab, telling the driver to meet him in a backstreet close by, then ran a hand through his unruly mop of dark hair and made his way down an alley. Only when he had emerged from the shadow of the theatre did he loosen the top button of his shirt and breathe in a luxurious lungful of cool night air.

CHAPTER THREE

So MUCH for sleeping for a week solid. Someone was making a racket on the landing. How inconsiderate could you get?

Mark sat up in bed, cold reality only just intruding on his nice, warm sleep haze.

After the awards ceremony he'd had the urge to get right out of the city, so instead of asking the cab driver to make the short trip to his flat on the river, Mark had made him very happy and told him the destination was Sussex.

There was another noise from the landing. Nothing loud, but someone was definitely out there. He hadn't dreamt it. There was only one explanation. It was after two in the morning and someone was in his house. Someone he hadn't invited because he was supposed to be here on his own. That wasn't good.

Mark jumped out of bed, wondering what he might have to hand in his bedroom that would help in a situation like this, but it was pitch-dark and he didn't have a clue where to start fumbling. He knew his squash racket was in the house somewhere…

But he didn't have time even to reach for the lamp by his bed. Just then the door slammed open. Mark tensed, unable to see who or what had just invaded his bedroom. A split-second later something—someone—barrelled into him.

He didn't have time to think, just reached out and grabbed

him. There was no way some snotty youth from the village was going to swipe his silver, or his high-tech audio gear, or whatever it was he was after.

A struggle ensued and he finally got the lad pinned down on the floor. Now what? How was he going to call the police without—?

'Ow!'

A searing pain radiated from his right collarbone. The little runt had bitten him! Actually sunk his teeth in and clenched hard! And now he was getting away, even though Mark didn't remember letting him go. He grabbed for the intruder and was rewarded with an ankle.

Well, it was better then nothing.

Time to take the upper hand. And the first thing was to see who he was dealing with. They were both shouting at each other—although it seemed to be more sounds than words that he was deciphering. He lunged for the bedside lamp and switched it on.

And that was when things really got confusing. Maybe he was dreaming after all.

This was no lad from the village. Not with those soft blonde ringlets and wide green eyes. And she was wearing…pyjamas! He flushed hot at the thought, though he hardly knew why. They were thick brushed cotton and only hinted at the curves beneath. Now, he knew some women could be a little over-keen to meet him, but this was just ridiculous!

And then she started babbling, and in the string of words he heard his own name.

'I know who I am. Who on earth are *you*?'

She looked up at him, breathless and blushing. The only motion he was aware of was the uneven rise and fall of the curves under her pyjama top; the only noise was their mingled rapid breathing. And then she spoke.

'I'm Ellie Bond—your new housekeeper.'

He'd been clenching his jaw in anger, but now it relaxed.

His eyes widened as the sleep fog cleared from his brain. She pulled her arms and legs into herself and sat ball-like at his feet, suddenly looking like a little girl. She began to shiver.

Truth was, he had no idea how to handle this. And it was better if she got out of here before he said or did something he'd regret in the morning.

'You'd better get back to your room,' he said.

She should have known something was up when she'd tripped over that stray shoe. She never left her shoes lying around. And last night had been no different. She'd kicked them off and placed them neatly beside her case before going to bed. At home, her make-up might be spilled all over the dressing table, her jeans might be hanging by one leg over the back of a chair, but she always put her shoes away. Mainly because she only wore something on her feet when absolutely necessary. Her feet liked freedom.

Ellie stretched. Apparently a bulldozer had run over her last night while she'd drifted in and out of sleep—and then had reversed and had another go. There was no point trying to drop off again now. She was an early bird by nature and she knew her body clock would refuse.

She gave up squeezing her eyelids closed and rolled over and looked at the curtains. Dawn wasn't far away. Maybe some fresh air would stop her brain spinning in five different directions at once. She pulled a huge cable-knit sweater on over her pyjamas. Since she didn't own a pair of slippers she tugged a pair of flip-flops from the jumble at one end of her case.

Once she was ready she paused, listening for any hint of movement from the room next door. There was nothing.

Now she was satisfied the coast was clear, she headed into the hallway and stopped briefly to reassess the scene of the crime, counting the doors on this side of the corridor. Four. There was a small cupboard opposite the bathroom that she could have sworn hadn't been there before.

Not wanting to get caught in her pyjamas a second time, she turned in the opposite direction and went down the narrow staircase towards the kitchen, a room far enough away from the bedrooms for her to finally breathe out and think. Once there, she switched the kettle on and looked aimlessly round the room. The passageway that led into the cobbled courtyard was visible through the half-open door. Her car was sitting out there, ready to go. One of her mad impulses hit her.

What if she just ran out through the door this minute, jumped in her car and bombed out of the front gates, never to be seen again? Tingles broke out all over her arms. The urge to do just that was positively irresistible. It was only six o' clock.

Breathe. Think...

She recognised this itchy feeling for what it was—another legacy of her head injury. It was all very well to know that her impulse control was permanently out of whack, but another thing entirely to tap into that knowledge when you were in the magnetic grip of what seemed like the best idea ever and find the strength to resist it.

She should be thankful, though. At least she was just a bit harum-scarum these days. Some of the other people she'd met during her rehabilitation had it far worse. How could she forget Barry, who didn't seem to realise that grabbing the rear end of every woman he clapped eyes on wasn't appropriate behaviour? Or Fenella, the posh old lady who swore like a trooper if she didn't have an even number of peas on her plate at dinnertime, all lined up in rows? Ellie nodded to herself. Oh, yes. Things could be a lot worse. She just had to keep remembering that.

As if she could forget, when last night's disastrous run-in with the boss was clearly going to get her fired.

She brewed herself a strong cup of tea and opened the French windows that led onto a wide patio. The garden was beautiful in the soft early-morning sunshine. She breathed deeply and walked along the smooth grey flagstones till she

emerged from the shadow of the house into the warmth of the
sunrise. She skirted the lavender hedge, sipping her mug of
tea, and stepped onto a rectangle of lush, close-clipped grass.
It was heavy with dew and springy underfoot. Her head fell
back and she stayed motionless for a minute or so, feeling the
sun's rays on her cheeks and inhaling the clean, pure scents
of the awakening garden.

This reminded her of mornings at her cottage years ago.
Sometimes she would wake early and sneak out into the
garden before Sam and Chloe stirred. The garden had been
Ellie's place to centre herself, to pause from the hectic pace
of life and just *be*. She would walk out barefoot and let the
soft blades of the lawn tickle her toes. Then she would wander
about, clearing her head by talking out loud. Sometimes she
just rambled to herself; sometimes she couldn't help looking
skyward and thanking God for all the amazing things that
made her life perfect.

When she returned to the cottage she would be able to hear
the machinery of the day starting to whirr—the clattering of
toothbrushes in the bathroom, footsteps on the stairs. However
busy the day got after that, she carried a sense of peace with
her that had been born in the quiet of the day. It had been her
secret ritual.

But she hadn't done it for years—not since Sam and Chloe
had died. There was no peace to be found anywhere. Did she
think she'd find it under a bush in her own back garden? Not
likely. And as for God, she'd been tempted to stand outside
late at night and scream at Him for being so cruel. They hadn't
been on speaking terms since.

Ellie bent down to examine a cobweb glistening between
the branches of a small shrub. Beads of moisture clinging to
each strand reflected the sunlight like a thousand tiny mirrors.

What was she going to do? She was all alone and in a
terrible mess. Her pretty dreams about being independent, free
from the past, had come crashing down around her ears in less

than twenty-four hours. What a fool she'd been to think she could outrun her ghosts.

A tear bulged in the corner of her eye. She sniffed and wiped it away with her middle finger. Thoughts were scrambling around inside her head, so she stood still and let the spring sun warm her inside and out. Then, when she was ready, she shook off her flip-flops and walked, and talked to the faultless blue sky until the words ran dry.

A floorboard on the landing creaked. Ellie stopped stuffing clothes randomly into bags and held her breath at the back of her throat.

She'd heard noises upstairs some time after noon, and had scurried up here not long after that. It was amazing just how long it could take a person to pack two cases and a couple of smaller bags. She'd made it last all afternoon.

But for once her reasoning panned out: the longer she left it before she saw him again, the less embarrassed she would feel and the easier it would be to handle her emotions when he asked her to leave. It couldn't hurt to delay the inevitable confrontation with her soon-to-be-ex-boss until she'd finished packing and was on an even keel.

She squashed the T-shirt she was holding into the case in front of her and reached for her wash bag. It slid out of her fingers, but she managed to snatch at it, gripping it between forefinger and thumb before it reached the floor. Unfortunately her quick reflexes didn't stop the contents spilling out and scattering all over the rug. With all her limbs occupied just preventing the bag from falling, she couldn't do anything but watch as her tube of toothpaste bounced on the floor, then disappeared deep under the bed.

So much for an even keel. The world was still stubbornly off-kilter and refusing to go right side up.

She lifted Chloe's blue teddy from where she'd placed it on her pillow the night before and pressed it to her face. For a while it had smelled of her daughter, but the scent of strawberry shampoo had long since faded. Ellie kissed it with reverence and placed it beside the case.

She'd only allowed herself a few treasures from home, and they had been the first things she'd pulled from her luggage when she'd unpacked. Propped on the bedside table was a single silver picture frame. The photo it held was her favourite of her and Sam together, taken on their honeymoon. They'd handed their camera to the retired couple in the next hotel room and asked them to take a snap on the day they'd travelled home.

She preferred this picture to the forced poses of her wedding photos. They were laughing at each other, hair swept sideways by the wind, not even aware of the exact moment the shutter had opened. She traced a finger over her husband's cheek.

Her beautiful Sam.

He had been so warm and funny, with his lopsided grin and wayward hair. When he'd died it had been like losing a vital organ. Living and breathing were just so hard without him.

They'd met on the first day of primary school and been inseparable ever since, marrying one week after they'd both graduated from university. Sam had taken a teaching post at the village school and she'd commuted to the City, working as a PA for a big City firm, and they'd saved to buy the rundown cottage on the outskirts that they'd fallen in love with. They'd transformed the tumble-down wreck bit by bit, scouring architectural salvage yards for stained glass, old taps and doorknobs. They had even rescued an old roll-top bath out of one of their neighbour's gardens—removing the geraniums before it was plumbed in.

When the last lick of paint had dried, they had proclaimed it their dream home and immediately started trying for a family. The following spring, they'd come home from the hospital with Chloe, a tiny pink bundle with fingers and toes so cute they'd verged on the miraculous. Ellie had almost felt guilty about being more happy than a person had a right to be.

But one wet afternoon had robbed her of all of it.

Her smile dissolved and she pushed the frame flat and folded the photo up in her pyjamas before tucking it into a well-padded corner of her sturdiest case.

When she'd moved back home after her rehabilitation, well-meaning friends and family had taken one of two approaches—some had wanted her to freeze-frame time and never do anything, the rest had dropped great clanging hints at her feet about moving on with her life. Their insensitivity had astounded her.

Move on? She hadn't wanted to move on! She'd wanted things back the way they were *before*. Chloe's pink wellies in the hallway. Sam bent over the kitchen table marking homework. But that was impossible. So she'd settled for hibernating in the present. But hibernating hadn't taken long to become festering. Perhaps she should be glad that events in the village had forced her to leave.

She zipped up her bulging case, then sat on the edge of the bed and stared at the elegant surroundings.

Her journey had led her here, to Larkford Place. Unfortunately only a brief pit-stop. She hadn't a clue what she'd do next. She could stay at the cottage for a few weeks if there weren't any holiday bookings. But that would be going back, and now she was finally ready to move forward she didn't want to do that.

However, she didn't really have much choice after last night.

It was time she hauled her things down to the car. She picked up a case in one hand and stuffed a smaller one under her other arm, leaving her hand free to open the door. She tugged it open and froze.

Mark Wilder was standing straight in front of her, fist bunched ready as if to knock.

Mark dropped his hand, stuffed it in his back pocket and pulled out a wad of folded twenty-pound notes. He held them out to Ellie.

'I thought you might need this.'

She stared at him as if he was offering her a hand grenade.

'For the shopping,' he added.

'Shopping?'

'Yes. Shopping. You know, with money…'

He waved the notes in front of her chin. Her eyes moved left and right, left and right, following the motion of his hand.

'Money?'

This was harder work than he'd thought it would be.

'Yes. Money. It's what we use in the civilised world when we've run out of camels to barter with.'

'But I thought…' She fidgeted with a small silver locket hanging round her neck. 'You'd… I'd be…'

Colour flared on her cheeks and she stepped away from him. He looked at the notes in his hand. She didn't seem to understand the concept of shopping, which was a definite minus in a housekeeper. His decision to view last night as an embarrassing one-off started to seem premature.

He stepped through the door frame and followed her into the room. There were cases and bags on the bed. They were lumpy enough to look as if they had been filled in a hurry. The zips weren't done up all the way, and something silky was falling out of the holdall nearest to him. He really should stop looking at it.

Ellie followed his gaze and dived for the bag, stuffing the item back in so deep that most of her arm disappeared. Now he was just staring at a pile of cases.

Cases? He tilted his head. Oh. Right. She thought he was going to give her the sack.

Well, as tempting as the idea might be, he couldn't afford to do that at present. Firstly because he'd never hear the end of it from Charlie, and secondly because he really did need someone here to look after the house while he was travelling. He was due on another plane in less than twenty-four hours and he simply didn't have the luxury of finding someone else.

It had been hard enough to fill the position at short notice when Mrs Timms had decided to leave.

Maybe it was time to work some of the legendary Wilder magic and put this Ellie Bond at ease. If he showed her he was laughing off the incident last night, it might help her relax.

Mark waited for her to finish fiddling with the bag, and then pulled a smile out of his arsenal—the one guaranteed to melt ice maidens at fifty paces.

'Well, I'm glad to see you're still in your own room, anyway.' He threw in a wink, just to make sure she knew he was joking. 'With your track record, we can't be too careful.'

Hmm. Strange. Nothing happened. No thaw whatsoever.

'There's no need to go on about that. It's just that I wasn't expecting anyone else to be here, and I'm not familiar with the layout of the house yet, and I just…the moon went in…I counted three instead of four…' The babbling continued.

There was one thing that was puzzling him. If she'd wanted a bathroom, why had she trekked down the hall?

'Why didn't you just use the *en-suite*?'

She stopped mid-babble. *'En-suite?'*

He walked over to a cream-coloured panelled door on the opposite wall to the bed, designed to match the wardrobe on the other side of the chimney breast. He nudged it gently with his knuckles and it clicked open. Her jaw lost all muscle tone as she walked slowly towards the compact but elegant bathroom.

She shook her head, walked in, looked around and walked out again, still blessedly silent. Actually, his new housekeeper seemed relatively normal when she stopped biting and yelling and babbling.

He had a sudden flashback to the night before—to the baggy blue and white pyjamas that hadn't been quite baggy enough to disguise her curves—and he started to get a little flustered himself.

'I have a…bathroom…inside my wardrobe?'

He gave a one-shouldered shrug. 'Actually, it's not quite

as Narnia-like as it seems. The wardrobe is that side.' He pointed to an identical cream door the other side of the chimney breast. 'We just had the door to the *en-suite* built to match. Secret doors seem to suit a house like this.'

The look on her face told him she thought it was the stupidest idea ever.

'I thought it was fun,' he said, willing her to smile back at him, to join him in a little light banter and laugh the whole thing off as an unfortunate first meeting. She just blinked.

'Anyway,' he continued with a sigh, 'let's just see if we can get through the next twenty-four hours without something— or someone—going bump in the night.'

'I told you before. It was an accident,' she said, scrunching her forehead into parallel lines.

It looked as if she was tempted to bite him again. Humour was obviously not the way to go. Back to business, then. That had to be safe territory, didn't it?

'Okay, well take this for now.' He placed the money on the chest of drawers while she watched him suspiciously. 'I'm getting a credit card sorted out for the household expenses, and a laptop so we can keep in touch via e-mail. I just need you to sign a few forms, if that's all right?'

She nodded, but her eyes never left him, as if she was expecting him to make a sudden move.

Mark wandered over to the bed, picked up the sad-looking blue bear sitting next to one of the cases and gave it a cursory inspection. He wouldn't have expected her to be the sort who slept with a teddy, but, hey, whatever rocked her boat. He tossed it back on the bed. It bounced and landed on the floor. Ellie rushed to scoop it up, clutched it to her chest and glared at him.

He raked his fingers through his hair. It was time to beat a hasty retreat.

'I'll see you at dinner, then?' He raised his hands on a non-threatening gesture. An insane image of him as a lion tamer, holding off a lioness with a rickety old chair, popped into his head. He wouldn't be surprised if she growled at him.

'Fine.' It almost *was* a growl.

'Would you join us? I've invited Charlie to dinner, to say thank you for finding me a—'

The word *hellcat* had been poised to fall out of his mouth and he stopped himself just in time.

Not hellcat. Housekeeper! Just try and remember that.

'—for finding me a *housekeeper* at such short notice. I thought it would be a good way to break the ice before I disappear again.'

'Thank you,' she said. Her eyes told him she'd rather walk on hot coals.

Fine. If she wanted to keep it cool and impersonal, he could keep it cool and impersonal. Probably.

'If you could be ready to serve up at eight o'clock…?'

Her eyes narrowed almost imperceptibly.

He backed out through the door and started walking towards the main staircase. Charlie had a lot to answer for. Her perfect-for-the-job friend was perfectly strange, for one thing! He took himself downstairs and sat on the velvet-covered sofa in front of the fire. Jet lag was making it hard to think, and he had the oddest feeling that his conversation with Ellie had just been weird enough for him still to be asleep and dreaming.

She was clearly barking mad. If the 'lost-my-bedroom' incident had planted a seed of suspicion in his mind, their talk just now and what he had seen early this morning had definitely added fertiliser.

His body clock was still refusing to conform to Greenwich Mean Time, and last night he'd dozed, tossed and turned, read some of a long-winded novel and eventually decided on a hot shower to clear his head. On the way to his bathroom a flash of movement outside the window had prompted him to change course and peer out of the half-open curtains.

Down in the garden he'd spotted Ellie, marching round the

garden, arms waving. She'd been talking to herself! At six in the morning. In her pyjamas.

Pyjamas.

Another rush of something warm and not totally unfamiliar hit him. The pleasant prickle of awareness from the close proximity of a woman was one of the joys of life. But he didn't think he'd ever experienced it after seeing a woman wearing what looked to be her grandad's pyjamas before. Silk and satin, yes. Soft stripy brushed cotton, no. There it went again! The rush. His earlobes were burning, for goodness' sake!

He'd practically had a heart attack when she'd charged into him in the dark last night. He'd been in such a deep sleep only moments before he'd hardly known *who* he was, let alone *where* he was. The small frame and slender wrists of his captive might have fooled him into thinking it was a lad he'd held captive, but when the light had flickered on he'd realised he couldn't have been more wrong. It certainly hadn't been a boy he had by the ankle, intent on dragging him down to the local police station. He'd started to wonder if he'd been dreaming. Those soft blonde curls belonged on a Botticelli cherub.

Just then the bite mark on his left shoulder began to throb.

No, not an angel—his instincts had been right from the start. A hellcat.

It would be wise to remind himself of that. He didn't have to like this woman; he just had to pay her to keep his house running. He would keep his distance from Ellie Bond and he would not think of her in that way—even if there was something refreshingly different about her.

Insanity, he reminded himself. *That's what's different about her. A woman like that is trouble. You never know what she's going to do next.*

A yawn crept up on him. He told himself it would be a bad idea to fall asleep again, but there was something very soothing about watching the logs in the fire crackle and spark. He pushed a cushion under his head and settled to watch the flames shimmer and dance.

When he opened his eyes again the flames had disappeared and the embers were just grey dust. Now and then a patch of orange would glow brightly, then fade away again. He pulled himself out of the comfortable dent he had created in the sofa.

From somewhere in the direction of the kitchen he could hear female voices. Was Charlie here already? He looked at his watch. He'd been asleep for more than three hours. He walked towards the dining room and met Charlie, coming to fetch him. His stomach gurgled. His sleep patterns might be sabotaged, but his appetite was clearly on Larkford time.

'Now, don't go upsetting my friend, Mark. She needs this job, and you are not allowed to mess it up for her.'

Hang on a second. He was the employer. Surely this was all supposed to be the other way round? Ellie was supposed to do a good job for *him*, try not to upset *him*. At the moment he was wondering whether his house would still be standing when he returned in a few weeks.

He opened his mouth to say as much, then decided not to bother. There was no arguing with his bossy cousin when she got like this. It had been the same when he'd tried to talk her out of taking a stray kitten home one summer, when he'd been fourteen and she'd been ten. Charlie had worshipped that cat, but he'd never quite forgotten the lattice of fine red marks the animal had left on his hands and forearms after he'd agreed to carry it back to the house for her.

Unfortunately it had taken another twenty years before he'd been cured of the habit of trying to rescue pathetic strays of all shapes and sizes.

Helena had been like that. Soft, fragile-looking, vulnerable. And he hadn't been able to resist her. Something inside him swelled with protective instinct when he came across women like that. And Helena had been the neediest of them all. Not that he'd minded. He would have gladly spent all his days looking after her.

Three months after Charlie had found the kitten, when its tummy was round and its fur had a healthy sheen, it had disappeared and never come back. That was the problem with strays. It was in their nature to be selfish.

So he avoided strays altogether now, both feline *and* female.

Oh, women always wanted *something* from him. But he made them play by his rules, only mixing with women who wanted simpler things: money, fame by association, attention. Those things were easy to give and cost him nothing.

Mark was pulled back to the present by the aroma of exotic herbs and spices wafting his way. Charlie didn't need to steer him any more. The smell was a homing beacon, leading him up the corridor and into the dining room. He dropped into a chair opposite Charlie and waited, all his taste buds on full alert.

There was a glimpse of an apron and blonde hair through the doorway as Ellie disappeared back into the kitchen to fetch the last in a succession of steaming dishes. Mark swallowed the pool of saliva that had collected in the bottom of his mouth. He hoped she wouldn't be too long.

She finally appeared. At least he thought it was her. She was cool and collected and quiet, and set down the last dish in an array of lavish Thai recipes. Not a hint of growling or biting about her.

Good. He was glad she'd pulled herself together.

His stomach, however, didn't care how the transformation had happened. It grumbled at him to just get over it and start shovelling food in its general direction. Which he did without delay.

CHAPTER FOUR

ELLIE dished up. Her heart jumped so hard in her chest she was sure the serving spoon must be pulsing in her fingers. What was happening to her? Mark Wilder had done nothing but walk into the room and sit down and her body had gone wild. She finished doling out the food and sat down, careful to keep her eyes on her plate lest her stampeding hormones concentrate themselves and get ready for another charge.

The man was *insanely* good-looking!

The TV cameras hadn't done him justice at all. No longer did she want to scold the reporter for drooling; she wanted to congratulate her for forming a coherent sentence.

Last night she'd been too shocked to register the weird physiological response he provoked in her, and this afternoon she'd been too angry. At herself, mainly, but she'd vented at him instead. It was her stupid brain injury that was to blame. She'd never had problems with runaway emotions before that. Now, any little thing could trigger overwhelming frustration, or rage, or despair.

Of course! She'd inadvertently stumbled upon the answer.

Her sigh of relief drew glances from her dining companions. She caught Mark's eye and quickly returned her gaze to the king prawn on the end of her fork while she waited for her heartbeat to settle.

How could she not have remembered?

The doctors had warned her that some people noticed a change to their sex drive after a traumatic head injury. This intense attraction, this wobbly feeling, it was all down to her head injury. She didn't like him *that way* at all, really. It was just her stupid neurons getting themselves in knots because of the damage they'd suffered.

What a relief!

It explained everything. She could never normally be attracted to a man like him—a man so…well, she didn't have words for what he was *so*… But she'd never seen the attraction of bad boys. Who needed the heartache? Give her a man like Sam—warm, dependable, *faithful*—any day. Not a charmer who thought everything with two X chromosomes ought to fall at his feet and worship.

Now she had that sorted out in her head she could relax a little and enjoy the food. But as she ate questions started to float to the surface.

Why now?

Why, after four years of seeming perfectly normal in that department—even completely uninterested at times—had this symptom decided to rear its ugly head?

It didn't matter. Whatever the reason, she needed to get a handle on it. This job was important to her and she didn't want to lose it. She'd just have to read up a bit on the subject, introduce measures to cope with it, just like she had with her other symptoms. By the time he got back from his next trip she'd have it completely under control.

She made the mistake of glancing up at that point, just as Mark smiled at something Charlie said. He wasn't even looking at her, for goodness' sake, but Ellie still felt her body straining at the leash.

Down, girl!

Oh, my. This evening was going to be torture.

Thankfully, she had an excuse to keep herself busy. She

would pay attention to the food, and only the food. And when the meal was over she'd plead tiredness and escape to her room. Charlie would understand. She'd have to.

Mark stole a handful of looks at Ellie as the clattering of serving spoons gave way to silence. She kept her eyes on her plate, only lifting them once to dish out another spoonful of rice.

The only information she'd volunteered during dinner had been about the plumbing disaster in the housekeeper's apartment, which cleared up the final mystery of why she'd been sleeping in the room next door to his. She'd barely acknowledged his thanks for organizing the repairs.

So much for 'breaking the ice'. It seemed the dining room was in the grip of a rapidly advancing cold snap. But he wasn't going to push.

Instead, he turned to Charlie and asked after her brother, which led to a raft of hilarious anecdotes about his recent backpacking trip to Indonesia.

Ellie said nothing. It was almost as if she knew she was sitting a few feet away from him but was desperately trying to wish herself invisible, or at the very least make herself blend into the background. Whatever she was trying to do, it wasn't working.

It was odd. She wore virtually no make-up, and the reckless curls were piled on top of her head and secured with a clip, and yet he couldn't stop glancing at her. It must be pheromones or something, because she wasn't his usual type at all.

Not any more, anyway.

A curl escaped from the long silver clip on top of Ellie's head and threatened to dunk itself in her meal, but before it could slim fingers tucked it behind her ear. That tiny hand had packed quite a punch last night. He stared at it, watched her fingers as they pleated her serviette, closed around her fork...

Charlie caught him with his cutlery frozen between his mouth and his plate, eyes fixed on Ellie. She smirked. He re-

taliated with a warning kick under the table. He knew how
much of a blabbermouth Charlie was, and he didn't want her
complicating things by teasing him, especially as he and Ellie
had reached an icy truce. Besides, there was nothing to tease
him about. She was his housekeeper.

Charlie glared at him and leaned underneath the table to rub
her leg. A second later searing pain radiated from his shinbone.

'Ouch!'

Ellie glanced up, puzzled by the exchange, and Mark
decided to deflect the attention from himself before she
realised the food wasn't the only thing that was causing his
mouth to fill with saliva.

He could do polite and businesslike. He could behave like
a proper employer rather than a best buddy. And, with a
sideways look at his cousin, he decided to prove it.

'So… Where are you from, Ellie?'

Ellie chased some glass noodles round her plate. Mark
stretched out, then rested his hands behind his head and waited.

'Kent,' she replied quietly.

'The whole of Kent, or one spot in particular?'

'Barkleigh.'

What was that edge in her voice? Was she angry with him?

That was a little unfair. After all, she wasn't the one with
teeth marks on her torso. And he'd done his best to wave the
olive branch by chatting to her earlier on, and got his head
bitten off for his trouble.

Pity. He liked a woman with a sense of humour.

Cancel that thought. She was an employee. He was her
boss. He would make polite conversation and help her to feel
more comfortable, right? Good. *Here goes…*

'So, what made you decide to—?'

Ellie clattered the empty plates together before he could
finish his sentence and vanished in the direction of the kitchen,
muttering something about coffee. Mark waited a split second,
then grabbed a couple of empty wine glasses as an excuse to

follow her. He got the distinct impression he'd said something wrong, although he couldn't think what it might be. His questions had been innocent enough—bland, even.

When he got to the kitchen Ellie was standing motionless near the sink, a couple of dishes still in her hands. She looked lost. Not in a metaphorical sense, but genuinely lost—as if she'd suddenly found herself in alien territory and had no idea of what to do or where to go next. Mark stepped forward to help her, and she jumped as if electricity had arced between them. The crockery leapt out of her arms and smashed against the flagstone floor.

She stammered her apologies and started to pick up the pieces.

'No. It was my fault,' he said. 'I startled you.'

He bent down to help her. She looked across at him as they both crouched beside the kitchen cabinets, picking up the remnants of the dishes. Their knees almost grazed, and whatever had startled her shot through him too. An anonymous emotion flickered in her eyes and she looked away.

When they had finished clearing away the mess, he pulled out one of the kitchen stools and motioned for her to sit down.

'I'll do the coffee.'

Her eyes opened wide, and he could feel the heat of her stare as he turned to the coffee machine.

'Dinner was stupendous,' he said as he placed a cup and saucer in front of her.

'Thank you,' she replied, looking even more surprised.

Suddenly he didn't feel like being the normal, wise-cracking Mark Wilder everyone expected him to be. He didn't want to *dazzle*. Some forgotten instinct told him to pare it all back, leave the charm behind and just talk to her, human being to human being. Actually, he did have something he wanted to ask her, something that might cement them in their right relationship without causing her to take offence.

'Actually, I was wondering if you could do me a favour.'

Her eyebrows raised a notch further.

'I mean, I love exotic food, but there is one thing I haven't had for a long time and I've *really* got a hankering for. I wonder if you wouldn't mind putting it on the menu some time?'

She looked at him, her eyes hooded and wary. 'What's that?'

He looked at floor before giving her a hopeful smile. 'Shepherd's Pie?'

Ellie Bond surprised him once again. Instead of scowling or rolling her eyes, she let go of all the tension she'd been holding in her face and laughed.

The kitchen was silent and empty when Ellie entered it the following morning. Dawn had come and gone, but the overcast sky produced an artificial twilight in the unlit kitchen. The state-of-the-art stainless steel appliances and barren worktop made the place look like a hotel. There was none of the usual clutter that made a kitchen the heart of the home. No family photos. No children's drawings. No pet bowls.

She found a note on the counter from Mark, letting her know he'd already left for the airport. An itinerary was stapled to it, in case she needed to contact him while he was away. She read the note in full, and cheered up instantly when she discovered he'd given her permission to buy anything she needed for the kitchen. Some women loved shopping for shoes; Ellie had a worrying love of shopping for kitchen gadgets—and this house could definitely do with her attention. It needed a food processor and measuring spoons and a griddle... And that was just for starters. It wasn't that there wasn't anything in the cupboards, but most of the equipment fell into the 'pretty but useless' category. The designer grater she'd found had been an odd shape, and they'd almost feasted on grated knuckles instead of grated ginger in their curry last night.

Outside it was grey and chilly, but the grounds of Larkford were still beautiful. Daffodils—not the garish ones, but blooms the colour of clotted cream—had burst through the lawn in clumps and were now whispering cheerfully to each other in the breeze. Wood pigeons cooed in the trees, and the first cherry blossoms were now visible on the silvery grey branches. It was almost a shame to be inside, so she went out for a walk, and continued walking long after the bottom of her teacup was visible.

Taking her cup of tea for a walk became part of her morning routine. On her return to the kitchen she would pass the super-duper, multi-highlighted calendar on the large fridge and mentally tick off the days until Mark returned.

Twelve more days of blissful solitude... Eleven more days... Eight more days...

And she ignored the fact that she felt slightly elated, rather than disappointed, as each day went by.

Mark lounged on a wicker sofa, high on the roof terrace of his hotel's penthouse suite. He was ignoring the traffic rushing round the corner and down Rodeo Drive in favour of the clear blue sky above his head. It had been an extremely long day schmoozing record company executives and their sharp-toothed lawyers in order to finalise the launch of Kat's album in the US, but he'd come away with what he'd wanted from the meeting—eventually. He was very good at schmoozing, after all.

He'd had an invitation to go clubbing this evening, with a rather strait-laced lawyer who looked as if she'd be a whole lot of fun once she let loose, but he'd turned her down. For some reason he wanted to be on his own at the moment. He didn't feel right, and he needed to relax a little and work out why.

Today he felt out of sorts, uncomfortable. As if he was wearing a suit that wasn't cut quite right. He closed his eyes and sank into the deep cushions of the sofa.

Well, he wasn't wearing a suit now. He'd changed into shorts and a T-shirt as soon as he'd got back to his suite. Unfortunately he still had that same itchy feeling, as if something wasn't quite right. He shook his head and pulled his sunglasses down over his eyes. Even with them closed the sun was still a little bright, burning strange shapes onto the backs of his eyelids.

Slowly the blobs swam and merged, until they solidified into an image that looked suspiciously familiar. In fact it looked suspiciously like his new housekeeper. He snapped his lids open and let the white sun bleach his retina instead.

What was up with him?

This was the third time something similar had happened. He was seeing her everywhere. And he didn't want to remember how sad and lost she'd looked when she'd smashed his best crockery to smithereens. He also didn't want to remember how warm and alive she'd looked when he'd mentioned Shepherd's Pie and she'd thrown her head back and laughed.

Housekeepers weren't supposed to be memorable. They were supposed to fade into the background and just do their job. He knew from personal experience how important it was to keep the lines between personal and professional firmly in place.

Somewhere in the back of his head he heard laughing.

Like you're doing with Kat?

That was different. He wasn't going to make the same mistake with Kat that he'd made with Nuclear Hamster. Stupid name. He'd advised them against it, but they hadn't listened. It was just that Kat was so young, she needed—

Okay, he was starting to act like a big brother towards Kat, but it didn't mean anything. Most importantly, it didn't mean he was setting a precedent of getting too close to his employees. He'd been cured of that fault a long time ago. Which meant he was totally capable of interacting with Ellie Bond without thinking of her as a woman—a woman who filled a pair of striped pyjamas very nicely, actually.

He sighed. He'd be back at Larkford in just over a week.

And Ellie would be there. It was what he'd hired her for, after all.

Suddenly the thought of the two of them alone in that big

old house together seemed a little…intimate. He stood up, walked over to the parapet and stared out towards the Hollywood hills. A house like his—well, what it really needed was to be filled with people. Lots of them.

On the day there were only five spaces left on the calendar Ellie got restless. All her tasks were done, and she'd finished the book she was reading. She needed something to do. Something to clean out. Sorting through cupboards and purging the rubbish was a therapeutic activity she rather enjoyed. It made her feel as if she were in control of something for once.

The infamous cupboard opposite the bathroom had become the object of her obsession. As far as she could see it was full of boxes of miscellaneous clutter that had been sent down from Mark's London flat and had yet to be sorted out. She'd found plenty of bedlinen, a squash racket and three boxes of books. The empty shelves in the study came to mind, so Ellie decided to liberate the volumes from the dust and cardboard and put them where they could be useful.

She carried the box down to the study and started pulling books out and putting them on the thick wooden shelves. As she got to the last book in one stack a slip of paper fell out of the pages and wafted to the floor. She picked it up and realised it wasn't a piece of paper after all, but a photograph.

Not any old photograph. It was a wedding picture.

Mark and an anonymous bride.

Well, well, who'd have thought it? The bachelor playboy hadn't always been a bachelor. Bet he'd always been a playboy, though.

She frowned almost instinctively and studied the photograph more carefully. Mark looked younger—maybe in his mid-twenties?—fresh-faced, and very much in love with his beautiful, sophisticated bride. Her expression softened a little. A man who could look at a woman like that *had* something.

Exactly what, she didn't know. Maybe he didn't either, because he'd thrown it all away and was living a very different life now. What a pity.

Turning the picture over, she saw the words 'Mark and Helena' scrawled on the back. The date underneath was twelve years earlier. Ellie slid the photograph back into its resting place and put the book on the shelf, feeling a little bit guilty for having found out what she sensed was a secret.

She reached for the next book, but was interrupted by the shrill beckoning of the telephone—the house line, not the one here in Mark's office.

Blast! She'd noticed the cradle in the hall was empty when she'd walked past with the box of books. She'd probably left the phone lying around again, which meant it might be anywhere.

She stood still and listened carefully.

The kitchen.

She raced down the passageway, skidding on the tiles in her socks.

It's in here somewhere!

The ringing was louder now, but oddly muffled. She ransacked a corner of the kitchen near the hob. Nothing! She leant closer to the worktop, then started frantically opening drawers.

Nope. Nope. Aha!

There it was, nestled amongst the wooden spoons. Where else?

She jabbed the button and uttered a breathless hello, then snapped to attention as she heard Mark's deep tones.

At first she didn't listen to the words, the content of what he was saying, because she hadn't been prepared for the way even his voice made her tingle. Oh, why couldn't he have e-mailed her? She wouldn't have had to concentrate on sounding normal if she'd been typing a reply!

Ah, but the phone call might have something to do with the fact she'd forgotten her password and hadn't been able to check her e-mails for a while.

It was just then that she realised Mark had stopped talking.

'Ellie?'

'Uh-huh?'

'Are you…? Is everything all right?' She could hear him suppressing a smile.

Unfortunately she was more than a little breathless—from all the phone-hunting, of course.

'Just…couldn't…find the phone.' She took a gulp of air and managed to croak, 'Can I help you?'

'Yep. I've decided to throw an impromptu party as a kind of housewarming when I get home. Only a few dozen guests—don't worry.'

A few dozen?

'My PA is handling the invites, and I'll get her to send you a list of caterers. We've decided on Saturday.'

'Saturday? This Saturday? That's less than a week away!'

'I know. I've been e-mailing for days, but you didn't reply. Don't stress. That'll be plenty of—hang on—'

Ellie huffed and tapped the counter as Mark chatted to someone on his end of the line. She thought she heard a woman's voice.

None of my business. I don't care who he's with.

'Got to go, Ellie. I'll be back on Friday evening.'

The receiver hummed in her ear.

He hadn't even given her time to tell him that she couldn't possibly organise a party in six days. She'd only just got to grips with the day-to-day running of the house, and the last thing she needed was something that was going to send all that into a tailspin.

However, it didn't seem as if she had much choice. If she wanted to keep this job she would have to cater to her boss's whims, no matter how inconvenient.

Catering.

Was that the best place to start? It was so long since she'd had a social life herself, thinking about planning a party seemed as run-of-the-mill as planning a trek up the Amazon.

She closed her eyes. Remember what you learned at the support group. Don't panic over the big picture. Take things one step at a time. Start with the obvious.

Her eyelids lifted again. The cleaners were coming on Friday anyway, so no problem there. And she could get Jim the gardener to help her rearrange the furniture in the downstairs reception rooms, and the florists in the village could provide some arrangements.

After her initial panic she realised it wasn't that different from what she'd done when she'd worked as a PA in the City after leaving college. Her cantankerous boss had had a penchant for drop-of-the-hat cocktail parties to impress the partners, where he would swan round being all sweetness and light, then return to being a sour-faced grump the next day. If she could create a party to blow Martin Frobisher's socks off, she could certainly succeed with a lovely backdrop like Larkfield.

Yes, but that was *before*…

Shut up, she told herself. It's all there inside your head still. She was just going to have to do a little…archaeology to uncover the buried bits.

She could do this.

Her brain began to whirr with excitement as menu ideas sprang up in her mind. This was her chance to prove to Mark Wilder that she wasn't a loose cannon, that she could do this job.

She reached for the phonebook and flipped it open to 'F' for florists, her smile wide. Passwords could wait for later. For now she would use the phone.

If Mr Wilder wanted a party, she was going to give him a party!

Ellie slipped the straps of the little black dress she'd borrowed from Charlie over her shoulders. She wasn't looking forward to this evening one bit. She'd tried hard to talk him out of it, but Mark had insisted she attend the party—partly to keep an eye on the caterers and whatnot, but partly to 'have a bit of fun'. She'd have much preferred to stay holed up in her apartment with a packet of biscuits and a chick-flick.

She smoothed the bodice of the dress over her torso and looked in the mirror. She turned from one side to the other, scrutinising her reflection. Not bad. The simply cut black dress accentuated her curves, but didn't cling in desperation. She slipped on a pair of strappy high heels—also borrowed from Charlie. Her ankles wobbled as she adjusted to the altitude.

Tyres crunched on the gravel outside. She exhaled wearily. Guests were starting to arrive, which meant it was her cue to go downstairs. While it wasn't her place to welcome the guests, she wanted to make sure that the pair of local girls she'd hired to help with coats and suchlike had retained the pertinent information from their briefing yesterday.

Perhaps she could just stick it out for an hour or so and then slope off when he—when *no one*—was looking.

She left her room and headed for the main staircase. It wound down into a hall that was larger than the living room in her cottage. The banisters were solid oak, and still as sturdy as the day they'd been made. Ellie was rather grateful for them as she made her way down the stairs in Charlie's disobedient shoes. They seemed to have a mind of their own. She watched each foot carefully as she planted it on the next step, and it was only as she neared the bottom that she looked up and caught a glimpse of Mark, standing by the huge marble fireplace, chatting to the first of the arrivals.

Unfortunately she'd discovered when he'd returned home the previous evening that time and distance had done nothing to dilute the sheer physical impact the man had on her. It was pathetic, really, it was. She knew better, knew what sort of man he was, and yet here she was, *twittering* along with every other female in a five-mile radius. She comforted herself with the knowledge that at least she had a medical reason for behaving this way.

She looked over at Tania and Faith, the girls from the village. Neither of them had thought to relieve any guest of a coat or a wrap; they were too busy standing in the corner and getting all giggly over a certain member of the male species.

Ellie forced herself not to look at Mark as she made her way across the hall and reissued her instructions to the two girls in a low, authoritative voice. They instantly sprang into action, relieving guests of their outerwear and delivering the items to one of the smaller rooms on the ground floor where Ellie had set up some portable clothing racks.

The only problem was that Tania and Faith were now so intent on proving themselves efficient they'd both darted off at once, leaving Ellie no choice but to act as hat-check girl herself when the next huddle of guests piled through the door. She approached the group that had just crossed the threshold.

Mark moved forward to greet them at the same time, and Ellie couldn't avoid meeting his gaze. It was like being hit in the chest with one of those Taser guns. Her heart stuttered, fizzing with a million volts, and she disguised the resultant quivering in her limbs by breaking eye contact and smoothing out a non-existent wrinkle on her dress. All the same, the hairs at the back of her neck lifted, full of static. She just knew he was still looking at her. He inhaled, as if he was about to say something, but before the words left his mouth, another voice gatecrashed the moment.

'Mark, you old dog!' bellowed a good-looking blond man in a dinner jacket, slapping him across the shoulders.

'Hello, Piers,' Mark replied in his good-humoured tone. 'Come in and find yourself a drink. What do you think of my new place?'

'Bloody difficult to find, that's what I say!' he roared, slapping Mark a second time.

Ellie was standing there still waiting to take any coats. She felt like a prize lemon.

'Let me introduce you to this trinity of lovelies,' Piers continued, ushering a group of bejewelled women into the house. 'Carla, Jade, and of course you already know Melodie.'

Of course. Ellie recognised her as the woman from the television. She didn't say anything, but silently willed Melodie to hurry up and hand that pashmina over. Ellie wanted an excuse to make herself scarce.

Mark didn't falter as he offered a polite greeting to all three women, but Ellie had a sense as she took hold of their wraps and coats that he wasn't as comfortable as his relaxed stance implied. She was just about to scamper away to the temporary cloakroom when the pair of girls returned and relieved her of her only legitimate means of escape.

Then, just to make matters worse, Mark turned to her and asked her something. She saw his lips move, heard the words, but her brain retained none of the information. Why had he done that? She was the help. And she'd actually like to keep their relationship on that footing, thank you very much. Things were complicated enough as it was.

Just then a waitress with a large tray walked past the entrance hall en-route to the drawing room. Caterers! She was supposed to be here in a professional capacity, after all. She would inspect each and every trayful of over-priced morsels and make sure they were just what she'd ordered. She mumbled something about food, not so much to Mark but to the room in general, then fell into step behind the waitress, lengthening the distance between her and the group at the doorway. As she rounded the corner she could still hear Piers's booming upper-class drawl.

'Ding-*dong*!' he said with a whistle. 'Who was that?'

She didn't wait to hear Mark's explanation of her existence, but scuttled away even faster—high heels permitting. The last thing she wanted to do was actually have to talk to people tonight. They would expect her to be dazzling and witty. And if she had ever been dazzling and witty in her previous life she had certainly forgotten by now. Socialising was something other people did. Even the prospect of a night down at the Anglers' Arms in Barkleigh filled her with fear and trembling. In comparison, this party was like purgatory with canapés.

A few dozen guests? Someone had underestimated a little.

The drawing room was like a *Who's Who* of popular music. Wasn't that…? You know, the guy who always seemed to be at number one? And that girl over there—Ellie had seen her latest music video only the other night on TV. Normal party nerves escalated into something far bigger and scarier. It would be really great if she could think of the girl's name— if she could recall *anyone's* name, actually. These were the sort of people who expected to be remembered.

She circled the drawing room, 'fluffing' the floral arrangements, hoping that no one talked to her and expected her to know who they were. But she wasn't really looking at what she was doing, and more leaves fell off due to her attention than she cared to notice. As soon as she could she slipped out and made her way to the kitchen.

CHAPTER FIVE

THERE was a strange calm to be had amidst the noise and movement of the kitchen. At least in here Ellie knew what she was doing. Her lists and charts were pinned to the cupboard doors, her timetable clung to the fridge door with the help of a few magnets, and waiters and waitresses were all jostling each other, doing exactly as they were supposed to.

It didn't take long before one of the catering company staff appeared with a question, and Ellie found herself busy for what seemed like a half an hour but turned out to be almost two hours. Eventually tiredness washed over her, the mind-fogging fatigue she knew she shouldn't ignore. Dodging dashing bodies and clattering trays suddenly became too much of an effort and she crept up the back staircase. Before she went to her room she carried on along the landing and looked over the banisters into the hall, where the party was still in full swing. She'd done well this evening, and she wanted one last mental picture of her achievement, to cement it firmly in her memory before she fled back to her bedroom and shut the door firmly behind her.

From her vantage point on the landing she watched the glittering crowd ebb and flow. The clink of champagne glasses and jumble of conversation drifted up from below. Surprisingly, she found the sound soothing now she was no longer in the thick of it.

Her eyes drifted here and there, searching. It wasn't until they fixed on Mark that she realised she'd been looking for him. He was the perfect host—she'd give him that. He was charming and smooth, always with a crowd around him. The group he was with laughed at something he said. So he was good company too, it seemed. But he didn't dominate the gathering, forcing people to look at him. They just flowed around him, accepting the good time he offered them.

That woman from the awards ceremony was talking to him now, batting her lashes and jutting her ample chest under his nose. Ellie rolled her eyes. And, funnily enough, when the woman turned to grab herself a cocktail from a passing tray, Mark did a microscopic version of the same expression. That made her smile. It also made her look a little closer.

He smiled. He talked. But every now and then he just drifted off and stared at nothing for a second, until the next excited guest drew him back into the conversation. It was almost as if…

No. That was a stupid idea. Why would someone throw a party if they didn't actually want to be at it themselves?

'What are you doing skulking up here? I've been looking for you everywhere.'

Ellie stopped breathing momentarily as Charlie appeared from nowhere.

'Don't do that!' Ellie whispered sharply, pressing her palm to her chest in an effort to slow her galloping heart. 'And I'm not skulking.'

Charlie stopped smiling and looked concerned. 'You're a bag of nerves,' she said, while giving Ellie's arm a reassuring rub. 'Come on, chill out. It is a party, after all…'

Ellie nodded. 'I know. But I need this to go well. I can't lose this job, Charlie, I can't—'

Without warning her eyes filled, and the party below glittered even harder than before.

'Hey!' Charlie's voice was gentle and her arm rested around Ellie's shoulders, pulling her close. 'What's all this about?'

She took a deep breath. 'Did you tell him…Mark Wilder… about me?'

Charlie's three frown lines appeared above her nose. 'All I told him was that you were an old friend of mine and I thought you'd be perfect for the job. I wasn't lying, Ellie.'

Ellie scratched at a non-existent mark on the banister with a blunt fingernail. 'No. I mean, did you tell him about how I have problems with…about my…?'

Charlie's voice was low when she answered. 'No, I didn't tell him about the accident or how it's affected you. It's up to you whether you want to share that information with him.'

Okay, so Charlie had believed her when she'd sworn blind she had it in her to be a top-notch housekeeper. Now she just had to prove her right. Ellie's chest rose then fell deeply as she let out a huge breath. 'Right. Thank you.'

A soft look appeared on Charlie's face. 'Do you really think being here, moving away from home, will help you…you know…get over things?'

Suddenly Ellie needed to sit down. Her legs folded under her with the grace of a collapsing deckchair and she grabbed on to the banister with both hands. Charlie's arm appeared, firm and protective, around her shoulders.

'There's more to this sudden desire for a new job than just needing fresh scenery, isn't there, Ellie? Why did you really want to leave Barkleigh in such a hurry?'

Blast. Why did Charlotte Maxwell have to be so perceptive under her devil-may-care exterior? Ellie stared at the milling guests below. Their only problems were deciding which diamond to wear or which sports car to drive.

A feeling of loss washed over her, so deep, so overwhelming that she thought she might just dissolve into nothing right there on Mark Wilder's landing.

Sometimes she wished her brain would just finish the job and give up working all together. Then she could just evaporate. She'd be happy then, feeling nothing, remembering nothing. It was this half-in, half-out thing her memory did that was driving her to distraction.

'I can't go home,' she whispered. 'I just can't.'

'Why?'

'Remember Ginny? Chloe's godmother and my oldest friend?'

Charlie nodded. 'Yes, I remember her.'

Ellie didn't want to say it. Hearing the words spill out of her own mouth would remind her of everything she'd lost. Of everything she longed for.

'She's pregnant.'

She didn't look up. Couldn't.

Charlie's hand stopped stroking her arm and slid down over her wrist until their fingers meshed, Charlie's red fingernails bright against her pale skin. Ellie gripped her hand, hanging on to it as if it would anchor her.

'I know it's awful, but I think if I have to see her every day for the next eight months, seeing her grow bigger, seeing how happy she is with Steve, I might just go *properly* bonkers. I just had to get away.'

She was happy for Ginny and Steve, really she was, but how could she watch them add to their happy little family when her own had been wiped from the face of the earth? It was too…too…*blatant*.

Charlie didn't say anything, just hugged her tight. 'Do you want me to get you anything? A glass of water?'

Ellie shook her head. 'No. I'm just tired. I think I'll just stay here for a few seconds and then go to bed. You go on and enjoy the party.' She nodded to the hall below, where the rather good-looking man she'd seen Charlie with earlier was searching the crowd. 'I think someone's looking for you.'

Charlie smiled, and her eyes never left the man as he moved this way and that. 'If you're sure?' she said.

'I'm sure.' Ellie gave her a shove in the right direction and Charlie headed off down the stairs. The man spotted her, and the look he gave her as she descended was pure magic. Ellie sighed. At least someone was happy.

She moved a little further to the left, so she could see more of the hall. Mark was still leaning on the mantelpiece, and he had that distant look in his eyes again.

Her mind wandered back to his smile in the wedding photo. She'd seen him smile plenty of times tonight, but not one of those smiles had lit up his face like his smile for the woman in the wedding photo. Where was she now? What had happened? For the first time she realised there were scars beneath his good-humoured persona. From wounds that maybe hadn't fully healed. Her hand flew to the locket around her neck. She knew all about the pain those kinds of wounds could cause.

As if he sensed she was watching him, Mark paused, his glass raised halfway to his lips. And then he turned his head and met her gaze. She froze. Could it be any more obvious she'd been staring at him and only him? She didn't think so.

Still, he didn't look cross. He wasn't smiling that irritating twinkly smile—wasn't mocking her. The other occupants of the room melted away, their conversation drowned out by a loud thudding sound.

Oh. That was her pulse.

Heat crept up her cheeks, but still she hadn't moved. And moving at this point would be a really good idea.

Still staring at Mark, she took a couple of wobbly steps backwards, then turned and fled along the corridor. For some reason she ignored her bedroom door and headed for the back staircase. She needed space, distance. And she didn't think she'd get that with only a ceiling and a couple of walls separating her from Mark Wilder.

The stupid stilettos strangled her ankles as she clattered down the back staircase. She paused at the bottom. No one was around, so she tiptoed down the corridor into the kitchen.

Ellie stole a smoked fish thing off a platter of canapés and popped it in her mouth. As she slid past a waitress carrying a tray of cocktails she pilfered one of those too, knocking it back and shuddering as whatever it was hit the back of her throat.

She edged past the round table near the French doors. An abandoned tray stood on the table, cluttered with champagne flutes, some empty, some full. She plucked one of the full ones and nipped out of her favourite escape route into the garden.

A wave of muffled laughter wafted past her on the clear night air. She took a sip of champagne, but barely tasted it. There was something she had to do first, before she could enjoy it properly.

Her feet were killing her.

She sat on a low stone wall and fiddled with the microscopic buckles. Pretty soon she'd flicked the shoes off and she hooked the satin straps under her fingers and headed into the garden.

The flagstones were cold and rough on the soles of her feet, and she veered in the direction of the lawn and sank her toes deep into it. Heaven! She closed her eyes and took another sip of champagne. The canapé was the first thing she had eaten all evening, and on an empty stomach it wasn't hard to feel the bubbles doing their work.

Funny how parties always sounded more inviting when you were on the outside. All she had wanted to do when she was in there was escape, yet now she was out here she felt strangely alone.

She took a few more steps on the springy grass, letting the blades invade the spaces between her toes. She wriggled them and drained the flute of its contents. Goosebumps flourished on her upper arms as she heard a low masculine voice behind her.

'Caught red-handed!'

A powerful pair of hands clamped down on Ellie's shoulders. The champagne glass slid out of her hand and bounced off her foot. She instinctively ducked down and forwards, wriggling out his grip, then swung round to face him.

He blinked groggily at her. 'What's the matter?' he slurred. 'Don't you like me?'

His name might have deserted her, but she hadn't forgotten this man. The floppy pale hair, the arrogant smirk. She didn't know who he was to Mark, but if the rest of his friends were like this, he could keep them.

He draped an arm across her shoulders. 'What d'you say we go for a little walk?'

She had to handle this carefully. He might be a pain in the behind, but he was Mark's guest too, so losing her temper would only get her in trouble. 'I'd rather not, thank you.'

His eyes were glassy and his breath reeked of whisky. She carefully peeled his arm off her shoulder. He lost his balance now he wasn't leaning on her for support, his feet sliding on the dewy grass. His smile faded.

'Hey! There's no need to be hoity-toity about it.'

'I didn't... I...' Oh, what was the use? He'd probably take any conversation as encouragement of some sort. The best thing to do was get out of here before she really did get *hoity-toity* with him.

She turned and walked back towards the house. He lumbered after her, stumbling slightly, and managed to grab hold of her arm and haul her towards him.

Something flashed white-hot inside her head. She dreaded these surges of anger, but could do very little to contain herself when they struck. She was going to blow, whether she liked it or not.

'Get off me!' she yelled.

He made a curious gurgle that she interpreted as a laugh, and clamped her to his chest. His lips made contact with the skin beneath her ear and slid down her neck in a slobbery trail.

'Ugh!'

Enough was enough. No more Miss Nice Guy. She swung Charlie's killer sandals wide and brought them crashing down on his temple.

* * *

Mark had suddenly had enough of standing around talking to the same people, having the same conversations he'd had last week. He needed fresh air.

Instinctively he headed for the kitchen, then paused at the threshold. Why had he come this way? He had the feeling he was looking for something but had forgotten what.

Nonsense, his conscience said. You know exactly why you're here…*who* you're looking for.

But it didn't matter. She wasn't there.

So he ducked past the busy catering staff and out of the French windows to the small lawn.

The floodlights on the outside of the house made the dark night even blacker, and it took him a few moments to realise he wasn't alone. A movement at the end of the lawn caught his eye and he made out two silhouettes. He almost grinned and shrugged it off as a couple of guests slipping away to get friendly, but something made him look again.

Piers was up to his old tricks, it seemed. He was a notorious flirt. The only reason Mark had invited him was because he needed his firm's specialist legal knowledge on a recording contract he was putting together. Still, Piers was relatively harmless, and most of the females in their circle of acquaintance knew how to deal with him. Mark peered deeper into the darkness. Just who was he with this time, anyway?

And then he was running, the sound of his own blood rushing and swirling in his ears. He worked out regularly enough, and his legs were pumping beneath him, but somehow he seemed to make torturous progress, like the slow-motion running in a dream.

The woman Piers was slobbering over was Ellie.

And there was no way he was going to let some jumped-up little twit who worked for his daddy's law firm foist himself on one of his staff. She might not know how to—

Mark almost slipped on the damp grass.

Perhaps she did.

He watched as Ellie gave Piers a first-class whack with her shoes. Piers stumbled and fell on the damp grass, clutching a hand to his head. Mark finally skidded to a halt in front of them and yanked Piers up by his collar. His right fist was itching to make contact with that pretty face. He ought to flatten him for treating Ellie that way.

'Mark, no!'

The panic in her voice was all he needed to make him reconsider. He released the slimy runt and gave him a shove in the direction of the house.

'Go home, Piers. You're drunk.'

Piers wiped saliva from the edges of his mouth with the back of his hand.

'Steady on, Mark!'

He marched towards Piers and stopped inches from his face. Piers might have a reputation for being a ladies' man, but Mark had never suspected how nasty he could be with it. How could a man who appeared so polished during the working week turn out to be such a rat? Once again he'd believed the best in someone, only to be utterly disappointed.

'No. You *steady on*,' he said, with more than a hint of controlled fury in his voice. 'Don't ever set foot in this house again. In fact, don't bother to set foot in my offices again, either. As of Monday I will be seeking new legal representation—you and your firm are fired.'

Piers tugged at his tie and stood as tall as the whisky would let him.

'Now, look here. I could sue you for assault, manhandling me in that way!'

'Yes, you could. And I could tell the paparazzi hiding in my front bushes how you got plastered at my party and tried to grope one of my guests. I'm sure the partners at Blackthorn and Webb would welcome the publicity, don't you?'

Piers turned tail and lurched towards the house. Mark

watched until he was out of sight, then faced Ellie. 'I'm so sorry about that. Are you all right?'

'Fine.' Her voice quivered enough to call her determined face a liar.

'You gave him one hell of a clout with those shoes!'

The shell-shocked expression gave way to a delightfully naughty smile. 'You should have warned him I was dangerous to mess with.'

The fingers of Mark's right hand wandered to the spot near his left collarbone, where she'd bitten him only a few weeks earlier. At the time he'd been livid, hadn't found it funny in the slightest. Tonight, however, he found he couldn't find it anything but, and he started to laugh.

To his surprise, Ellie joined him. Softly at first, with a giggle that hinted she was holding more of it in than she was letting out. But eventually she was laughing just as hard as he was, and the more he saw her eyes sparkle and her cheeks blush, the more he wanted to keep the moment going.

Look at her. When she smiled like that, lost the glare and the frosty expression, she was... Not beautiful. At least not in the way Hollywood and the media defined the word. But he couldn't stop looking at her.

And why would he? She was laughing so hard she'd gone pink in the face and her eyes were squeezed shut. Any minute now he thought she'd keel over. It was adorable. Just as she threatened to make his prediction come true, she clutched at the air to steady herself. Her hand made contact with his upper arm and all the shared laughter suddenly died away.

Ellie looked away and tucked and escaped curl into the clip on top of her head. It bounced back again, unwilling to be leashed. His desire to reach forward and brush it away from her face was almost overpowering, but he'd done that so many times with other women. It would be too much of a cliché.

She looked up at him and shivered.

'You're cold.'

She started to protest, but he swung his jacket off and carefully hung it round her shoulders. It must be the night for clichés. This, too, was something he'd done more times than he could remember too—one of his *moves*, part of the game.

But it wasn't like that with Ellie. She'd been cold, and he'd done something to remedy that. He wasn't playing any games. Mainly because he didn't know what the rules were with her. She made him feel different—unpolished, uncertain—as if he wasn't in control of whatever was going on.

He looked at the warm light spilling from Larkford's every window. He really ought to get back to his guests.

She moved slightly, and the friction of material between his fingers reminded him he was still holding the lapels of the jacket firmly. He really should let go. But Ellie was looking up at him, her eyes soft and unguarded, just as they had been when she'd stared down at him from the landing.

He'd liked that look then, and he liked it now. There wasn't a hint of greed or artifice in it. And that was a rare thing in his world. It was as if she saw something that surprised her, something that everyone else missed.

He'd seen her skirting the edge of the party, boredom clear on her face. And when he'd turned back to Melodie and the record producer he'd been chatting to he'd suddenly seen the whole gathering through Ellie's eyes, as if he'd been given X-ray specs that cut out the glare and the glitter, revealing everyone and everything for who and what they really were. Not much of what he'd seen would benefit from close scrutiny.

But out here on the lawn everything felt very real indeed. Uncomfortably so. His heart was hammering in his chest—and it wasn't from his race across the lawn.

She was tantalisingly close, her feelings clearly written in her face, floating across the surface. He felt her warm breath on his neck, sending shivers to the roots of his hair. He clenched the lapels of the dinner jacket, pulling her closer until only a molecule of air prevented their faces from touching.

Normally he'd go in for the kill now, take the advantage while he had it, but he waited.

What for, he wasn't exactly sure.

The world seemed to shrink into the tiny space between his lips and hers. At least Ellie was aware of nothing but this, nothing beyond it. And, since remembering past or future was a struggle sometimes anyway, she finally let go and just existed in the moment. This particular moment revolved around a choice, one that was hers alone: to flow with the moment or push against it.

She was so tired of fighting herself, tired of pushing herself, of always keeping everything under constant surveillance. Just once she wanted to follow an impulse rather than resist it.

She wanted *this*.

Hesitantly, she pressed her lips against his, splaying her hands across his chest to steady herself. For a moment he did nothing, and her heart plummeted, but then he pulled her to him, sliding his hands under his suit jacket to circle her waist, and kissed her back.

All those women who fluttered and twittered merely at the sight of him would have melted clean away if they'd been on the receiving end of a kiss like this. Every mad hormonal urge she'd been fighting for the last few weeks roared into life and she didn't resist a single one.

It was a kiss of need, exploration...perfection.

She didn't need to think, to struggle to remember anything. And she wouldn't have been able to if she'd tried, not with Mark's teeth nipping at her lower lip, his hands sliding up her back until they brushed the bare flesh of her shoulders. Ellie reached up to feel the faint stubble on his jaw with her fingertips. He groaned and pulled her close enough to feel the muscles in his chest flexing as his arms moved. She let her head drop back when his lips pressed against the tingling skin just below her jaw, and she slid her fingers round the back of his head, running them through the short hair there and feeling him shiver.

A tray clanged inside the kitchen, and the noise cut cleanly and smoothly through the night air. They both froze, and the moment they'd shared shattered along with the glasses landing on the kitchen floor.

There was a horrible sense of *déjà vu* as they stared at each other, neither sure of what was going on and what they should do next.

Mark grasped for words inside his head. *Say something!*

He reached for her. 'Ellie…'

Come on, smooth talker! Where's all your patter now?

She stared back at him, wide-eyed and breathless. Then, before he could get his thoughts collected into syllables, she bolted into the house.

See? Unpredictable. He couldn't have guessed she was going to do that. After all, it wasn't the normal response he got when he kissed a woman—quite the reverse.

He raced after her and burst through the French windows into the kitchen. Precious seconds were lost as he collided with a fully laden waiter. The clattering of trays and muttered apologies masked the sound of her bare feet slapping on the tiles as she tore out of the kitchen and down the passageway that led to the back stairs.

He dodged another waiter and ran after her, only to be corralled by a group of guests.

'Mark!'

He turned to find Kat, looking all dishevelled and misty. Her puppy-dog eyes pleaded with him.

'It's Razor…'

She sniffed, and a single tear rolled down her cheek. Mark looked hopelessly at the staircase to his left, then at Kat, and back to the staircase. Kat hung on to his sleeve. He knew her well enough by now to realise that full meltdown was only seconds away. He put his own desires on the back burner and guided her through the crush in the drawing room to his study.

The boy wonder had undoubtedly been his usual considerate self, and Mark's shoulder was the one designated for crying on these days. He'd resisted that in the beginning, but he was too much of a sucker for a forlorn female to just pat Kat on the head and say, *There, there.*

As he ushered her into the study and shut the door he reasoned to himself that Ellie wasn't going anywhere for the moment. It would probably be better to give her a few minutes before he went after her—some thinking time. So he allowed Kat to spill out the whole sorry story and soak his shirt with her tears.

Ellie sat in the dark, shivering despite the central heating. She couldn't bear to turn on the light and see Sam's picture on the bedside table. Her eyes were sticky with tears and her nose was running. With a loud sniff she toppled back onto the mattress and curled into a ball.

'What was I thinking?'

Oh, but *thinking* hadn't been the problem. It was what she'd *done* that had messed everything up. Thoughts were fleeting, easily lost, erased or misplaced. Actions, however, were a little more concrete. And in this case definitely more memorable.

Just the memory of Mark's lips on hers was enough to make her flush hot and cold again.

How could she have done this to Sam? Wonderful, loving, dependable Sam? She was sure he would have been happy to think she would find someone else and rebuild her shattered life, but Mark Wilder! He was the worst kind of womaniser there was.

She searched the darkness above her head for an answer, desperate to make sense of it all.

But Mark hadn't seemed like a womaniser tonight in the garden, quite the reverse. He'd sent Piers Double-Barrelled packing, backing her up and taking her side, and he hadn't even taken advantage of the situation when she'd been vulnerable and heaving with hormones. She could have walked away...

Maybe it wasn't about Mark. Maybe it was a symptom of her decision to break free, to learn to live again. Perhaps part of herself that she'd thought had died and been buried along with Sam had sprung to life again. She was a young woman still. It was just a healthy interest in the opposite sex, a natural response to a good-looking man.

But that train of thought derailed just as fast as the last one had.

It was only since meeting Mark that she'd been anything but numb. He was a catalyst of some kind. And…and if it was just about pent-up desires, she wouldn't have rejected Piers. He was suave and attractive, but it didn't stop her experiencing a wave of revulsion every time she thought of him.

So she was back to Mark. Her brain was swinging in wild arcs, but it always came back to Mark. What was she going to do about that…about *him*?

His attraction to her was genuine, there was no mistaking that, but it wouldn't last. Men like him didn't stay with women like her. After a couple of months it would fizzle out and she'd be left alone again. And in search of a new job.

She didn't want an affair, or a fling, or a one-night stand. Settling for less than the all-encompassing love she'd had for Sam seemed like being unfaithful to his memory. It would be like losing the Crown Jewels and replacing them with paste and nickel that made your skin turn green. This thing with Mark, whatever it was, it couldn't go anywhere. It couldn't be anything.

She sniffed again and stretched out a little. Why? Why be interested in someone like him? She could say it was the money, or the success, his looks and his charm, but it wasn't any of those things. Tonight she'd glimpsed something else behind the cheeky, boyish charm. Something darker and deeper that resonated with a similar *something* inside her too.

A faint hint of Mark's aftershave drifted into her nostrils. She looked up, half expecting to see him standing there, waiting for her, but the room was empty. Then she realised she was still wearing his jacket. His masculine scent clung to it, and she was reminded of the moment he'd put it on her in the garden.

He'd seemed so vulnerable standing there. For a man who had women drop at his feet on a daily basis he'd almost seemed unsure of himself. Not at all what she'd expected.

She whimpered and covered her face with her hands, even though there was no one there to see her blush.

How was she going to face him in the morning?

CHAPTER SIX

MARK stumbled downstairs some time after ten. He'd intended to get up earlier, but he hadn't dropped off until dawn and then his sleep had been heavy, full of dreams where he was running from unseen predators. He'd wanted to be fresh and calm this morning, to deal with the aftermath of last night's events with just a little panache.

He didn't have to search hard for Ellie, though; he could smell something delicious wafting from the kitchen, and he followed the mouthwatering smell like a zombie.

Well, almost like a zombie. His heart rate was pattering along too fast for him to be considered officially dead. Was he…was he *nervous*?

He'd spent hours last night in his study, going over and over it all in his head. Not that he'd come to any earth-shattering conclusions. He had a housekeeper. She kissed like a dream. That was about the sum total of it.

All he'd done was kiss her. It was hardly a big deal.

All he'd done… He should listen to himself.

If it had just been a kiss, his heart wouldn't be flapping around inside his chest like a fish out of water.

He liked Ellie. And not in the let's-have-dinner-at-the-Ivy kind of way he normally liked women. It felt different. As if this kind of *liking* had a different shape, was a different kind of entity all together.

Now, that was a scary thought.

Like Helena, Ellie was one of those delicate beings, beautiful in their frailty like an orchid or a butterfly. And that made her even more dangerous. He knew he couldn't resist getting drawn in by women like that, finding himself wanting to protect them, to care for them until they were whole again. It was a weakness, he knew, but one that he channelled into his clients these days, by being the best manager in the business. At least they paid him for his devotion.

That kind of woman sucked everything out of a man until he had nothing left to give. And then she took what he'd done, all the tender, loving care he'd given, and bestowed it on someone else, someone who didn't remind her of the pain. Someone who didn't remind her of who she used to be when she was just a shell, empty and hurting.

He couldn't do that again. He couldn't be that for anyone again.

So he would just have to deflect Ellie, dazzle her, and move things back to where they should be—on a purely professional level.

If he could talk a highly strung diva down from demanding three-hundred-pound-a-bottle mineral water that had been blessed by a Tibetan priest in her dressing room, he could surely manage this. And then he would invent a reason to go and stay at his flat in London for a few days. It wasn't running away; it was self-preservation.

'Morning,' he said, overcompensating a little and sounding much too relaxed as he entered the kitchen. Ellie had her back turned to him. She was stirring something in a saucepan on the hob and returned his greeting in a cool, clipped voice, not looking up from the pan.

'What are you doing?'

Ah, yes. This is the smooth wit and banter you are famous for… This will charm the socks off her and sort everything out.

Ellie didn't say anything, just stirred harder.

'It smells great. What is it?'

'I decided to make a big batch of bolognaise and freeze it in smaller portions for quick suppers,' she said in a starchy voice. 'Would you like me to stop and fetch you breakfast?'

That was the last thing he wanted. Far too awkward.

'It's okay. I'm more than capable of getting my own coffee.'

He grabbed himself a mug of coffee and sat down at the circular wooden table near the French windows that led to the garden. Ellie was pushing what he now recognised as beef mince round the pan with a wooden spoon. It spat and hissed, the only sound in the rapidly thickening atmosphere.

He cleared his throat. 'Ellie, listen…'

'Look, Mark, I know where this is going.'

'You do?' He rubbed his nose with the heel of his hand.

'I do. And let's not go there.'

Good. They were reading off the same page. Why, then, had his stomach bottomed out like a plummeting lift?

'Okay,' he said, not trusting himself with anything more complicated. It seemed as if Ellie was doing fine on her own, anyway. She took a deep breath in readiness for another speech.

'You're my boss. You spend your time flitting around the globe and living the high life. And I'm…' She looked at the ceiling, searching for the right word.

'I know I'm your boss—of course I know that—and you're…'

Surprising? Appealing? Unforgettable? Those were the words that filled his head. None of them were the right ones to come out of his mouth, though.

'You're…'

Ellie's gaze wandered down from the heavens and settled on him. 'I'm your *housekeeper*.'

'Right.' That was correct. But it didn't *feel* like the right answer.

She shook her head, her curls bouncing slightly. 'To be honest, you and me, it's just—'

'Complicated?'

She shrugged one shoulder. 'I was going for tacky or predictable, but your word works too.'

Ouch.

'I'm your employee, and I think we should keep our relationship on a professional basis,' she said, turning to face him fully.

'I agree with you one hundred percent.'

He looked hard at her, trying to work out what she was thinking. Her words were telling him she was fine, but her tone said something entirely different.

'You seem upset…'

She waved the wooden spoon in dismissal.

'Upset? I'm not upset!'

'Good.'

She gave him a blatantly fake smile, and returned her attention to the meat in the pan.

'Annoyed, then?'

More frantic stirring.

'Nope. Not at all.' She started jabbing the wooden spoon at the remaining lumps.

Ellie might be different from a lot of women he knew in a lot of ways, but the whole pretending to be fine when she clearly was not was horribly familiar.

'Ellie, I know I may have been a bit impulsive last night, but I don't think we…*I* did anything wrong.'

'Oh, you don't?' she said through clenched teeth.

'No. Do you?'

Now he was totally lost. Why did women have this secret agenda that read like code to normal human beings—men, in other words?

The pan spat ferociously as Ellie added a jar of tomatoey gloopy stuff and mixed it in. She turned to face him and took a step away from the counter, still holding the dripping spoon.

'You're unbelievable, do you know that? You live in a lovely little Mark bubble where everything is perfect. You haven't got a clue what real life is like!'

He thought he did a pretty good job of living life, thank you very much, and he didn't much care for someone he hardly knew judging him for it.

'I don't?'

'No! You don't. Real people have real feelings, and you can't just go messing around with them. You live in this rarefied world where you do whatever you want, get whatever you want and everything goes right for you. Not everybody has that luxury. And you waste it, you know? You really do.'

Something in her stare made him hold back the smart retort poised on his lips. Through the film of tears gathering in her eyes he saw determination and an honesty that was surprising—and not a little unnerving.

Something was very wrong, but as usual he was totally mystified as to what was going on inside her head. Why was she blaming him? He hadn't been the one to start it last night. *She* had kissed him, remember? And he certainly hadn't meant to mess around with her feelings, but perhaps he had…without realising it.

Maybe he *was* clueless. He needed to consider her accusation a little more fully before he gave a real answer.

Ellie made use of the silence to ram her point home. 'I think it's best for both of us if we just put that…you know, the…'

A crack in her anger showed as she desperately tried to avoid using the word 'kiss'. It would have been funny if she hadn't been giving him the brush-off.

'Let's just put what happened last night down to champagne and temporary insanity, okay? I don't want to lose this job.'

He nodded just once. 'And I need to start looking for a new housekeeper like I need a hole in the head.'

Finally she breathed out and her shoulders relaxed a little.

'I'm glad we understand each other,' she said with a small jut of her chin, and turned her attention back to the bolognaise sauce.

She was right. He knew she was right. It was just…

Aw, forget it. He'd spent the last decade fooling everyone—even himself—that he was 'living the dream'. He might just as well return to that happy, alpha-wave state and forget that he'd ever yearned for anything more.

If you can, a little voice whispered in his ear. *If you can…*

Mark disappeared back to London the next day, much to Ellie's relief. But it didn't stop him coming back to Larkford again the following weekend. Or the one after that. During the week she could relax, enjoy her surroundings, but the weekends were something else. Stiff. Awkward. And, although she'd never expected anything more than a professional relationship with the man, now they were operating on that level it just seemed, well…weird.

And that was how it continued for the next month or so.

So, there she was on a Saturday afternoon, hiding out in the kitchen, preparing the evening meal, even though she needn't start for hours yet. But it was good to keep herself busy and out of a certain person's way. Not that it had been hard today. He might be at home, but he was obviously working; he'd hardly left the study all day. They were keeping to their separate territories as boxers did their corners of the ring.

She was still cross with herself for being too weak to control her brain's fried electrical signals. They still all short-circuited every time he appeared. It was as if her neurons had rewired themselves with a specialised radar that picked up only him as he breezed around the house, as calm as you like, while her fingernails were bitten so low she'd practically reached her knuckles.

Blip. Blip. Blip.

There it went again. Her core temperature rose a couple of notches. He was on the move; she just knew it. She stopped chopping an onion and listened. After about ten seconds she heard what she'd been waiting for—footsteps in the hall, getting louder.

She kept her eyes on her work as Mark entered the kitchen. The coffee machine sputtered. Liquid sloshed into a cup. The rubber heel of a stool squeaked on the floor. Silence. The tiny hairs on the back of her neck bristled.

Just carry on as if he's not there.

The knife came down hard on the chopping board—thunk, thunk, thunk—so close she almost trimmed her non-existent nails. She threw the onion pieces into a hot frying pan where they hissed back at her. According to the recipe they should be finely chopped. The asymmetrical lumps looked more like the shapes Chloe had produced as a toddler when left to her own devices with paper and safety scissors.

She sliced the next onion with exaggerated care and flipped the switch for the extractor hood above the hob. It was too still in the kitchen. Too hot. She plucked a papery clove of garlic from a nearby pot.

Only one more left.

That gave her an idea, stunning in its simplicity. She turned to face Mark with what she hoped was a cool stare. He sat looking straight back at her, waiting.

'I need to go out—to get some things I can't find at the local shops from the big supermarket. Is there anything you'd like me to get you that's not on the shopping list?' She nodded to indicate a long pad hanging on a nail where she always listed store cupboard items as soon as they'd run out. She even managed a smile on the last few words, so delighted was she at the thought of getting out of the house and into fresh, un-complicated air.

He just lifted his shoulders and let them drop again. 'Nope. Nothing in particular.'

Most housekeepers would be glad of having a boss with such an easygoing nature, but the contrast with her own jangled emotions just made her want to club him over the head with his large wooden pepper mill. She strode to the other side of the room and snatched her handbag from where it hung on the back of a chair.

It wasn't more than a minute later that she was sitting in the driver's seat of her car, turning the key in the ignition.

Nothing.

'Come on, old girl!' she crooned, rubbing the dashboard. 'Don't let me down now. You are my ticket out of here—at least for the afternoon.' She tried again, pumping her foot frantically on the pedal. Her old banger coughed, threatening to fire up, then thought better of it. She slapped the steering wheel with the flat of her hands.

'Traitor.'

She collected her bag and strutted back into the kitchen, chin in the air. Mark was still sitting on the stool, finishing his coffee.

'Problems?'

'Car won't start. I'll have to go another day, after I've had the old heap looked at.'

Mark stood up and pulled a bunch of keys from his pocket. 'Come on, then.'

'What?'

'I'll take you.'

'No, it's okay. Honestly. You're busy.'

'No problem,' he said with that lazy grin of his, the one straight out of a toothpaste ad. 'I could do with getting away from my desk and letting things settle in my head, anyway.'

Ellie groaned inwardly. Now the afternoon was going to be torture rather than escape. She followed him reluctantly to his car. It was a sleek, gunmetal-grey Aston Martin. She could almost see his chest puff out in pride as he held the passenger door open for her.

Boys and their toys. What was the theory about men with flash cars?

* * *

Mark didn't need to take his eyes off the road to know that Ellie had shifted position and was now staring out of the window. He was aware of every sigh, every fidget. And her body language was yelling at him in no uncertain terms—*back off*!

What if she'd been right all those weeks ago when she'd shouted at him? He'd given the whole thing a lot of thought. Did he live in a 'Mark bubble'? A self-absorbed little universe where he was the sun and all revolved around him? Did he now waltz through life—well, relationships—without a backward glance?

If he did, it hadn't always been that way. His thoughts slid inevitably to Helena. That woman had a lot to answer for. He'd have stayed by her side until his dying day. Hadn't he promised as much, dressed in a morning suit in front of hundreds of witnesses? Stupidly, he'd thought she'd felt the same way, but it turned out that he'd confused *loyalty* with *neediness*. She'd stuck around while he'd been useful and then, when he'd needed her to be the strong one for a change, she'd walked away.

And he hadn't seen it coming. Before the news had broken, he'd been thinking to himself that Helena had finally reached a place where she seemed less troubled, and he'd even been thinking about broaching the subject of having kids.

But then his first management company had gone belly-up because he'd made the same mistake with Nuclear Hamster. He'd really believed in them, had remortgaged his house, emptied his savings accounts to give them a start in the business. Friends had warned him not to take a cut of the net profit in their first contract when most managers took a percentage of the gross. The album had sold well, but on tour they'd run up huge bills—having parties, chartering private jets—and at the end of the day fifteen percent of no profit whatsoever and creditors knocking at the door meant he'd had to declare himself bankrupt. It hadn't been any comfort at all to know he'd walked into a trap of his own making because he made the mistake of trusting people he'd got close to.

He'd thought Helena's coolness, her distance, had been because she'd been worried about money. Heck, he'd been terrified himself. He'd known how expensive it was to take a rock band to court. But what else could he have done? He couldn't have let one bunch of freeloaders ruin his career and reputation, could he?

All at once the love and care she'd demanded from him for the previous four years had been deemed suffocating, and without the nice lifestyle there hadn't been much incentive to stick around. Helena had declared she needed space, that it was time to stand on her own two feet. You name the cliché and she'd flung it at him.

Of course that hadn't lasted more than two minutes. She'd soon found herself a rich TV executive to pander to her needs and the whole cycle had started all over again. Oh, she'd sniffed around again when he'd won his court case and rebuilt his company, but he hadn't even returned her calls. If she couldn't stand by him through the tough times—through living in a bedsit and eating beans on toast for months, through losing all his so-called friends and business associates—then she didn't deserve even a minute of his attention. He'd surprised himself at his own hardness.

And it gave him a grim sense of satisfaction to know she'd burned her bridges too soon. Half a ton of debts was all she'd been entitled to in the divorce proceedings. If she'd waited a couple of years before she'd bailed she would have done a lot better for herself.

Light drizzle peppered the windscreen. He watched it build into a pattern of dots. A flick of a switch round the steering wheel created a blank canvas where a new and completely different design was free to form.

He turned off the main road into a narrow country lane and determined to concentrate on the road in front of him. The

Aston Martin was heaven to drive. Normally he didn't have time to sit back and enjoy it, always hurrying from A to B, always focusing on the destination instead of the journey. Ellie's presence as his passenger made him want to savour the experience.

The trip to the supermarket had been fun, in a way. Spending time with her on neutral territory had been different. She'd relaxed a little. He felt strangely comfortable pushing the trolley along behind her as she'd browsed the aisles, squeezing avocados and reading the backs of packets. Of course he'd had no idea what she was doing half the time, or what she'd make with the assortment of ingredients she'd flung in the trolley, but the fact *she* knew gave her an air of wisdom.

The raindrops on the windscreen got fatter and rounder. They were going to have to get a move on if they were going to get home before it tipped down. The purr of the engine seduced him into going faster. He was pretty confident in his driving skills and was starting to become familiar with these lanes, anticipating the sweep and curve of the overgrown hedgerows as they got closer to Larkford. He glanced at Ellie. She was staring straight ahead, a grim look on her face.

He swung round a corner into a flat, fairly straight stretch of road and picked up speed. He loved the growl of satisfaction as the engine worked harder. It responded with eagerness to every nudge on the accelerator.

The sky darkened and the wild hedgerows whipped past, clawing at the car as if they were jealous. Inside the low-slung sports car the air was full of static. He could almost feel the crackles arcing from Ellie's thigh as he changed gear, his knuckles threatening to stroke the warm denim of her jeans.

A pheasant burst from the hedge in a flurry of feathers. He heard Ellie's sharp intake of breath, and out of the corner of his eye saw her grip the edge of her seat. After he'd braked slightly, he turned his head fully towards her, meaning to reassure her.

'Mark…' The trembling plea hardly escaped her lips.

'It's okay. We weren't going to—'

'Mark…please…!'

The urgency in her voice panicked him. Her face was frozen in stark horror. He looked back down the lane and his stomach lurched as he saw the farm vehicle pulling out of a concealed entrance. He squeezed the brake harder, slowing to a smooth crawl, and allowed the rust-speckled tractor to rumble past them. He pulled away and silently congratulated himself on not even leaving a skid mark on the tarmac.

'Stop the car.' Her voice was faint, but determined.

'But we're almost home.'

Her voice came in breathy gasps. 'I said…stop the car…I want to get out.'

Mark's faced creased into a scowl of disbelief as Ellie scrabbled at the door lever, desperate to free the lock. He pulled deftly into a passing place. Before the car had fully stopped Ellie had popped her seat belt and staggered out of the car, stumbling forward, gulping in damp country air. She was shaking, her whole body quivering.

Mark sat paralysed in the driver's seat, too stunned to move. Then, coming to his senses, he unbuckled himself and ran after her. It didn't take long to catch her as she straggled up the lane, half in a dream state.

He grabbed her wrist and pulled her firmly to him. Her head lodged just under his chin, and for a split second she moulded against him before pushing him away again.

He should have remembered she was surprisingly strong for a woman so soft and rounded-looking. He managed to grab one of her wrists before she darted off again down the middle of the road.

She turned to face him, fury in her eyes. 'I asked you to *stop* the car!'

Her free arm waved around wildly and she pulled and tugged the other, trying to twist it out of his grasp.

Mark stared at her. What on earth was wrong with her? Why such angst over a stupid tractor? Puzzled as he was, he held on to her as gently as he could without letting her run down the lane into oncoming traffic. Ellie swung towards the middle of the road as she attempted to wrench her arm away from him again, all the while pressing a flattened palm to her chest and breathing in shallow gasps.

The nasal blast of a horn pierced the air and Mark grabbed her back out of the path of an approaching car. He stumbled backwards with her until his feet were on the grassy verge, the gnarled twigs of the ancient hedgerow piercing his back.

Ellie's mouth worked against his chest. He could feel her jaw moving, feel the moist warmth of her breath through his pullover. She might have been trying to shout at him, but nothing remotely resembling a word was included in the few noises tumbling out of her mouth. Her tiny hands balled into fists and she punched him on the chest. Twice.

He might not know what was going on here—clueless, as always—but one thing was certain: whether she knew it or not, Ellie needed him in this moment. She needed someone to be angry with, someone to fall apart on. And, hey, wasn't he the most likely candidate to light her fuse at the moment, anyway? He might as well take the brunt of whatever this was.

No way was he about to brush this situation off with a joke. It was time to face the challenge he'd walked away from so many times over the last decade. No amount of sequins or cash would defuse the situation. He was just going to have to be 'real' too. He hoped to God he still had it in him.

She was still trying to push away from him, but now the tears came. She gulped and cried and sobbed as if she'd never stop. He swallowed rising fear at such intense emotion, whispered words of comfort in her ear and waited for the squall to wear itself out. Eventually the sobbing became shallower and she surrendered to it, burying her face in his jumper. All those crying sessions with Kat now just seemed like practice sessions leading up to this moment—and he was thoroughly glad of the training.

How he wished he could do something to ease her pain. It was so raw. Perhaps if he held her long enough, tight enough, something of him she needed would seep through the damp layers between them in a kind of osmosis. He wanted to make up the missing parts of her. Loan her his uncanny ability to shield himself from everything, to feel nothing he didn't want to.

His fingers stilled in her curls as he thought what a poor exchange it would be. He had nothing to give her, really. She could teach him so much more. Her determination, her ability to say what she felt whether she wanted to or not. She knew how to live, while he only knew how to dazzle.

The sky turned to lavender-grey as afternoon retreated. Mark let the thump of his heart beat away the minutes as Ellie became motionless against him, pulling in deep breaths. She peeled her face from his chest, the ridge marks of the wool knit embedded on her hot cheek, half blinded by the thick tears clogging her eyelashes. Mark held her face tenderly in his palms and looked deep into her pink-rimmed eyes, desperate to soothe away the tempest he didn't understand.

Ellie stared back at him.

He could see weariness, despair, the ragged depths of her soul, but also a glimmer of something else. Her eyes were pleading with him, asking him to give her hope.

His voice was soft and low. 'Tell me.'

It was not a demand, but a request. Ellie's lips quivered and a tear splashed onto his hand. Never taking his gaze from her, he led her to the passenger door and sat her on the edge of the leather seat, crouching to stay on her level, keeping her hands tight between his.

Ellie let out a shuddering sigh as she closed her eyes. Her top lip tucked under her bottom teeth. He could see she was searching for words. Her pale green eyes flipped open and looked straight into his.

Her voice was low and husky from crying. 'It was just a panic attack. I get them sometimes… Sorry.'

He wasn't sure he was buying this. A forgotten voice inside his head—his conscience, maybe?—poked and prodded him and dared him not to let this slide. Whatever she needed to say was important. And it was important she said it now. So he did the only thing he could do. He waited.

For a few minutes no one spoke, no one moved, and then she dipped her head and spoke in a low, hoarse voice. 'My husband and daughter were killed in a car accident on a wet day like this,' she said, looking down at their intertwined fingers.

'I'm so sorry.'

Well, that was probably the most inadequate sentence he'd ever uttered in his life, but it was all he could come up with. Lame or not, it was the truth. He was sorry for her. Sorry for the lives that had been cut off too early. Sorry he hadn't even known she'd been married. He squeezed her hands tighter.

'It was almost four years ago now. We were driving home from a day out shopping. I'd bought Chloe a pair of sparkly pink party shoes. She never even got to wear them…'

There was nothing he could say. Nothing he could do but let her talk.

'The police said it was joyriders. They'd been daring each other to go faster and faster… There was a head-on collision at a sharp bend on a country lane. Nobody could stop in time—the road was too wet.'

How awful. Such a tragedy. He wondered how she'd found out. Had the police come knocking at her door? A word she'd muttered earlier came back to haunt him.

We?

He rubbed the back of her hand with his thumb. 'You were in the car too?'

She sniffed and hiccupped at the same time, then looked at him, a deep gnawing ache in her eyes. 'I was driving.'

Mark pulled her back into his arms. He could feel her salty

tears on his own cheek, smell her shampoo as she laid her head on his shoulder. He closed his eyes and drank in her gentle fragrance. Her soft ringlets cushioned his face, a corkscrew curl tickling his nose.

'Feel,' she said. At first he didn't understand, but she pulled his hand away from her back and placed it on the right side of her head. Where there should have been smooth bone beneath skin and hair there was a deep groove in her scalp. Mark stroked the hair there too. Gently. So gently.

'The police told me there wasn't anything I could have done,' she said quietly. 'But I don't remember. And it's like having a huge question mark hanging over my life. I'm never going to know that for sure. What if I could have reacted a split second faster or turned the wheel another way?'

She drifted off into silence again.

His voice left him. He'd never imagined…

And he realised how stupid he'd been now. He should have curbed the adolescent urge to show off around her, racing his car down the winding lanes. All this was his fault.

Ellie sighed and relaxed into him. It felt perfect, as if she'd been carved to fit there. In recent weeks he'd not been able to stop himself fantasising about holding her close like this, kissing her brow, her nose, her lips. Well, not exactly like this. But he knew if he gave in to the fierce pull of his own desire now he would desecrate the moment, and he knew it would never come again.

She stirred, pulling back from him slightly to drag her hands across her face in an effort to mop up the congealed tears.

'I'm sorry.' Her voice was so faint it was barely a whisper.

'No. *I'm* sorry. For starting all this in the first place…'

'You couldn't have known.' All the fizzing, spitting irritation she'd held in her eyes every time she'd looked at him since the night of the party was gone.

'Well, I know now. And I am sorry. For anything—every-thing—I did to upset you. You must know I would never do that on purpose, however much of an idiot I may seem sometimes.'

Her mouth curved imperceptibly and her eyes never left his. He felt a banging in his chest just as hard as when she'd been thumping on it with her fist. He stood up and rested his hand on the door to steady himself.

'Let's go home.'

CHAPTER SEVEN

No lights were on in the drawing room. The firelight flickered, playing with the shadows on the wall. Mark sat in his favourite chair and savoured the aromatic warmth of his favourite whisky as it smouldered in his throat. The only sounds were the cracking of the wood on the fire and the laborious ticking of the antique clock in the corner. Ellie had gone to bed early, and he was left to relentlessly mull over the events of the afternoon.

They had driven back to Larkford in complete silence, but it had been different from the combustible atmosphere of their outward journey. The calm after the storm. He hadn't wanted to jinx the easy comfort by opening his big mouth. He hadn't been sure if Ellie was lost in the recent past, or plumbing the depths of earlier memories, and it hadn't felt right to ask.

The vivid evening sky had deepened to a velvety indigo by the time they'd drawn up in front of the house. Mark had carried the shopping in, forbidding Ellie to help, and had suggested she have a long hot bath. He'd realised, as he'd struggled with the dilemma of where to put the dried pasta they'd just bought, that he didn't have a clue where stuff went in his own kitchen. He'd got down to a shortlist of two possible cupboards when he'd heard the unmistakable sound of Ellie's bare feet on the tiles.

'Top left,' she said quietly.

'Thanks,' he replied, shutting the cupboard door he was holding open and walking to another one on the other side of the room. When he put the linguine away next to the other bags of pasta he turned to look at her. She was dressed in a ratty pink towelling robe that was slightly longer at one side than the other. Her hair was wet, the blonde curls darkened and subdued, but struggling to bounce back. Her face was pink and scrubbed, eyes bright. He had never seen her look so gorgeous.

She walked towards him. His heart thumped so loudly in his chest he thought she was bound to hear it. But she didn't stop and stare at him. She didn't laugh. Instead, she was smiling, eyes hesitant but warm. He was hypnotised.

'Thank you, Mark. For everything.'

She was only a foot away from him now, and she stood on tiptoes and placed an exquisitely delicate kiss on his cheek.

'Goodnight,' she said gently, and she headed for the door.

'Night,' he replied absently, still feeling the sweet sting of her lips on his cheek.

Now, hours later, he could still feel the tingle of that kiss. He took another sip of the whisky and rubbed the spot with the tips of his fingers.

At least he understood that tragic look in her eyes now. Ellie was haunted; the ghosts of her lost family still followed her. She had lived through more hurt than he could possibly imagine and yet she had found the strength to carry on living.

He looked back at his own life over the last decade and berated himself for his self-centredness and cowardice. He'd been afraid to let anyone close because he'd allowed one gold-digging woman to discolour his view of the rest of her sex. Instead of moving on and growing from the experience he'd sulked and cut himself off from any possibility of being hurt again, learning to cauterise the wounds with sarcastic humour and a don't-care attitude. He'd taken the easy way out.

Not like Ellie. She was brave. How did you pick yourself up again and keep on living after something like that?

He downed the rest of the whisky and sat for a long time, holding the empty glass. Once upon a time he'd written her off as fragile, but she was possibly the strongest person he'd ever met.

Be careful what you wish for, Ellie thought, as she exited the kitchen through the French windows and took her usual route round the garden. All those months in Barkleigh, longing for breathing space, the chance to be on her own without anyone fussing…

Well, now she had air and space in bucketloads. And for a while it had been good, and she thought she'd escaped that creeping sense of loneliness that had seeped into her bones at the cottage, but it had just followed her here.

Okay, most of the time it was pretty perfect. Like now, when the early-morning sun was gently warming her skin as she wandered a subconscious route round the gardens, her habitual cup of tea cradled in her upturned hands, but sometimes all this room, this space, it was a little…well…

She shook her head. She was just being silly.

It was hardly surprising she was finding life a little solitary. Only a couple of days after the disastrous trip to the supermarket Mark had disappeared, mumbling something about putting a big deal together, and she hadn't seen him for more than a fortnight. She guessed he was staying up at his flat in London, going to meetings all day. She tried not to speculate on what he might get up to at night.

The view of the Thames from his flat must be stunning, the vibe of the warm summer nights exciting, but if she had a choice of living in a crowded city, full of exhaust fumes and scary commuters, and being here at Larkford, she knew what she'd pick.

She kicked her flip-flops off as she reached the edge of the lawn and sighed in pleasure as the soles of her feet met soft grass that was dry, but still cool from the early-morning dew.

It was silly, but she couldn't shake the feeling that Mark was staying away deliberately. Maybe he was embarrassed. He wouldn't be the first person not to be able to handle her unique circumstances. She'd tried to run away from that feeling too, hadn't she? And now it had tracked her down and turned up on her doorstep.

She looked around the garden. The roses on the wrought-iron arches that lined the main path were in flower, a variety with frilly shell-pink petals. The smell was fantastic.

She sighed. Well, if Mark wanted to stay away, she couldn't stop him. It just seemed such a pity he was missing how beautiful his home looked. Every day there was something new to admire in the garden, another flower opening its buds or shooting out new green leaves. Maybe Mark wasn't the sort of person to notice these kind of things, but even if you didn't notice the details you couldn't help but feel rested here.

When she went back inside the house and checked her laptop she found an e-mail from Mark, and this time, instead of giving another boring, bland reply, she decided to add a little bit about Larkford—about the rose walk and how the wisteria on the back of the house was fairly dripping with flowers, how the hazy summer mornings burnt off into hot, bright afternoons. At least he wouldn't miss the magic of his house totally, even if he wasn't here to see it for himself.

Just as she was about to turn the laptop off she heard a ping, announcing the arrival of an e-mail. Thinking it might be from Ginny, informing her of the latest in a long line of pregnancy-related stories about absent-mindedness, she almost ignored it, but at the last minute she clicked on the little window and opened up the message.

She blinked and opened her eyes a little wider. It was from Mark. He must be online right now.

Hi Ellie
Thanks for the update on the plumbing situation. I'm sure you'll be glad to have your own space when the repairs are finished in your apartment. Feel free to decorate as you'd like.
I'm glad the wisteria is stunning and the roses are happy!!! I didn't realise you were a poet as well as a housekeeper ;-)
Mark.

What a cheek! Still, she couldn't erase the image of Mark's devil-may-care smile as she read it, and she was smiling too when she typed back her reply.

Fine. Now I know my boss is a Philistine I won't bother sending any similar observations with my next message!

Of course he couldn't leave it at that. And a rapid e-mail battle ensued. Ellie was laughing out loud when she finally admitted defeat and switched the laptop off. Maybe he was busy, after all. Maybe this whole 'deal' thing wasn't just an excuse to avoid her.

And that was how communication continued the next week or so. The e-mails got less businesslike and more chatty. Mark always added winky faces made out of colons and semicolons—Sam would have said that he used far too many exclamation marks—and Ellie forgot her threat not to tell him anything about Larkford and ended up describing the way the wonderful house looked in the pale dawn light, losing herself in the images and getting all flowery about it…

And Mark, true to form, would reply with a teasing quip and burst her lyrical little bubble, causing her to laugh out loud and send back something equally pithy. She decided it was nice to communicate with someone who didn't remind her constantly of what she'd been like before the accident, who just accepted her for who she was now and didn't patronise her. He wasn't just her boss now; he was an ally.

But she knew he couldn't be any more than that. And that was fine, because that was exactly how she wanted it. Really, it was.

London late at night was stunning. Mark pressed his forehead against the plate-glass wall that filled one side of his living room and used his own shadow to block out the reflection of his flat so he could see the city beyond. Multi-coloured lights blinked on the black river below, endlessly dancing but never wearying.

When he'd bought this place he hadn't thought he'd get tired of this view, but lately he'd found himself wanting to trade it in for something else. Maybe a leafy square in Fitzrovia or a renovated warehouse near the docks?

He decided to distract himself from his restlessness by turning on the TV, but everything seemed pointless, so he wandered into his bedroom, crashed so hard onto the bed that it murmured in complaint, then picked up the book on his bedside table. *A Beginner's Guide to Head Injuries*. Only one more chapter to go and he'd be finished.

He got it now. Why Ellie had moments where she zoned out, why she forgot common words. It wasn't just that she was scatterbrained. Not that it mattered, anyway. And he wasn't entirely sure that *all* of Ellie's unique qualities were down to a rather nasty bump on the head. He had the feeling that even if the head injury could be factored out of the equation she'd still be pretty unique.

He read to the end of the bibliography and put the book back where he'd got it from. He hadn't checked his e-mail yet this evening, had he? And he had started to look forward to Ellie's slightly off-on-a-tangent e-mails. She had a way of making him feel as if he were right there at Larkford, with her little stories about village life and descriptions of which plants were in flower in the garden.

Bluebells.

In her last e-mail she'd said that she'd seen a carpet of bluebells in the woodland at the fringes of the estate. Although he'd never been a man to watch gardening programmes, or take long country walks to 'absorb nature', he'd suddenly wanted to stand in the shade of an old oak tree and see the blue haze of flowers for himself. He wanted to see Ellie smile and turn to him, as if she were sharing a secret with him…

No.

He couldn't think that way. He liked Ellie. He respected her. Hell, he was even attracted to her—majorly—but he couldn't go down that path.

It had been a long time since he'd held a woman in such high regard. And that was why this was dangerous. All the things he thought about Ellie… Well, they were the basis for a good relationship. Friendship, compatibility, chemistry. But he couldn't risk it. And not just for himself. What about Ellie? He wasn't the man for her. She didn't need someone who would probably cause her even more pain.

He jumped off the bed and started moving. Not that he had any particular destination in mind. He just seemed to get a burst of speed whenever he thought about a certain housekeeper.

And that was why he'd stayed away from Larkford. Because he was scared of what he was starting to feel for her. Yet even then she'd burrowed even further under his skin. Staying away hadn't worked, had it?

He found himself by the window in the living room again, and placed his palm on the glass.

So why was he here? Bored and wishing he was somewhere else? If keeping his distance hadn't worked, he might as well go and enjoy the house he'd bought for himself, because that was what he really wanted to do.

He wanted to go and see the bluebells for himself.

* * *

The gentle chiming of distant church bells roused Ellie from her Saturday morning slumber. Almost subconsciously she counted the chimes, not realising when she'd started but knowing the total by the time they'd finished. Eight.

Warm sunlight filtered through the curtains. She half sat in bed and rubbed her eyes. Her mouth gaped in an unexpected yawn. She shuffled herself out of bed, threw back the curtains and drank in the beautiful morning. The plumbing in her apartment above the old stables was now all fixed and she'd moved in. While her little kitchen looked over the cobbled courtyard, her bedroom had a wonderful view over the gardens. They were glorious this morning, bursting with life. She felt decidedly lazy as she watched a bee worrying the clematis beneath her window. It seemed completely unimpressed with her and disappeared into the centre of a large purple flower.

She turned from the window, full of great ideas for an al fresco lunch, and the sun glinted off the picture frame on the windowsill. She stopped to look at it, head tipped on one side. The photo had been taken at Chloe's fourth birthday party. Chloe was grinning like the proverbial Cheshire cat, her freshly lit birthday cake in front of her on the table. Sam and Ellie leaned in behind her, faces warmed by the glow of the candles.

They all looked so happy. She kissed her index finger and pressed it onto the glass where Chloe's smile was. It had been a wonderful day.

The memory came easily and painlessly now. She smiled as she recalled the incessant squealing of little girls and the pungent smell of blown-out birthday candles. Chloe had spent the whole party bouncing up and down in excitement, even when she was devouring pink birthday cake. She remembered Sam's smile later that evening, when he'd silently beckoned her to come and look at Chloe. They'd crept through the post-party devastation into the lounge and found her fast asleep on the sofa, chocolate smeared all over her face and clutching the doll they had given her in her sticky hands.

She'd found it so hard to look at this photo in the past. Even so, she'd kept it on prominent display as a kind of punishment. What she was guilty of, she wasn't sure.

Being here when they weren't. Being alive.

Since their deaths she had lived life as if she was walking backwards—too terrified of the unfamiliar territory ahead to turn and face the future. She'd blindly shuffled through each day, just trying to keep going without meeting disaster again. Pain was to be avoided at all costs. No risk. No attachments. But no love, either. Her smile dissolved completely.

What would Sam think of the way she'd been coping?

She knew exactly what he would say. Her face creased into a frown. She could almost see his hazel eyes scowling at her, the trademark tuft of wayward hair slipping over his forehead.

Life should never feel small, Ellie.

That was what he'd always told her. Despite her secure family background she'd always been a shy child, but Sam had seen beyond the reserve. He'd asked her to play tag while the other schoolchildren had ignored the quiet girl on the wooden bench with her coat pulled round her. She'd been desperate to join in, but much too scared to get up and ask in case they laughed and ran away. But Sam had won her over with his gentle smile as he'd grabbed her hand and pulled her off the bench. Within minutes she'd been running after him, the wind in her hair and a smile beneath her rosy cheeks.

It had always been like that with Sam. He had encouraged her to dare, to believe. To make life count.

'Sorry, sweetheart,' she whispered, the glass misting as she talked to his face in the photo.

She sighed and pulled her tatty robe from its hook on the back of the door. Since the incident in Mark's car, she'd felt different. Liberated, somehow. Perhaps the whole embarrassing scenario had done some good after all. She'd been clutching on to her grief for so long, and her reaction to Mark's driving had finally provided an outlet—the last great emotional lurch in her rollercoaster stay at Larkford so far.

Ever since she had got here she'd been plunging into some forgotten feeling—panic, shame, anger—desire, even. She'd experienced them all in vivid richness. And somehow Mark Wilder stood in the middle of the maelstrom. Instead of making her feel safe, as Sam had, he made her feel nervous, excited and confused all at once. It was as if the universe had shifted a little when she wasn't looking and she suddenly found herself off-balance when he was around.

Yet he'd surprised her with his understanding and sensitivity. Not once had she felt judged for her behaviour that afternoon. It had been so nice to sink into his strong arms and know that she wasn't alone.

She tied the sash of her gown in a lumpy knot. With a heavy sigh she acknowledged that her relationship with Mark had changed in that moment. A boundary had been crossed as she had stood shivering against him in the lane.

She'd also noticed a change in Mark in the couple of weeks since he'd started living at Larkford again. But the way he was treating her now made her feel uncomfortable in a completely new way. Now he came home more evenings than he stayed away, even though the hour's drive from London could double if the motorway traffic was bad. He was always witty and entertaining, and she no longer fumed at his humour, but laughed along with it. There was even the odd quip at her expense, but it was a gentle nudge rather than sarcastic teasing.

He obviously thought she was too fragile to be toyed with now. What a pity, because suddenly she was ready to find out if there was an upside to all these impulses and strong emotions she'd inherited from the accident, to see if love and joy and happiness might just be brighter and more multi-coloured than they had ever been before.

* * *

Ellie was working on a salad for lunch when she heard a car pulling up outside. That was odd. She'd assumed Mark had been sleeping late, because he'd had to attend a function the night before, but that sounded like his car. She blinked in surprise when he strode into the kitchen a few moments later.

'You're up early,' she said, inspecting a bottle of rice vinegar to see how much was left—a complete cover for the fact her insides were doing the tango. He still made her catch her breath every time he walked into the room, but it was different. It wasn't all about hormones fizzing and pure physical reactions. Somehow those sensations had grown beyond the superficial things they were, and now she sometimes felt as if there was a dull ache inside her chest that grew stronger the closer he was to her.

'I had things to do,' he said.

She noticed the little shopping bag he was carrying with the logo of a high-end electrical store and shook her head. '*More* gadgets?' He was a typical man in that respect.

Instead of giving her a boyish grin and proudly showing off his latest piece of kit, he just looked a little awkward as he nodded his answer to her question.

'Actually, I bought this for you.'

Ellie put the vinegar bottle down on the counter and stared at him. 'For me?'

Mark handed her the bag and she pulled a small glossy box from it. A handheld computer. She stared at it, hardly knowing what to say.

'You got me a PDA?'

He nodded again, still unusually serious and silent. 'You can link it up to the laptop and keep all your calendars and notes with you wherever you go. It even has a voice recorder function. I thought it might be…you know…useful when you need to make a note of something in a hurry, before you forget.'

Ellie felt like crying. She hadn't even thought of using something like this, but it was perfect. Just what she needed.

'Thank you,' she said, her voice wavering. 'Why did you…? I mean, what made you think of getting me this?'

He shuffled backwards. 'Just something I read…'

She frowned at him. Where was the normally cocky and devil-may-care Mark Wilder? Why was he looking so sheepish?

Oh, great. He'd been researching her condition—probably read up on it on the Internet. While it was still an incredibly sweet gesture, it just confirmed that his view of her had changed. Now she was just the poor brain-damaged housekeeper who couldn't keep her facts straight without the help of a bit of technology.

She wanted to be cross with him, but she couldn't rev up the energy. Instead she put the box back in the bag and stowed it in an empty cupboard. 'I'll have a look properly later.'

'You like it? You think it'll be useful?'

He looked so hopeful, so eager, that she couldn't help but smile and nod. 'It's wonderful. It'll be a big help.'

And it would. There was no need to be sad about a tiny computer just because it signalled what she knew already—that anything more than a professional relationship between them was a total impossibility.

Mark grinned. Suddenly he was back to his old self: cheeky, confident…impossible. Ellie picked up a cook's knife and went back to chopping something—anything—to keep her mind occupied and her pulse even. But after a few moments he walked over to the chopping board and looked over her shoulder. Ellie fanned her face. It was very warm. Had he closed the window? She glanced over at the French doors, but the embroidered muslin panels were still billowing gently.

'What are you cooking?'

Ellie put the knife down a little too quickly. It clattered on the worktop. Despite the fact her brain told her the crush she had on Mark was pointless, the neural pathways carrying that information to her body seemed to have gone on strike.

'Vietnamese salad,' she said, the words tumbling out.

'Which is—?' He waved his hand in a circular motion as her mouth moved soundlessly.

'Chicken and noodles and a few vegetables, with a sweet chilli dressing,' she replied, a wobbly finger pointing to each of the ingredients in turn.

Great! Now she was babbling like a bad TV chef.

His cheek twitched, yet his face remained a mask of cool composure. 'Hot stuff, then?'

Under different circumstances, Ellie would have thought he was flirting with her. Heat licked at the soles of her feet. She swallowed. 'It depends on the size of the chilli.'

The look her gave her was positively wicked. 'And you girls try and tell us boys that size doesn't matter.'

Ellie almost choked.

Mark picked up the half-chopped chilli from the chopping board. 'How hot is this one?'

Ellie tried very hard to focus on the bright red chilli and not on Mark's warm brown eyes.

'Medium, sort of. The small ones are the hottest, funnily enough.'

Stop babbling! He already knows that. Everybody knows that!

She bit her lip and turned to peel the outer stem off a stick of lemongrass.

'Do you want this back?'

She felt Mark's breath warm on the back of her neck as he stood close behind her. She failed to still the tiny shiver that rippled up her spine as she turned slightly to take the chilli back from him.

'Thank you.'

She carefully eased it from his grasp, avoiding brushing his fingers, and offered up a silent *hallelujah* as Mark stepped back and headed for the door.

'I'm going for a shower.'

'Okay. Let me know if you want any of this when you come out.'

He ran his hand through his hair and rubbed the corner of one eye with his thumb. That early-morning start must be catching up with him.

But then she realised what he was about to do. 'Don't put your—'

Mark yelped, screwed his eyes shut tight and slapped his hands to his face. She rushed over to him, wincing in sympathy. She peeled the hand from his face and led him over to one of the breakfast stools, where she ordered him to sit down. His right eye was squeezed shut and watering.

'Try and open your eyes,' she said gently.

'Very funny!'

'I mean it. If you can manage to open them and blink a bit, the eye can do its job and wash the chilli juice away. It works a lot faster than sitting there with your fingers pressing into your eyeballs, making it worse!'

Mark groaned again, removed his hand and attempted to prise his watery eyelids apart.

'Wait there!' she ordered, dashing to the sink and washing her hands vigorously with washing-up liquid and scrubbing under her nails with a little brush.

'Here, let me see.'

She moved in close and delicately placed a thumb on the smooth skin near Mark's eye. He flinched.

'Sorry! Did I hurt you?'

'Um…no, it's okay.'

She gently pulled downwards, helping to open his eye. 'It looks a bit pink. Is it still stinging? Try blinking a few more times.'

'It's fading now, thank you, Nurse. How did you know what to do?'

She blushed. 'You think with a memory like mine that I haven't done this to myself a million times?'

Mark's laugh was deep and throaty. He blinked a few more times, opened his good eye, then attempted to do the same with the other, but it stayed stubbornly at half-mast.

Ellie's partial smile evaporated as she became conscious of the warmth radiating from him. They were practically nose to nose. He was sitting on the stool, one long leg braced against the floor, the other hooked on the bottom rung. She was standing between his legs, only inches from his chest. She knew she should move. Mark was looking back at her through bleary eyes. She picked a spot on the floor between her feet and stared at it.

'You're lucky,' she said, succeeding in inching backwards slightly.

Try not to look at him.

'You only touched the chilli briefly. It would have been much worse if you'd been chopping them…'

Mark caught her hand as she attempted to shuffle back further. She made the mistake of looking up. A soft, tender look was in his eyes, despite the fact that one eyeball was still pink and watery.

'Thank you, Ellie.' The sincerity in his tone was making her feel all quivery.

She managed to shift her gaze to her hand, still covered by his. Static electricity lifted the hairs on her arm.

'That's—that's all right,' she stammered. Her hand jerked from his as she shook herself loose. She turned and headed for the door. 'I'll go and have that shower now, then,' she added.

Perhaps a cold one.

She started to scuttle off down the passageway.

'Ellie…?' he called after her, a laugh underscoring his words.

The urge to keep going was powerful, but she turned and popped her head back through the open door. 'Yes?'

Mark was grinning at her. She had the sudden sinking feeling she didn't want to know why.

'*I* was going to have a shower, remember? *You* were cooking.'

Ellie closed her eyes gently and darted a moist tongue over her bottom lip, trying to work out how to salvage the situation. She looked at Mark with her best matter-of-fact expression. 'Of course.'

For some reason he looked very pleased with himself. He wasn't going to tease her about this for months to come, was he? What if he guessed it was him who had got her all in a fluster?

Once her cotton wool legs had taken her back to the chopping board she set about peeling the garlic, trying to block Mark's view of her shaking hands with her body. She heard the scrape of his stool across the floor as he rose from his seat. Every part of her body strained to hear his movements as he left the room. She stripped the skin off a clove of garlic, leaving it vulnerable and naked, and listened to Mark whistling something chirpy as he bounded up the stairs at least two at a time.

CHAPTER EIGHT

'MARK!'

His head snapped up. Nicole, his PA, stood with hands on hips, a buff folder clutched in one hand, scowling hard. This wasn't good news.

'Huh?'

'What is wrong with you this morning? That has to be the fifth time I've caught you admiring the London skyline while ignoring every word I say. You're making me feel like my old maths teacher, Mrs McGill.'

Mark stopped staring through the glass wall of his office and turned to face Nicole fully. She was right. He hadn't been paying attention. But now that he was she still wasn't making any sense.

'What?'

'She was always throwing chalk at Billy Thomas for staring out the window during double algebra. I mean it, Mark! If you make me sound like Mrs McGill I'm going to do something drastic.'

He hunched over his desk and scribbled feverishly away on the pad in front of him. Nicole flopped into the chair on the other side of the desk and massaged her temple with her free hand.

'What are you doing now? I'm feeling too grotty for your stupid games.'

When he had scrawled a handful of lines, he ripped the

sheet off and thrust it in Nicole's direction. She snatched it from his hand and started to read it out loud.

'"I will not daydream in Mrs McGill's class. I will not daydream in—" Very funny!'

He easily dodged her missile as she crumpled the paper into a ball and threw it back at him. He did the puppy-dog thing with his eyes he knew she could never resist.

'Sorry, Miss.'

'You'd better be! You were saying something about pushing the record company for a three-sixty-degree contract for the new band's next deal, and then you just drifted off.'

'Sorry, Nic. I promise I'm listening now.'

He rested his elbows on the desk and propped his chin on his fists, deliberately focusing on her and only her.

'And I need to know what you want to do about this video shoot. We've only got five days before we leave for the Caribbean, and Kat's in a state because Razor went AWOL. The director has changed his mind about one of the locations, and the stylist has had a strop and isn't taking any of my calls.'

Mark did his best to listen as Nicole continued to brief him on the latest string of disasters to hit the upcoming shoot. It had been a nightmare from start to finish. He was starting to wish they'd opted for the other treatment, which had involved lots of time on a soggy moor in Scotland. When they'd set it up he'd been looking forward to going to Antigua. He'd planned on taking a few days off after the shoot—the closest thing to a holiday he was going to get this year.

But now the date was looming close he was starting to wish he could wriggle out of it. He didn't want to leave Larkford. A week on the other side of the planet would be a week away from Ellie. Coming into London was different. He was away for the day, but in the evening he would be stranded on the M25 in the rush-hour traffic with a smile on his face, knowing he was on the way home.

Home. Ellie had made his house a home. He loved arriving

back there and seeing a warm glow in the windows instead of faceless black. He would park his car, walk through the door and find Ellie pottering in the kitchen, cooking up something fabulous.

He had started to fantasise that she was there waiting for him, not because he paid her to, but because she wanted to be.

She worked so hard. Now he'd read up on brain injuries he understood how difficult it must be for her. And she never seemed to want a day off to go home. Perhaps there were too many memories waiting for her there. But it would be good if he could get her to relax now she had the household running like clockwork. He'd even cover the cost of a holiday if he thought she'd accept it from him. He almost felt guilty for jetting off to the Caribbean and leaving her behind.

Maybe there was something he could do about that…

Nicole slapped her folder down so hard that the papers on Mark's desk lifted in the resultant breeze.

'If you're not going to listen, I'm going for a girlie chat with Emma at the end of the hall!'

He was only partially aware of the slam of the door and the meant-to-be-heard muttering as she click-clacked out of the office and down the hallway. He swung his chair round again and continued studying the busy city below. The Thames glinted between the mixture of glass office blocks and the pollution-stained masonry of older buildings.

The last few weeks had been both heaven and hell.

The prickly, reclusive Ellie who had arrived at Larkford in the spring was only a memory. The Ellie he returned to each night was warm and caring and funny. Clever and resourceful. He loved hanging around the kitchen watching her cook, savouring each bite of the meal and making it last as long as possible to prolong his time in her company. He always felt a little deflated when the coffee cups were cleared away and the mechanical whooshing of the dishwasher was the only sound in the kitchen.

She was still a little shy, but it added to her charm. He loved the way she was totally original—one of a kind.

Mark stood up. The afternoon sun was bouncing off the windows of the other office blocks, giving the whole city a warm yellow glow. He took a moment to process the revelation that had just hit him smack between the eyes.

He loved her.

His stomach lurched as he recognised his own vulnerability. Whether she knew it or not, that fragile woman had tremendous power over him.

But he didn't want to push her, even if he guessed she might be feeling at least some of what he was feeling. He watched a jet puff out its white trail in the clear blue sky, the plane so high up it was only a silver speck in the air. Part of him exulted at the knowledge that she found him attractive, that he put her off-balance, but another part of him ached with the uncertainty of any deeper feelings on her part.

'I need a sign!' he whispered, waiting for something to happen.

But the plane kept on its course, its trail a no-nonsense line. No writing appeared in the sky saying *Go for it.* He scanned the horizon for a hint of divine thunderbolts, but the pale clouds refused to comment.

He continued to ponder his position as he sat behind a truck on the M25 later that evening. The crawling traffic gave him plenty of time for self-analysis. He sat for many minutes trying to predict the outcome of any romantic entanglement with Ellie and decided that prophecy was not his thing. It didn't matter, anyway. Whether she loved him back or not wouldn't change how he felt about her. He would just have to be patient. Wait in this horrible limbo until a sign appeared.

Butterflies wrestled in his belly as he turned the car into his driveway. His pulse quickened as he jumped from the car and bounded up the steps to the front door. As he put the key in the lock a mouthwatering aroma assaulted his nostrils. He followed the trail into the kitchen. Ellie bobbed up from behind the kitchen counter, causing his already racing heart to skip a beat.

'That was good timing! I was just about to dish up. You're much later than you said.'

'Traffic jam,' he said absently, his eyes following her every move. She reached to get a couple of plates from the cupboard and passed them to him.

'Your PA called about an hour ago.'

Ah. He'd forgotten all about Nic, and had left the office without telling her.

'She said she will not be coming back into work until you ring and tell her she is no longer Mrs McGill—whatever that means!' said Ellie, searching for the oven gloves and finding them in the dishwasher.

Mark reckoned an apologetic lunch somewhere nice would probably help. And maybe a big bunch of flowers. Nicole's bark was worse than her bite, and he didn't know what he would do without her. His stomach complained noisily, returning him to the present.

'What's for dinner?'

Ellie opened the oven door and stood back from the blast of hot air before she reached inside to remove a scalding-hot earthenware dish. She looked very pink as she stood straight. If it wasn't for the heat from the oven, he could have sworn she was blushing.

'Shepherd's Pie.'

Mark almost dropped the plates he was holding.

'Thank you,' he mouthed to the ceiling, before following her to the table.

Ellie was in the chemist's in the village, picking up some supplies, when her mobile rang. The caller ID told her it was Mark, and she took a steadying breath before she punched the button to answer.

'Hello?'

'It's me. Are you busy?'

Ellie looked at the tube of toothpaste, a box of plasters and the hand soap in her shopping basket. 'I'm in the village shopping, but I'll be finished in a few minutes. Do you want me to come straight back?'

'Yes. I've got a bit of an emergency on my hands.'

And, without explaining anything further, he rang off. Ellie stared at the phone. Very mysterious. She quickly paid for the items in her basket and hurried back along the lane to Larkford Place, cutting through the gardens to make her journey quicker.

When she reached the back door and entered the kitchen she found it all quiet. Guessing Mark must be in his study, she dumped her shopping bag on the counter, prised off her trainers and socks—it was too hot for shoes—and headed off to find him.

He was sitting behind his desk listening to someone on the other end of the phone when she poked her head round the half-open door. She coughed gently and he motioned for her to come in and sit down, still listening to whoever it was on the line.

She sat in the small but rather comfortable leather chair on the opposite side of the desk and waited, noticing as she did so that the colour of her painted toenails clashed with the rug. He finished the call without saying much but 'mmm-hmm' and 'bye', and replaced the phone carefully in its cradle before looking at her.

'I have an idea to run past you. I hope you don't mind?'

Ellie shook her head. Although she was a bit puzzled as to why Mark would want her help with what was obviously a business problem.

'I'm due to fly to Antigua at the end of the week and my PA, vital to keeping me organised during what is likely to be a chaotic few days, has come down with the flu. I need someone to fill in for her.'

Ellie studied her toenails again. Tangerine really didn't go with the aubergine shapes on the abstract rug.

'Can't someone from the office fill in?'

'Difficult. The whole place is in turmoil with a newly signed band. Their first single is out this week and it's all hands on deck. Anyone who isn't already with a client is involved in that. I did have two people in mind, but one is on holiday and the other is pregnant and throwing up every ten minutes. I seem to have run out of employees to commandeer.'

Ellie smiled at that. Nobody to boss around? What a hardship.

When she looked up, a wolfish grin was on his lips.

'Well, *almost* run out of employees…' he added.

She didn't like the look of that smile. She felt like Little Red Riding Hood, lost in the woods. Mark's eyeballs didn't move a millimetre as he stared straight at her. Ellie began to shake her head.

No way! Don't you even think it!

He nodded in slow motion as her ringlets bounced from side to side. Without warning he sprang from his side of the desk and bounded towards her. He crouched in front of her and tugged her hands into his.

'I have got one employee who could help me out.'

Her heartbeat accelerated. It was difficult to think whilst looking into those bottomless brown eyes.

'Come on, Ellie. I know you can do this. Charlie told me about how you used to be a PA.'

Ellie tried to stammer *no,* but her mouth refused to cooperate. His eyes looked like a spaniel's. She'd bet this was the puppy-dog thing Charlie had warned her about. It would be like stamping on a poor abandoned animal if she refused. And it would be to help Mark out of a tight spot. She couldn't really do this, could she?

Mark pressed on while he had the advantage.

'Look at the way you run the house. You're quick to pick things up, and you've got bags of initiative. Even with all your challenges you seem to handle any unexpected thing I throw at you. I know this is a different ball game, but I have confidence in you. Please!'

Ellie grabbed the lifeline he had thrown at her. 'The house!' she blurted out.

Mark frowned. 'What house?'

'This one! We can't leave it unattended. Who's going to look after it?' She let out a relieved sigh and relaxed into the padded leather chair, feeling oddly deflated at her own success.

'Mrs Timms could manage for a few days. I've asked her already and she said her daughter would be able to help her out.'

Ellie sat, mouth open, trying to find another valid objection. She'd only just got used to Larkford. To go somewhere else, somewhere completely foreign—literally—and do work she wasn't used to doing. Well, the idea was just plain terrifying. And she hadn't even factored in how difficult it would be to spend days upon end in a tropical paradise working even more closely with Mark.

He was smiling at her, his voice low and rich. Ellie could feel herself slipping. 'Mrs Timms used to work here before you started. Mind you, she wasn't nearly as good—or pretty.' His eyes twinkled. 'And she smelled of peppermints and disinfectant—'

'Mark!'

'I know. Not important.'

He took hold of her hands again, eyes pleading. 'It's only for a few days. I just need someone to handle the red tape while I look after fragile egos and deal with hissy fits—and that's just the tea lady I'm talking about.'

Ellie couldn't help laughing. She suspected he could persuade her that black was white if he put his mind to it.

She folded her arms across her chest. 'I will *think* about it.'

'Basket case!'

Ellie mumbled to herself as she watched the planes taxiing back and forth in the evening haze, her nose pressed hard against the plate-glass wall of Heathrow's first class lounge. The sunset was tarnished by the pollution of the busy airport.

What an idiot to think she could do this.

She turned, leaning back on the cold window to survey her fellow travellers sprawled over the comfy sofas on the far side of the lounge. Mark was chatting to Kat and the other members of her entourage. He looked completely at ease. In fact he'd been looking pretty darn pleased with himself since she'd told him she would fill in for his sick PA at breakfast this morning.

Ellie sighed and banged the back of her head lightly against the glass. She'd made a valiant attempt to say no to Mark's offer, but she hadn't quite been able to bring herself to turn him down.

Of course her decision had everything to do with a free trip to Antigua, and nothing at all to do with spending the next few days with Mark instead of rattling round Larkford Place on her own. At least that was what she'd thought this morning. Somehow the universe had done a one-eighty between then and now. The fantasy of jetting off to a palm tree filled island in a sarong and flip-flops had fallen flat once they had arrived at the airport. Well, slightly before that, Ellie admitted, looking down at her un-flip-flopped feet and sarong-less legs.

She hadn't realised they were going to be travelling with Kat and her 'people'. Immediately she'd gone into tortoise mode, feeling she had nothing much in common with the assorted bunch of strangers. Kat seemed nice—very young, and much shorter than she'd expected.

She studied the other members of the entourage. There was a tall, burly guy with a pair of shades who she presumed was a bodyguard or something. The girl with the funky white-blonde hair had to be a make-up artist or hairdresser. But she couldn't even guess what the others did. The woman in the lurid boob tube could be Kat's personal grape-peeler for all she knew.

The young guy with the pierced nose finished telling a funny story and the whole group erupted into laughter. Ellie's eyes followed Mark's every move as he grinned away, pleased with the reaction. The funky-haired woman put a pressureless hand on his arm as she wiped a tear from her eye.

Ellie frowned and turned back to face the anonymous jets parading round the runway. Her forehead met the cool glass with a delicate thud.

Basket case.

At thirty-five-thousand feet she was still wondering what she was doing with these people. Sure, she'd been on aeroplanes before, but it had been rubber food, cramped leg room and fighting about who had the armrest. Not this. Not champagne and seats you could fit a small family into. It all seemed so foreign—yet it shouldn't. Nobody else seemed to be pining for garish seat covers and lager louts singing football songs.

She felt like an impostor. Any minute now people would start pointing and staring, and she'd be dragged back to Economy, where she belonged. This wasn't her world. What a huge mistake to think she could slide in here with Mark and find it a perfect fit.

However, the outsize chair was definitely comfy, and she sank into it, her eyelids closing of their own accord.

The next thing she was aware of was something brushing her cheek, something soft and slightly moist. She swatted it away without opening her eyes.

'Ow!'

She pulled her eyelids apart with enough force to unstick her eyelashes and squinted at the fuzzy shape in front of her. As it came into focus she realised it was Mark, and his lips were slightly pursed.

'Why are you holding your nose like that?' she asked, shifting in her seat to get a better look.

'I was trying to wake you up when you walloped me.'

'I didn't wallop. I swatted. There's a difference.' She rubbed the spot on her cheek that was still tickling her. 'And how did I end up hitting you on the nose? What were you doing that close?'

In the semi-dark of the cabin she could have sworn his face turned a shade pinker.

'I was just… Never mind what I was doing! I was waking you up because the pilot just announced we'd be landing in half an hour. I thought you'd want to get yourself together.'

She stretched her arms past her head, yawned and looked out of the window. It was so dark out there they could have been flying through a black hole.

'What time is it?'

'Our time or local time?'

'Whichever.'

'Well, it's just after midnight local time. At least we get a few extra hours to catch up on sleep.'

Ellie made a face. 'I think I could do with a whole week!'

He smiled, and she forgot to be grumpy.

'You know, you look very cute when you've just woken up,' he said.

Ellie snorted, then pulled a mirror out of her bag and inspected the damage. Just as she'd thought. All her mascara had migrated into a gloopy lump in one corner of her eye. Very cute.

'You need glasses, then,' she said as she threw the mirror onto her lap and searched for a tissue in a bag pocket.

'Here—let me.'

Before she could refuse he'd whipped a handkerchief out of his pocket with a flourish and tipped her chin towards him with his other hand. He leaned so close all the hairs behind her ears stood on end. She did her absolute best not to look too pathetic as he gently dabbed her eye. Somehow, with him taking care of her like this, she didn't feel so lost.

That incident set the tone for the rest of the journey. When she hauled her cases off the carousel at baggage reclaim Mark was there with a trolley before she even blinked. He shepherded her into one of the cars that appeared like magic out at the front of the terminal and saw her settled at the hotel.

It had been so long since she'd felt like this. Safe. Taken

care of. Not struggling to do everything by herself. It was very tempting to give in and forget they'd be home in a few days. And that, technically, she was being paid to look after him.

Ellie shivered as yet another spider scuttled across her foot. The first time one had crawled over her today she'd almost freaked out. Big time. But the cameras were rolling, filming at the first location for Kat's video, and she hadn't wanted to sprint round the set like a lunatic in front of the crew.

Or re-live the incident when they watched the rushes at the end of the day.

Or feature in some TV out-takes compilation next Christmas.

So, although she felt as if she'd imploded with the effort, she stifled the screams, put on a stoic face and stood her ground.

She sighed and ran her fingers through the damp curls sticking to her forehead. The whole crew was packed into a tight knot at the end of an idyllic bay where the narrow beach met the rocks. Ellie was hiding out in the jungle-like greenery that fringed the white-hot sand. Hence the spiders. She'd thought she'd do anything to escape something with eight legs, but the need for shade and even a few degrees less heat had overruled her natural instincts. It was only *after* they'd arrived at the hotel that Mark had explained that summer could be hot and horribly humid on the island. Most of the tourists came in the winter months.

Kat was knee-deep in water, singing along to the track that was due to be her next single. The surf behind her looked mighty inviting. Ellie was fantasising about diving into the sea, acting like a fish and hoping nobody would notice. Nice dream, but in reality she was stuck under the nearest palm tree, wilting, while everybody else did something vastly important.

The heat was making her clothes stick to her skin. Even her skin was sticking to her skin. She longed for the air-conditioned haven of the hotel. Typical of many resorts on the island, the elegant low-rise main building was surrounded by lush tropical gardens and luxurious cabins. She wanted to be doing jobs she knew how to do: faxing things, shredding things. An evil glint flickered in her eyes. She wanted to be stapling things—preferably to Mark's head.

No, that wasn't fair. It was her own fault she hadn't found out what she was letting herself in for. It was the jet lag making her tetchy. And she'd never been on friendly terms with this kind of heat. It made her hair frizz.

The director stood up and bellowed, 'Cut!'

The music died instantly, but Ellie knew the song so well by now that it kept playing inside her skull, pounding against her temples.

The director barked instructions to anyone within earshot. 'Baz, zoom out a little so I can see the sand. Jerry, check that last take to see if the light is still okay. Kat, my darling, could you just move to that rock on your left?' Kat waded obligingly to the rock and took up her position. 'That's it. Can you put one foot on top of it? Good.'

Ellie admired her stamina. They'd all been standing on this beach for most of the day. She'd have dived in and floated away hours ago if it she'd been in Kat's shoes. She massaged her forehead and listened to the pounding of the surf. She'd expected a little time to collect herself after they'd arrived, but it had been straight to work. No lounging by the pool under a yellow umbrella. No sipping coconut-flavoured cocktails in a hammock. Time really was money when video cameras were involved, it seemed.

'Playback!'

The director's yell was like a crack from a shotgun. Birds scattered from the treetops in terror. Ellie checked her clipboard. All her tasks were done. There was nothing left to do but drift over towards the director and watch Kat's progress on one of the boxy little monitors.

The minute hand on her watch dragged itself listlessly through the next few hours and the sun began to set. They moved position a few times, and each move meant ages of checking the lighting, setting up cameras and other kit. Then Kat would have to sing her song another thousand times, this time in close-up, this time on a long-shot. See? She was even starting to learn the lingo.

Just as the sun had finally set, and Ellie was about to scream with the monotony of it all, Mark suddenly waded into the sea and scooped Kat into his arms.

'Cut!' the director bellowed, impotent with fury.

Ellie could only imagine the myriad expletives scalding the tip of his tongue. He spluttered, searching for the right word to unlock the torrent. Ellie turned quickly to face the trees and hid a smile. The prima donna on this set was definitely not the singer!

Mark said nothing as he carried Kat out of the water, but his eyes were blazing a warning as clear as if he'd shouted it. The director swallowed his rant. Mark unhooked his arm from under Kat's knees and let her bare feet touch the ground in one controlled motion.

'That's a wrap for today, everybody,' he said.

His voice was calm, but everyone from the director to the runners knew that negotiations were useless. The generator coughed to a halt. No one moved.

Ellie broke the tense silence with a scurry of movement. She tugged a fluffy towel out of the bag of provisions she'd hauled along with her and slung it over Kat's shoulders. All that time standing in the water! The poor girl must be prune-like on the bottom half and baked on the top half. She glanced at Mark, and flushed as she saw the flicker of approval in his eyes.

Kat whispered her thanks as they headed to the speed boats that had brought them on the short trip round the coast into the small crescent-shaped bay. It had been chosen because they were practically guaranteed an uninterrupted shoot, with no on-lookers or journalists to deal with as it was inaccessible by road.

Mark and Kat headed for the smallest boat, followed

closely by Rufus, Kat's bodyguard—or personal protection officer, as he preferred to be called. Ellie trailed along behind, still feeling like a spare part. The rest of the crew concentrated on unplugging and packing the expensive technical thing-ummy-jigs in foam-padded metal cases. They would follow on shortly, in the larger two boats.

They arrived back at the small marina in the neighbouring bay and made their way to the cluster of anonymous black people-carriers that were waiting for them in the car park. Mark pulled Ellie back to let Kat and Rufus walk ahead.

'I'm going to wait here for our illustrious director and give him a piece of my mind. If he plans to roast Kat alive in the midday sun tomorrow he's going to have to think again.'

'You act more like her big brother than her manager.'

Mark frowned a little. 'Babysitting the star is part of my job description. On the business side, I wouldn't be doing my job if Kat couldn't finish the shoot.' His matter-of-fact manner softened. 'But you're right. I do feel protective towards her. It's easy to forget she's only seventeen and all her friends are still at school.'

He shielded his eyes with a hand and looked up the walkway after Kat as she slid the back door of the people-carrier open and climbed inside. 'She's a great kid. If she can get through the next couple of years without self-destructing she'll have a long and successful career.' He looked Ellie straight in the eye. 'It would be such a waste if she burns out.'

The compassion in his eyes made something inside her feel very gooey indeed. She'd thought Work Mark would be different—harder, more remote. If it were possible, he was even nicer than Home Mark.

He turned away, stuffed his hands in his pockets and scoured the headland for a hint of the other boats.

'She's had a tough time recently,' he said, and turned back towards her. 'Will you look after her for me while I wait here?'

Ellie rubbed his arm lightly and nodded.

The clouds in Mark's expression were banished by a smile. He planted a feather-soft kiss on the tip of her nose and walked down the pontoons to wait by the empty berths.

That kiss was the cherry on top of the weird feelings she'd been having since they'd arrived in Antigua less than twenty-four hours ago. It was as if she was in a parallel universe where, even though she was working for Mark, the 'employer' and 'employee' labels they'd stuck on themselves had peeled off in the heat, leaving only a man and a woman who were really, really attracted to each other.

CHAPTER NINE

WHEN Ellie reached the car she tapped on the mirrored window, assuming that Kat was taking advantage of the relative privacy to change her clothes.

'Ellie?'

'Yes. Are you okay?'

An exasperated grunt preceded Kat's reply. 'Well, yes and no—it's okay to open the door.'

Ellie eased the sliding door open an inch or two. Kat looked more like a half-drowned cat than a sex kitten. Her eyes pleaded and she wore a weary smile.

'The knot in my bikini top won't come undone.'

'Come here.' She turned Kat to face the other way with the same kind of deft handling that she had used when making Chloe stand still to have her hair brushed. As Ellie set to work on the knot she couldn't help noticing the angry pink on Kat's shoulders.

'You look like you've caught the sun, despite the lotion you slathered on.'

'Great. And I've got to do it all over again tomorrow.'

Ellie released the tangle in the bikini top straps and stood back outside the car as Kat finished changing, leaving the door slightly ajar so she could catch her conversation.

'The director will probably have me snorkelling with sharks or something,' Kat said with a tired laugh.

'I'm sure Mark would have something to say about that.'

'He's great, isn't he?'

Ellie tried not to comment for fear of incriminating herself. She made what she hoped was an ambiguous noise to cover all eventualities, but knew she'd failed when Kat slid the door open for Ellie to climb in. Kat had obviously absorbed some of Mark's mannerisms while she'd been working with him, because that smirk was pure Wilder. Ellie busied herself by doing up her seat belt.

Kat leaned across and whispered in a conspiratorial manner, 'Don't worry. Your secret is safe with me.'

Ellie's eyes jumped from Kat to the back of Rufus's head as he drove the car out of the car park.

'Don't worry about him, Ellie. Rufus knows all my secrets and his lips are sealed—aren't they, Rufus?'

Rufus agreed by remaining silent, his thick neck motionless.

'See?'

Ellie groaned. Was she really so transparent that every passing stranger could read the contents of her head?

'I trust Mark one hundred percent,' Kat said, giving her a meaningful look. 'Some managers sign up young talent and work them like crazy until they drop. Then it's on to the next fresh young thing. But Mark's not like that. He always looks after me.'

Kat looked down at her lap. 'I just split up from my boyfriend. I thought he was perfect. They do say love is blind, don't they?'

Ellie squeezed her hand softly. Kat sniffed.

'It's hard to get over it when I see pictures of him in the papers almost every day. On a beach with some girl. In a nightclub with some other girl. At a premiere with—you get the picture, right? But Mark has been great. I can't count the number of times he's handed me tissues as I told him the latest sob story.' A fat tear rolled down her cheek and she sighed and looked out of the window at the lush tropical scenery. 'Sometimes I wish I could run away for a bit and have a little time to myself to get over it. But just when I think I'm on my own, *bam*! There's a telephoto lens sticking out the bushes. I can see the headlines already: "Kat's Secret Anguish Over Split."'

Ellie felt her own eyes grow wet. Mark was right. Kat was a great girl, and she lived a difficult life for a seventeen-year-old. When she spoke, there was a croaky edge to her voice.

'My husband used give me a piece of advice that I'm going to pass on to you—'

Kat jumped round to face her, eyes stretching wide open. 'You're married!'

'I *was* married. I'm not now,' Ellie said quickly. 'Long story. Anyway, Sam used to tell me that life should never feel small. I'm a bit of a tortoise by nature, I'm afraid, much happier if I'm all tucked in inside my shell, where I'm safe and warm. But I'm starting to remember that *safe and warm* can be incredibly dull and lonely. Sometimes we've just got to have the courage to step out and live, no matter what happens.' She turned to look Kat in the eye. 'I can see that kind of strength in you. You *will* get through this.'

They hugged as far as the seat belts would allow, then Kat shifted in her seat and stared out the window.

'What happened to…to your…? Did you get a divorce?'

Ellie tried to eliminate any trace of emotion in her voice. 'No. He died.'

Kat's head snapped round. An involuntary hand covered her mouth, trying to catch the words that had already escaped.

'And here's me snivelling about a man who doesn't deserve my tears…'

Ellie's smile was braver than she felt. 'It's okay.'

'When did it…? I mean, how did he…?'

'He and my daughter were killed in a car accident a few years ago.' Ellie glanced down at the date function on her watch. 'In fact, it will be exactly four years in a week's time.'

A tear ran down Kat's face. 'Oh, Ellie!'

'Don't you start!' She pressed the heels of her hands into her own soggy eyes. 'Now you've got me going.'

A small noise from the front seat made them both look up. Did she really see Rufus dab a finger under his eye?

'Does Mark know?'

Ellie nodded. 'About my family? Yes.'

'No, I mean about next Friday.'

Ellie shook her head as the car pulled up under the canopied front awning of their hotel. Rufus got out of the car, leaving it to the valet, and headed round to open Kat's door for her.

Kat continued, despite Ellie's shaking head. 'You should tell him—you ought to, Ellie. He's really sweet and supportive. You know, he even postponed an important business trip to come to an awards thing a couple of months ago. I was petrified—more of winning than of sinking into the background—and Mark cancelled everything to be there for me. You could do with a friend like that right now.'

Ellie had no chance to respond as Rufus opened the door and bundled Kat through the hotel lobby before anyone could mob her. Ellie followed in their wake, taking advantage of the invisible path before it was filled by holidaymakers and bell-boys with trolleys. They walked out into the hotel gardens and Kat headed for her cool white cabin with its low tiled roof and wraparound veranda. Ellie stood alone on the terrace steps and watched their progress. Just before the mismatched pair disappeared behind a clump of bushes lining the path, Ellie saw Kat mouth a message to her: *Tell him!*

Tell him? Tell him *what*, exactly? There was so much to choose from.

Tell him it was the first time the dreaded anniversary hadn't filled her with panic? That something had made it different this year, and that he was the something? There was too much to say, and most of it needed to be left unsaid.

She weaved her way back through the bustling lobby, confident in the knowledge that no paparazzi were going to be somersaulting from the light fittings in order to snap *her* picture, thank goodness.

The yellow umbrellas by the pool were calling to her. Time to get intimately acquainted with an outlandish cocktail with pineapple bits and paper parasols. She marched up to the poolside bar and ordered one that came in a glass the size of a small goldfish bowl.

The thick icy liquid struggled its way up the straw and she aimlessly watched the tanned bodies diving into the pool.

Kat was right. Mark was sweet and loyal and dependable—absolutely nothing like her first impressions of him. She'd been so blinkered. But now… Now she could see it all.

It reminded her of the visual neglect she'd experienced for a couple of months following the accident. For a while she'd only been aware of half the things in her field of vision. The weird thing was she hadn't even realised anything was wrong. But she'd found reading confusing, because when she'd read a magazine she'd only seen half of each sentence on the page. And she'd only washed one side of her face. When the nurses had realised they'd developed strategies to help, and gradually, as her brain had started to heal itself, she'd been able to process information from both sides of her visual field again.

Why and how had she chosen to see only half of Mark? And only negative things too? Ellie put her glass down on the bar. She'd made up her mind about him, set its trajectory, before she'd even met him. Her thought patterns had got stuck in one of their grooves yet again.

But now she saw all of him…

Oh.

And she saw all of herself too—all the things she felt for him.

A jumble of images, sensations and smells hit her all at once. As if every moment she'd spent with Mark flashed before her eyes. All her blinkers dropped away and she felt as if she was floating, with nothing left to anchor her to cold, hard reality.

It was quite possible she was desperately in love with him. How could she not have known?

And how had this happened in the first place? He was nothing like Sam, and she'd always expected that happiness only came in that size and shape. How would it work with someone totally different? *Could* it work? Their lives were so different. Could she find joy in his fast-moving, flashbulb-popping world?

Talking to Kat earlier had stretched her conceptions of what being rich, successful and famous was like, had given her a fresh look at life from her side of the lens. Kat was surprisingly human. In fact she was just like thousands of other seventeen-year-olds who cried into their pillows every night because they'd fallen for the wrong guy.

Maybe it wasn't all as impossible as it seemed. Maybe she could have a future with Mark. Everybody needed love, whether they were rich or poor, somebody or nobody.

Her head swam. Too much pineapple-rum stuff on an empty stomach. This was no time to be thrashing this problem out.

What she needed was a clear head—and a shower.

And with that thought she plopped the straw back into the half-full cocktail glass and walked through the gardens to her cabin, thinking that even if she never qualified for the former she could definitely manage the latter.

A knock on the half-open slatted door of the cabin caused Ellie to jump off the sofa she'd been dozing on. For a second her mind was blank and she was totally in the present, hardly aware of where she was and what she'd been doing to make her so sleepy.

There was another knock, and she swivelled to face the veranda. She knew it was Mark standing out there, knew it in a way that had nothing to do with the height and shape of his silhouette and everything to do with the way her skin prickled in anticipation.

'Come in,' she called out, and then realised too late that she'd been fresh out of the shower when she'd collapsed on the sofa and was still dressed in her old pink robe. Too late to do anything about it now; he was already pushing the door fully open. She tried to smooth her damp hair down, and pulled at the edges of her robe to get rid of the gap.

'I...er...' He stopped and swallowed. Where was the carefree, free and easy Mark Wilder banter? Probably evaporated in the heat. He tried again. 'I wondered if...if you'd like to grab some dinner?'

'Oh. Okay. That would be lovely.'

Although they'd finished early, the third and final day of shooting had left her absolutely ravenous. On the previous couple of evenings they'd joined Kat and some of her entourage in the rather trendy hotel restaurant. Ellie had enjoyed the gourmet food, but had felt a bit superfluous to requirements.

'I'll just go and get dressed,' she said, pulling herself to her feet.

She wasn't really in the mood for sitting on the sidelines of another round of industry chat and gossip, but the only alternative was sitting alone in her room, and at least this way she got to be with Mark.

As she emerged from her bedroom, wearing a simple long skirt and spaghetti-strap top, she glanced at the clock. 'It's only four-thirty. Aren't we a bit early for dinner?'

'I've been up since six this morning and I'm starving,' Mark said. 'I don't know about you?'

Ellie nodded enthusiastically.

'Anyway, there's something I want you to see first.'

Instead of heading for the hotel restaurant, Mark set off in a different direction, his long legs helping him to stride ahead. She was too busy just keeping up with him to ask questions. He led them into the hotel car park, hopped into a Jeep with a driver at the wheel and sat there, grinning at her, as if he'd done the cleverest thing in the world.

Ellie put her hands on her hips. 'Where are we going?'
She didn't add *alone together*.

'I'm taking you to the best place on the island.'

Ellie looked down at her floral-print skirt and flip-flops.
She wasn't really dressed for fine dining. And she was too
tired to be on her best behaviour. When she felt all fuzzy-
headed like this she knew she was apt to forget words and
bump into things more easily.

He patted the seat beside him and gave her a meaningful look. Ellie climbed in, too tired to be bothered to walk
back down to her cabin, flop onto her sofa and dial Room
Service. At least doing it Mark's way she wasn't going to
have to use her legs.

The driver put the Jeep into gear and they rattled their way
through the neatly manicured resort, but it wasn't long before
they'd left it behind them, heading uphill. The road was lined
with palms and aloes and breadfruit trees. Occasionally she
saw pretty little clusters of yellow orchids dancing in the light
evening wind.

Ellie breathed out and relaxed back into her seat. This was
lovely, actually. Although they'd been to three different locations over the island in the last three days, she'd always been
too caught up with her clipboard and 'to do' lists, terrified of
missing something, to sit back and admire the scenery. This
island truly was stunning, everything a tropical paradise
should be. The beaches were soft white sand, the sea shades
of cobalt and turquoise. If it wasn't all so pretty it would be
a giant cliché. But there was something comforting about
having her expectations met rather than defied for once.

It was almost a shame that everything was over and they'd
be flying back tomorrow. At least she assumed it was
tomorrow. If Mark had told her the time of the flight, she'd
already lost that bit of information in the maze of her brain.

Looking down the steep hill and out to sea, she asked,
'What time do we need to get to the airport tomorrow?'

Mark didn't answer right away, and eventually she stopped looking at the stupendous view and turned to face him.

'Mark?'

He looked away, studying the scenery through the windscreen. 'Actually, I'd planned to take a break—stay on for a few more days.'

Oh.

That meant she'd be going home alone. Suddenly all the hours of flying she'd be doing seemed a lot emptier. She nodded, following Mark's lead and looking straight ahead.

Mark cleared his throat. 'And I wondered if maybe you wanted to stay on too? Have a holiday?'

Ellie found her voice was hoarse when it finally obliged and came out of her mouth. 'With you? On our own?'

'Yes.'

There was a long pause, and all the air that had been whipping past their faces, ruffling their hair, went still.

'I'm not ready to go home yet,' he added.

She glanced across at him, and her heart began to thud so hard she felt a little breathless. He didn't look like the normal, cocky Mark Wilder she knew at all. He looked serious and honest and just a little lost.

She had to look away. Scared that she might be imagining all the things she could see in his eyes. Scared this was just another impulse or trick her brain was playing on her.

'Neither am I,' she said softly.

And then the air began to move around them again. They both breathed out at the same time. After a few moments something tickled Ellie's hand. She didn't look, not wanting to spoil anything. And as Mark's fingers wound themselves round hers she felt something hard inside her melt.

The Jeep climbed higher and higher, the road twisting and turning, and the lush banana trees and palms gave way to scrub and cacti. Now she could see down into the harbour, dotted with the white triangles of hundreds of yachts, and somewhere in the distance she could hear the unmistakable sound of a steel band.

Moments later the Jeep swung round a corner and was parked not far from a few old military buildings, obviously left over from the days of British rule. Reluctantly she let Mark's hand slide from hers as he jumped out of the Jeep and then came round to her side to help her out. They left the Jeep behind and walked towards a huddled group of buildings on the edge of a steep hill.

Unlike the other ruins they'd seen on this part of the island, these had been restored. A crowd was milling around in an open-air courtyard, bouncing along to the calypso music played by a band under a roofed shelter. Mark handed Ellie a plastic cup of bright red liquid. One sniff told her it was rather toxic rum punch, and she sipped it slowly as she swayed to the rounded notes of the steel drums.

Oh, this was better than fancy-pants cooking and business talk. This was just what she'd needed. She looked at Mark, who was sipping his own punch and smiling at her. How had he known?

'Come on,' he said, putting his cup down on a low wall and holding out his hand.

Ellie shook her head. 'I'm a terrible dancer—really clumsy.' Especially these days, when remembering her left from her right was a monumental effort.

'Nobody cares,' Mark said, nodding towards the more exuberant members of the crowd, who'd obviously been enjoying the punch and were flinging their arms and legs around with abandon. 'You can't look any worse than they do.'

She put her cup down too, laughing. 'I can't argue with that,' she said, and he led her to the uneven dusty ground that served as a dance floor.

Ellie discovered that she loved dancing like this. There were no rules, no steps to remember; she just moved her body any way that felt right. And, unsurprisingly, that involved being in close contact with Mark. He hadn't let go of her hand since he'd led her to the dance floor, and she gripped it firmly, determined not to let it slip from between her fingers again.

As they danced, Mark manoeuvred them further away from the main buildings and towards a low wall. After a rather nifty spin Ellie stopped in her tracks, causing Mark to bump softly into her.

'Wow!'

'Told you it was the best place on the island,' Mark said, as Ellie just stared at the scene in front of her.

The view was stupendous. The sun was low on the horizon, and the undulating hills and coastline were drenched in soft, warm colours. Ellie recognised this view as the one they always stuck on the tourist brochures for Antigua. It had to be the most beautiful place in the whole world. She moved forward to rest her hands on the wall, unaware for a moment that Mark hadn't moved away and that her back was being heated by his chest.

'Will you take a photo of us?'

Ellie looked round to see a sweet young redhead with an English accent holding a camera hopefully towards her. She was standing with a lanky guy in long shorts and rather loud, touristy shirt.

She shrugged and smiled back. 'Okay. Sure.'

The girl beamed at her, handed the camera over, then snuggled up to the violent shirt. 'It's our honeymoon,' she explained, glancing adoringly at him.

'Congratulations,' Mark said from behind her, and Ellie became aware of a slow heat building where their bodies were still in contact.

'You've had the same idea as us, I see,' the girl babbled. 'Get here early to get a good view of the sunset. It's our last night and we've watched every one. We're hoping we'll get to see the green flash before we go home.'

Ellie held the camera up and snapped a picture of them grinning toothily at her.

'Green flash?' she said as she handed the camera back to the redhead.

'It's a rare sight,' the woman said as she checked the photo on the screen and smiled. 'Sometimes, when the last part of the sun dips into the sea, you can see a flash of green light as it disappears.'

Loud Shirt Guy nodded. 'Atmospheric conditions have to be just right. It's all to do with astronomical refraction and—'

His wife laid a hand on his arm and he stopped talking. 'Don't bore them with all that, darling,' she said, laughing. Then she whispered behind her hand at Ellie, 'Honestly, he's a scientist, and sometimes he just doesn't know when to stop.'

Ellie could *feel* Mark smiling behind her. Although how you could tell someone was smiling only by being in contact with their chest she wasn't sure.

'Anyway, we're not watching it for the physics, are we, Anton?'

Anton shook his head, and got a misty look in his eyes. 'Island folklore has it that couples who see it together are guaranteed true love.'

A pang of incredible sadness hit Ellie right from out of nowhere. This couple were so sweet. She remembered being that besotted with someone, sure she was going to have a long and happy future with him. She almost wanted to go and give them both a great big hug, to whisper in their ears never to take the time they had together for granted, never to waste even a second. Instead she smiled at them, feeling her eyes fill a little.

'Well, I hope you see it—and congratulations again.'

They nodded their thanks and turned to watch the sun, now dipping dangerously close to the clean line of the ocean. More people were wandering over to watch the sunset and Mark tugged Ellie's arm, leading her down a path, away from the crowd. The view wasn't quite so breathtaking here, but it was framed by trees and she relished not being hemmed in by lots of people, free to feel all the emotions washing over her without being watched. Her fingers crept up to the locket round her neck and she stroked it as she watched the sun go down.

Somehow Mark had hold of her hand again, and he stood beside her, warming her with his mere presence.

Slowly the air grew thick and silence fell as everyone further up the path concentrated on the wavering orange disc that was now dipping itself into the horizon. Ellie didn't move. She hardly dared breathe as she watched the sun inch its way down.

She hadn't thought it possible, just a few short months ago, that she could love again. But here she was, watching the most mesmerising sunset she'd ever seen, with a man who had turned all her rigid expectations on their heads. But did he feel the same way? Was it even possible this was more than a passing attraction for him? She wanted to believe that the look she'd seen on his face in the car was the truth, but she just didn't trust her instincts any more.

A wayward curl blew across her face and she brushed it away so she could stare harder at the setting sun. He was here with her now, and that was what mattered. Who said love lasted for ever, anyway? She knew better than most that you had to grab the moment while you could. Maybe it was time just to 'go with the flow', as Sam had always encouraged her—as she had been doing when she'd danced to the hypnotic calypso music. Maybe it was time to let life feel something other than small again, no matter what that meant. No matter if *for ever* wasn't part of the package.

Mark leaned forward and whispered in her ear. 'Look.'

The sun was almost gone now, the very last traces only just visible, and she'd been so busy daydreaming she'd almost missed it. Why was it so difficult to live in the moment and not get distracted by wounds of the past or fears for the future? She concentrated hard on the sun, knowing that capturing this moment for her memory banks was important somehow.

And then it happened.

Just as the orange lip of the sun disappeared there was a sizzle of emerald on the horizon. Ellie froze. It lasted only a second or two and then faded away. Mark was standing slightly to the side and behind her. She could hear his breathing, soft and shallow, in her right ear.

Then he began to move, and she moved too, turning to face him.

He looked at her for a long time, a solemn, almost sad expression on his face, and then, just as her mind started to go wild with questions, he leaned in close and kissed her, silencing them all.

Later that evening Ellie wandered on to her veranda alone. She leant on the criss-cross wooden railing and stared in amazement at the confusion of stars jostling for space in the midnight sky. Light from Mark's cabin, a short distance through the gardens, was casting a faint glow on the waving palms, but there was no sign of him.

It had been a magical night—starting with *that* kiss.

By the time they'd returned the short distance up the trail from where they'd watched the sunset the sky had been a velvety dark blue, the sun long disappeared. They'd danced to the steel band, eaten sticky barbecue food with their fingers, and hadn't been able to stop smiling at each other.

Her relationship with Mark had definitely crossed into new territory, but neither of them had brought the subject up, preferring just to live in the moment, rather than spoil it with words and theories.

She wasn't just a fling to him.

The knowledge was there, deep down in her heart—in the same way she'd known after that first day of primary school that Sam's life and hers would always be joined somehow.

There was something between them—her and Mark—something real. Only she didn't have the words to describe it. And for the first time in a very long while the fact she couldn't find the right word, couldn't label something instantly, didn't bother her in the slightest.

The next few days were almost too much for Ellie's mind to deal with. She'd been so accustomed to guilt and pain and misery, clanging round her ankles like shackles, that the light, airy happiness she was feeling took a bit of getting used to. And the glorious island she was on and the wonderful man she was with just made life seem even more surreal.

But who needed real life, anyway?

She'd rather live this dream, where she spent almost every waking moment with Mark. They'd eaten at the most amazing places, ranging from surfside shacks to exclusive restaurants. They'd been sailing and had walked across countless beaches. Some evenings they'd gone out into the bustle of nearby St John's; sometimes they'd just found somewhere quiet to watch the sun set. They hadn't seen the green flash again, but Ellie didn't worry about that. Once must be enough, surely?

And Mark...

He astounded her. He knew her every mood, anticipated her every need. He knew when to hold her tight and when to give her space without her even having to try and get the jumble of an explanation past her lips.

Marrying up this version of Mark with the grinning playboy she'd seen on the television all those months ago was almost impossible. She'd been so blinkered. But, even so, she was sure the way he was behaving wasn't something she'd conveniently blocked out. He was different. More free. He was changing too.

And it only meant she loved him more.

As the week wore on, she felt the shadow of the approaching anniversary looming close on her horizon. With that blocking her view of the sun, it was hard to think about where her relationship with Mark might go, what it would become when they flew home on Saturday.

She'd just have to get Friday out of the way first. Then she'd be able to think clearly. Then maybe, when the plane took off and she watched the ground drop away, the houses and cars all become miniature versions of themselves, she'd be able to leave her small life behind her once and for all.

CHAPTER TEN

MARK finally spotted her, walking down near the shoreline, kicking the wavelets with a half-hearted foot. He walked to the edge of his veranda and focused more carefully, just to make sure he was right. He was. It was Ellie, looking very much like a lost soul on the deserted beach.

A storm had passed over the night before, and he'd lain awake in the early hours, listening to the creaking of his wooden cabin as the rain had gusted against it, the rustling of the tall palms in the hotel gardens as they curved and swayed in the wind, wondering if Ellie was awake in her cabin too. This morning it was grey, and slightly overcast, but everything was clean and fresh and new.

Normally that was a good thing.

He watched Ellie as she turned to face the wind and stared out to sea, lifeless as a statue. Yesterday he'd thought all his prayers had been answered. Her smiles across the dinner table had been warm and sweet and just for him.

As they'd headed home the sky had darkened, and by midnight rain had been hurling itself out of the sky with the force that only a tropical storm could manage. He and Ellie had spent their time snuggled up on the sofa in his cabin, watching a bad action movie. He couldn't remember the last time he'd had so much fun.

Yet there had been no glitzy nightclub, no suffocating shirt and tie, no polished mannequin on his arm, laughing on cue at his jokes. Just him and Ellie having a late-night Room Service picnic on the carpet in front of the television. They'd talked about anything and everything, and sometimes nothing at all.

His celebrity-hungry girlfriends would have balked at such an evening. There was no point going out with Mark Wilder unless you were going to be *seen* out with him—and it had better be somewhere expensive! They would certainly have frowned upon scanning the film credits for the most interesting-sounding bit part. Ellie had won with 'second tramp in explosion'. It had beaten his 'teenager with nose-stud' hands down.

Relaxing on the sofa with Ellie snuggled up under his arm, he'd realised that this was what *normal* felt like. He liked it. In fact, he could see himself doing it for a long time to come with her, and he hardly remembered why he had been so terrified of it for almost a decade. Now he had tasted it he wasn't sure he could go back to living without it. It was kind of addictive.

What did that mean?

He tried not to think of the 'm' word, but no matter how he diverted his thoughts they kept swerving back to images of Ellie, dressed in white, a serene smile on her face as he slid a delicate gold band on her finger.

The wind ruffled his hair and his daydreams scattered like the bulbous clouds hurrying towards the skyline. Overnight something had happened. This morning she was withdrawn. No smiles. No bubbling laughter. Today, he hardly existed.

He kicked the railing of the veranda hard. Which was a big mistake—he had bare feet.

What was going on with her? Had she finally taken a good look at him and decided there was nothing more than schmooze and show? Hadn't he criticised himself enough in recent months for the lack of substance in his life?

He raised his foot, ready to take another kick, but thought better of it. Instead he turned and walked through the cabin to his bedroom to get dressed. It was time to find out what was going on, whether the last few days had just been a mirage or not.

Five minutes later he felt the wet sand caving under the weight of his heels as he strode across the almost deserted beach. Ellie was now only a billowing speck in the distance. A remnant of last night's wind lifted her loose skirt as she wandered along the shoreline.

He lengthened his stride.

She didn't hear him come up behind her. She was busy drawing in the wet sand with a long stick. He didn't want to startle her, so he stopped a few feet away and spoke her name so gently it was only just audible above the splash of the waves near their feet.

She stopped tracing a large letter 'C' in the damp sand. Mark's heart pounded like the waves on the distant rocks as he waited for her response. Her head lifted first, but her eyes remained fixed on her sandy scrawlings a few seconds longer before she found the courage to meet his enquiring gaze. The rims of her eyes were pink and moist.

Any words he'd had ready dissolved in the back of his throat. Devoid of anything sensible to say, he held out the single pink rose he'd lifted from the vase in his room. Ellie started to reach for it, then her face crumpled and silent tears overflowed down her cheeks. He dropped the rose and stepped towards her, intent on gathering her up in his arms, but could only watch in horror as she buckled and sat weeping in the sand.

'Ellie? Ellie, what is it?'

He sank down next to her and pulled her firmly into his arms. She tried to answer him, but her words were swallowed in another round of stomach-wrenching sobs. So he waited. He held her and he waited. Waited until the tide turned and the hot flood of tears became a damp trickle. She pushed away from his chest and stood up, shaking the sand from her skirt.

Her voice wobbled. 'I'm sorry.'

Mark leapt to his feet and reached for her.

'Don't be.' He pulled her close to his chest and stroked her wind-ruffled hair. 'Is there something I can do?'

She swept her fingers over her damp eyes and straightened, seeming to have made a decision about something. 'I need to tell you something…' She took a deep breath and held it. 'It's the anniversary today. Four years since…since Sam and Chloe died.'

Her hand automatically reached for the silver locket she always wore. Mark didn't need to be told what pictures it held. He'd had an inkling, but now he knew for sure.

He didn't say anything. What could he say that wouldn't sound patronising or trite? So he just continued to hold her, love her, and hoped that would be enough.

'I didn't mean to shut you out or push you away,' she said. 'I just needed some time to think. It's different this year. So much has happened in the last few months…'

Slowly she unclipped the flat oval face of the locket and showed its contents to him. On one side was a little girl— blonde curls like her mother, as cute as a button. On the other side a sandy-haired man, with an infectious grin and a gleam of love in his eyes for whomever had been taking the photo. It was hard to look at the pictures, because it made him scared that she wasn't ready to move on, but he appreciated what a big step it had been for her to show him.

Ellie stooped to pick up the discarded rose and peeled the crushed outer petals off to reveal undamaged ones underneath. Mark felt ill. What if she was still in love with her dead husband? And how horrible was he for being jealous of him? He was polluting the pure emotions Ellie had provoked in him by thinking this way.

'It was the rose that set me off,' she said, picking up the bud and bringing it to her nose. 'Pink was Chloe's favourite colour.'

He almost thought the conversation was going to end there, the gap was so long, but just when he'd decided she'd lapsed back into silence she continued.

'I didn't get to go to the funeral—I was only barely conscious, couldn't walk, couldn't talk—but my mother showed me the pictures. She thought it would help. Maybe it did.'

She broke off to look out to sea again.

'Chloe had a tiny white coffin with silver handles, and Mum had chosen a wreath made only of pink roses that covered it completely. I planted a bush in the cemetery for her when I got out of hospital.'

Mark felt moisture threaten his own eyelids. She reached out and touched his cheek, stroking it with the fleshy pad of her thumb. 'Thank you for coming to find me. Thank you for never telling me how *lucky* I was to survive. You have no idea how much that means to me.'

How did she do it? How did she think beyond herself so easily? She had every right to spend the day cut off from the world, wallowing as much as she wanted. Ellie had lost part of her life to a fog her brain had created. What must it be like to not have been able to go to the funerals? To never get closure? Part of her must yearn to remember something from those days.

In contrast, he was a coward. He'd *chosen* to forget Helena, forget about love and commitment. And that hadn't helped him heal either. If anything it had just made him more shallow, less brave.

He gazed into her beautiful damp eyes. The pale green was even more vivid against their slightly pink tinge, and he caught her face in his palms.

'You're amazing, Ellie Bond.'

She lowered her lids. 'I don't *feel* very amazing. I've spent the last few years feeling terrified mostly, and recently—' She looked back at him. The warmth in her weak smile quickened his pulse. 'Recently I've just felt plain old crazy.'

'How can you say that?'

Her lashes lowered and she gave a derisive laugh. 'I would have thought our first meeting would have been ample proof!'

He smiled. 'I think that, despite first impressions, you're probably the sanest person I know. At least you know what's real—what's important. I'd forgotten.'

That made her smile, the thought that someone else might have to wrestle with their memories too, that she wasn't entirely alone in that predicament. Their lips met briefly, tenderly. He could taste the salt from her tears.

'How you survived what you went through I'll never know. Lesser women would have crumbled.'

'But I did crumble. That is until I met—' she stopped and swallowed '—you.' Her voice dropped to a whisper. 'I'd forgotten how wonderful life could be.'

'I still think you're pretty amazing.' He held her close and his words drifted softly into her ear. 'You don't see it in yourself. That's one of the reasons why I love you.'

She froze in his arms and Mark's stomach churned. Ellie pulled back slightly and scrutinised his face, analysing his expression. He willed his facial muscles to keep still, however much they wanted to collapse. He hadn't a clue what she could see in his face. Honesty, he hoped. All he was aware of was the slicing agony as he waited for her to say something. Anything...

A couple more seconds and he was going to scream.

She blinked away a fresh tear. 'You—you love me?'

Mark recognised that feeling he got in dreams, when he suddenly discovered he'd been walking down the street naked and everybody knew it but him. The familiar urge to bolt was so strong he could taste it. In response, he ground his heels a little deeper into the sand as an anchor.

'Yes. I do. I love you.'

Just as he thought he was going to suffocate on the tension-thick atmosphere Ellie launched herself into his arms and covered his face with a hundred little kisses. At first he couldn't move. He hardly dared ask himself what this meant, hardly dared to hope.

What was that sound?

She was laughing. In between kisses, she was laughing! That was all he needed. He hugged her so tight her feet lifted off the floor. Their lips sought each other out and he lost all sense of reality for a while. When they finally pulled themselves apart rays of sunlight were punching holes in the gruff clouds. He looked at her face, alive with joy, such a difference from the mournful expression she'd worn when he'd first found her. Tears still followed the damp tracks down her cheeks, but he hoped for a very different reason.

At that moment he knew he wanted to love her so completely, so thoroughly, that every speck of pain would be soothed, every wound healed. He might not be able to change her past, but he was going to make darn sure her future was filled with all the adoration and happiness he could give her. He felt strangely unafraid at the thought of for ever.

He linked his fingers in between hers and they strolled back along the shoreline. Every now and then he would spot one of Ellie's random sand doodles. He knew now that the 'C' had been for Chloe. The selfish part of him dreaded seeing a letter 'S'. But he hadn't—yet. Only some squiggles, her name and a flower.

There was another one up ahead he couldn't quite discern. He strained his eyes, trying to read it upside down. When he eventually made it out his heart nearly stopped.

It was an 'M', encased in a gently curving heart.

The words were out of his mouth before his brain had a chance to intervene.

'Marry me?'

What had he just said?

There must still be static left in the air from the storm, because she felt tiny electric charges detonate all over her body. Then a sick feeling of disappointment hit her in the pit of her stomach. She'd heard him say something like this before. She yanked her hand out of his. How could he ruin the moment like this?

'Don't joke with me, Mark.' If he was bright, he'd heed the steely warning hidden in her reply. She turned to face him, expecting to see the trademark grin across his big smart mouth, but it wasn't there.

Another jolt of electricity hit her.

'You're serious, aren't you?'

He scooped her into his arms and kissed her until she nearly forgot the subject of this surreal conversation. Nearly.

'Of course I'm serious!'

She didn't know whether to laugh or cry. Mark started to kiss her again, but she stepped back, holding him at bay.

'Hang on a second, Mark. I can't think straight when you're that close.' She'd thought he'd laugh, but he didn't. She smoothed her wind-blown hair and turned a slow circle in the sand, scanning the horizon for an answer. He came up behind her and hugged her close, his warmth delicious against her cool skin.

'What's there to think about? I love you. Don't you love me?'

'Mark, it's not that easy!'

He nuzzled in close to her neck. 'It could be.'

Could it? Could happiness really be that easy? It was as if someone had told her it was okay to reach out and grab the stars if she wanted to.

For four long years she'd been living in the past. Trying to remember… Trying to forget… Recently she'd actually managed to live in the present, enjoy the moment. But did that mean she was ready to think about the future? That was something she hadn't done for such a long time, she realised, for all her big talk about 'breaking free'. She hadn't really been looking forward when she'd taken the job as Mark's housekeeper; she'd been looking back over her shoulder, running away from ghosts.

But now, standing here on this beach, she was starting to think that the future might be wonderful instead of scary. Today she'd found some peace. And Mark was a wonderful man, so much more than he gave himself credit for. Maybe it *was* that easy. Maybe this was one impulse she should follow one hundred percent, because, boy, she really wanted to say yes.

He turned her to face him without breaking contact, keeping her in the protective circle of his arms. 'Ellie. I love you. I've never felt this way about anyone. Ever. I can't imagine spending another second of my life without you.' In a solemn gesture he took her hands in his, kissed them and lowered himself onto one knee.

Now she knew she really was dreaming! There was no way this could be happening to her. Still, she hoped the alarm clock wasn't going to go off any time soon.

The earnest look on his face made her eyes sting again. 'Ellie Bond, will you do me the honour of becoming my wife?'

She could feel his whole body shaking as she lowered herself to sit on his raised knee and kissed him sweetly, passionately.

'Is that a *yes*?'

Her breath warmed his earlobe as she whispered, 'Yes.'

Mark's ferocious kiss destroyed their precarious balancing act and they both fell onto the sand, tangled but still joined at the lips. Ellie wasn't sure how long they stayed there 'celebrating'. Long enough for the tide to creep in a bit further and take a peek.

'Mark, my feet are getting wet.'

'Do you care?'

'Not really.'

More jubilant celebrations.

By the time the salty water was lapping at the hem of her skirt she surrendered.

'We can't stay here all day, you know.'

Mark fell back into the sand and stared at the vivid blue sky. 'Shame. I was hoping we could just float away to a desert island and never be heard of again.'

That night at dinner they suddenly remembered they needed to think practicalities if they were really serious about getting married.

'What sort of wedding do you want?' Mark asked Ellie as she dug into her creamy dessert, desperately hoping it wouldn't be the three-ring circus Helena had insisted on. Weddings like that felt like bad omens.

Ellie swallowed her mouthful and thought for a moment. 'Something simple.' She dug her spoon into the coconut and rum thing again, but it stopped halfway to her mouth and hovered there, threatening to drop its contents back into the bowl while she considered his question further. 'Something small...private. Just you and me on a sunny day, somewhere beautiful.'

That gave him an idea. 'Somewhere like here?'

Ellie put her spoon back in the bowl and smiled at him. 'That would be perfect! You mean come back in a few months?'

That was exactly what he'd been thinking. But then he thought about all the to-ing and fro-ing, all the hideous preparations and tensions in the run-up to a wedding. That would just spoil everything, ruin the atmosphere of perfection that was clinging to them at the moment.

'How about we get married here? Now. In a few days.' He looked at her earnestly. 'As soon as possible.'

She opened and closed her mouth. Then she made that scrunched-up face she always did when she was trying to process something unexpected.

'We'll have a big party for friends and family when we get back home,' he added. Ellie looked horrified, and Mark remembered the last party at Larkford. He took hold of her hand. '*Real* friends only, I promise.'

'This isn't another one of what *you* think are your hilarious jokes, is it?'

He was deadly serious. How did he make her see that?

'Ellie, I've been hiding for too long, waiting for too long.' He watched as the tension eased from her face and she smiled at him, nodding in agreement. He stopped smiling and looked straight into her eyes. 'I don't want to wait any more.'

She let out a happy sigh. 'Mark, you're asking the right girl, then—because I have this horrible impulse to go along with anything you say, and I just can't be bothered to fight it.'

Ellie stared at herself in the bathroom mirror.

'I'm getting married tomorrow!' she screamed at the idiot grinning back at her. Then she screamed again, just because it was fun. Oh, get a grip, girl! You can't just stand here all day smiling at yourself. You've got some serious shopping to do today. And a fiancé to corner before he disappeared off to do whatever secret things he'd planned and wouldn't tell her about.

One more grin in the mirror for luck, and then she ran out of her bathroom and got dressed in the first things she found in the wardrobe.

The last few days had been madness. Her cheeks hurt from smiling so much. She'd thought she would be flying home days ago, but she was still here in paradise with Mark, and things were going to get even more perfect. She couldn't think about anything else. Her mind just refused to prise itself from that track and she wasn't inclined to let it.

Of course a voice in the back of her head whispered to her, asking her if this was all too quick, asking whether there was unfinished business she needed to sort out first. But she didn't want to listen to that voice, so she drowned it out with a slightly off-key rendition of 'Oh, What a Beautiful Morning'.

Happiness was within her grasp, here and now. She was going to snatch it before the whole dream disappeared in a puff of smoke. No more fear. No more trepidation. Just facing the future with Mark at her side.

But what about the past? the voice said. *What are you going to do with that?*

Ellie belted out the chorus of the song and ran through the garden. She burst through the unlocked doors of Mark's cabin like a miniature whirlwind.

He was in the sitting room, poring over some faxes. His

face lit up as he saw her. 'Good morning. And what have you come as today?'

'Huh?' Ellie stopped and looked down, then burst into laughter as she took in her floaty floral-print blouse and her pyjama bottoms.

'I had other things on my mind while I was getting dressed,' she admitted with a wry smile.

'Pyjama bottoms…hmm…' Mark claimed his morning kiss. 'They remind me of the first time we met,' he said, making a feather-soft trail from her neck to her ear.

Ellie flung her arms around him. 'If you really want to recreate our first meeting I think we need to be a little more— how shall I put it?—horizontal,' she said, and let her weight fall backwards, pulling them both down onto the large sofa behind her. 'And you! You should be wearing considerably less!'

'You know I'm not that sort of girl,' he quipped. 'I thought I'd made it very clear. You have to sign on the dotted line before you get to sample the goods.'

'Spoilsport!'

'Only twenty hours to go. Surely you can wait that long?'

'Only just.' She pulled him close for another kiss. 'Just a deposit,' she assured him, making sure she got her money's worth. Both sets of parents and Ellie's brother were due to fly in for the wedding, so they'd planned a meal at the hotel after the ceremony. 'Do we have to stay through *all* of the wedding breakfast? Can't we leave early?'

Mark threw his head back and laughed. He pressed his lips against her forehead as he untangled himself and stood up. 'We won't have to stay long.'

'Five minutes?'

'Three at the most.'

It was her turn to laugh. He walked back to the desk. 'Now, as for the rest of today, you have to go shopping. You can't get married in another outfit like that. Carla, the stylist from the shoot, has faxed me a list of shops in St John's that you can visit for a dress. Thank goodness Antiguan red tape is just as laid-back and flexible as everything else on this island, and I can go and pick up the marriage licence today, once some essential documents have arrived. And, talking of essential elements of our wedding, I have one last surprise for you.'

He grabbed her hand and dragged her with him to another cabin. When they got onto the white-painted veranda he gave her a little nudge in the direction of the open door. Ellie gave him a quizzical look, then stepped inside.

'Charlie!'

Charlie jumped off the sofa and bounced over to Ellie, squealing, and dragged her fully inside the cabin. Then she flung her arms around Ellie's neck and yelled her congratulations in her ear. Ellie was already having trouble catching her breath, and Charlie's bear hug left her practically airless. She patted her friend's back in a pathetic attempt to return the gesture.

'I don't understand. What are you doing here?'

'Do you think I'd miss this? Mark called me the day before yesterday, broke the news, and asked me to fly over with birth certificates and such. I'm a rather stunning, elegant, designer-clad courier!' She did a little twirl just to prove it.

Ellie grinned. 'You're more than that! And the first thing you can do to make up for almost giving me a heart attack is to come dress shopping. It's the least my bridesmaid can do.'

Charlie's high-pitched squeal almost shredded Ellie's eardrums.

Sunrise.

Ellie and Mark walked towards the minister arm in arm as the sun lifted above the horizon. She loved Mark for suggesting her favourite time of day for the wedding. There was something so pure and fresh about the early-morning sun. And it was a beautiful symbol for her life. A fresh start, new hope. Light and warmth where she'd thought there could only be darkness.

Her bare feet sank into the cool, silky sand as they passed

the few guests up early to share the ceremony. Charlie and Kat, who'd insisted on cancelling something important to be there, stood beside the minister in their bridesmaids' outfits, smiling at Mark and Ellie as they approached. Charlie looked as if she'd already had to break out the emergency hanky. It was just as well Ellie had insisted she wear waterproof mascara.

Ellie took a deep breath and looked down at her feet. Her softly flowing white chiffon dress was blowing gently round her ankles. Her feet looked almost as creamy as the pale sand. Her toenails were painted a shade of deep pink to match the exotic blooms woven into her hair and in her bouquet. And on her left foot was a white gold toe-ring, beautiful in its simplicity. Mark's gift to her this morning. Just until they got a proper engagement ring, he'd said. But she didn't care; she thought it was perfect.

She wore no other jewellery. Not even her locket. Much as she loved it, she couldn't wear it any more—especially not today. It wouldn't be fair to Mark.

As they reached the minister they halted and turned to face each other. How could she be this lucky? Finding love once with Sam had been wonderful enough, but finding it with Mark was a miracle. She never thought she'd have a second chance. She was so thankful he'd made her see that happiness didn't always come in identically shaped packages.

She almost didn't hear the minister as he started the ceremony, she was so busy staring at Mark. She'd never seen him looking so devastatingly handsome. Her eyes never left him throughout the vows. They might as well have been standing on the beach alone for all she knew. Finally she heard the words *husband and wife*, and the minister gave Mark permission to kiss the bride.

She should have known from the naughty grin on his face that he was up to no good. He lingered a little longer than propriety suggested on the kiss, then swept her up into his arms, hooked one arm under her knees and headed off down the beach with her, leaving her dress billowing behind them and the small band of guests open-mouthed.

'Mark!' she gasped, when he'd gone a dozen or so steps. 'Where are you going? We've still got the reception to get through!'

He slowed to a halt. 'I thought you wanted to disappear as soon as possible after the wedding?'

'I'm tempted, believe me, but we can't leave our guests waiting.'

'Just for you,' he said, and let her legs glide down to meet the sand, then kissed the tip of her nose. Laughing, they walked back to the small group of guests, who were sharing indulgent smiles.

By the time they congregated in the hotel gardens under a flower-draped pergola for their celebratory feast, the sun was glowing gold and fully above the horizon. The hotel chef had been very inventive with the food, and a stunning array of mouthwatering dishes was ready for them. Since the numbers were small they all sat around one large table, sipping champagne and chatting.

After they had eaten, made the toasts and cut the cake, Kat surprised them by picking up her guitar, which had been cleverly hidden behind a planter, and proceeded to serenade them with a song especially composed for the occasion. Tears welled in Ellie's eyes as she listened to the beautiful lyrics.

All my tomorrows are nothing but yours, all my yesterdays my gift to you.

It was the best wedding present anyone could have given them. The chorus stuck in her mind, and she found she was humming it as they prepared to leave for the honeymoon.

'Where are we going, then?' Ellie asked, puzzled, as Mark led her not to the front of the hotel, as she'd expected, but on to the beach. Mark just smiled an infuriating smile that said *you'll see*.

A small speedboat, with a satin ribbon tied bridal-car fashion on the front, was sitting a few feet from the shoreline.

'I thought we'd float away to that desert island we talked about and never be heard of again,' he said, as he lifted her into his arms once again and waded out to deposit her in the boat.

CHAPTER ELEVEN

MARK was as good as his word, Ellie thought, as she rolled sleepily over in bed. Two weeks on their very own private tropical island had been absolute bliss. She snuggled back against him. A heavy arm draped over her waist and his breaths were long and even. Heaven.

The villa they were staying in was small, but luxurious. The local owners brought fresh food and supplies every day, but were discreet enough that Ellie had not caught sight of them yet. She found enough lazy energy to smile as she remembered how Mark had laughed when she had referred to them as the 'shopping fairies'.

If only they could stay here for ever. But today was their last day. Tomorrow it was back to England. She frowned, and snuggled even further into Mark's sleeping body. The last couple of weeks had been like a wonderful dream and she wasn't sure she was ready for the cold grey slap of reality yet. Here they were just Mark and Ellie, besotted newlyweds. No labels, no outside expectations, free to be themselves. The thought of going home made her shiver. She loved Mark desperately, but she had an inkling that getting used to being Mrs Wilder was going to take some effort.

Warm golden light filtered through the sheer curtains. She guessed the sun had been up a while; it was maybe nine or ten o'clock. Her tummy rumbled in confirmation. No wonder!

Their half-eaten dinner still lay on the dining table, abandoned in favour of traditional honeymoon recreation.

Wonderful as it is, lying here tangled with my husband, a girl's gotta eat!

She wriggled out from under his arm and reached for her robe. Thankfully she had managed to buy something a little more appropriate for a new bride than her old ratty pink one. The ancient garment certainly didn't come under the category of *sexy honeymoon lingerie*. She'd been astonished when Mark had seemed disappointed she hadn't packed it. Weird. She slung the wisp of ivory silk over her shoulders, only bothering with it because she was afraid of running into the 'fairies'. She left it unfastened and walked away from the bed. A sudden jerk of the sash trailing behind her arrested her progress.

A sleepy voice mumbled from under a pillow, 'Don't go. Come back to bed.'

'I'll be back in a sec. I'm starving!'

'So am I.'

She laughed. 'Why don't I think you've got breakfast on your mind?'

A naughty chuckle from under the pillow told her she was spot-on. In a moment of feminine contrariness she decided to make him wait, and continued her journey to the kitchen. The sash pulled taut as he tried to stop her, but the slippery silk whooshed through the loops and she disappeared out through the door. She laughed gently as she imagined what he must look like with the sash dangling uselessly from his outstretched hand.

'Ellie?' he yelled from the bedroom.

She was still smiling as she reached into the fridge for the jug of fresh orange juice. 'Sorry. Forgot what you said. You'll just have to wait,' she called back, pleased with her own self-mockery.

Mark's effort at secretive footsteps was atrocious, but she pretended not to hear him and readied herself for his attack.

She detected a flicking movement out of the corner of her eye, and before she could work out what it was her missing sash looped over her head and dragged her backwards into the hard wall of his chest.

His voice was very nearly a growl. 'I said, Don't go!'

'Mark! I just spilled orange juice all over myself.' She looked down and watched a bead of liquid travel down her torso towards her belly button.

He loosened the sash just enough to let her turn to face him. 'We'll just have to clean it up, then, won't we?' he said, a truly wicked glint in his eyes.

Ellie sighed as he started tugging her back towards the bedroom. She was pretty sure he wasn't going to fetch a towel.

Ellie wandered outside and sank her feet into the dewy grass. The vibrant green carpet welcomed her feet and she sighed. It was wonderful to be home. She might have lived on in the cottage after Sam and Chloe had gone, but it turned from a home to a shell of bricks and mortar the day they died. She turned and looked at the majestically crumbling manor house. Larkford Place felt like home—but then she'd feel at home in a caravan if Mark was there.

She was surprised at how easy the transition had been. She'd been so worried that she would feel different when they returned from the Caribbean. Over three weeks later she still felt alarmingly peaceful. She'd experienced a strange sense of foreboding on the flight home, but if trouble was looming in the distance it was hiding itself round a dimly lit corner.

She looked at the open French windows and wished that Mark would stroll through them any second and join her. The curtains rippled in promise, but she knew he wouldn't appear. He was off on business for a few days and due home first thing tomorrow. She'd had the opportunity to go with him. She'd already travelled with him once since they'd been back, but she'd been feeling a bit below par for a couple of days and had decided to stay home and recharge her batteries while Mark flew to Ireland. The idea of sleeping in her own bed rather than a hotel one, however luxurious the surroundings, was too much of a lure. She took a careful sip of her hot tea.

Yuck!

It tasted awful. The milk must be off. She would just have to make a new one. She walked into the kitchen and poured the rest of her tea down the sink, then put on the kettle for a fresh cup. While she was waiting for it to boil she went in search of the offending milk in the fridge.

A row of unopened bottles stood like pristine soldiers in the door. Where was the one she'd used earlier? She moved a couple of items around on the nearby shelf to see if the half-used bottle was hidden away behind something. Nope. Hang on! What were the teabags doing in here?

Oh, well. She popped open a fresh pint of milk and sniffed it, while keeping her nose as far away as possible. No, this one was fine. Having done that, she made herself another cup of tea and sank into one of the wooden chairs round the table. She took a long sip, scowled, then spat it back into the cup. What was wrong with the tea today? It would have to be orange juice instead. She returned the rather chilly box of tea bags to its proper resting place in the cupboard—or would have done if a bottle of milk hadn't been sitting in its spot.

Obviously her absent-minded tendencies were getting worse. She'd been under the mistaken impression she'd been improving recently, but she was clearly deluded. She laughed quietly to herself as she returned the milk to the fridge.

Then she fell silent. These weren't her normal memory lapses. This was something new. Should she be worried about that? She'd never been scatty like this before, unless you counted that time years *before* the accident when…

Oh, my!

Ellie continued staring into the open fridge, the cool air making no impact on her rapidly heating face. When she let go of the door and let it slam closed she realised her hands were shaking. She sat back down at the table, her thirst forgotten, and tried to assemble all the evidence in her cluttered brain. The milk, the tea, the lack of energy—it was all falling into place.

She'd completely gone off both tea and coffee when she'd been carrying Chloe—hadn't even been able to stand the smell when Sam had opened a jar of instant coffee to make himself one. She'd made him drink it in the garden! And then she'd developed an overwhelming craving for tinned pineapple sprinkled liberally with pepper.

Her palm flattened over her stomach. She stood up, then sat down again.

I can't be pregnant! Not already.

She hadn't even considered the possibility, although it would certainly explain her sudden lethargy. A creeping nausea rose in her throat, but she was sure it was more a result of shock than morning sickness.

How could this have happened?

Er...stupid question, Ellie! You spent more time with your clothes off than on on honeymoon. Yes, they'd been careful, but nothing was guaranteed one hundred percent in this life.

She wasn't sure she was ready to have another baby! Life was changing so fast at the moment she could hardly keep up. She needed to get used to being married before she could consider all the possibilities for the future.

And what was Mark going to say?

She hoped he would be pleased, but what if he wasn't? They hadn't even talked about this stuff yet, having been too caught up in a whirlwind wedding and being newlyweds to think about anything sensible.

Calm down! You're getting ahead of yourself!

She didn't even know if she *was* pregnant yet. All she knew for sure was that she'd had a dodgy cup of tea and had misplaced the milk. She didn't have to turn insignificant minor events into a major crisis, now, did she?

Ellie shook her head. Talk about her imagination running away with her. What she needed to do right now was take a few deep breaths and have a shower. Which was exactly what she did. However, all the time she was washing she couldn't shake the nagging voice in the back of her head.

You can't run away from this one, Ellie. You can't bury your head in the sand. But she hadn't been running away from things recently, had she? She'd run *to* Mark, not away from something else. At least that was how it had felt at the time.

She stepped out of the shower and got dressed. She needed to find out for sure. She'd go down to the chemist in the village and buy a test. Strike that. She'd already got to know the local residents, and if the village drums were doing their usual work the news that she might be expecting would be round the village in a nanosecond. The fact that dashing Mr Wilder had married his housekeeper was still the main topic of local gossip. A baby on the way would be too juicy a titbit for the village grapevine to ignore.

She'd be better off going into town and shopping at one of the large chemists. Much easier to be anonymous then. At least when Mark got home tomorrow she'd have had a chance to absorb the outcome herself.

The thought that the test might be negative should have made her feel more peaceful. Instead she felt low at the prospect. If the test *was* negative, she would make a light-hearted story of it to tell Mark over dinner tomorrow. She'd tell him how freaked out she'd been, see what his reaction was, test the waters.

Two hours later she was standing in the bathroom, holding the little cellophane-wrapped box as if it was an unexploded bomb.

You're not going to find out by staring at it.

She removed the crinkly wrapping and opened the box.

How could something as mundane as a plastic stick turn out to be the knife-edge that her whole life was balanced on? She sat on the closed toilet lid while waiting for the result, the test laid on one thigh. Two minutes to wait. If someone had told her she was only going to live another two minutes, it would seem like a measly amount of time. How, then, could this couple of minutes stretch so far they seemed to be filling the rest of the day?

First the test window. Good. One blue line. It was working. Then wait for the next window. She waited for what seemed an age. Nothing. She stood up, threw the test onto the shelf over the sink and ran out of the room crying.

All that stress for nothing. She ought to be relieved! It gave her a little more time to think, to plan, to find out what Mark wanted.

Suddenly she wished he was there. She wanted to feel his strong arms wrapped around her, wanted him to hold her tight against his chest and stroke her hair.

She grabbed a wad of tissues from the box beside her bed and blew her nose loudly. She should get out of here, get some fresh air. Perhaps she should pick up the papers from the village shop. Mark liked to read a selection, from the broadsheets to the tabloids, mostly to keep track of what attention his clients were attracting in the press.

She went back to collect the pregnancy test and picked it up, with the intention of putting it in the bin, but the moment she looked at it she dropped it into the sink in shock. The breath left her body as if she'd been slapped with a cricket bat.

The tears must be blurring her vision! She dragged the hem of her T-shirt across her eyes and stared at it again.

Two blue lines?

She took it to the window to get more light. Her eyes weren't deceiving her. Granted, the second one was very faint, compared to the first, but there were definitely two blue lines.

The hormones had to be only just detectable. She could hardly believe it, but there it was—in blue and white.

I'm going to have a baby. Our baby.

Suddenly the rambling old house seemed claustrophobic. She needed to get outside, feel the fresh air on her skin. The garden called her, and she ran down to it and kicked her flip-flops off. Her 'engagement' toe-ring glinted in the morning sun as she stepped onto the grass and began to walk.

A stroll through Larkford Place's grounds should have been pleasant in high summer. The far reaches of the garden, unspoilt and untended, were alive with wild flowers, butterflies and buzzing insects. But Ellie noticed none of it. All she could think about was having a little boy, with a shock of thick dark hair like his father and eyes the colour of warm chocolate.

Was this how she'd felt when she'd realised she'd been expecting the last time? It seemed so long ago now, a memory half obscured by the fog of the accident. But her last pregnancy had been planned. This one was…well, a surprise to put it mildly.

She stopped and looked a bright little poppy, wavering in the breeze. Through the confusion and doubts, joy bubbled up inside her, pushing them aside. She wanted this baby. She already loved this baby—just as much as she'd loved…

Images of golden ringlets and gap-toothed smiles filled her mind, but there was something missing. A word missing.

Her hands, which had been circling her tummy, went still. Just as much as she'd loved…

No. Not now. Not this name. This was one name she was *never* allowed to forget, never allowed to lose. It was too awful. Ellie looked back at the house and began to run.

This couldn't be happening. She couldn't have forgotten her own daughter's name.

Mark burst through the front door with a huge bunch of wilted flowers in his hand. They had looked a bit better before they'd spent two long, sticky hours in the passenger seat of the Aston Martin.

'Ellie?'

No answer. She was probably out in the garden. He almost sprinted into the kitchen. The French windows, her normal escape route, were closed. On closer inspection he discovered they were locked. He ran back to the entrance hall and called her name more loudly. The slight echo from his shout jarred the silence.

Okay, maybe she was out. He was half a day early, after all.

He looked at his watch. Nearly four o'clock. She couldn't be too far away. He'd just go and have a shower, then lie in wait. He chuckled and loosened his tie as he hopped up the stairs two at a time.

But as the afternoon wore on Ellie didn't appear. He ended up in the kitchen, wishing she'd materialise there somehow, and he found her note near the kettle. Well, it wasn't even a proper letter—just a sticky note on the kitchen counter, telling him that she'd gone.

He sat down on one of the chairs by the kitchen table and put his head in his hands.

Not again. She'd seemed so happy since the wedding.

That's when they leave—when they're happy. They don't need you any more.

No. This couldn't happen with Ellie. He loved her too much. More than Helena. So much more. He stood up. He'd be damned if he lost a second wife this way. But if she was really intent on going she bloody well owed him an explanation. He wasn't going to let her waltz off without a backward glance.

The keys jumped from Ellie's fingers as if they had a life of their own. She muttered through her tears and bent to scoop them up from the front step. Thankfully the holiday company had told her they'd had a cancellation this week. The cottage was empty. Perhaps if she went inside it would help.

Although she'd remembered Chloe's name almost the second she'd reached Larkford's kitchen, she still couldn't shake the clammy, creeping feeling of disloyalty and guilt. She'd needed to come somewhere she could rid herself of this horrible feeling of being disconnected from her past.

She slid the key into the lock and started the familiar routine of pulling and turning to ease it open. It was feeling particularly uncooperative today. She gave the key one last jiggle and felt the levers give. The door creaked open.

For no reason she could think of, she burst into tears.

The cream and terracotta tiled hallway seemed familiar and strange at the same time. The surfaces were cleared of all her knickknacks and photos, but the furniture was still *in situ*. Even devoid of personal items it seemed more welcoming than when she'd left on that grey, rainy day months ago.

Ellie hadn't planned to end up here. She just had. An impulse. She walked into the sitting room and slumped into her favourite armchair.

I should never have left this chair. I should have stayed here eating biscuits and never gone to Larkford. Then I would never have forgotten you, my darling girl.

But then she wouldn't have this new baby. And she really wanted it. She clamped her hands to her stomach, as if to reassure the tiny life inside, and her eyes glittered with maternal fierceness.

If Mark didn't want it, then she'd just bring it up on her own.

Ellie shook her head. She hadn't even told Mark yet, didn't have a clue what his reaction would be. She was just making the same mistake she always made: an idea had crept into her head and she'd sprinted away with it like an Olympic athlete, not even bothering to check that she was running in the right direction. Maybe she was so terrified of losing Mark that deep down she almost expected something to come along and demolish it. And at the first hint of trouble she'd been only too ready to believe her luck couldn't hold out.

Sitting here moping was doing her no good. She pulled herself to her feet and started to walk round the house. As she visited every room different memories came alive: Chloe riding her truck up and down the hall; Sam marking homework at the dining table; the kitchen counter where she had made cakes with Chloe, more flour down their fronts than in the mixing bowl. And she realised she'd never been able to do this before, never been able to look at her cottage and see it alive with wonderful warm memories of her lost family.

As she sat trying to process all the new information Kat's song from the wedding drifted through her head:

> *Yesterday is where I live, trapped by ghosts and memories.*
> *But I can't stay frozen, my heart numb, because tomorrow is calling me...*

Ellie guessed the song had been about her break-up with Razor, but the simple lyrics about learning to love again had been so right for their wedding day too. 'All My Tomorrows' was the title. And she'd promised the rest of hers to Mark, willingly. Nothing in the world could make her take that promise back. So there was only one thing to do: she had to go back home—her real home, Larkford—and let Mark know he was going to be a father. Whatever fallout happened, happened. They would just have to deal with it together.

Her instincts told her it was going to be okay. She hoped she was brave enough to listen to them.

She grabbed her keys off the table and took long strides into the hall, her eyes fixed on the front door. A shadow crossed the glazed panel. She hesitated, then walked a few steps further, only to halt again as a fist pounded on the door.

'Ellie? Are you there?'

She dropped her keys.

'Ellie!'

'Mark?' Her voice was shaky, but a smile stretched her trembling lips. She ran to the door and pressed her palms against the glass.

'Let me in, or so help me I'm just going to have to break the door down!'

She patted her pockets, then scanned the hallway, remembering she'd dropped her keys. She ran to pick them up, but it took three attempts before her shaking fingers kept a grip on them. As fast as she could she raced back to the door and jammed the key in the lock. An ugly grinding sound followed as she turned it, then the key refused to move any further. She wiggled and jiggled it, pushed and pulled the door, trying all her old tricks, but it wouldn't budge. The key would not turn in either direction, so she couldn't even get it out again to have another go.

'Ellie? Open the door!' The last shred of patience disappeared from his voice.

'I'm trying! The lock's jammed.'

'Let me try.'

The door shuddered and groaned under Mark's assault, but remained stubbornly firm.

Ellie sighed. 'They don't make doors like this any more.'

Between pants, she heard Mark mutter, 'You're telling me.'

She pressed her face to the stained glass design, able to see him through a clear piece of glass in the centre. He looked tired, disheveled and incredibly sexy. Without warning, she started to cry again.

He stopped wrestling with the door and looked at her through the textured glass. 'We have to talk.'

She gulped. He sounded serious. Was serious good or bad? Good. Serious was good. Please God, let serious be good!

'I know,' she said.

'Why are you here, instead of at home?'

She took a deep breath and turned away from him, pressed her back against the door, then slid to the floor.

'How did you know where to find me?'

'I phoned Charlie in a panic and she suggested I might find you here. I'd already been to your parents' house and your brother's.'

She nodded. Charlie knew her so well. Maybe too well. If her friend hadn't guessed where she was she might have made it back to Larkford and Mark would never have known how stupid she'd been this afternoon. But why had her first impulse been to run? To come here? Did that mean something?

'Ellie?'

She took a deep breath. 'Do you think we got married too fast, Mark? I mean, did we get carried away? Should we have waited?' Everything just seemed so confusing today.

She heard him sit on the step. His feet scraped the gravel path as he stretched his legs out. 'Are you saying you want out?' he said quietly. 'Are you saying you want to come back here for good? I thought you loved me, Ellie. I really did.'

Ellie spun onto her knees and looked through the letterbox. He looked so forlorn, so utterly crushed, she could hardly speak. 'I do love you,' she said, in a croaky whisper. He looked round, and her stomach went cold as she saw the sadness in his eyes.

He tried a small smile on for size. 'Good. Come home with me, then.'

Her fingers got tired holding the brass letterbox open and she let it snap shut. Carefully, because she was feeling a bit wobbly, she pulled herself to her feet. He stood too, and leaned against the door, trying to see her through the multi-coloured glass. Ellie raised her fingers to the clear green diamond of glass where she could see his left eye. It reminded her of the colour of the sunset flash. Of true love. Of coming home.

'I'm sorry, Mark. It's just…I just needed to be somewhere that reminded me of Chloe.'

The green eye staring at her through the glass blinked. She knew what he was thinking. He thought she'd come here to remember Sam too. But while she had unearthed forgotten memories of both the people she'd lost, it didn't make the slightest impact on what she felt for Mark.

'I love you, Mark. And as soon as we work out a way to get this door open I'm coming back home. I promise.'

He nodded again, but she could tell he only half believed her. Another wave of emotion hit her and she began to cry again. What was wrong with her today? 'I don't know why I'm doing this,' she said, half-sobbing, half-laughing. 'I can't seem to get a grip…'

'Perhaps it's the hormones?'

Hormones?

She jumped as the brass flap of the letterbox creaked open again. Something plastic rattled through and clattered onto the floor. Her pregnancy test! She'd left it in the sink. So much for a cool, calm testing of the water on that subject.

'When were you going to tell me?' he asked, his voice going cold. 'I didn't expect to find out I'm going to be a father from a plastic stick. You could have called me at the very least.'

'I *was* going to tell you, but then I…I forgot Chloe's name. And that just freaked me out. I was scared. What if I forget her altogether when this new baby comes along? I couldn't live with myself. You do understand, don't you?'

She heard him grumble something under his breath. The heavy crunch of his feet on the gravel got quieter.

'Mark!' Ellie ran to the door and pressed her nose against the glass.

No answer. She'd finally scared him away with the ghosts from her past. Her unfinished business had caught up with her.

'Mark!' She sounded far too desperate, but she didn't care.

She dropped the test and flung her full weight against the door. Unimpressed, it hardly rattled. She banged it with her fists, hoping to catch Mark's attention. She needed to tell him how stupid she'd been, that she thought he'd be a wonderful father.

'Mark!' Hoarse shouts were punctuated by sobs as she continued to bang on the door.

She stopped.

No faint crunch on the gravel. No hint of a shadow moving up the path. She used the door for support as she slumped against it, exhausted. He couldn't leave now, could he?

She managed one last hollow plea, so quiet he couldn't possibly hear it. 'Don't go.'

'I'm not going anywhere.'

She spun round to find him striding towards her down the hallway.

'How did you—?'

He nodded towards the back door, not slowing until he crushed her close to him. His lips kissed her wet eyelids, her nose, her cheeks, and came to linger on her mouth. She might be confused about many things, but here in his arms everything seemed to make sense. When she finally dragged herself away, she looked into his face. All the passion, tenderness and love she had ever hoped to see there were glistening in his eyes.

'Ellie, there is room in that massive heart of yours for all of us. Easily.' He stroked the side of her face. 'Just because we're going to make new memories together—the three of us—it doesn't mean you have to erase the old ones.'

He dipped his hand into his pocket and pulled something out of it. It was only as she felt cold metal round her neck that she realised he had brought her locket with him, and that he was fastening it at her nape, underneath her hair.

Her lip quivered. 'But what if I *do* forget? My brain's not reliable all the time, is it?'

He looked at her with fierce tenderness. 'You won't forget. I won't let you. If you lose a name or a date I'll remember it for you. We're in this together, Ellie. You and me. And I want all of you. We have the future, but your past has made you who you are now, and that's the woman I love.'

She raised both hands and stroked the sides of his face, looking just as fiercely back at him. 'Oh, I love you too,' she whispered, and pressed her trembling lips to his.

She had one thing left to ask. Just because she needed to be one hundred percent certain. 'You do want children?'

Waiting for his reaction, she swallowed, trying to ease the thickening in her throat.

His hands moved from her back to splay over her still-flat stomach. She laughed. He looked as if he was expecting evidence there and then. He was just going to have to be patient.

'I want it all. I want our baby. I want to change nappies and clean up sick and crawl around on the floor with him. I want to give him brothers and sisters and teach the whole lot of them to play cricket. I want to help our children with their homework, teach them how to drive, give our daughters away at the altar. And I want to do it all with you by my side. Will you do that with me, Ellie? Do you want that too?'

Ellie threw back her head and laughed with joy. Mark always had made everything seem so simple. She was the one who made it all so complicated. She kissed him with a fervour that surprised them both.

Then, for the second time that month, she said, 'I do.'

EPILOGUE

ELLIE crept across the carpet in her bare feet and peered into the empty cot.

'Shh!' A low voice came from a dim corner of the room. 'I've just got him off to sleep.' Mark was pacing up and down, their two-week-old son cradled against his shoulder.

Baby Miles was sleeping the boneless sleep that newborns did so well. His mouth hung open and his brow was tensed into a frown. Mark and Ellie smiled at each other.

'The trick to putting him into bed is to treat him like a stick of dynamite,' he said, sounding like a total expert already as he lowered the infant into the cot with precision. 'One false move and—'

'The explosion is just as noisy and twice as devastating. I know. You've made that joke a hundred times in the last fortnight, and unfortunately I haven't forgotten a single occasion.'

Mark grinned at her, then went back to what he'd been doing. He eased his hand from under his son's head. They both froze as the little tyrant stirred and made a squeaky grunt. Mark's mask of stern concentration melted.

'I love it when he makes those noises,' he said, reaching for Ellie's hand and leading her from the room. She lifted their joined hands to look at her watch.

'Midnight! Just the right time for a chocolate feast,' she explained, and pulled him towards the kitchen. She delved into the fridge and pulled out a large bar of her favourite chocolate.

He turned the radio on low, and they ate chocolate and chatted until they were both doing more yawning than munching.

Ellie cocked her head. 'Listen, Mark.' He turned the radio up a notch. It sounded deafening in the quiet kitchen. They both looked at the ceiling and waited. When they were sure it was safe to make a noise, she added, 'They're playing our song.'

He started to hum along to Kat's latest single, 'All My Tomorrows'. It had been number one for three weeks already. The music-buying public couldn't seem to get enough of the simple love song, performed with just the expressive huskiness of Kat's voice and her acoustic guitar.

Ellie smiled and remembered the first time she'd heard it. She could almost feel the warmth of the Carribbean dawn on her skin and smell the hibiscus blossoms. Mark joined in the second chorus. She stood up and ruffled his hair before sitting on his lap. 'Don't give up your day job, sweetie. Kat might have you up on murder charges for doing that to her song.'

Mark pulled a face and Ellie hummed along with the music.

Treasure my heart and keep it safe, and I'll spend all my tomorrows loving you.

Ellie wagged a finger at him. 'Better do as the lady says, Mark.'

'Always,' he said, as he leaned in and stole a kiss.

His Housekeeper
Bride

MELISSA
JAMES

Dear Reader,

This book has been very near to my heart since I wrote it—first draft in 1997. In the writing of this Cinderella story, Mark and Sylvie became very special characters.

I hope, as you read about them, they become beloved to you as well, and find a place on your keeper shelf.

Happy reading!

Melissa

Melissa James is a mother of three, living in a beach suburb in New South Wales, Australia. A former nurse, waitress, shop assistant, perfume and chocolate demonstrator—among other things —she believes in taking on new jobs for the fun experience. She'll try anything at least once, to see what it feels like—a fact that scares her family on regular occasions. She fell into writing by accident, when her husband brought home an article stating how much a famous romance author earned, and she thought, *I can do that!* She can be found most mornings walking and swimming at her local beach with her husband, or every afternoon running around to her kids' sporting hobbies, while dreaming of flying, scuba diving, belaying down a cave or over a cliff—anywhere her characters are at the time!.

To the woman who inspired this book with an extraordinary life: I am privileged to be your friend. You raised a family from the age of eight, survived the worst horror a young girl can imagine, and yet you're constantly giving. You have no idea how special you are.

To Vicky, a woman of true giving, strength and compassion: you don't even know how you inspire others as you do what needs to be done.

To my beloved Mia: thank you for loving these characters, and never giving up on this book.

My friend, my sister, we're always a continent apart, yet our friendship goes from strength to strength. Remember you are never as others define you; you are what your heart is, loving and giving.

My deepest thanks go to my dear friends and CPs Robbie, Barb and Rachel, particularly Rachel, for showing me where and when I wandered off track, and Barb, for taking the time to read for me while on retreat. Special thanks to Nikki for reading at short notice. I thank you all.

PROLOGUE

St Agatha's Hospice, Sydney, fifteen years ago

THERE she was again, standing just outside the window, giving
him her sweet smile, her little encouraging wave. His friend
with the sunny red-gold curls, big brown eyes and brave,
dimpled smile that made her look like Shirley Temple.

She was in the copse of trees and flowering shrubs in the
middle of the hospice that she called the garden. The secret
garden, she called it—named for her favourite book, which she
read over and over to herself, as well as to her little brothers.

It was her escape from a reality and a future even grimmer
than his.

She was his escape. They'd met only in the confines of this
hospital during the times her mother's and Chloe's hospitalisa-
tions coincided, yet she *saw*, understood him, as his family no
longer did. Sometimes he felt as if he was standing in a black
and blinkered place, screaming for help, but surrounded by
people who saw only Chloe's needs, who were tuned only to
Chloe's voice.

Except for this thirteen-year-old girl who knew almost nothing about his life—a girl he never saw unless he was here.
'Shirley Temple' was his light and warmth in a dark, cold

world, his colour and life. Everything had faded to black or white except for her.

Mark waved back at her, letting her know he'd join her soon. Their brief exchanges of maybe twenty minutes made her day bearable, just as they did his. They talked, or didn't talk; it didn't matter. It was the only time in the day when she wasn't playing the adult, and when he actually felt like the kid he still was.

He glanced briefly back inside the room, but everything in there was a blur of white, a deathly shade of pale. The blankets, the walls, the gown Chloe wore, her face—even the blue oxygen tube going into Chloe's nostrils—had somehow faded into the pale thinness of her. Beneath her knitted pink cap her hair was in a plait, roped over her shoulder, thin and dull. Even shining with lipgloss her mouth looked defeated, transparent. Her eyes were like a delicate cobweb on a winter morning, rimed with frost. Broken with a touch. She was *sixteen*, and she was dying….

He was seventeen, and he was watching his best friend die— just as he'd been watching it for five endless years. Chloe had turned from childhood pal to his lover and bride of four weeks, and, watching her, he wanted to scream, to punch holes in the walls, to bolt as far away from this place as he could.

Oh, help—that sounded so *selfish* when he'd loved her almost all his life! But part of him felt as if *he'd* begun to die too when she'd got cancer, or as if he was chained to a cage: he wasn't *in* the cage but he couldn't fly away, either—and the only person who understood how he felt was a thirteen-year-old kid.

Carrie and Jen would be here in five or ten minutes. Chloe's best friends came every day after school, to tell them who was dating who, who'd broken up with who, and how ugly it had got. About the fight between Joe Morrow and Luke Martinez over who'd lost the opening game of the football season, and '—*don't choke*—Principal Buckley is getting *married*—like, at forty. How gross is that? He's so *old*.'

When Carrie and Jen came, Mark took off for a while. It was his time to breathe, to *be*. Chloe would fill him in on the Big News after. It gave them something to talk about.

Waiting for his escape time, he let his gaze touch all the reminders of life and normality. There was the massive Get Well card—as if she had a choice—signed by the whole school—even old Buckley and Miss Dragon-face Martin; the flowers-and-hearts and stick-figure finger paintings by Katie, his six-year-old sister, and Jon, Chloe's eight-year-old brother; the flowers his other sisters Bren and Becky picked for Chloe every day…

There was also a photo of Chloe, Jen and Carrie in a group hug, from when their school year had gone to the Snowy Mountains. Clear-skinned, tanned and laughing, Chloe looked so beautiful and healthy—as if nothing could hurt her. He remembered her smell that day. Like wind and sunshine and smiles. To her, it had been as if taking a six-hour trip on a bus was Everest and she'd conquered it.

It was the last time she'd gone out with her class.

As he stood by the bed he kept trying to calculate when he'd last had a day not spent in hospital, or at a doctor's office or thinking about illness and death. It was all a blur—as if he was a slow car stuck on a fast freeway. Everyone else around him rushed and flew, while he chugged along, unable to go faster. Just waiting.

It was a sunny day outside, a soft spring afternoon, perfect for testing the capabilities of his new motorised go-cart. But he was stuck in this room, watching the life drain out of Chloe, and there was *nothing* he could do about it.

'Prof…? Prof?'

The pain lacing her voice tore at his guts, but Mark couldn't make his head lift. The girl in the bed—strained, so thin, the hollows beneath her eyes the biggest and most colourful part of her—wasn't his best friend. This girl had given up.

Secondary cancer had gone from her bones to her lungs, and finally her brain. It was over—apart from the endless *waiting*.

'Come on, Prof, look at me.' Chloe's thready voice gained strength by that hard-headed will of hers—the same will that had talked him into playing with her when they were four and he'd hated girls. The same stubborn faith that had made her believe he'd marry her one day—she'd been saying it since they were five—and had seen her become his research partner in the inventions he made in his backyard workshop. The same adorable persistence that had given him acceptance at school when the other kids had thought his flow of ideas strange and stupid. Because Chloe had believed in him, because beautiful, popular Chloe Hucknall had said she was going to marry Mark Hannaford, he'd become part of the inner circle.

'I know you hate looking at me now, but I wouldn't ask if it weren't important.'

He didn't hate it—or her—but he hated what she was about to ask, what he knew she'd say. Because she'd been asking the same thing for days—for weeks now. He felt like a sleepwalker bumping into the same wall over and over.

He'd turned seventeen five weeks ago. Last time he'd looked he'd been twelve, asking what osteosarcoma was and when was Chloe getting better, because he had this *massive* idea he needed to work on with her. Then the days and years had become like potatoes under a masher. Though he'd gone to school and found a part-time job, got his learner's permit and his driver's licence, had worked hard and passed all his exams, created things for her to marvel at or give ideas for improvement, this place, this *pain*, was all that was real.

'Mark—*please*. I need you.'

I need you. The words he'd answered from the time she'd roped him into fixing her Barbie doll after Milo Brasevic had ripped its head off. He felt encased in darkness, with dark shutters fallen over his soul, yet he made himself look at her, and from somewhere deep inside he even forced a smile. It felt weak and hollow, but he managed it—for her, his best friend, the girl he'd loved ever since he could remember.

'Yeah? Whaddya want, Slowy?'

Mark and Chloe—the Mad Professor and Slowy. Always had been, always would be.

Chloe's answering grin was weak, but her thin, pale face was radiant with the love she'd never tried to deny in all the years they'd known each other. 'You didn't promise yet, George.' For no reason he'd ever known, she called him George when she was trying to be funny. 'I swear, I won't die until you promise,' she joked, her eyes glistening with tears of cheated wishing for all the years they'd never have together.

'Then I'll never do it,' he replied huskily.

Chloe stopped smiling. 'Stop it, Mark. It doesn't help—and I'm so *tired*. I know you're not gonna do so well without me, but you have to promise…' She closed her eyes, but the tears kept squeezing through. 'Don't spend all your time going for a scholarship, or hanging out in your shed alone with your inventions. You—you have to find another girl to love when you grow up, have kids…'

What was he supposed to say to that? *Yes, dear*? He knew how much it cost her to keep on asking day after day, because he couldn't *stand* to think of another guy touching her even if he'd been the one lying in that hospital bed.

Chloe was dying, and he had to live the rest of his life without her.

The bile rose hard and hot and fast, like a burning catapult. He turned and stumbled out of the ward—he wasn't going make it to the bathroom.

He made it outside the swinging doors, past the metal garbage can, and ran through the first door—the one leading to the tiny walled-in garden—before the sickness hit.

His hands and legs shook so badly he couldn't make his knees or his feet work. His breathing hurt, and there was a burning pain all the way up his chest and throat—but it was better than going back and having Chloe see him like this.

He knew that she'd try to force him to give the promise—or get their parents to talk to him again. *Give her the promise, Mark. Do it for Chloe.*

The same words he'd been responding to for five years—from going with her to her specialist appointments, to going back to school, to marrying her in a hasty backyard ceremony a few weeks ago.

Sometimes he just wished he'd *had* a choice to make. He'd like to know he'd have done all he had *without* the family's persuasive tactics.

'Here,' came a sweet, piping voice from behind him.

Mark's voice was croaky as he realised she was there. 'Hey, Shirley Temple.'

He liked calling her that as much as he liked the fact that she never used his name. If they didn't say Mark and Mary this wasn't real, it wasn't happening to them...and without names their shared time seemed a harmless dream, far from grim reality.

She was holding out a wet flannel to him. Crouching on the path beside him, she seemed luminous as the sun dipped behind the wire fencing at the end of the garden and framed her reddish-blonde curls. He knew those big fox-brown eyes of hers would be filled with the silent understanding only she could give. 'Put it on your face and your neck. It helps take the burning away.'

He took the cloth and wiped his face and throat. The pain eased a little. 'Thanks.'

'Keep it there.' She handed him a glass of water. 'Sip it slow.'

He nodded and sipped, and it eased the pain a little more. He felt it again—the unspoken connection. This pale, tired girl, looking so young until you looked in her eyes, felt like his only ally in a war he hadn't signed up to fight. 'Thanks.'

'You're welcome.' She reached out and touched his hand.

He could feel her hand shaking, could see her corkscrew curls bobbing with the effort to stay steady. 'Bad day?' he asked quietly.

She gave him a smile that wobbled. 'The doctor told us to say goodbye. Mum told me to be a brave girl and look after the boys.'

Oh, God help him. God help them both in what they had to face when they left here.

'Want to hit something with me?' he asked, to see what she'd do. Maybe she needed to lash out, to scream or yell, do *something* to let her suffering out.

She gave a gulping laugh, then two fat tears welled in her eyes. 'I have to set a good example for the boys.' Her slight body began to shake and lurch forward.

'Come here.' He held the trembling girl in his arms, feeling safe, at peace. She lived inside a similar cage to his, and she wasn't asking anything from him but to hold her, to understand.

Weird how a girl barely out of childhood could become his only haven…even weirder how he'd become hers, too. But he sure couldn't seem to make anyone else happy.

When she lay still against him, the only sound her hiccupping now and then, he wiped her tears with the cloth she'd brought for him. 'Hey, you want a drink or something?'

A soft, catching double breath told him she hadn't heard. Probably she'd spent the night caring for her youngest brother, who had croup.

Nobody knew the Brown family's story, for none of them talked about themselves. They all knew 'Shirley Temple' was the oldest of four kids. Local gossip said that Mrs Brown shouldn't have had the last of her children because she was too sick; she had something wrong with her heart that could threaten her life. She'd had him three years ago by C-section, and had been slowly dying since then, her heart too weak to pump. She'd been on the list for a transplant, but when one had finally come she'd been too sick for the operation.

So while Mr Brown was crying over the imminent loss of his wife, Shirley Temple was caring for the needs of her little brothers. It was the scandal of the hospital, but the girl did it all with a serene, defiant smile, neither complaining nor welcoming any sympathy. Social workers had come and gone, amazed by the strength of this girl who played a mother's part with seeming ease, refusing to admit she needed any help from the networks.

But she had to sleep some time…someone had to let her sleep. Poor kid.

His back was aching from sitting up unsupported. Holding her awkwardly in his arms, he wriggled back until he found the trunk of a big, thick old pine tree in the centre of the garden. He rested against it and closed his eyes, feeling a deep sense of life and hope emanating from her. Peace enveloped him.

'Mary! *Mary!*'

The panicked bellow woke them both with a start. Mark peered around the darkening garden with bleary eyes. The last thing he'd remembered was yawning. Now the sun was behind the western wall. Dusk had come and was almost gone.

'Mary!'

'Shirley Temple' jumped in his arms; Mark let her go, and she scrambled to her feet, rubbing her eyes, still swaying with tiredness. 'Da-Dad?'

A man was peering out of the slide-up aluminium window on the opposite ward to Chloe's. He had that poleaxed look of grief that Mark had seen on too many faces in the past few years.

'She's gone.' He didn't even seem to notice that a strange boy was standing beside his daughter, had been holding her in his arms. 'She's gone, Mary.'

A child's cough and a wail came from inside the room behind him.

Mark watched 'Shirley Temple'—Mary—sway again, her lip tremble and her eyes blink. He waited for the tears to come. Then she squared her shoulders. 'I'm coming.'

Mark turned to stare at Mary's father. In disbelief he saw the man's face crumple with relief. 'You're my good girl…' He withdrew from the window.

Mark watched Mary walk away with a poise that seemed totally wrong. She was *thirteen* and she'd just lost her mother. How could she be so—so *calm*?

'Mary?' he said, using her real name for the first time.

Mary turned her head, looking over her shoulder at him. In that moment he saw not the girl but the woman she would become. No: there was a woman already inside her—a person of more courage and strength than he'd ever have. Her eyes were open windows to a beautiful soul—and Mark grieved for the maturing of this girl to a woman he'd want to know. Because this was the last moment he'd have with her. She was leaving—going to that unbearable future without him.

'Will you be—all right?' Inadequate words for all he wanted to say.

Her bottom lip was sucked under the top one, and tears were falling down her cheeks, but the delicate body was tight and straight. He saw the contours of her body in the silhouette of shadowy lights against the wall, the last light of the falling sun, and for the first time he saw a girl poised on the brink of womanhood. It was a reaction as physical as it was emotional, and guilt pierced him that he could even *think* that way when Chloe was in the room behind him, dying….

'I promised,' Mary said simply. 'Goodbye, Mark. I have to go now.'

And then she was gone.

Mark stood in the garden until darkness filled it. Then he walked back into the ward, to Chloe's room. The entire family was there, and each of them had identical expressions of grief and accusation on their faces as they looked at him—even Katie and Jon.

The tense, exhausted look on Chloe's thin face broke him. It was obvious she'd spent most of the afternoon fighting her wasting body, summoning up all her reserves of courage and strength to continue her quest for his promise. It meant that much to her to believe that one day he'd find happiness again.

He waved the family out with the cold fierceness that was starting to feel like a second skin over his heart and soul. 'I'll do it,' was all he said when they were alone.

Those cobweb-delicate eyes slowly closed; her face relaxed. She brought his hand to her cheek—the hand that had for four weeks borne his ring. 'Thank you,' she whispered, and drifted back into a ghost-like sleep, releasing his hand as her body unwound like a coil with its pressure released.

Mark's hand moved over her limp hair. Even now Chloe was beautiful, yet all he could see at this moment was the face of the girl who'd just left him behind. Perhaps because he saw a mirror of Mary's reflection in Chloe's acceptance of death, the dignity, grace and courage to say goodbye, to make a promise and keep it.

Filled with hatred at the thought of what he'd promised, Mark clenched his free fist and sat on the chair beside his wife's bed, watching her face. Waiting again…and already missing his only friend.

CHAPTER ONE

Office of the CEO, Howlcat Industries, Sydney Harbour, the present day

'WHY, Bren? Why the—?' Mark skidded to a mental halt, remembering his three-year-old niece was sitting on his lap. Shelby was prone to repeat anything he said and then bat her long golden eyelashes at her father when she got in trouble for it, saying, *'But Unca Mark says it.'* He amended his words. 'You think she'll do, so why do I have to interview this woman? She's a *housekeeper*. I have better things to do with my time than—'

Brenda Compton, née Hannaford, pulled her thick dark-blonde hair back off her face and fanned her neck, but grinned at Mark's careful pruning of his language. 'Well, of course, if you *want* me to conduct the interviews for you, find another… um…*suitable* woman…'

He set his jaw at the reminder. He might be CEO of Howlcat Industries, Australia's most successful engineering firm, in total control of the company he'd built from the ground up— but at home he had too many reminders of his humanity. His family knew him well, as no one else did—his hidden weaknesses, the way he spaced out when caught by an idea…

And they never failed to reminder him of the promise he still hadn't kept. But why had Bren chosen now, *today*, to make that reminder, to find him another *suitable* woman?

Today was his wedding anniversary. In six weeks it would be the anniversary of the day he'd become a widower.

His mother and his sisters had interviewed every house-keeper he'd ever hired. Before he gave them a contract he had them vetted by the best security firms in the country, and he paid them well. He also forced them to sign a confidentiality clause.

None of his precautions had stopped his employees selling their story about him to the tabloids, or bringing along their daughters or nieces, who happened to be pretty and single and, who'd love to be taken out on the town, marry a multi-millionaire and give him the family and kids his parents and sisters so romantically believed was in his future.

Today was a reminder that he'd *never* risk his heart and soul again. He'd never risk becoming a person so lost in grief that he'd almost—

Grimly he blocked out the memory, and answered Bren. 'I'll interview her myself…but she can wait in the outer office until I'm da—good and ready.'

Bren grinned and pretended to bow to him—which earned her a paper bird tossed in her hair. He often made origami when he was thinking up the dimensions of new inventions, needing to keep his hands busy while his mind worked.

His family were the only ones who could get away with any kind of irreverence with him. Everyone else was too afraid of his cool sarcasm. 'Heart of Ice' was his nickname in the press, and he was happy to keep it that way. It kept the nice women away from him—and fame-and-fortune-hunters deserved all they got—which was nothing but an occasional good time and their faces in the glossies.

'What's da—good, Unca Mark?' Shelby's big bright eyes were alight with curiosity.

He grinned down at his niece and pulled her ponytail, until she mock-shrieked and tugged hard at his nose. 'It means really, really good.'

'Okay,' Shelby replied, her face thoughtful. She knew he'd covered the truth and was trying to work out what he'd been about to say. She was a Hannaford, all right.

Bren got to her feet, rubbing her very pregnant belly. 'I'll tell Sylvie to wait. You'll pick me up tonight? Glenn felt so bad about asking, but since his trip is for Howlcat—'

He smiled, soft as he only ever was with his family, and handed Shelby to her mother. 'Can it, Bren. I can handle a couple of Lamaze classes as long as you introduce me as—'

His sister rolled her eyes. 'Yeah, yeah—as if calling you *George* is going to fool anyone when your face is in the papers every week.'

'Not every week,' he retorted mildly. He liked being called George every now and then. It made him smile.

She'd been waiting almost an hour.

Sylvie Browning smiled to herself. If he expected her to be put off or storm off he'd be disappointed. In the initial interview his sister Brenda had warned her that meeting her prospective employer would be no picnic. Mark Hannaford was hard-edged and cold, and he didn't like his routine or privacy challenged—he had no use for women, apart from the obvious.

That was why she was here. She had a fifteen-year-old promise to keep.

After ninety minutes, the fanatically neat secretary rose to her feet, and said, 'Mr Hannaford will see you now.'

The older woman showed Sylvie in through the massive oak double doors, opulent without ostentation. 'Ms Browning to see you, sir.' Then she closed the doors behind her.

Feeling the nervous grin stretching her face—she always

laughed or joked through stress, and this was a tremendous moment—Sylvie walked on low-polished floorboards and for a few moments looked anywhere but at the CEO of Howlcat Industries. There was a soft blue and grey scatter rug on the floor. Pictures of the harbour and the Blue Mountains lined the walls, comfortable in their places.

What a lovely office, she thought to herself. It suits—

'No. *No*.'

She blinked, and focussed on the sole occupant of the office. 'I beg your pardon?' she said softly, putting her hand out to him.

With the golden-brown hair and eyes, the lithe, athletic male body obvious even beneath the designer suit, she recognised him at once… But then, what Aussie *wouldn't* know him? He was one of the most famous men in the country. He hadn't inherited his empire, but pulled himself up by the bootstraps to this level of success by sheer brilliance. Inventor and lone wolf—tagged 'Heart of Ice' because no woman had ever come close to him.

Only his family—and she—knew better than that.

But at the moment he was living up to his reputation. He didn't stand to shake her hand, didn't touch her. His eyes were frozen as he said, with chilling clarity, 'I said, *no*. If you're Sylvia Browning, you are *not* being offered the position of housekeeper.'

Unfazed, she lifted her brows. This, too, she'd expected. She would change his attitude soon enough. She'd done it before, and she'd do it again. 'I know I look young, but I'm twenty-eight.'

Eyes filled with scepticism roamed her face. 'Twenty at the oldest. *No*.'

Since it was obvious he wasn't going to observe the most basic of social niceties, she dropped her hand and sat in the chair facing his desk. She rummaged in her handbag, pulled out her wallet and handed him the driver's licence and birth certificate from her CV packet.

He read them in silence, and handed them back without changing expression. 'Your age changes nothing, Ms Browning.'

'I was under the impression it changed *everything*.'

Her gently amused tone seemed to perturb him, for he frowned at her. 'Don't be impertinent.'

'I beg your pardon, Mr Hannaford,' she said gravely, but her telltale dimple quivered—she had only one, in her right cheek. Her brothers swore it gave her away when she was teasing. 'But, since you are *not* employing me, I'm free to be as impertinent as I like.'

His face stilled, then his mouth moved in a half-smile, slow as a rusted gate. '*Touché*, Ms Browning.'

Sylvie grinned at him, rose to her feet, and again put her hand out to his. 'It was nice meeting you, Mr Hannaford. I hope you find a housekeeper of the right age and appearance for you.' Her heart raced so fast she could barely keep up to breathe. Would it work?

He stood, too, but was still frowning. 'You're not going to try and convince me to give you the position?' he asked abruptly, again not taking her hand.

Her heart kicked up yet another notch—*yes*, there was the faintest tone of challenge there, as well as surprise. She made herself shrug. 'What's the point? I can cook and clean—but you don't care about that. I can make a home for you—but that isn't why you rejected me. I can only grow older in time, and I can't change the way I look.'

'There's nothing wrong with the way you look.'

His tone was still abrupt, but again something faint beneath it made her breath catch and her pulse move up a touch. 'Thank you,' she said as she turned towards the doors. 'I like to think I'm not totally repulsive.'

'You have to know you're a pretty woman.' But the comment was so far removed from a compliment—almost an insult in the hardness of his voice—that she didn't thank him.

'Are the curls natural?' he asked as he followed her to the door—he was actually coming with her. She wanted to rejoice. Yes, she'd intrigued him.

'Yes, they are.' The answer was rueful. She touched the tumbling dark auburn curls escaping from her attempt at a chignon and looked up at him…really *up*. The top of her head barely reached his shoulder. 'Any attempt to straighten them only makes them frizz. Combine that with freckles, being only five-one and size eight, and I have to put up with everyone thinking I'm sixteen.'

She'd used the number deliberately, to see how he'd react. It was why she was here—why she'd come on this particular day—and she might as well start now.

His mouth tightened, but he only nodded. Then he frowned again, as if the number had triggered something inside him. 'Pardon me, Ms Browning, but I'm having the strangest sense of *déjà-vu*. Have we met?'

He'd remembered! She nodded, with a grin that felt silly on her face. He *remembered* her… 'For years I've wanted to thank you for all you did for my family. You'll never know what it meant to us—giving us the house, setting up the trust fund to send Simon to medical school, Joel to university, Drew to engineering college. When I found out this job was for *you*, it seemed a good chance to meet you again and thank you.'

For the first time he looked in her eyes, and she saw the change as he took in the face, the curls, and emotion dawned in him—recognition. 'Shirley Temple?' With his low growl, it was as if deep winter broke, giving way to a reluctant spring, and the warm-hearted boy she'd known when she was a girl peeked at her from beneath the frozen heart of the famous man.

'I go by Sylvie now.' For the third time she put her hand out, hoping he'd take it. She needed to know if the illusion she'd held for so many years would crumble under the force of reality—if she'd shrink or find him as terrifying as every other man she'd met since she turned fifteen.

'Sylvie?' His voice was deeper, rougher than she remembered it, but a warm shiver still ran through her. 'But your name's Mary Brown.'

'It's Mary Sylvia, actually, and we—the boys and I—liked Browning better. It was less common—especially for me, with a name like Mary.' Feeling embarrassed by the admission, she shrugged. 'I changed my name by deed poll, and the boys did the same.' She'd never tell him why she'd done it, or why the boys had followed her lead without hesitation. Although none of them had changed their first names, as well, as she had....

'Then Joel must have changed his only a few months ago.'

He knows how old we all are. He's kept up with us. The knowledge that he cared enough to know them, even from a physical and emotional distance, made her feel—feel—

Just *feel*. He hadn't forgotten her—as she'd never forgotten him.

Looking dazed, he put his hand in hers just as she was about to drop it. 'Look at you. You're all grown up.'

'So are you.' Her voice was breathless—but how could she help it? He was touching her again...and for the first time since she was fifteen a man's touch didn't repulse or terrify her. She felt warm and safe—and, given what her life had been, those feelings were as precious as gold to her.

From the first time she'd seen him at the hospital, when she'd been only eight, the prince of her fairytale dreams had changed from black-haired to dark blonde, from blue-eyed to golden-brown. Every time she'd met him after that, though months had passed, she'd felt the connection deepen, and when he'd held her in his arms and let her sleep the day her mother had died she'd known that, though it was the last day she'd see him for a very long time, no other boy would ever take his place.

Quiet lightning still strikes once—and never in the same spot. But he had lovers in abundance—all far more beautiful than she'd ever be—and they didn't come with her issues. Years ago she'd accepted that he was her impossible dream. That wasn't why she was here.

'So you really are twenty-eight?' He shook his head, as if trying to clear it.

'Yes.' As the juxtaposed longings to reach out and touch his face and to jerk her hand out of his and run all but overwhelmed her, she had to force her hand to stay where it was. Though she'd never been to counselling, she'd learned to conquer her fear to a manageable degree, by dint of the simple need to eat. If an employer thought she was crazy, he wouldn't employ her, and she couldn't always work with women.

His gaze swept her again. 'Your hair grew darker.'

'Red hair quite often does that.'

He was still holding her hand. Looking at his expression as they touched, she sensed that it had been a long time since he'd truly touched anyone. 'Strawberry blonde.' He was smiling. 'You looked like a china doll.'

'According to some people I still do,' she said, sighing. 'Sometimes I'd give anything to be a few inches taller, if nothing else.'

'People don't take you seriously?' His voice held sympathy.

'You didn't,' she retorted, disliking the tone that seemed too close to pity, too close to how she'd been treated for so many years of her life. She pulled her hand from his.

'You're right.' He was looking at the broken connection, a strange expression in those frozen dreamer's eyes. 'Why do you want this position—or did you only come to thank me?'

His tone had lost the gentle warmth that made her glow. He

wanted to be thanked even less than he'd appreciated her pointing out when he'd been in the wrong. By the look in his eyes, he also didn't want to hear any personal reasons for her answering his advertisement, on this of all days.

'I need the job,' she said abruptly. 'I'm in the final year of my nursing degree. I need somewhere to live and I need to pay the bills.'

'Why now?'

The simple question drew her out—the not-quite-cynical tone, the weary implication of *there must be a catch in this*. She stiffened her spine. It was all she could do not to walk out— but even her unconquerable pride was less important than keeping her word. But, oh, if she'd known it would be so hard to come back into his life this way, to stand before him and ask, she would never have made that promise to Chloe.

She heard the flat curtness in her voice as she finally answered. 'My flatmate Scott's getting married in a few weeks, and Sarah, his fiancée, wants to move her stuff in. I could live on campus, but I'd still need a job.'

'You still have the house?' It wasn't quite a question, more of an interrogation.

'Drew married his long-time girlfriend a while back—they had a baby boy five months after. They needed the house. He's in his third year of mechanical engineering, and with his study workload he can only work long enough hours to keep the family. Simon, Joel and I can get out there and pay rent.' She smiled at him, as if it was no big deal.

'I see.' And the tone, though restrained, told her he really did.

Mark looked down at the face of memory, an echo of sweetness long submerged. He saw in the pretty face of Sylvie Browning the girl she'd been. She didn't look as he'd expected except for her eyes—eyes still ancient in a young face—and her smile. The sweet, defiant smile of a girl who'd had to go to school while caring for her father and brothers, taking on a mother's role long before her mother had died.

Yes, he did understand her—too well. She'd accepted his money *for her family*. The one person he'd wanted to help through the years probably hadn't taken a cent for herself.

He shut himself off from the world with ice. Sylvie did it with a smile.

Behind the shutters he could make of his eyes, his famous brain raced. If she was desperate enough to play on a past so painful and intensely private, then she truly needed help—but she wouldn't accept his charity.

'Do you have references from past positions?'

As he'd judged, his cool detachment reassured her. Her shoulders relaxed and she breathed in deeply before she replied. 'Here's a reference from my boss at Dial-An-Angel, and some from many of my regular customers.'

She thrust a plastic sleeve at him, filled with letters.

His brows lifted as he read one glowing referral after another. *Honest, hard-working, discreet.*

She made our house a home.

She became part of our family.

We offered her double to stay. We're so sorry to lose her.

'Impressive.' He noted she'd updated the references that stretched back a dozen years to fit her name change. She obviously wanted to leave her past behind for some reason—a reason he'd have to find out. He hadn't come this far in life by trusting anyone.

A wave of colour filled those soft-freckled cheeks. 'I didn't ask them to say it.'

The 'Heart of Ice' was famed for never descending to argument or reassurance on minor points. 'I have a contract all employees sign—including a confidentiality clause. If you sell a story or steal anything from me I'll sue you out of all human existence.'

She stared at him, and her flashing eyes—eyes the colour

of old sherry, enormous, their curling lashes made thicker with mascara—held insult. The colour grew in her face. Sweet indignation and adorable anger. Yet she was so much a woman at that moment the image of little brave Shirley Temple wavered and fell in his mind, shattering like glass on a tile floor.

'You'll sign it?' he pressed, fighting the ridiculous urge to take it back, to say he *knew* he could trust her. He hadn't seen her in fifteen years. He knew nothing about the woman apart from her stiff-necked refusal to accept help. That much about her hadn't changed a bit.

She nodded. 'I have one condition.'

He lifted a brow. None of his housekeepers had ever tried to bargain with him before; he made sure they didn't need to. 'Well?'

'I want to live in the cottage that comes with the job, but—' her eyes held the smiling defiance he'd seen in her as a girl, setting boundaries as well as he did, with all his cold control '—you don't come inside. *Ever.*'

He almost laughed in her face. What did she think? He hobnobbed with the help? He hadn't been in that place since he'd had it renovated years ago. 'Done. Now, please wait outside. If your references check out, the job's yours.'

'Thank you.' The words were cool, reserved, but he felt *relief* inside. Oh, yeah, he understood that desperation and that pride, the need for personal space and dignity.

She walked out, her little feet in low-heeled sandals making no sound on his wooden flooring. He watched the sway of her gently flaring hips beneath the swishing skirt, saw the way her fists curled, her head held high, and didn't bother to call her former employers.

He was neither stupid nor blind. He knew inevitability when he saw it. Sylvie had the job, and she would live in the housekeeper's cottage behind his house for as long as she needed. If warning signs were flashing, if he felt as if he was standing in quicksand, he still couldn't do anything but hire her. If he let her down for the sake of his own security she'd haunt him for life: he'd be wondering where she was, what job she had, if they were good to her. He'd taken care of her by proxy for too many years to stop now.

Suddenly he wondered. *Did Bren know how he'd cared for the Brown family? Did she know it was Shirley Temple when she brought her here?*

Anger flooded his soul. Oh, yeah, Bren must have recognised Sylvie. By now the whole family must know that the child Sylvie had been made her the only woman who could break his defences on this day of all days. Why she'd come to him he didn't know, but he knew his family—still trying to rescue him from a life they abhorred, trying to break the ice around his heart. They were always trying to find him a woman like—

Didn't they know if he ever found another woman like Chloe he'd only run like hell? People like Chloe weren't meant to live long lives with guys like him. Just as Chloe had done, as little Mary had done, they touched your life and then left you— bereft, empty.

As empty as his heart and soul had become in the past fifteen years.

It was too late for redemption. None of his success changed what he'd done. No amount of money could take away the damage he'd inflicted on others—and Shirley Temple had come fifteen years too late.

Her name's Sylvie, and she's not a kid anymore, his mind taunted him. *Small, delicate, haunting, but she's a woman, head to foot*.

He clenched his fists, hating that just by telling him who she was she'd breached his defences. Her gentle face with its freckled prettiness was vulnerable and genuine, and it made him feel warm in a place he'd forgotten existed. But he couldn't let her get too close or she'd destroy him—and, worse, he'd destroy her.

He shuddered. *Never, never again.* No. It was time to erect a few barriers.

With cold deliberation he reached for the phone and, instead of calling Dial-An-Angel, he called a woman he'd dated once or twice—a model-actress as callous and uncaring as he'd been for years, who wanted only fun and a few minutes of fame.

If Sylvie was in the cottage behind his waterfront mansion tonight, she'd be alone. He'd be out on the town with Toni, doing what he did best: forgetting there had ever been someone who loved him just as he was, and who pushed him to be his best.

On this day he had two choices: drink, or take a woman to a hotel.

As usual, he chose the latter.

Balmain

Sylvie wandered through the house, wide-eyed, whispering, 'Oh,' every few moments. Built in 1849 by a ship's captain, right on Sydney Harbour, Mark's house was a fascinating waterfront blend of colonial, naval and Victorian, with open beams, leadlight windows and wide-planked flooring; the outside was sandstone blocks.

It was a dream come true—the kind of dream she'd have had if she'd known this wonderful, eclectic, *homey* house existed. It was almost perfect…*almost.*

She grinned. So he had a date tonight? So what? Because of him, she now had a home, and a job that would pay the bills and allow her to save while she finished college. She was so deeply in his debt she doubted she'd ever be able to climb out—and she'd promised Chloe she'd take care of him. It was time for her to do some giving…and she knew where to start: the Friday night markets at The Rocks.

By running all the way to the ferry stop on the harbour, she just made the next ferry.

CHAPTER TWO

Later that night

Mark had to hold back from slamming the door.

What was wrong with him?

After the Lamaze classes, where he hadn't missed a single opportunity to get the message across to Bren, he'd dropped her home and taken Toni, a stunning woman, for a late dinner and dancing at the best clubs. And he'd made sure his sister knew where he was going.

He'd fulfilled his part, given Toni the exposure she needed. She was currently between jobs, and being photographed with him would make all the tabloids. It was a guarantee that producers and casting agencies would remember to call her. In return, she'd have been happy to spend the rest of the night with him at a hotel—she didn't want the intimacy of spending the night at her place or his, either—and yet he'd still said, 'Another time…'

Toni's amused acceptance of his being so able to keep his hands off her perfect tanned body hadn't helped things, either. 'So, what's her name?'

He'd had a ridiculous urge to snap back, *Shirley Temple*.

And it was the truth. Oh, not sexually—it was guilt. After she'd signed the contract, he'd tossed his spare keys at a bemused Sylvie, scrawled the address on a piece of paper for her, and told her the housekeeper's cottage was out at the back and to move in over the weekend. He'd said he expected breakfast at six twenty-five Monday morning, and he wouldn't be home tonight.

All she'd said was, 'Of course. Thank you for everything.'

Her good manners in the face of his rudeness had made him all the more appalled that he'd lost his manners with the wrong person. She'd come to thank him—to answer a job advertisement. He'd taken out his anger with Bren on Sylvie.

He owed her an apology, and he didn't like its effect on him. She'd stayed on his mind, haunting him with her brave, defiant smile and her acceptance of his bad temper, until he hadn't even felt Toni when she'd kissed him.

So now he was home alone, thinking of *his housekeeper* when he could have been naked with a gorgeous blonde, forgetting the past for an hour. And now he probably wouldn't sleep because he felt totally screwed up, screwed over, angry and *ashamed*. And Sylvie was bound to be sleeping so he couldn't offload his conscience until morning—

And then every thought vanished.

He flicked on the lights and stood in the middle of the entryway, breathing. What was that amazing smell? Inhaling again, he felt the turbulence inside his soul vanish, leaving only traces of its memory behind. He felt uplifted, energised, *inventive*…

The house was different, too—wasn't it?

He went into one room after another, flicking on lights. He'd never seen that stained-glass sailing ship on the living room wall before, or that chart beside the entry to the ballroom—a print of Captain Cook's pencilled route to Botany Bay. Funny, he had to look at them twice to notice, but now he looked there seemed to be little changes everywhere.

Even the lights weren't the same—the lights themselves

were softer, lending a gentle night radiance to every room it hadn't had before.

What had Sylvie done to his house?

Breathing in the amazing scent, he wandered from room to room, seeing the touches so sweet and subtle he still had to look twice to find them. It was as if they'd grown here while he'd been gone. A funny little scarecrow doll sat proudly on his kitchen windowsill, bearing the legend 'Housework Makes You Ugly'. A plain grey river stone sat on his study desk in front of his monitor, with a single word on it: *Believe*. Two of his stupid origami pieces sat either side of the stone, as if to say *Your creations*.

Dried herbs hung from the edges of curtains. There was a bright flowered tablecloth on his grandma's dining table, a vase filled with purple flowers from his garden. Tiny pictures hung on the kitchen walls, old soap and butterscotch ads in wooden frames. A distressed wooden hanging was on the dining room wall, proudly bearing a kookaburra in military get-up, proclaiming the efficacy of Diggaburra Tea. Another faced it, this time a teddy bear saluting him, telling him to drink Teddy Beer.

Everything was scrupulously clean, polished, but it looked... He didn't know—but after his fury of a minute before, now all he wanted was to smile. The glowing floors, the scent, the additions to his furniture made him want to laugh. Stupid clutter to him—he'd *never* have bought it himself—yet somehow it announced her presence in his life. *I'm here, Mark.*

She knew how to make an impact.

It was just so—so *Sylvie*, he thought grimly, trying to muster up some negative emotion and failing. Confused by all the foreign emotion churning in him—he was feeling *happy* when he should be mad—he stalked to the back door, jerked it open and shouted in the general direction of the cottage, 'Sylvie!'

He refused to repeat himself. He'd yelled loud enough the first time.

Moments later a light came on in the cottage, then the door opened and a sleepy voice said softly, 'I think knocking would be kinder to the neighbours at this time of night.'

He cursed beneath his breath. 'Could you come inside, please?' he asked, in as reasonable a manner as possible.

'Answering to the boss at 2:47 a.m. wasn't in the contract... sir.'

She was right. He was caught in the wrong again—and the fact only made him want to fight more. 'Tomorrow at six.'

'Technically, it's today, sir—and it's a Saturday. Do I have weekends off?'

The word *sir* got him all fidgety. It wasn't right coming from her, after their shared past, and he suspected she only did it now to make a point. 'Just come inside *now*!'

He heard a distinct sigh, but a figure emerged from the warm darkness.

Mark caught his breath. Tumbled curls, mussed with sleep, fell around her shoulders, catching the light until they looked like dark fire. Her face was rosy, her eyes big, cloudy—and she was wearing a slip nightie in a soft clear blue that showcased her pale skin like pearls in shimmering water.

She stood outside the door, dropped some slippers to the mat, and shoved her feet into them. She sent him an enquiring glance. 'You did want me to come in now?' she asked, nodding at the door he still held.

'What? Oh, yes.' He moved back and she walked into the kitchen, throwing a cotton robe over her nightie.

He nearly growled in protest. She'd looked so sweet and silky, so touchable with her bare feet, and her body—the curves were small, but in the iridescent half-light she'd looked like a creature of magic and moonlight.

She rubbed her eyes and blinked. 'Is this kind of awakening going to be a regular occurrence, sir? If so, I'll have to go to bed earlier.'

'Stop calling me *sir*,' he snapped.

Sylvie sighed again. 'Mr Hannaford is such a mouthful…but whatever you wish.'

'I've already warned you about impertinence. I won't tolerate it.'

She frowned and tilted her head. 'I'm sorry, but I'm not at my best this time of night. Are you saying that calling you Mr Hannaford is impertinent?'

'I'm saying—' He shook his head. How had they descended to this level so fast? And how could he have fallen in lust so fast with someone he'd thought of as Shirley Temple? Until he'd seen her like this, as if she'd come fresh from a lover's bed. 'I don't argue with employees.'

She smiled at him, a sleepy thing of flushed beauty that made him catch his breath and his body harden with an urgency all Toni's kisses hadn't been able to rouse. 'You can't imagine how glad I am to hear that—given our…um…conversation of the past few minutes. So, to sort matters, what *would* you like me to call you?'

Locked into the unexpected desire that had hit him with the force of a ten-pound grenade, he said huskily, 'Mark will do.'

The way that single crinkle between her brows grew told him what she thought of *that*. 'I thought you wanted some professional distance between us?'

He shrugged, trying not to laugh. Oh, she knew how to call him on his pronouncements, and she wasn't a bit intimidated by anything he did or said. 'Distance seems fairly silly at the moment, given where we are and what you're wearing—and our shared past.'

With an endearing self-consciousness she pulled her robe

around her. 'I'd feel better if you smiled.' Her eyes were big as she stared at him with haunting uncertainty. China-doll lovely, and so tempting…

'Please, Sylvie, call me Mark,' he murmured—and smiled.

She swallowed and moistened her lips, her eyes still huge, unsure. 'Thank you—Mark.'

A little half-smile lingered on her mouth. She always smiled—unless her prickly pride was touched. She seemed to have hidden laughter lurking around her, a delicious mirth he thought she might share with him if he got close enough. He took a step forward, obeying the imperative urge to imbibe her sparkling warmth, to touch—

Sylvie caught the back of her slipper on a mat as she took a hasty step back.

And he remembered at the worst possible moment what he was doing, where this was going. She was his employee, in a vulnerable position—and, much as he wanted to forget it, she *was* Shirley Temple. Her memory shone in his mind like starlight: for five years she'd been the girl who'd given him silent empathy when no one else had understood he didn't *want* to talk, who'd been there for him when he'd felt lost and alone, cared for him when she'd had no one to care for her. She'd simply given him what he'd needed when he'd needed it, in a no cost or agenda way.

She was still doing it now—giving without taking back— and while his craving body was reminding him that she was most definitely a woman, she was only here because he'd ordered her inside. Hours after duty ended.

Her duties haven't even begun yet, jerk. She's barely had time to move her stuff in.

She'd suffered enough in her life, if the report he'd received this afternoon was true. She didn't know the shallow games he played with women; she'd been too busy caring for her father until his death, bringing up her brothers. She'd only begun to have a life of her own when Joel had moved into the dorm rooms at his university. *Three months ago.*

His hands curled into fists of denial. He couldn't be the hard-hearted man on the town. No matter how much he wanted to forget what this day was, he couldn't do it to her.

'So…what did you want to talk about?' she asked, the breathless sound in her voice sweet and pretty.

Everything about Sylvie was pretty—from her tousled curls to her pink-painted toes peeping out from the open-ended slippers. And so were the changes she'd made to his house.

His anger seemed ridiculous now. 'I owe you an apology for my rudeness at the office.'

She yawned behind her hand with a puzzled look. 'You yelled the street down at 2:47 a.m. to apologise?'

He felt heat creeping up his neck.

Her grin was as sweet as the look in her eyes—a mixture of woman and imp. 'I was sure you were going to bawl me out for the presents I brought you.'

'Why did you do it?' he asked abruptly.

She shuffled her slippers on the floor, staring at her feet. 'Every good thing in my life has come from you.' She shrugged with one shoulder, her neck tilting to meet its uplift, and he knew what she was about to say. 'It isn't in me to do nothing but take, Mark. I know there's nothing I can give you to thank you for rescuing my family—but I wanted to try.'

Any lingering anger, any urge to bawl her out or freeze her out, withered and died under the pure, humbling honesty of her. 'Anything I ever gave you can never repay what you did for me.'

She looked up again, her smile shy and eager, and though he saw an echo of the Shirley Temple he remembered, she was a rosy, tumbled woman at the same time. She was both and more—and she fascinated him too much for her own good. He had to get her to stay away from him, because he wasn't having any success in staying away from her.

'When the deed for the house came, and the trust for us, and the card from you… You have no idea what you did for me—us.'

Her words, sincere and choked with emotion, annihilated his normal method of making a woman keep her distance. 'You, Sylvie,' he said quietly, wondering why he said it. 'I did it for *you*.'

'You saved my life.' She looked at him as if he was wonderful. 'Literally, you saved me, Mark. When the money came I was drowning. Dad was too sick to work, I was working part-time at a restaurant to make the rent, going to school, cleaning houses, doing homework at midnight. I—' She swallowed, and then said abruptly, 'Owning the house helped me put food on the table, paid for a housekeeper. I could stay at school, study and pass my exams.'

'It was just money.' He wanted to turn away, but he couldn't stand not to see her flushed prettiness, the shining gratitude and hidden pain in those lovely eyes.

'No.' She took a step towards him, tender, hesitant. 'Your house is so beautiful. I can feel your love for it in all the old furniture. I love it, too. It's like you.'

Too many emotions crowded him; he hadn't felt this confused since he was about thirteen, and her last comment heightened his bemusement. 'Like me?'

She nodded, her face serious. 'I walked in this afternoon and felt as if it was a haven in a crazy city. I felt peace. You could have made this a showplace. Instead you chose furniture that made it mellow, gentle and welcoming. It's a family house for a family man.'

Alarm bells shrieked in his head. *Don't do it. Don't lose it with her.* And still he stepped forward, looking over her—such a delicate woman—and snarled in a freezing tone, 'Do you *see* a family here?' She jerked back fast, breathing unevenly, her face white, and with such terror in her eyes he felt horrified. 'Sylvie, I didn't mean to—'

She lifted a shaking hand and he stopped. Just like that. He who hadn't obeyed any woman but his mother for over a decade. Was it their past, or the shimmering tears in her eyes that halted him before her?

When she spoke it was in a half-whisper, with the shadows of her fear hovering around her like an aura of night. 'I see the ghosts of the family that *should* be here. This house is the real you…it's your haven from being the Heart of Ice. You bought this house for *her*. For Chloe, for both of you—it's everything you should have had with her. The family, the babies.'

He felt the blood drain from his head, leaving him dizzy. By God, she met a sword-thrust with gentle atom bombs—and he couldn't take any more reminders of what he'd become, what he'd always be now: a man alone.

'Go to bed, Sylvie. Have the weekend off to settle into the cottage. Don't worry about my breakfast. Just don't come in here until I'm gone.' The words grated like sandpaper in his throat.

'All right.' She turned and walked to the door, not wishing him a goodnight. Probably she knew it wasn't, and it wouldn't be. All he wanted now was for her to leave him alone. All he wanted was to drown himself in Scotch. If only he had any of the stuff in the house.

An echo rang in his heart and head—an anthem of unending loss. Not of Chloe herself—he'd accepted that a year before her death—but loss of hope. He'd lost something vital inside himself long before her death, and he'd never found it again.

At the door, Sylvie spoke again. 'Mark?'

He gripped a dining chair, knowing that whatever she was about to say would be unexpected. She wasn't fooled by his cover. She didn't see him as the Heart of Ice, wasn't intimidated by his anger, wasn't over-awed by his power or wealth. She saw

Mark. She knew what he'd once been—believed that boy was still inside him somewhere—and that scared the living daylights out of him. He couldn't be that person again. He couldn't open his heart to any woman. Even Sylvie.

Especially Sylvie. She was everything he'd avoided for fifteen years—the kind of woman who'd take what was left of his heart and soul and rip it to shreds.

'What?' He closed his eyes, waiting for the blow. He already knew she had that power.

When she spoke, he heard the shaking in her voice as strongly as he felt the trembling in his limbs. 'Chloe deserves you to have bought this house for her. She deserves to be remembered and to be loved still. And you deserve this refuge. Time out from the cold and uncaring person you never were inside.'

He hung on to the chair like grim death as pain raced through his body and soul like a heat blast, leaving him scalded and weak. *She doesn't know the truth. Don't tell her. Don't say it!*

'Just go. *Please.*' The words came out in a strangled voice.

The door closed behind her, and he was left alone with the endless ghost of grief, guilt and regret. All he wanted now was to talk to a friend in a black-labelled bottle.

He'd been wishing that for the past fifteen years. All he could drown himself in now was meaningless sex…and it never helped him forget who he was. *What* he was.

Sylvie closed the door of her new home, closed her eyes and gulped in shaking breaths.

She should never have said it. The agony in his eyes had told the truth about the infamous Heart of Ice. He wrapped himself inside a coldness that could shatter at a touch. But it was nothing but a delicate veneer, hiding his private emotions from a world that didn't want to see, didn't want to know the man beneath the legend.

So *stupid*! She'd known it was too early.

If he snarled at her like that again he wouldn't have to fire her; she'd run like the frightened jackrabbit she was—even though she *knew* he'd never hurt her.

Leaning against the door, because she didn't think her legs would carry her further, she kept trying to breathe while her ears strained for the sound of his footsteps. She was pulling herself together, ready to smile in the face of disaster. Waiting and waiting.

Only the soft lapping of waves behind her cottage greeted her.

He wasn't coming. Of course he wasn't—because he was Mark and she was Shirley Temple, the girl who'd handed him a wet flannel, a few glasses of water, given him some hugs and held his hand. And yet he'd treasured what little she'd done for him enough to seek the family out and save them when she'd reached desperate measures to pay the rent and put food on the table, with threats of Welfare stepping in to take the boys away.

From the moment Brenda had recognised her at the job interview today, her words had cemented what Sylvie had long suspected. Mark's family loved him but didn't understand him. They wanted to *push* him into happiness so they could stop worrying about him. It was love, but not the love he needed.

Just like her brother Simon, who tried to match her up with men all the time: men who were gentle, who wouldn't rush her. Men who might as well have been invisible for all she could feel for them.

'Stop reaching for the stars,' Simon always said. 'You'll never see him again.'

But she'd rather live her life alone than with any man who wasn't the one. Mark had been her childhood prince, but he might have faded from her memory if he hadn't saved her life, saved her family…saved her from the unbearable choice facing her when the money came. And the prince of her little-girl fantasies had become her teenage hero. Then finally, when she'd

seen the tabloid stories on him, seen the frozen suffering beneath the wolfish smile, he'd become her love, so entwined in
her heart she'd never leave him behind.

The Heart of Ice wasn't the boy she remembered, who'd
stood beside a dying girl for years, even marrying her rather
than running when it all became too hard. The boy who'd felt
sick at the thought of giving a promise to love another girl because it would be a lie. Maybe all he wanted was to be left in
peace with his memories but she'd given a promise, made
sacred by death. At the right time she'd given up her home, her
job security—and most importantly, her secure anonymity—
to come to Mark and keep her vow.

Though she had nothing to speak of, she had something she
could give Mark that he didn't have: a true home, a *friend*…
And if she could pull off a miracle, maybe she could help him
learn to live again.

CHAPTER THREE

SYLVIE was in the kitchen Monday morning, making breakfast
while Mark was out running, when the phone rang. She checked
the oven clock: six-fourteen. She was sure Mark carried a
mobile phone and a pager. She shouldn't take his private calls.
But by the fourth time it started ringing she'd realised the caller
knew Mark was out. She picked up.

'So, how's it going, Sylvie?' Brenda's eager voice came the
second she said hello.

'Fine,' she said warily. How would you describe a weekend
where your employer had seemed to work all hours while you
moved non-existent furniture around, aching to move your feet
thirty metres but you'd been banned until Monday? And how
did you say that to your employer's sister whom you barely
knew—hadn't seen in fifteen years?

'So, how's Mark? Is he talking to you? Has he said anything?'

She bit her lip. This was her first real day of work. The
course of wisdom was telling her to take her time—but, being
Bigmouth Sylvie, she did the opposite. 'Brenda, I appreciate
you helped me get the job, but whatever Mark says to me remains between us. End of subject. I need this job, and I'm not
about to risk it by being unprofessional—'

'Sylvie, Mark needs you,' Brenda said bluntly. 'You've seen how he is. He's not our Mark—the boy you knew.'

Sylvie sighed. 'You can't throw women at Mark like mud and hope one sticks. You can't heal him; he can only do that himself. And calling me for updates is something I never agreed to. I'm only here to cook and clean.' She almost added, *For all you know, I could be romantically involved*, but she remembered Brenda's specific questions on her romantic status, with the excuse that Mark would welcome no overnight guests. 'I haven't seen him in fifteen years, but I'm sure of one thing: your anxiety probably makes him feel bad that he can't make you feel better—and that makes it worse for him.'

Silence greeted her declaration for a few moments. 'I'm sorry.' Brenda's voice had gone stiff and cold. 'Wouldn't you be anxious about your brother if he was like Mark?'

Before Sylvie could answer, the bleeping sound of disconnection filled her ear. She sighed and hung up, turning back to the breakfast she was making.

'Thank you.'

She whirled around..Wearing exercise gear that moulded to his body like a second skin, he stood in the open doorway between the kitchen and dining room, hot and sweaty from his run, his dark-blond hair plastered to his skull. He was still breathing heavily.

'You're welcome.' Her throat was thick, her heart pounding so hard it was as if she'd been running with him. Shocked by the depth of her response to him, she whirled to face the oven. She'd never felt desire in her life before, but the aching of her body, the itching in her fingertips to touch him, couldn't be anything else. 'I know I crossed the line, but she kept calling. She said…' Hot colour scorched her face. She was talking about his *sister*!

'I knew she would. Persistence and interference are the Hannaford middle names.' He spoke with loving resignation.

'The only mystery is why the other girls haven't called or come over yet—you remember my sisters Becky and Katie—or my mother. You ought to expect them, though. Beware: they'll dig and dig until they get what they want,' he said, sounding surprised he'd said anything so personal.

To cut off the coldness she sensed was coming—his way of trying to keep a professional distance—she spoke in a flat tone. 'I'll be at college.' She opened the oven door. 'I hope coming in early to make breakfast is acceptable?'

'For something that smells like that, you can come in before dawn.' He breathed in deeply. 'That smells incredible. What is it?'

Trying to hide a grin of delight—Brenda had told her that he preferred health foods—she said neutrally, 'Just some home-baked muesli and fresh coffee.'

'Home-baked? I don't think *that* was in the contract.' But the way he inhaled, the smile as he did so, told her he wasn't about to argue. 'I usually eat fruit.'

'I made fruit salad, too.' She turned back to the food before he could comment, unsure whether he would say something kind or would freeze her. 'It'll be ready when you are.'

Fifteen minutes later he was wolfing down breakfast as she cleaned. 'That was superb,' he said as he brought the bowls and cup to her. 'Thank you, Sylvie.'

'You're welcome.'

Strange how such polite words and praise could hide so much. Somewhere between his coming in on her conversation with Brenda and his return from the shower he'd remembered her interference on Friday night. The air was strained, the tension almost visible; it would only become worse if she apologised. All they were leaving unsaid hovered in the air between them like a comic dialogue balloon—you could choose not to read it but it was still *there*.

He said a curt goodbye as he was leaving—before seven.

'I'll have dinner waiting,' she said, not knowing why she'd said it or what she was hoping for.

His cold reply was all she deserved for poking her nose in again. 'I'm rarely home before nine.'

He worked fourteen-hour days on a regular basis? 'I'll have it ready for eight, in case.'

She cursed her clumsy mouth—setting rules in his home. She didn't expect an answer, and didn't get one.

When he roared out of the garage she shrugged, ate her share of breakfast, put on her cleaning music, ran through the house until it was sparkling, and left for college before the family he'd forewarned her about could arrive.

'So how's the new housekeeper?' his brother Pete asked after the morning meeting was done, and he, Pete and Glenn, his brother-in-law, were alone.

'Tell Bren if she wants an update to ask me herself.'

Glenn chuckled, and Pete grinned. 'The Heart of Ice stuff doesn't work on me, bro. I've shared a room with you, punched you up, stood beside you when the football jocks attacked us, and covered up for you when you and Chloe did midnight flits to invent something.'

Glenn laughed again, and agreed.

Mark smiled reluctantly. They'd all been close from school days. Pete, only a year younger than him, was his Chief IT Officer, and Glenn, besides being Bren's husband, was Financial Controller for Howlcat. Nerds United, they used to call themselves; but they'd stuck together through good times and bad, and there were no two men he trusted more.

'So, how is she? You know Mum's sure to call me and ask.'

Mark gave an exaggerated sigh. 'We fell in love at first sight, made passionate love all night and we are eloping on our first day off. *Now* will you get off my back?'

Pete's brows lifted. 'I only meant to ask if she can cook and clean all right, since I know you did her a favour in hiring her,' he said mildly.

Mark found himself flushing. 'She makes muesli to die for, keeps the house in perfect order.' He tried to stop himself, but the stress in him had been building like a pressure cooker on high all weekend, and it had to come out. 'She also says everything she shouldn't, gives me presents that make my house hers somehow, then says something so *sweet* I can't tell her off. She doesn't act like any employee I've known, but I can't fire her because—' The words burst from him. 'She's Shirley Temple—all right? Remember the kid whose dying mother was in the hospice the same time as Chloe a lot? She's been through hell since then, and she deserves a break.'

His brother and his friend both nodded, but there was a suspicious twinkle in both sets of eyes, and he knew what was coming. 'I saw her the other day. She's a real cutie,' Glenn said.

'Adorable, if you like the type,' Pete added, grinning. 'Pretty and sweet. Just as well you prefer sophisticated women to china dolls.'

He was lying, and they all knew it. He growled in agreement and stalked out of the conference room to his haven in Howlcat Industries, pulling off his jacket and tie on the way. Nobody bothered him in the basement lab except in an emergency— even his mother.

Why he was home by seven-thirty he didn't know. She was his *housekeeper*, he wasn't accountable to her—but the good manners his mother had instilled in him came into play. If dinner was ready by eight, he'd be there.

Though he was still angry at her less-than-subtle manipulation of his working day, after the breakfast she'd made this morning his stomach was reminding him he didn't have to get takeout, heat a frozen meal or eat at his parents' tonight and answer the inevitable questions.

He came in the back way, and his reward for leaving work was immediate. The smell from the oven made his mouth water and his stomach growl double-time. Baking garlic, cheese and pasta…and music wafted from his ballroom.

He walked as far as the entryway and saw a fairy sprite tripping across the floorboards.

Literally.

She was barefoot, wearing cut-off denim shorts and a lavender tank top, her hair in a ponytail, with dark red spirals falling around her face and shoulders. Her arms were stiffly held out to an invisible partner, her face serious, her kissable mouth pursed as she dipped her head with each first movement. '*One*, two, three…*one*, two, three…'

And she tripped sideways, stumbled and recovered with a sigh.

Adorable Sylvie might be—graceful she was not.

He halted three times on his way, before he threw caution to the winds for the first time in years, crossed the room and moved into her arms. 'Straighten your back.'

She gasped and fell against him—but, ignoring his body's reaction to her gentle curves, to the soft scent of her skin, he pulled her up and held her with the right distance and strength.

'Your posture's off, which is why you keep tripping, Sylvie. Now, straighten up and follow my lead.'

She blinked, and blinked again, gulping and wetting her mouth. Her face was filled with a mixture of wonder and trepidation, and something lurking beneath he couldn't identify. 'You—you can dance?'

He nodded, intrigued. Yeah, Glenn had it right: she *was* cute, but something he couldn't work out caught and held him.

'Three years of lessons, on and off.' Chloe had nagged him into it the year before her cancer diagnosis. 'Now—*posture*.'

After a hesitation so palpable he thought she was going to walk away, she stood as tall as her delicate frame would allow. She was stiff in his arms, her gaze focusing straight ahead on nothing, as if he wasn't there. Or she didn't *want* him to be there.

'What's next?'

The two brusque words didn't invite questions. 'Feet facing mine, five inches apart.'

She checked her feet in evident anxiety, then looked back at him with the same anxiety quickly masked.

'Look up at me. I'll tell you when it's right.'

Big mistake. She looked in his eyes, hers earnest and apprehensive all at once—and she was *blushing*. He almost forgot what he was doing.

'Is this right?'

Her voice was breathless, the heat in her cheeks filling her throat, and the alarm bells in his head were shrieking. She'd either danced herself into high blood pressure, was terrified of him—or his touch was affecting her as much as hers did him.

'It's right.' He almost croaked, but controlled it with a strong effort. When he touched other women the silky-softness he felt was bought with expensive lotions in stores. Sylvie was a slip of moonlight in his arms, and the satin of her skin was as natural as the simple clothing she wore. 'Now, follow. Your count was right, but it's hard to dance the woman's part without a lead.'

Without a word she followed him when he stepped forward.

Now she moved well. In following him she lost her endearing clumsiness, became graceful—and the situation lifted to high alert without her even trying to flirt with him.

Why had he forgotten the rule? *Never touch the kind of woman he liked best*. That way led to madness and loss, the road to fury, drinking, regrets—and rehab. He never wanted to repeat *that* time. So he played with women who wouldn't expect more than his money could give. He couldn't get over his loss, find someone new and move on. He felt too much, hurt too much. Fell apart when—

'*One*, two, three…*one*, two, three…'

So serious, concentrating on each step. The tip of her tongue popped out between counts as she thought about her feet. He didn't tell her she didn't have to think beyond her posture now. A good male lead could keep his partner in step in most social situations—and he was guessing Sylvie wasn't practising for a contest or celebrity show.

'This is for the wedding, right?' he guessed.

She nodded, looking flustered still, a little scared—and so kissable it was all he could do to hold back. 'I'm maid of honour. Sarah wants a real waltz for her bridal dance. She and Scott have been taking lessons for two months.' Her voice held a wealth of love and a multitude of dark secrets—and he didn't have to ask why she hadn't paid for lessons.

A *ping* sound floated in from the kitchen.

'Dinner's ready.' She stood staring at him, the blush growing by the moment—as was his urgency.

For years sex had been a physical release on days when he needed to forget the pain—occasionally urgent when it had been months since he'd bothered with a woman. Now the urgency was hitting him like a king tide…but this was *Sylvie*. He didn't deserve a woman as luminous and pure as her—and she sure as hell didn't deserve the screw-up beneath his wealth and fame.

'Please let me go.'

It was only then he realised he'd been holding her so tight she couldn't break out of his arms without struggling. Feeling like a fool, he dropped his hands. 'Smells delicious. I'm hungry. What is it?'

She'd already stepped out of his dance zone—out of his zone

altogether. She did the one-shoulder shrug thing again, look-ing at the floor. 'Just vegetable lasagne and some garlic bread. Nothing special.'

'If it's anything like the home-baked muesli this morning, I'll be home for dinner any night you make it,' he said, won-dering why she always demeaned her skills.

The colour intensified in her cheeks, and he wanted to hit himself. 'I didn't mean to make you feel compelled to cook for me every night, Sylvie.'

Another half-shrug, defensive, keeping him at a distance. 'It's what I do.'

He remembered the references he'd read about offering her double to stay, making a house a home, and he no longer felt special or flattered that she was going out of her way for him.

What a jerk, imagining more, based on lustful hopes and her blush, which could so easily be simple embarrassment at the boss touching her.

Since he couldn't avoid her, it seemed there was only one way to get through this: cauterisation. He'd have to touch her and touch her until he felt nothing.

'How about a deal?' He made his voice casual as he led the way into the kitchen. 'Your food is so wonderful it makes me feel like I owe you. You need to learn the waltz. I know how. So, you cook for me and I'll teach you to dance.'

He took two dinner plates from the cupboard without think-ing about it, and handed them to her. After a second's hesitation she put them down and began ladling food onto one, then the other, and took two sets of cutlery from the drawer. She didn't answer him about the dancing, and he didn't push the offer.

Strangely delighted by her tacit acceptance—that she wasn't making more of a simple sharing of a meal than it was—he got out a bottle of chianti from his wine rack and lifted it in silent query, wondering if she'd notice that, though it was imported from Italy, it was non-alcoholic. A permanent reminder that he'd never be normal again.

She nodded and smiled at him, her face all rosy again, and though it could easily be the oven's heat, she looked so lovable....

No! She was *likable*, that was it. Not *love*. Never love.

But it was funny how they communicated so well without words.

And, for no reason he could fathom, cold fear gripped his soul. He *wanted* to spend time with Sylvie, talking or silent, and yet only three days ago he'd felt nearly sick with relief when she'd left him alone. Things had changed so fast he couldn't get a handle on it—on what was happening or why he wanted her company.

What did it matter? When she wasn't with him he thought of her anyway, and it would be a terrible lapse in manners to withdraw the unspoken invitation. He might as well have the pleasure of looking at her.

As he cut off his first mouthful of lasagne, he asked, 'So, how was college? You said you're doing nursing?'

She nodded, smiling. 'I think it was inevitable—that or a kindergarten teacher. I like looking after people.'

'You do it well.' A burst of flavour exploded in his mouth and he groaned. 'This is marvellous. Did you ever think of becoming a chef?'

She shook her head. 'I love to cook. It's fun for me. If I had to do it for a living it wouldn't be fun anymore.'

'I still love inventing.' In fact, during his sojourn in the basement today he'd come up with a new use for the original Howlcat patent: a way to reduce engine noise pollution in planes on takeoff and landing if he could find the right materials for the application.

'Of course you do. What's not to like?' She grinned, and he

began to relax. Whatever was bothering her, she was finally letting go—at least for now. 'In charge of your company, able to tell people to hike off when you're thinking, making millions every time you say, "I've got an idea...."'

'It's not quite that simple.' He laughed.

'It can't be if you're the boss and you still have to work thirteen, fourteen hours a day.'

'Well, I do have to actually make the things—you know, gather materials, work engines, make it work in practice, as well as on paper.'

Her eyes twinkled. 'You mean you have to *work* for those millions?' she asked in mock-horror. 'And here I thought you spent all day playing the part of famous playboy.'

He didn't answer that. In his opinion, being a playboy was one of the best and worst parts all at once—because though he had fun it was still, as she'd so beautifully put it, *playing the part*; it wasn't Mark. 'There are some downsides to the life.'

She sobered immediately. 'I'm sorry. My sense of humour sometimes takes me to strange and exotic places. Simon always says it'll be the death of me.'

Sylvie said the words with light deliberation, smiling in the hope that he would accept the words without going too deep.

'Death by laughter? An appropriately Sylvie thing to happen—and typical of me that I'd hire you. I'm sure there's a hint of the masochist in me somewhere.'

Relieved far more than she'd show that he hadn't overreacted to her death comment and asked her to leave, she lifted her wine-glass and saluted him. 'To men who make a living by howling cats, and women who want to laugh themselves into oblivion.'

He touched his glass to hers. 'That's just a goofball way of saying "To us".' But he was chuckling, and she joined in, hiding the tightening of her chest at the mere thought of there ever being an 'us' for them.

She had to get over this ridiculous infatuation! So stupid to dream when she *knew* there could be nothing. He'd seen her reaction to his touch; he knew something was wrong with her. She *had* to get over him. She had no choice, because she knew three things with all her soul: she was nothing like the beautiful, sophisticated women he dated now; she could never live up to Chloe in either his eyes or her own—and she'd never be a normal woman.

'So, you think you know me after a few days?' she challenged him after they'd eaten in silence for a minute or two.

He shrugged. 'Expect the unexpected is your motto, I suspect.'

Her mouth twitched in acknowledgement, but she said, 'I knew what to expect for too long. Now the boys are settled and happy, Dad died peacefully at home, and I want to rejoice in every day—to celebrate life, always looking forward.'

And never look back to what I was—what I had to do to survive.

Instead of seeing the message for him in her words—why could she never shut up and enjoy his company without trying to heal him?—Mark leaned forward, his hand almost touching hers. She jerked back before she could stop herself, and though his gaze followed the movement, he didn't comment on it.

'After all you've been through you deserve to celebrate life, to be happy. I hope you find reasons to celebrate each day.'

She frowned, tilting her head as the implications of his words sank in, going far deeper than the little she'd told him. 'You had me investigated?'

His gaze was dark, hooded. 'I have everyone I employ investigated, Sylvie. I have to.'

But why me? she wanted to yell at him. *Surely you trust me?*

A thought as insidious as poison crept into her soul. *What does he know? What else did he find out*?

But he couldn't know. Though her younger brothers and

Scott suspected something had happened to her, nobody knew but Simon and Mr Landsedge. If he ever decided to tell—

He won't unless it becomes worth his while—such as if I became involved with a rich, famous man. And that was why fulfilling any part of her promise to Chloe was fraught with danger. Yet here she was…

'I'm amazed you didn't do it years ago—before you sent the money,' she bit out.

He stiffened, didn't speak for long, uncomfortable moments, and she almost squirmed, waiting for what she deserved. 'I found out where you lived and whether you needed money. That was all. I had no reason to invade your privacy…then.'

The implications of that—he'd found out how very poor they'd been, and he might suspect her of something underhand, with far less cause than *she* had to believe the worst of him—made her even angrier. But worst of all was the fear. What else had he discovered? Had he sent the money because he knew what happened just before?

Mark spoke when the turbulence in her heart left her too confused to answer. 'You could have changed more than your name.' He looked her right in the eyes. 'I've had trusted friends, lovers and employees sell stories and lies for thousands and feel justified in doing it if I don't give them what they think they deserve. One of my housekeepers stole some personal things from the house and sold them online.'

'I know.' She remembered that story with the same bubbling fury she'd felt when she'd read it three years ago. She'd read almost every article on him, rejoicing in his successes, indignant at what she'd seen as the lies.

Now, seeing the look in his eyes, she saw it as more than a way to feed her fascination with him. She'd fed the media machine, too, by wasting her hard-earned money on the tabloids to clip pictures and articles about him. She'd made his life worse with her silly crush on a famous playboy—like so many girls and women in the country.

And *that* was why he'd had her investigated like everyone else. He couldn't know he'd become so much more than her childhood prince through the years. He'd been her therapy...but she'd healed herself at his expense.

'I understand.' Ashamed of herself, she pushed her chair back. 'I've eaten enough, and it's been a long day. I'll clean up, and head to the cottage and read a book.'

He looked up from his food, his eyes probing without asking, and she knew he saw more than she wanted him to—but when he spoke it wasn't what she'd expected. 'Did my family come to see you today?'

Caught out, she nodded.

'Who?' His voice was grim.

Embarrassed she hadn't seen this coming, she shrugged. 'Your mother, Becky and Katie were waiting when I arrived home,' she said, wondering if he'd catch her slip. After only a few days Mark's warm, beautiful house was her palace, her dream house—had become a word she'd never truly felt in her heart before: *home*. 'They're as nice as I remember.'

'I'll bet they were.' He shook his head. 'I'm sorry.'

About to leave the table, she sat again, arrested by the rueful words. 'For what?'

He didn't look away as he said it. 'For their putting you in the awkward position I know they did simply because Bren told them who you are.'

She felt a stupid blush moving up her cheeks. 'Do I look so weak that a few awkward questions would make me cry?'

'I've rarely met anyone who's been through what you have, done the things you've done, and not merely survived but emerged optimistic—no, joyful.' His tone was curt; he downed the last of his wine before he spoke again. 'You have the deepest sense of self I've ever known in a woman. So why don't you stop avoiding what I haven't asked, and tell me what they said?'

Touched by his opinion of her, she said, 'It's fine, Mark. I handled it all right.' She shot him a glance brimming with mischief. 'They...um...know now to expect the unexpected from me.'

His eyes widened for a moment, before he grinned and leaned his chin on his hands, staring at her with mock-earnestness. 'So, are you involved, gay, or did you really shock them by finding me so unattractive even the money didn't do it for you?'

'The last, of course,' she retorted. 'I said you were downright ugly.'

He threw his head back and burst out laughing.

Delighted, she grinned. This kind of light banter took away all the *don't talk about it*—either about Chloe, or her own secrets.

So many undercurrents—and the fact that he didn't ask about the things she wanted to keep buried showed her a side of Mark that left the 'Heart of Ice' myth behind. This was the man he could have been had his youth not been stolen by enduring tragedy so young. Yet his experiences had made him the man who now mesmerised her. He looked beautiful, masculine, with a strong sense of decency and self. He seemed so far from the Heart of Ice she wouldn't recognise him from the hundreds of photos with those glamorous women.

How long had it been since he'd laughed like that—as if he'd been let out of a cage?

He pushed back his chair and held out a hand to her. 'Come on, Ginger, let's waltz.'

Her body's reaction was predictable, urgent—but beneath the expected fear a deeper fascination called to her and wouldn't be denied. As fearful as she'd been, dancing in Mark's arms had made her feel like a princess in a fairytale....

'Ginger?' She turned her face half away, frowning and peering at him in amused suspicion. 'Is that a reference to my hair or my lack of dancing skills?'

'Whichever you prefer,' he replied without missing a beat. 'And if you don't like it, too bad. You say things to me no one else would dare, change my house without asking, feed me when I say no and dance in my ballroom without permission.'

'You don't seem very angry about it,' she pointed out.

He shrugged. 'Must be the lasagne and wine mellowing me—or maybe it's your two left feet…Ginger. But we'll get you ready for that wedding.'

She stood, biting the inside of her lip to stop a smile forming, but it did anyway. 'I have to wash up…Fred.' Her hand slipped into his even as she spoke, and she wondered that she'd done it—touched him without its being a traditional expected formality. And she wondered even more that she didn't want to pull away. She felt warm, happy, *safe* with Mark—and she wanted to curl her fingers around his, drink in his skin.

He smiled down at her, those golden-brown eyes warm. 'We can do it later.'

She caught her breath at his casual use of the word. *We* can do it. As if this was their house, their dishes to wash, just like any normal couple. But she could never be part of a normal couple, because she was not and never would be normal. She had to accept that.

Lost in tangled emotions, she barely noticed as Mark drew her back to the ballroom.

'You need a slower song. Try this.' He flicked the stereo on with a remote, and soft strains drifted from the speakers.

He spoke as if she was one of his sisters. He didn't seem bothered by her touch, she thought, fighting a weird mixture of elation and depression. *It's never going to happen, Sylvie. You have to accept it.*

How many years had she been telling herself? And yet being

near him, having his hand in hers, the other resting on her waist without intimacy, had gone to her head. *He* had gone to her head. Within only days she was terrified he was already—or still—in her heart, and would always be there. Even if the miracle occurred and she found another man whose touch she could endure, and she married and had ten kids.

No! Infatuation. That's all it is. He's always been a safe love, distant as a star. If he really touched me he'd know what a freak I am….

'Feet in position, facing mine.'

He was so close she could feel the heat of his body again, could feel the warm rush of his breath on her hair. *Breathe, Sylvie…in, out…*

'This is your dance space; this is mine. Strictly, in a waltz, you never invade that space.'

What if I want to? her heart whispered. *Do you want to as much as I do*? And it shocked and scared her that she really did want to…

'Posture is always straight. Think tall.'

Concentrating on his commands, she drew herself as high as she could.

'Now, look at me.'

That was never a hardship—but would the agonised longing of so many years of dreams show in her eyes? Her lashes lifted, her chin followed, and she drank in the face of the one person whose simple existence had made the unbearable bearable for so long. Who'd even helped her put the worst nightmare a girl could face behind her because he was alive and she could dream of him and feel as if it had never happened.

His eyes and smile held a strange kind of tenderness that reassured her. 'There's no need to be embarrassed with me, Sylvie. You're taking care of me, and I'm teaching you how not to land on your butt at your friend's wedding. It's just a deal between old friends. So, let's try the basic moves. We can go on to something more elegant when you're ready.'

Yes, he was speaking to her as if she was Becky or Katie—and still the rush of heated colour in her face grew, until she felt like one big scarlet neon sign pulsing in the soft-lit old-fashioned ballroom for him to read: *I'm crazy about you*.

She had to stop it—had to stop hoping life and her body could change…

'*One*, two, three,' she counted, her voice strangled with acute humiliation. Because she was a tangled mess of desire and adoration and to him she was merely *his old friend*. She really was safe with him, because he saw her as a little sister. '*One*, two, three.'

His hands tightened on her body. He stepped forward and she moved back. To the count she kept up he moved and she followed, backwards and sideways, slowly round and round in swirls and dips, he looking in her eyes and she into his.

He led her to the middle of the floor, dancing with strict instructions as the next song began.

She should never have given in to temptation when Brenda had called her for the interview and she'd known she'd be working for him. She'd been here not even four days, and she already knew she was in way too deep. She'd thought to be safe because she couldn't bear a man to touch her. But with one touch she'd had her dream come true—Mark had made her normal again, a young woman wanting a man.

Only *one* man…

She was heading for a fall here—big-time.

But tonight, in his arms, resting in his embrace as he led her around the floor, swirling and dipping her in their own private world of moonlight and shadow, feeling graceful and almost *pretty*, she couldn't make herself care.

CHAPTER FOUR

THE next night, when Mark came home, he found her dancing in the ballroom, this time in a simple sundress and low heels.

'I'm trying to practise how it will be for the wedding,' she said, in a tone so serious and so adorable that even with a mountain of paperwork to do he came toward her with an enquiring look. She nodded gratefully, and he took her in his arms. And though he didn't speak to her apart from severe dance instructions, she more than filled the silence.

'How was work?—*one*, two, three—I have a practical stint in hospital next week—*one*, two, three— Orthopaedics. Great— nursing a bunch of raging male hormones in traction, with no one to practise on but us—*one*, two, three—I made *nasi goreng* tonight. Hope you like Malaysian food—*one*, two, three…'

What could a frozen heart *do* with an unpredictable darling who didn't take any amount of hints but just kept on being… adorable?

Invite her to stay for dinner, of course. The Malaysian dish was incredible, she was a sensational cook, and then—again at his instigation—they returned to the ballroom.

She was looking at him as she danced, but he could tell that, though her eyes stayed on him, she was still counting in her head—trying to concentrate on not falling over.

'Trust me, Sylvie, I won't let you fall,' he said, feeling almost tender.

'You won't, but Angelo probably will,' she replied with a sigh. 'He's Scott's best man. He's got two left feet and is so sensitive about his clumsiness he won't take lessons.'

He'd have laughed but for the fact that she sounded almost tragic about it. 'So how will you even get him on the dance floor?'

'That's Sarah's department. Guilt should do it. She introduced Angelo to a dozen girls—including me—until he met Sandi. And now they're the next to walk down the aisle.'

'He won't even take lessons for Sandi?' he asked, wanting to add, *Why didn't* you *like him*? Because there was no way a guy couldn't be intrigued by this mercurial angel with her pretty face and her heart of gold.

'Sandi loves him as he is, the big goofball.' Sylvie smiled with an affection bordering on tenderness. 'She's banned the waltz from their wedding.'

'She sounds perfect for him.' He was amazed by the shot of wistfulness in him. He didn't *want* to risk his heart again, so why would he deny that joy to others?

She nodded, smiling. 'I'm so glad for them. I like seeing others as happy as they are.'

Was it deliberate, the way she'd said *others* like that?

She was dangerously close to the stereo. He guided her away and, on impulse, dipped her, grinning when she laughed in delight. 'You don't want that for yourself?'

The sudden look on her face—sad and resigned—made him wish he'd never asked.

'There's no use. I don't think I'll ever marry.'

He frowned. That seemed so wrong. If anyone was made for marriage and babies and a happy-ever-after ending it was Sylvie. 'Why?'

'I met my prince years ago, but he loves someone else. I've

met a hundred men since, kissed a few, but—' She sighed and
shook her head, looking up at him with a smile as bright as the
soft shimmering of unshed tears in her old-sherry eyes. 'I have
a good job, a lovely waterfront cottage, a pretty decent boss.'
Her eyes twinkled in a mercurial mood change only Sylvie
could produce. 'And in nine months I'll be a registered nurse.
I have a good life. So, can we change the subject before we both
become maudlin?'

Something in her resignation bothered him. She was young,
pretty and made others happy just by being in the room. The guy
lucky enough to marry her would smile until the day he died.

Stop thinking like that!

'We've been dancing for an hour. Maybe we should do the
dishes,' he suggested, aiming for friendly distance—hard to do
with certain parts of his body still pounding with a weird mixture
of joy and want. Kissing Sylvie would be the *happiest*—

Stop it, you dumb jerk!

'Am I doing any better?' she asked, in evident anxiety.

Torn from a fuzzy world of desire, guilt and pain, he saw
the look in her eyes and softened. 'You're doing well enough
to miss a lesson, since I'm out tomorrow night. We can take it
up again Thursday.' He was already anticipating having his
barefoot sprite in his arms again, all soft silkiness and surprisingly addictive conversation.

She turned away, frowning. 'I have midterms at the end of
the week. I should probably eat in the cottage and study.'

'Fine,' he said, trying to keep the cold stiffness from his tone.
For the first time in years he *wanted* to spend time with a
woman, and she was rejecting him.

Perhaps she'd told his family the truth: she *didn't* find him
attractive.

'Just so we're clear, Sylvie, I don't seduce my employees.
I wasn't trying to hit on you.' Now his voice *was* cold and stiff.

He was so unused to rejection these days he didn't take it well. The old shy schoolboy in him would have laughed at the man he'd become.

Still she didn't look at him. 'I know that.' Her hands were so tight-fisted her knuckles showed. Sylvie was made for laughter and sunshine, but right now she was unhappy—and he'd made her feel that way. He'd hurt her, and all she'd said was she needed to study.

He called himself all kinds of names—Heart of Ice being the least of it.

'Go and study, Sylvie. I can clean the kitchen,' he said quietly.

Still looking at the floor, she shook her head. 'It's my job.'

'Your job is what I say it is. You have exams, and I can stack a dishwasher. My mother makes me do it whenever I eat there, to remind me of my roots. I wasn't always an infamous playboy, you know.' And he winked, angling for a smile from her.

For a moment her sweet face lifted, she smiled—and then, as his body began to thrill to it, as he began to feel the happiness he could imbibe by osmosis just by being near her, she turned away.

'Thank you.'

'Thank you, *Mark*,' he replied softly, not knowing why he pushed—but she hadn't said his name for hours, and he wondered why.

Her back still turned from him, she nodded. 'Thank you, Mark.' She looked wilted, a little daisy pushed away from the sunlight. No—she looked as she had the day her mother had died. Brave in the face of suffering, willing to keep trying though she was in pain.

Now, as then, she shamed him with her strength. He had the money, the success, yet she, the housekeeper, knew how to *live* through tragedy, while he'd merely survived. He couldn't be angry with her for showing him all the things he wasn't, because she said nothing. She just *was*.

'Goodnight, Sylvie. Sleep well.'

'Thank you.' There was a little catch in her voice. 'You, too.'

Had he taken his eyes from her for a moment? He must have, because when he looked at where she'd been standing she was gone, leaving only her memory, like an insubstantial dream of a smile, behind her.

The next night, on a date to a movie premiere with all those who were seen or wanted to be seen, he did his part with a woman—Mimi was lively, fun and beautiful—and again he went home after a supper that was awkward instead of an intimate prelude to a night on satin sheets.

He found himself checking for lights in the house or in the cottage when he came in, and felt the bite of disappointment when everything was dark and still.

Leaving a date out of guilt last week he could handle. But this—the *need* to be with her—this situation was becoming dangerous.

Five days later

'Hey, Sylvie,' Mark called as he ran in through the door and up the stairs for a shower. 'I'll be down in twenty.' Unable to sleep much the past three nights, he'd overdone his run this morning in an effort to exhaust himself into sleep tonight. In consequence he was twenty minutes behind schedule, and he had a vital meeting with a conglomerate of auto manufacturers at eleven.

'Okay.'

He stopped in his tracks. Singular as the word was, he felt as if it had raced from her body to his, bouncing off him with its unspoken angst. He almost went back to look at her, to ask—

She'd only shut down if he tried. Last night she'd had something on her mind that had refracted off her body in waves of tension. She'd barely touched him even to dance.

By having a lightning shower, he made it back down in the

exact time. He didn't look at her, but he felt the intensity of lockdown in a person he'd never seen lock down in all life had thrown at her.

He wolfed down the muesli, as usual, but kept watching unobtrusively. 'I'm running late,' he said, with a carelessness he hoped wasn't overdone. What was wrong with her? Was she angry at the long-standing date he hadn't been able to break last night? It had been an important event. If he'd backed out, Angie—and the media—would have wanted to know why…

'I noticed.'

Her answer was colourless, so un-Sylvie, he stopped eating and looked at her; she wasn't looking.

'I forgot to ask last night—did you get any exam results back?'

'Two distinctions.'

'That's great—congratulations,' he said, burning to know what was going on in that closed-off section of her. 'Want to celebrate tonight? Fish and chips in the backyard, and another dancing lesson in which I *swear* I won't yell at you?' He laughed.

After a heartbeat, she said, 'No. Thank you,' she added, in obvious afterthought.

'Well, thanks for pretending to want my company at least,' he retorted, stung by the lightning-fast rejection.

'I have plans tonight.'

He looked right at her at last, and saw dark eyes dominating a pale face so white her freckles stood out in stark contrast. She was scrubbing the counter with enough vigour to leave grooves in the granite. She didn't say where she was going, but the plea inside the ongoing silence cried out to him. *Help me.*

'What's up with you today?' He didn't have to try to make it sound indignant; he felt it. He *liked* her, they were friends, and she'd thrown his invitation in his face as if he'd insulted her. 'Is it because I went out last night? I told you we couldn't dance—'

'Your love-life is none of my business.' But though she

spoke with hard defiance, she'd stilled so completely he thought she might turn, look at him, say what was really on her mind. 'I have to go. I'll clean up later.' And she was out of the door without her usual cheery *Have a good day*, or tempting him home early with a promise of a mouth-watering dinner.

No smiles. No blushes, adorable comments or deep insights. None of the uniqueness that had kept him at home far more than he ever had been before; nothing that made her *Sylvie*. And it worried him far more than it ought. So he pretended to leave, drove out and came in again through the back door ten minutes later.

She was playing her cleaning music—she had a habit of playing upbeat stuff and dancing as she did the house, he'd caught her at it—but though the music blasted from the stereo, Sylvie was dashing at tears that fell so fast she probably couldn't see the vacuum cleaner she was pushing on the rug.

Go in to her, Prof. She needs you.

The voice of the past, so sure it was right, felt so *real* he didn't hesitate. He strode across the room to where Sylvie cried in silence, yanked the vacuum from her hand, switched it off and pulled her into his arms.

Well, he'd broken her silence at least. Her screams rang right through the house.

Her terror echoed in his heart—and he no longer needed to ask her what was wrong. He was so shocked he didn't even stop her flailing fists as she fought to get away from him, just took the blows. 'You're safe, Sylvie. It's only me,' he murmured as she struggled and whimpered. He held her until her screams became soft sobs that tore at his soul and her head fell to his chest. She laid her cheek against his heart.

'I'm sorry,' she whispered, when she was finally calm.

He shook his head, caressing her hair with a tender hand, hiding the fury within him against the jerk who'd cut her gentle heart into ribbons this way. 'It's okay.' He didn't ask her if she wanted to talk about it, though she desperately needed to talk; any fool could see that. And if he got the name of the—

'It's a bad day today,' she hiccupped.

'Okay.' He knew pushing her would only hurt her more— but he wanted to find out the name of the creep who'd done this to her. He knew she hadn't gone to the authorities, or he'd have seen what had happened on the file his detective had compiled.

She gulped. 'My mother…'

Then he wanted to knock his thick skull against a wall. Of *course*! Fifteen years ago today her mother had died. He knew because in less than a month his own black anniversary would come round: the day he'd become a teenage widower. 'I'm sorry, Sylvie. I should have noticed the date.'

But it couldn't be her mother's death that made her react with such terror to his touch. Not *his* touch—any man's touch… The sense of being haunted, there from the start, gelled to horrifying reality.

He knew her secret, and there was no turning back now.

'How old were you when it happened?' he asked, and though he made it gentle and non-threatening she knew he wasn't talking about this day, this painful anniversary.

She stiffened, pulled away and didn't look at him. 'I don't ask you about Chloe, or why you drink non-alcoholic wine.'

The shock ran through him. She was right—and yet the fact that she knew sent silent shrieks of protest through him. She only had half the story. If she found out the whole truth she'd have the leverage to destroy him.

As if she would. You know her better than that. Help her!

He no longer knew if Chloe spoke to him or if it was his dormant heart coming to life, *believing* in a woman for the first time in what felt like a lifetime. Though he knew he was opening Pandora's Box between them, he obeyed the imperative directive. 'I don't scream when someone touches me.'

She whirled around to face him, her eyes burning. 'And that means you've healed? You think never having any form of meaningful relationship outside of your family, only touching people who mean nothing to you, means you've accepted the past and you're stronger than I am? At least I'm trying to find a real life, and I'm honest when I scream. Who are you lying to more with your image—the world, or yourself?'

She snatched up her tote bag filled with books, ran out through the door and bolted headlong for the bus stop, leaving him with more questions than answers—and the few answers he had were too ugly to deal with.

He barely worked all day for worrying about her. He let Glenn and Pete take the meeting with Macron Motors while he whiled away endless hours tinkering in his lab, making nothing, her words ringing over and over in his head, as loud as her screams.

At least I'm honest…no meaningful relationship…who are you lying to?

That night, there was no music playing when he came home. Dinner was in his slow cooker—a casserole with rice.

And though he knocked on her door it remained closed. Though he kept watching her windows until midnight the lights in the cottage stayed off.

The next morning all Sylvie wanted to do was leave his breakfast for him and disappear again, but she caught the 5:30 a.m. bus from Drew and Shelley's place, where she'd spent the night playing with baby Nicky while pretending to give Drew and Shelley a night on the town. And her brother, grateful for the time out, knowing the date even if barely remembering their mother, had said nothing about the day or why she was so tense.

She came in when he should have been in the middle of his run, hoping to get everything done and bolt for the cottage—

'Where have you been all night?'

The harsh demand made her halt halfway in the back door, her hand flying to her throat. She stared at him, standing in the alcove between the kitchen and dining room, dressed in jeans and a T-shirt, feet bare, his streaky hair tousled, and wondered how she could find him so beautiful and so frightening at the same moment.

He looked like a storm cloud about to erupt in lightning.

But she was years beyond the terrified, silent acquiescence that had ruined her innocence; she'd never go there again. So she lifted her chin and said calmly, 'I don't think that's any of your business, sir.'

'Don't call me sir.' His jaw worked as he took a step closer. 'Indulge me.'

She faced him down from her eleven-inch disadvantage. 'I don't think so. I'm not one of your sisters.'

'I know that.' His voice sounded as if it had been shoved through a grater, gritty and broken with anger. 'I've been up all night worrying about you.'

She tightened her jaw, refusing to soften. 'That's not my problem. It was your choice. So long as I keep the house clean and provide meals, what I do at night is my business.'

She'd barely finished the words before she was off her feet, in his arms, with his face buried in her hair. 'I know you're still angry with me, but I was worried sick about you,' he growled, holding her with a sweet tenderness that turned his anger into something wonderful to her starved heart; she felt *safe*. 'Don't do that to me again.'

In his arms, feeling his exhaustion and his caring, Sylvie felt her anger melting faster than ice cream on a searing summer's day. She gulped down the hurting lump in her throat, and whispered, 'Okay.'

'I'm an idiot,' he whispered back. 'I should have known not to push you on that day of all others.'

'Yes, you are—an idiot,' she clarified with twinkling eyes when he pulled back, his eyes filled with questions. 'I'm still mad at you.'

He chuckled and rubbed his unshaven jaw against her cheek, and her heart drank in the intimate punishment as if he'd kissed her. 'Let me make it up to you. A fish and chips and white wine picnic in the backyard tonight.'

Her gaze dropped. 'I—I can't. It's a bad idea.'

'Why?' He lifted her chin, tilting his head so he could see her eyes. 'Is it to do with my reputation, or with what happened to you?'

'Don't.' The word barely made it from her tight throat. 'Please.'

'Who was it?' His voice was rough and tender. 'Who hurt you?'

All she could do was close her eyes and shake her head.

'I trusted you with my pain once,' he said softly, holding her with such gentleness the little hole in her heart cracked open wider and she bled. 'Trust me with yours, Sylvie.'

Overcome with the burden of a secret she'd told no one but Simon, then a thirteen-year-old boy, she laid her head over his heart and shook her head again. Oh, how safe she felt in his arms, and how she *wanted* to open her wounds, to say the words—but the shame, the self-loathing, stopped her mouth like the tape *he'd* threatened to use on her to stop her screaming.

'You said I saved your life—that the money came when you were going under. I sent you the house, the money and trust funds when you were fifteen.' He probed her wound with delicate surgery. 'You were only *fifteen*?'

She couldn't lift her head, even to nod. She could barely breathe the constriction in her chest and throat was so tight.

'Was it a boyfriend?'

Somehow a watery chuckle escaped her. 'Like I ever had time for that.'

The long silence unnerved her. 'A boy at school?'

Her head moved a fraction in negation. She didn't know if he'd feel it as that, or as a shudder.

The quiet felt portentous, because she knew what he was going to say. 'Your father…?'

'No.' Her father had never once laid a hand on her—even when she was naughty or rebelling against her responsibilities, he'd only begged forgiveness for putting such awful burdens on her. It had always made her feel resentful and strong, glad and furious—had stiffened her spine. Her pride had been inherited from him. Their family would not accept outside help unless they were desperate.

He carried her to the sofa and sat down beside her, his arm circling her shoulders. He lifted her face with his free hand, his eyes not filled with the pity or revulsion she'd dreaded, but with a *caring* that made her feel safe and cherished. 'I want to be your friend, sweetheart, but I can't if you don't let me in.'

'Stop.' Her voice wobbled. 'Please. It's not you. I—I just want to be happy.'

His eyes softened even more. 'We're a pair, aren't we? I bury my past with ice, you do it with a smile. But neither way is working—not for either of us.'

She sighed, fiddling with his T-shirt without thinking of how intimate it was; she felt so secure in his arms. 'I know. But—'

'You're still not ready to talk about it.' He shook his head with a rueful smile. 'Hypocrite,' he whispered, brushing his mouth over her cheek. And the delicate whispers of arousal in her body didn't frighten her, because soft words chanted in her mind: *safe, you're safe with Mark.* 'You keep pushing me out of my hole, but you stay in yours. If you don't talk it out with someone it's going to catch up with you. Your happiness is nothing but pretence until you face your past and leave it behind.'

'Look in the mirror, Hannaford,' she retorted, but its severe effect was ruined by a hiccup. 'What are you doing now?'

'I was talking about the worst parts, not the good parts. Those you keep.' He winked at her, surprising her; she'd expected him to turn dark and cold at her remark. 'I never promised to be consistent.' After a brief hesitation he kissed her cheek again, his mouth a half-inch closer to hers.

She felt his longing as a physical presence inside him. He wanted to kiss her mouth, but he was holding back because he was her boss, because she'd screamed yesterday. She sensed he was giving her the power of choice—but the beauty of his touch overwhelmed her and the ugly past faded to white. With an almost timid eagerness she put her hands on his shoulders and turned her face.

A flood of unbearable bliss filled her being with the barely there touch of his mouth. Intoxicated by his nearness, by the kiss she'd waited a lifetime to know, she moaned and pulled him closer, her hands winding into his hair.

With a groan he drew her against him, but he kissed her so gently tears flooded her eyes. He knew she couldn't bear passion yet. He caressed her hair, her cheek, her throat, wiped hot tears away with his thumbs, and kissed her over and over, whispering her name. She wanted to cling to him, but she knew this was just for now; he was only hers on borrow from another girl, from a life that could never include her.

Soon, too soon, he'd remember Chloe, and then she'd have to let him go with a smile… But she'd have these few treasured moments in his arms. It wasn't all she'd dreamed of in her girlish fantasies, but it was so much more.

'You're shaking,' he whispered against her mouth, concern shimmering in his eyes.

She lifted one of those trembling hands and put it over his mouth. She didn't know what she was going to say until she said it. 'It's not fear. Not of you. I—I trust you, Mark.' Then she closed her eyes, drawing him closer.

He pulled back, frowning. 'You shouldn't, Sylvie.' But he caressed her face, his eyes never leaving hers. The desire was there, but far stronger was the storm of self-hate.

'I do. I know you,' she whispered. 'I *know* you—the real you.'

'No, you don't. You don't know the things I've done since you left my life.' Gently he put her back on the sofa and jerked to his feet, pacing the room.

She watched him, aching. 'They're just things. You're still the same person I knew.'

'No. *No.*'

She saw him shudder. 'Do you want to talk…?'

'No.' The word was so harsh she jerked back on the sofa. Seeing it, he sighed and set his jaw for a moment. 'So it's your turn to call me a hypocrite.' But again his voice had come down from the callous tone, was warm and rueful.

Her mouth quirked. 'I was a hypocrite to ask. What a pair we are.' Her eyes twinkled.

His gaze drank her in for a moment, and a thrill ran right through her.

'I'm going to be late for work,' he said quietly, withdrawing without the ice.

He was healing already, becoming the Mark she'd once known….

It's too soon. I can't bear to leave him yet!

The bleeding in her heart grew stronger. She knew if she stayed, she'd have to see him fall in love with a woman truly worthy of him—one who wouldn't bring him public ridicule and shame. He'd probably even invite her to the wedding.

She stood on legs almost too shaky to hold her. 'Only if you still go for your run. We weren't—' She blushed, then said it. 'We weren't kissing that long.'

'No, we weren't.' In a voice gentle yet uncompromising, he went on, 'So, the fish and chips tonight isn't such a bad idea now, is it, Sylvie?'

She bit her lip, fiddling with the throw cover she'd bought for the sofa to relieve the unrelenting green his great-grandparents had obviously liked. 'Not tonight. I wasn't making an excuse. I have three exams this week. I have to pass all of them or risk repeating a year.'

Slowly, he nodded. 'You want to leave this life behind. I don't blame you.'

The deep black of a winter night was in his voice, in his heart. 'Not you. I don't want to leave you behind, or our…friendship,' she faltered.

'Why not? You did before. You never even called to say hi and thanks for the money,' he said, with a quiet harshness that left her shivering.

Her eyes closed. 'That's not fair.' But it *was* fair from his perspective, she realised a moment too late. Why *hadn't* she called?

'Isn't it?'

She felt his eyes boring into her.

'Look at me, Mary.'

Startled by her real name, she obeyed the imperative command.

'I waited for you. I sent you a card with my office and home numbers. I left instructions that if you called the office, day or night, you were to be put right through to me.' He stared at her, hard. 'I waited months to hear from my friend before I gave up.'

She stared at him in horror. 'I was fifteen. I—I didn't think… You'd become so important by then, inventing Howlcat at nineteen…'

The look on his face cut off her protest. 'Yes, I was nineteen—only nineteen—in a life that overwhelmed me…and we were *friends*. I remembered you—Mary.' He didn't say any more. He didn't have to.

He'd been reaching out to her years ago. He'd been giving her help, but also reaching out in the wilderness of his cold isolation, the new and already infamous Heart of Ice crying out for a friend. And she, soaked in gratitude for his rescue, dreaming of seeing him again, still hadn't called, hadn't thanked him.

Hadn't reinstated their friendship because—

The words came out like gravel from a tight throat, from a heart filled with a double-barrelled shame as deadly as any rifle. 'It happened four weeks before...' Her head fell. It was her reason, but no excuse. Mark had saved her from its ever happening again, saved her from a life of degradation—and, lost in the shame she still couldn't conquer, she hadn't felt worthy of speaking to him. She'd come to him in the end, but she'd waited thirteen years too long.

All because of five hundred dollars...

She was snuggled in his arms, hearing his heart beating against her ear, before she knew he'd come to her. 'Sweetheart,' he whispered, 'I'm sorry. I'm sorry I put that guilt on you just because I wanted to see you again. I could have come to you and didn't.' He caressed her hair. 'What is it about us? The best things come at the worst times.'

She nodded against his chest, feeling cherished, feeling *safe*. 'Things can change. We can make it better.'

'Yes, we can.' He spoke with slow wonder, as if she'd delivered a revelation instead of foolish, inadequate words. 'You always see the beginning of a rainbow in a storm cloud.' He dipped down to kiss her, almost heartbreaking in his tenderness.

Warmth as sweet as hot honey ran through her.

Yet she could see the inevitable ending of their unlikely pairing rushing at her like a skier on a downhill run. This couldn't last; they both knew it. Born in the same world, they now stood planets apart.

But he didn't know *why* whatever it was starting between

them could never go public. She'd leave both the job and him rather than let him find out the whole truth of what had happened to her thirteen years ago.

CHAPTER FIVE

'HERE you are,' Sylvie said cheerfully, putting a plate loaded with eggs, tomatoes, mushrooms and toast before Mark's bemused gaze. 'I got it all fresh from the market this morning—the lot for ten dollars!'

'You don't work Saturdays,' Mark said, as she put her own plate across from his, as if she'd been invited. 'Why are you in here?'

'Feeding you, silly,' she chided, rolling her eyes as if he should have been expecting it.

And in a way he had. She'd been waiting for him all week when he came home from work; they'd danced, eaten and washed up together—and they'd repeated it last night.

They hadn't kissed again. The situation hadn't been intimate in any way. It felt more as if she was trying to make it up to him for never calling. As if she wanted to be his *friend*.

Sylvie brought coffee mugs to the table, smiling with that sweet pixie-look that made him feel like Scrooge when he argued with her. And she was so *pretty*, in her weird stripy pink and blue pants and her favourite lavender top, with her cheeks flushed from the stove's heat and a bunch of curls escaping from a headband. He didn't *want* to argue.

'I thought you'd like to share my bounty. And, by the way,

in most polite societies *thank you* is more acceptable than "Why are you in here?".'

Only Sylvie would call a ten-dollar breakfast bounty—and only she would call him on his lack of manners when she was in *his* house, uninvited, cooking for him barefoot.

'Thank you, Sylvie,' he said, in blatantly sarcastic obedience, hating her pity. 'Thank you for breaking into my home on my day off and inflicting your ten-dollar breakfast on me.'

'And my company, Ice Man. Don't forget I'm inflicting *that* on you, too,' she retorted with a grin, putting the coffeepot on a cork coaster and the milk jug beside it. She leaned over him without coming too close to set two glasses of fresh juice on the table, and her shampoo and talcum powder scent touched him, adding to his inner smile. 'Since you're obviously not in the mood to give thanks for the food, I'll give you the hungry man's prayer: one-two-three-four, praise God, eat more.' She tucked into her food without any more ado. 'Yum, oh, yummy...*eat*,' she ordered, shoving his plate closer with a frown. 'When millions of people are starving around the world, ignoring good food is selfish and arrogant.'

He blinked, wanting to laugh, but he had more self-discipline than that. He wasn't about to let her know that the thought of breakfast without her sunshine and starlight company had sent him on a much longer run than usual this morning—and he hadn't liked the burst of sweet light in him when he'd seen her in here when he came back.

Like the things she'd bought for his home, she'd transplanted herself here, growing as naturally as if she'd always been in his life. And he liked it too much for his peace of mind.

He lifted a forkful to his mouth, groaning in delight at the taste of fresh herbs and just-picked vegetables cooked in butter. 'I can feel my cholesterol count rising as I speak.'

'Once a week won't kill you, Ice Man. Tomorrow I have

pancakes for us—a Browning Sunday special. Organic maple syrup and strawberries to go with them.'

He frowned. 'Don't call me Ice Man.'

She lifted a brow and grinned over a full mouth. When she could speak, she said, 'Then don't play the part with me and I won't.' She waved her fork at him as she ended the mock-lecture. 'You should know by now it's of absolutely no use.'

He filled his mouth with food. No point in saying anything to alienate her when she wouldn't *be* alienated. But what *was* this between them? Not employer and employee, not quite friends.

How did you redefine a relationship that had never had a definition in the first place?

After the next mouthful Sylvie spoke again, her chin on her palm. Her thoughtful tone betokened she was about to say something startling. 'I can't work it out. All the magazines talk about your good looks and smooth charm. Okay, the looks are obvious…a woman would have to blind to miss that and I don't need glasses yet. But where's the charm—or is it that you don't need to waste it on your poor housekeeper?'

He choked on a mushroom and started coughing. She jumped up, ran around the table and began hitting his back in a rhythmic method that actually helped. She handed him his glass of juice when he stopped choking. 'Drink that or you'll get hiccups.'

He broke into helpless laughter, bringing on the prophesied hiccups. She promptly gave him advice on that, too.

'No, don't drink yet! A tic in your diaphragm from the coughing is the cause of it, so…hold the muscle down tight, breathe in and out, same pace again and again….*now* drink all the juice without breathing, then release the breath with the same slow rhythm. That's it. See?' She beamed as the hiccups subsided.

He pushed his plate away and buried his face in his arms. 'Thank you, Sylvie,' he said, aiming for deadpan. But it came out as laughing despair. 'And *that's* why I don't waste my so-called charm on you.'

'Why?' Her curiosity sounded genuine.

He looked up at her—she was too pretty, too genuine, too sweet—too *everything* he couldn't ignore. 'What's the use of trying to charm someone who's stopped me choking and cured my hiccups?'

'You're right, it'd be as useless as the Heart of Ice routine.' With a thoughtful expression, she added, 'I probably wouldn't like it anyway.'

It was his turn to demand, 'Why not?' Feeling a bit offended that she'd write off his charm without ever having experienced it.

'I've seen the best of you at the hospital and here,' she said simply. 'I like you as you are. Anything else but the real you would feel like a lie.'

Stunned by the truth of it, he saw what she'd probably known from the start: *why* he couldn't say no to her, *why* he couldn't freeze her out or turn her away. She *liked* him. Not Howlcat Man or Heart of Ice, but Mark. What the *hell* did he do with that?

Beneath all his defences he was a simple man. Until now he'd defined his life into two eras. With Chloe he'd been one person. When he'd finally come to terms with losing her and accepted the man he'd become he'd already been the Heart of Ice—unless he was with family and his few trusted friends.

But Sylvie was unique: an old friend who knew him, but didn't know the worst of him, only the best. She'd known him when they were kids, but not again until now. The fact that she wasn't taken in by the Heart of Ice routine left him confused, as if she'd taken away the comforting boundaries and categories he put people in—including himself.

So now, though he knew he should push her away, he heard himself saying, 'Thank you,' and he sounded as touched as he felt. She *liked* him.

For the first time in half an hour she wasn't cheeky or shock-ing him with her pronouncements. Her smile was as soft as starlight, her eyes as comforting as a fire in winter. 'You're wel-come, Mark.'

Why her honesty scared him down to his soul he didn't know—or maybe he did, which was why he scraped back his chair and said, 'I have to get ready. I have a lunch date.'

'Me, too,' she said in cute surprise, as if they shared a secret. 'Have fun on yours. Is she nice?'

'She's great,' he replied on auto-pilot, darkness slamming down on him. Sylvie was going on a date? With whom? What was he like? Was he good enough for her? Would he make her happy?

It's none of your business, Hannaford.

He took his plate, glass and mug to the counter, rinsed them and stacked them in the dishwasher as if he wasn't burning to ask. And he hadn't lied: *she* was his boat, and he was keeping his usual Saturday date with her. For years *Harbour Girl* had been his refuge, his place to be alone, to be Mark. No woman had ever been on her.

And now the one day he'd been tempted to ask a woman to come with him she had a date.

Sylvie was home again before four, ready to face another Saturday night alone. Honestly, why had she bothered? Rob, her lunch date, a junior doctor at the hospital where she'd done her last practical stint, was a terrific guy with a nice personality—but she'd only wanted to find him a nice girl who'd *see* him.

With a sigh, she dragged her books from the cottage and set them on Mark's coffee table. She put on his stereo, curled up on his lovely oak and tapestry sofa and prepared to study human biology. Two final exams to go; she might as well be prepared.

'What are you doing here?'

She squealed and jumped, dropping her notes in a jumbled

mess over the table and floor. She glared up at Mark, standing on the landing between floors, dressed in shorts and a T-shirt, and felt her breath catch. Those long, muscled, tanned legs... '*Now* look what you made me do,' she complained, and to cover her blushing cheeks and racing heart she leaned over to gather them up.

He strolled down, crouched beside her and helped her pick up the papers, put them in order, and handed the bunch to her. 'You shouldn't lean so far over in a top like that,' he remarked in a neutral tone.

She dropped the papers again as she yanked her top up. 'I don't have enough there to make a cleavage,' she snapped, her cheeks on fire.

'Small or large doesn't matter; they still dominate the male hormonal reaction. We poor men are slaves to what we see—or want to see.' He handed the papers to her again—and though he wasn't looking *there* her heart was still in her throat.

Panic clawed at the sweet bud of excitement in her—but to her shock the arousal fought back and was winning. She lost her breath and the ability to speak, and sat there waiting for him to look again, to make a move, to touch her....

'So, why aren't you still on your date?'

She felt like a hot air balloon shot down by a bazooka of ice. 'Nice guy. Not my type,' she said with a shrug. No point in saying *none of your business* when she was in his house without excuse. 'What about you?'

'Unsatisfying.'

The curt tone made her heart kick up yet another notch. 'What was wrong with her?'

'Nothing wrong with her. It's me.' He didn't look at her. 'She wasn't the one I wanted to be with.'

Chloe.

She lowered her gaze, too fascinated by the simple movement of his mouth, wishing it was on hers. 'I'm sorry,' she said softly, hating the dark jealousy in her. Hating that her competition was a dead girl he couldn't forget.

Competition? The thought made her freeze inside. She'd come here expecting nothing, hoping for nothing for herself— *And she's lying to herself again, folks.*

'So do something about it.'

Confused, she glanced up, and was caught by the half-smile lurking about that riveting mouth. 'What?'

'It's your fault I was with my favourite Saturday date and could only think *Sylvie would love to be here.*' Still wearing that enigmatic smile, he held out a hand to her. 'So, if you have a few hours you can take off studying, come with me. I'll introduce you to my favourite Saturday girl.'

Rearing back, she stared at him, caught between another bout of horrifying jealousy and wondering if he'd lost his mind. 'Won't the lady think that's a bit on the sick side?' *And won't it make the tabloids?*

It was the one thing she was doing her utmost to avoid in this crazy thing between them—past and present, shadow and sunlight, two people who knew the darkest of each other's souls and so little more. If Mark ever discovered her secret, she'd want to curl up in a corner and die.

He lifted a brow. 'She won't think a thing about it.' He pointed out through the back windows. '*Harbour Girl* has been my regular Saturday afternoon date for five years.'

Confused, she turned her head, and saw a small white yacht with pink edging bobbing on the water at the end of his private jetty.

A vision flashed into her mind: Chloe had always had a little bit of that shade of pink on her somewhere. She'd had a pink knitted cap on the day she'd asked Sylvie for her promise. *Make him happy again, Mary. He'll need a friend.*

She'd never been on a yacht....

She saw that irresistible smile and the strong brown hand held out to her—and, caught between the rock of desire and a fast-falling heart and the hard place of a promise to a dead girl, she did the only thing she could: she put her hand in Mark's.

She was already dressed in her favourite shorts and top, which he deemed appropriate for sailing, but he sent her into the cottage for a pair of rubber-soled shoes and a hat. Within five minutes they were on *Harbour Girl*.

She sat down and hung on to a rail as he released the line, the sails caught the wind, and the boat moved into deeper waters.

'Come here,' he called, beckoning to her.

The boat was pitching with the small waves racing to shore. 'I don't think so.' She kept a tight hold on the rail.

'We're barely moving. People have probably pushed you harder when the Manly ferry is in the Heads.'

Giving in with a loud sigh, she released her death grip on the rail and, shuffling foot by foot, made it to him. 'Well?' she demanded, caught between delight at the new experience and fear of falling overboard.

'You look terrified. I thought you'd like the experience.' He tilted his head, studying her. 'So, is it the boat or my sailing skills you don't trust?'

'It's the size of the thing. It's so small, the rails are low, and— I can't swim. I never learned,' she blurted, feeling the heat scalding her cheeks. 'If I fall overboard either I die and you lose a housekeeper, or you dive in after me and you could lose your boat.'

His eyes softened. 'That's easily fixed. Come here.' He reached back and pulled a life jacket from behind him. 'This is why I called you back here—that and sunscreen.'

He pulled off her hat and pulled the life jacket on, tying it less tightly than her insecurity wanted—but then she wouldn't be able to breathe. Then she forgot all about her fears when he began smoothing sunscreen on her arms and shoulders in soft, rhythmic strokes that left her quivering inside—and not with fear.

'Um, thank you.'

'You're so fair, an hour in this heat will roast you.'

His practicality made her want to sigh. Why did his simplest touch do so *much* to her, and yet he seemed so unaffected?

'I can do it,' she protested with a breathless note she despised. Why was it every man's touch made her terrified except the one man who was as far out of her reach as the moon?

'That would necessitate letting go of the rail—and I think I'd have to break your bones to force that.' He laughed.

She had to admit he was right. About to retort, aching to show him how much of a woman she was beneath the façade, she closed her mouth—because for the third time in a couple of minutes he was laughing.

'He's barely laughed in years,' Brenda had told her.

So what if he laughed at her expense? It was what she was here for, right? To give him laughter and love and happily ever after—only not with her. So what did it matter how he saw her? She was his pit-stop on the way to life.

'So, where are we headed, Captain?' she asked in a jaunty tone. The smile of hidden sadness, the tears of a clown—but if it helped him live again she'd do it.

'Brooklyn's quite a way, but if you have the time there's warm, calm pockets of water there to learn to swim. Especially in the evening, when it's quiet.' He shot her an enquiring glance.

'If it's all the same to you I'd rather learn somewhere a bit less—less deep. Like a kiddie pool.'

He tipped up her chin with a finger. 'You aren't that little, or that young.'

'I know.' Her body quivered with the simple touch, with the step closer. He was only a breath or two away. 'Old enough to vote, to work, to marry and have half a dozen kids,' she retorted, her heart beating hard and her fingers trembling.

His eyes roamed her face. The softness had a touch of desire—and her pulse went into overdrive.

'Is that how many you want?'

Without warning the shutters slammed over her soul. She felt her right shoulder lift and hunch. 'I did as a child: the prince, the palace, half a dozen beautifully behaved and appropriately royal children. What girl doesn't dream of the whole shebang?'

'Then leave the kiddie pool for them, when you marry your prince and the kids come. You're a woman who's missed the joy of swimming in the ocean. Come to Brooklyn and swim with me. I'll be with you all the way. I won't let you drown. Trust me, Sylvie,' he said softly, close enough to touch, his breath warm and smelling of mocha coffee.

She all but melted at his feet. 'I do,' she whispered, her eyes enormous as she drank in his face—the high cheekbones, the bump on his nose, the crooked smile and the eyes she'd been swimming in for so long she could barely remember a time she hadn't. 'I don't have my swimmers on.'

His smile grew. 'Me neither, since I wasn't planning on a swim today. We'll just wear what we have on. I have towels, though, and some sandwiches and hot chocolate mix in the galley. We'll eat on deck after our swim to dry off and sail home tonight.'

A boating adventure with Mark; swimming and a picnic and a night sail home….

'All right,' she whispered. Where had her voice gone? Out into the harbour along with her good sense, no doubt. Thrown overboard by the one word she should never allow when it came to him.

Hope.

CHAPTER SIX

'I CAN'T. It's too deep,' Sylvie babbled for the fifth time.

She stood beside Mark at the edge of the yacht, where he'd dropped the ladder, looking down at the lapping water as if there were dozens of hungry crocs and sharks circling below her. Then she looked at him helplessly. 'I just can't.'

She was shaking, and her tremors were real.

Mark could see she'd gone as far as she could on her own. She'd taken the wheel as he trimmed the lines, she'd learned to avoid the boom as she crossed the boat—she'd even let go of the side rail and begun to run. She'd loved the sunshine on her face and the salt wind in her hair, even laughed at the splashes of water drenching her when they reached the Heads, the notorious rough patch of water heading to Manly. She'd landed on her butt more than once and didn't care.

She'd had a ball today. He knew that. She'd let go of her fears and enjoyed the adventure. But that was with the life jacket tied securely around her. Now her face was so white her freckles stood out in sharp contrast. Her courage had left her.

Maybe he was going too far, but he *knew* that if he could get her into the water…

'Here.' He climbed down the ladder and jumped in, feeling the summer-warm water envelop him like a lover's arms—and why he always had to think of lovers when he was with Sylvie he didn't know. He could control all but the most fleeting lust with all women but the one who was way off-limits. She was too high above him, too pure and giving for damaged goods like him.

To banish the thought, even knowing he was flying right into a no-go zone, he lifted his arms. 'Come down to me.'

Her face so white her eyes stood out in sharp contrast to the pale skin, she shook her head, edging back.

At this point he knew he should stop—but something perverse forced him to try one more time. 'Just shut your eyes, hold your breath and jump. I'll catch you. I promise,' he said with gentle persuasiveness. Was he pushing for her sake, or because he wanted to feel her in his arms, warm and slippery, in the buoyant ocean? 'I know you're scared, but you'll never conquer it unless you try. You'll spend your life terrified of the unknown.'

As he'd hoped, his reference to fear did it. As her predictable pride kicked in, a wave of colour hit her cheeks, she dragged in quick, hard breaths, and she screwed her eyes tight shut. Instead of climbing down the ladder, she stepped off the edge.

A moment later his arms were full of the forbidden; the satin skin of her bare legs flew past him. He wrapped his arms around her waist before she could go under and panic. 'That's it, Sylvie. Hold on to me—not so tight. I need to breathe,' he mock-complained to make her laugh, loving the feel of her arms wrapped around him so close her face was buried in his neck.

She'd never let him this close to her before. Even when they'd kissed he'd sensed part of her holding back, watching, waiting for the panic to kick in. But right now she trusted him completely—she had no choice.

Could she feel what she was doing to him? That he was more aroused than he'd felt since his teens and she was fully clothed? *You're her boss. You're teaching her to swim. Get over it!*

'It's cold,' she muttered near his ear, her teeth chattering.

He held her against him, trying to reassure her, to make her feel safe. Trying to ignore his rebel body's *I've got to have her* response he couldn't shut down. 'That's fear speaking. It's really warm.'

'No, it's freezing! I want to get out!' she cried, suddenly struggling against him.

Was it really the cold that caused her terror? Or had she felt his body's reaction to the sweetest armful of woman he'd felt in half a lifetime?

To test her, he said softly, 'Come on, my fearless girl, you took on the Heart of Ice and won a job and a friend. A little water can't beat you, surely?'

She stiffened; he literally felt her spine moving tight into place. Her reliable pride kicked in once more and she stopped moving— apart from her feet, kicking to stay up in natural reaction.

'Well?' She spoke through what sounded like lockjaw, but she wasn't giving in. She'd fight her fear to the end now.

He laughed, low and soft. 'Now you release your stranglehold on me, take my hand, lift your body to the top of the water and float.'

'I can float,' she retorted, with that adorable indignation he loved to see. 'Well…in a bathtub,' she amended, blushing.

In the glow of her blush he saw a vision of her sweetly naked, floating in a hot tub, with her lovely curling hair rippling across the water like a pillow….

He gritted his teeth, breathed out and made himself smile. 'Salt water's a little different to the bath. Here—let me show you.' He turned her body with a hand at her back.

Then he lifted her so she floated on the bobbing water. He disciplined his eyes to remain on her feet, hands and face. Looking anywhere else left him feeling as if he was the one needing the life jacket. Her hair spread across the warm salt water in rippling dark waves, and her chest rose and fell against his skin with every anxious breath.

He held her hand for reassurance as he taught her first to float, then to turn and kick. She floated well, and learned to swim basic strokes on her back. She was awkward with freestyle—principally because she wouldn't let go of his hand—and began to sink every time she even thought of letting him go. So he tried breaststroke, with far greater success, because he could follow her arm movements without head-butting her.

'You're a natural,' he told her half an hour later, when he could see she was flagging and they climbed back on the deck to dry. 'You'll be swimming in no time.'

Her cheeks glowed with pleasure. 'Once I learned how to do it I didn't want to stop. I didn't know it would feel like that.'

She took the towel he handed her, then bent over and alternately shook and squeezed the water from her hair. She undid her shirt by two buttons, squeezed that out, too, and tied it in a knot above her navel. Without even looking at him, she squeezed out her shorts, too, bending over a little as she did.

Nothing she did was provocative, yet Mark's mouth was dry and his heart was pounding like a jackhammer. He wanted to turn away, to give her privacy—how wrong was it for him to lust over an old friend this way?—but he couldn't make his body obey his will. How did she make him want her so much, light up his inner darkness without trying?

'Didn't know it would feel like what?' He heard the husky note in his voice, and threw up a fast prayer she wouldn't recognise it for the yearning it was.

That was the worst of it. Simple lust he could handle. This was more—it was way too much. Why was he standing here, dripping water, fascinated by a woman he couldn't slake himself with and walk away?

'So free, so joyous,' she answered in a dreamy voice that heightened his sense of danger to the red zone. 'Like we were alone in the world, surrounded by warm water and sun and…'

She turned her face to share her joy. He masked the intensity of his reaction too slow, and her words dried up.

Her eyes were enormous as she stared at him, her sweet skin dappled with salt water and sunshine. She wet her mouth and he groaned quietly.

'Listen to me talking like I'm some kind of poet. Why didn't you tell me to be…?' She swallowed, blinked and stepped back. 'I must have swallowed too much sea water. I need a drink.'

She fled down the stairs to the galley.

Mark was left standing on the deck, heart pounding, mouth dry, body aching. It had come to this—the famed playboy and Heart of Ice, the man who'd felt *nothing* for almost half his life, who'd played the game with some of the most beautiful women in the world, reduced to the level of any other dumb jerk in the world, in thrall to the one woman he couldn't have.

Despite her kissing him last week, the complete fear in her reaction just now couldn't be faked. He'd *frightened* her with his feelings…and he *terrified* himself.

As he debated with himself over the wisdom of following her, he frowned. He'd frightened her with a simple look, yet she'd trusted him to touch her until then—and the *why* of her trust suddenly made sense: he'd touched her, held her, *before* what had happened to her.

The ugly suspicion he hadn't wanted to think about the other day crystallised to bleak knowledge: if she was going to heal, it was up to him to do it.

He followed her down a few minutes later.

What would he think of her? Would he have seen she was as aroused as she was terrified? Did he think her a scared doe, bolting at the first scent of danger?

'I hope you left some water for me. You've been down here long enough to fill a camel's hump.'

The total normality in his tone, as if nothing had happened, forced a rush of breath from her lungs. She didn't know she'd been holding it. 'Oh, there's a drop or two.' Her voice was rusty, as if she hadn't used it in days. As if she hadn't been laughing and chattering all afternoon with each new discovery on the boat.

'Good.' He came into the galley, poured from the bottle into a glass, and drank long and thirstily, rivulets of sea water trickling down the rough brown skin of his throat.

Suddenly she needed more water. Lots of water.

She turned to the water bottle, heaving in a dry breath, her whole body aching to see that look on his face again and this time to *do* something about it.

Yeah, you'll do the same old thing. Run.

Did she seem as crazy to him as she did to herself? Her see-sawing emotions were impossible to control. During all the years he'd been her therapy her love and desire for him had been *safe*—because he'd been as distant as the moon. Even when she'd come here she hadn't felt threatened, because a man like Mark—rich, handsome, playing the field—couldn't possibly find a tiny china doll attractive.

But he did…or at least he had for a moment. She didn't count the kisses the other day which he'd meant in comfort—she'd known that all along. But today he'd seen her as a woman, had looked at her with aching desire…and that had resurrected all her fears that her secret would come to the surface. Being with a man as intensely media-magnetic as Mark would ensure the truth would out some day. It would destroy the boys, and Mark, too—and it would risk everything she'd planned for her future.

She should never have come today. What if the media—?

'Are you hungry? I have a pack of sandwiches I bought at a local deli this morning.' He reached over her in the cramped room to pick up a basket. 'Let's head up on deck. We can dry off as we eat.' He turned to the stairs.

He was talking to her as if she was a sister again—and she felt the exact same mixture of relief and resentment as the last time. She released another breath, said, 'Lead the way, boss-man,' and headed for the stairs.

'Don't call me that!' But the words were teasing. 'Ginger.'

She laughed, and followed him up to the deck.

The sun was beginning to sink; the soft rose hue of its setting touched the edges of the lapping waves with gentle fire. She sank onto one of the towels he'd laid over a blanket and accepted the glass he held out to her, giving a smile that felt uncertain.

'It's nothing fancy—sandwiches and wine.' He looked tense as he said it. 'I hope you like white.'

'I do.' She sipped at the wine and again tasted the difference. But if she kept her secrets he had the right to his. 'It's fresh—perfect for the outdoors.' She reached into the basket. 'I'm starving, and—'

He relaxed and laughed. 'I know—we can't waste a scrap.' He unwrapped a sandwich. 'So, tell me what you plan to do with your degree when you're done. What branch of nursing do you want to go into?'

She dragged in a breath, knowing what would happen as she said it. 'Terminal illnesses,' she said quietly. 'I've already applied for St Agatha's. They've accepted me—contingent on my passing all subjects, of course.'

He stiffened. 'I see.'

Her eyes met his. 'You know how it is, Mark. Doctors and nurses do their best, but they're so busy with all their patients. Until you've lived through the slow death of a loved one you don't realise the empathy is missing. The families of the dying *need* that—just as we needed it. But we were kids, and back then they didn't think to provide grief counselling for the children. We were lucky we found what we needed in each other.'

'Until you left.' He put down his sandwich. 'I was so damn *alone* after you went, just watching her die.'

Tender compassion filled her for the strong, loving boy left alone with his loss. Forgetting her fears, she laid a hand over his. 'I'm so sorry. I had you when I needed you most. I should have come, should have called—'

He gave her a humourless smile. 'You were a girl with more than enough to do. If only you could do it all. You had far more on your plate than I did after she was gone.'

He was right. Until now she hadn't thought of it that way, but after Chloe's death he'd probably fallen into a gaping hole of *nothing*. She'd had years of being there for her family— having a reason to get up every day, a higher purpose in everything she did—but he'd had nothing. Now she understood why, when Joel had gone off to university, it had seemed the perfect time to fulfil her promise to Chloe and come back into Mark's life: she'd needed to fill the gap.

Mark had never learned how to do that. He'd filled it with the work that had brought him fame and fortune but only temporary satisfaction; with women who meant nothing. He'd had his family, but they *worried* about him rather than helping him to find a new purpose in life.

He'd had half a lifetime of Chloe always being beside him; after five years of being her significant other, her support, her friend and finally her husband, loving her through her illness, he must have felt like a rudderless ship after she'd died. No wonder he'd thrown himself into his inventions, done so much through the years....

'I wish you'd come to see me,' she said softly, feeling her way. 'There were times I felt so alone, so weighed down I could scream. Every time I had a free hour Joel or Drew would cry, or Dad would get sick. Simon did what he could to help me, but he was the clever one, the one who was going to save the family, so he had to be free to study.' She frowned, looking out over the water. 'I used to think of you as I rocked Joel to sleep at night. I thought of you when the kids at school thought I was a freak and I spent lunch hours with my dreams. You made everything bearable for me even when you weren't there any more.'

After a long moment in which the only sound was a seagull's cawing cry he said, 'I thought of you, too. I would have come, but I—' He closed his eyes, shook his head. Whatever he'd been going to say was still too painful for him.

'You were my best friend.' She bit her lip as she made the admission. 'Always, when I felt lost or alone or scared, I remembered how you held me that day, and I imagined you were there, with your arms held out to me.'

He'd buried his face in the crook of his elbow, his knees holding him up. 'I'm nobody's hero, Sylvie. God help me, I couldn't even save myself.'

She nodded, accepting the meaning behind his words without letting him know she suspected his secret. 'But you still saved me,' she said quietly.

He made a deprecatory gesture. 'Just money.'

'A home when we were about to be thrown out of it. A trust fund for the boys that saw them through university—and for me…' She choked, unable to say it. 'You'll never know what you've been to me, Mark—more than just the money. *You.*'

He shook the head still resting in his arms, as if the load he carried was too heavy for him to bear.

A little hole in the dam of her bursting heart cracked open. 'You,' she repeated, and as lost in compassion as he was in despair of the past, she leaned over, lifted his face and brushed her lips over his. 'God only knows what I would have become if not for you. You saved my life. Thank you, Mark. *Thank you.*' With tears in her eyes she kissed him again, filled with gratitude and drenching sweetness, then she drew back as unbearable beauty hit her like a bullet to the heart. She'd kissed him, and it made her feel aroused and so very *beautiful*....

The sun fell to the horizon beyond the open sea, deepening the sky above them to lavender and the water to grey-black as he stared at her in silence. Then he leaned forward, brushing his mouth over hers like moth's wings, tender and unsure.

He knew something was wrong and he gave her the choice: draw back or accept. But she had *no* choice; the sweet lassitude filling her held her in chains. Terrified, longing, she took her turn again, leaning into him, drinking in the hot summer salt scent of him as her mouth moved on his, over and over. Feather-soft tastes of paradise forbidden....

They didn't touch. Neither deepened the kisses. They never descended to passion, but it remained there, hovering between them unspoken. Faerie kisses filled their souls as, through speaking of the past and yet leaving so much unsaid, childhood friends and new acquaintances became something more. Barely moving, boss and employee crossed the line, both knowing this time they couldn't go back, but needing each other too much to stop. Both held hostage to the past, unable to open up to anyone else, they trusted the people they'd once been and opened unseen gates to trusting who they were now.

Strange to know so much about him and yet barely know him at all....

And then he pulled away, put his food back in the basket, downed the wine and stood, lifting her to her feet, as well. 'We should go.'

Though his voice wasn't cold, it was quiet. Too quiet—and the words hovered around them unspoken, like everything else today, a memory beautiful and poignant, but leaving them both feeling cold and dead.

Night fell, and it was as if he had taken part of it and wrapped it around him, lifting the drawbridge to his heart, locking himself in cold darkness. Sylvie grieved in silence for something precious she hadn't truly had to lose.

After a nightmare day at work, Mark came in a few minutes before midnight on Monday night to find the lights on. He frowned, entering the back way, and though he was getting used to it now he still took a deep breath, inhaling that amazing, uplifting scent again.

The oven was on low. Flowers picked from his garden stood in a vase on the table—

And Sylvie was curled up sleeping on his sofa.

He came towards her, the smile growing; she was so *beautiful* like that, in shorts and a T-shirt obviously inherited from a brother, miles too big and advertising a heavy-metal rock band. Her hair was a tangled mess, her hand under a cheek flushed with sleep—and she did more to him, body and heart, than the glamour of any woman he'd touched in half a lifetime.

He'd tried to avoid her. He'd gone out all day yesterday, spoken to her as little as possible this morning. But no matter what barriers he put up she slipped under his false cold skin and warmed him with her presence, her sunshine smile. She made the women he'd dated until now seem hard and callous with her sweet, pretty freckled face and her shining honesty.

Still smiling, he bent to her. 'Sylvie.'

'No,' she mumbled, and flipped over.

He chuckled. 'Sylvie, wake up.'

'Go *away*, Simon.' She sighed and curled up again.

Giving up on waking her, he lifted her in his arms. He loved the way she snuggled into him, as though even in sleep she knew who he was and trusted him.

Inhaling the scent of her—sweet flowers and shampoo—moving his fingers like a whisper against her silky skin, he carried her to the cottage, opened the door—

He stopped after a single step inside. Horrified, he looked around.

After her demand that he never enter her cottage he'd expected simple furnishings—but not this. *She had nothing but a mattress, a rug and an old wardrobe.*

No TV. No fridge or microwave. No furniture. Not even second-hand stuff. Just that rug on the floor covered with books. A picture of her with her brothers and one of her parents hung on the back living room wall, but that was all.

No wonder she practically lived in the main house and chose to study there. No wonder she danced to her music on his stereo. She had nothing...*nothing*. And still she'd bought presents to make *his* house, already magnificent, more of a home.

He should have known! It was so ridiculous and yet so *Sylvie*. Of course the girl he'd known would become a woman who'd spend her hard-earned money to buy gifts for a lone wolf multi-millionaire when she had nothing herself. He'd bet his entire fortune that her brothers lived in well-supplied homes filled with furniture *she'd* given them, and that she always visited them so they wouldn't know the truth.

What debt was she paying off that her brothers—one of whom a resident doctor, earning reasonable money—didn't know about?

Her father's medical bills. He'd give his entire fortune away if he was wrong.

Giving in to the temptation gnawing at him body and soul, he bent and kissed the flushed cheek, inhaled the uplifting, intoxicating scent of her. Just shampoo and five-dollar cologne. Yet because it was *her* it was beautiful. He turned his face and touched his lips to hers, as he'd done on the boat... He touched, then brushed over her mouth with his, once, twice and deepened it so tenderly he hoped it wouldn't wake her.

But after a few moments a soft sigh filled his mouth, fluttering fingers touched his face, and sleeping lips kissed his. Dreaming kisses filled with the wonder and joy he could have shared with her for life.

Once upon a time.

When he finally stopped, a soft whisper touched his mouth. *'Mark.'* Just his name, yet so filled with longing that unexpected pain shafted through him.

After a long time he carried her back into the main house. He couldn't leave her here. Step one in Sylvie's life change was about to begin. He knew what he had to do—and he prayed he was right and he'd found the only way to make her accept what he had to give.

When the alarm went off the next morning, Sylvie woke up with a sense of luxurious confusion. She scrunched up her closed eyes and stretched, feeling a sweet, shuddering *ah* of relief, not needing to work out the kinks in her back and neck.

Her bed was *comfortable*. And the alarm didn't play the radio, but made a muted beeping sound.

Her eyes flew open. From cleaning the house, she knew exactly where she was: one of Mark's spare rooms. The bed was a king single, with solid bedposts and rail slats—good, solid forties furniture. The mattress was thick and cloud-soft.

Still dressed in the shorts and T-shirt of the night before, she leaped to her feet, turned off the alarm—it was six-thirty-five!—stripped the bed of its lovely pure cotton percale sheets for washing, and headed down the stairs.

He was dressed, seated at the table and eating the last remnants of the muesli she'd made the day before. 'Morning,' he greeted her, with a cheerfulness that seemed overdone to her paranoid ears. 'I'd ask if you slept well, but I know you did judging by the snoring.'

Arrested despite herself, she blushed. 'I do *not* snore.'

'No—you do this funny triple-catch of your breath. Huh, huh, *huh*.' He made the sound, each *huh* higher-pitched than the last.

She stopped where she stood, glowering but undecided. 'Why did I wake up in your spare room?'

He kept eating, and turned a page of the morning paper and read while he chewed and swallowed. Sylvie fumed.

'Well, you told me to stay out of your place. I tried shaking you, but you told me to go away—oh, and you called me Simon.' He looked up and grinned. 'Did he have the same trouble waking you that I did?'

She thought of her brother's complaints when she'd been studying for her Higher School Certificate and had commonly fallen asleep on the old sofa. *'You sleep like the dead,'* he'd always said when she woke up, being dragged by her feet through the hallway to her room. Lucky for her they hadn't had a staircase, or she'd probably have had concussion on a regular basis.

'You carried me to—to the room?' She felt her cheeks and throat heat up.

He shrugged. 'It wasn't hard. You really don't weigh much, do you?' He turned another page. 'By the way, I'll be home early tonight. We have to go out.'

Delight streaked through her. 'We do?' she asked shyly, for-getting to ask why he'd set her alarm for six-thirty instead of five-thirty.

He nodded, his attention absorbed in the international news pages. 'Well, it's either that or give you the ten thousand dollars I owe you up-front.'

'Ten—' she choked on the words. *Ten thousand dollars*. And he'd said it as if it was nothing. It was more than she'd seen or had in her life—for her own trust fund had gone on medi-cines for her dying father. Thoroughly intrigued, she demanded, 'You owe me money? What for?'

His answer was vague as he kept on reading. 'My lawyer

went over your contract and he'd forgotten the clause regarding a furnished residence in the terms. I'd forgotten too, because the last three housekeepers brought their own stuff and took the cash instead.'

She shook her head, trying to clear it. 'I don't understand. Why are we going out?'

'Pierson Brothers is having a private pre-stocktake sale tonight for their special customers. I have to go personally to get the bargains.' He looked up and smiled, still in a distracted way. 'I'd appreciate it if you came.'

Now she was really suspicious. 'Why?'

He sighed. 'You commented on my homey, old-fashioned furniture—that's because it's all my grandparents' stuff; they left it to me in their will. I don't know what you want for your place, but since it's going to be yours for the time being, you might as well pick what you like.' He returned to the newspaper. 'If you don't want to bother I could ask one of the girls, but they'd spend all their time pumping me about you—'

'I get it.' She lifted a hand, unable to argue with his logic—but she'd be checking her copy of her contract when he was gone. 'I'll come.'

'Good.' His gaze remained on the paper but she felt something simmering in him—an emotion she couldn't identify. 'Be ready at six. We can eat out after. What do you like?'

Long moments ticked on the wall clock before she answered. 'I don't have a dress suitable for the kind of places you go to...*sir*. And I have no desire to be on page three tomorrow as your latest squeeze.'

His brows snapped together. 'Who do you think you're speaking to? Some prince of the blood? I grew up as you did, Sylvie, and I haven't forgotten it even if you have. I still love a burger or a kebab, and I eat Chinese takeout regularly.'

She felt her stupid cheeks heating up again. Her suspicions

on why he'd brought the entire subject up in the first place hadn't abated, but there was no way she could ask now without seeming churlish. 'I'm sorry, Mark. That was uncalled-for.'

He nodded. 'So, what food do you like?'

'I like anything, and I love to try new foods,' she offered, feeling embarrassed even giving her opinion to him after the way he'd put her in her place.

'Excellent. I know a great place not far from Taylor Square. It's a Spanish place—lively and fun when they start the dancing.' He gave a careless shrug. 'We could try waltzing to a Salsa beat. It'd be good practice for you.'

In his arms, doing a sensuous Latin American dance…

Oh, her ridiculous cheeks—would they never stop giving her away? Why not put up a sign saying *Woman with intense crush on her boss*? 'How dressy should I be?'

'A simple dress will be fine, but wear heels if we're going to dance. You need to practise in what you'll be wearing for the wedding.'

He didn't look up, didn't see her hot cheeks or respond to the breathlessness in her tone. He spoke as if he'd asked her to polish the floors again.

'All right,' she replied, squashing a ridiculous urge to sigh.

He pushed his chair back. 'Have a good day at college.'

'You too,' she called, caught up in an absurd mixture of trepidation and excitement. She was going on a second date— well, a second *non*-date—with him.

A single backwards wave was Mark's only answer, and in his avoidance of speaking to her as normal she felt a chill as cold as his face had been when he'd walked out the door.

CHAPTER SEVEN

I DON'T seduce my employees.

But that didn't mean he hadn't thought about it constantly since that first kiss. It had grown to unbearable proportions since smoothing sunscreen over her silky skin, holding her body against his in the water. Each day felt like torture—trying to treat her like a sister when all he ached to do was sweep her into his arms and carry her to his bed. Not to a hotel, to *his* bed—and the worst part was it didn't even terrify him. She was in his life already; she *knew* him, cared about *Mark*, and the thought of having her in his bed was as natural as taking her to a hotel was alien.

He also thought constantly about making her life better. He could still taste the exquisite relief when she'd agreed to shop with him…and when she clearly hadn't read her contract thoroughly before he'd replaced it at 5:00 a.m. with the one he'd paid triple for his lawyer to draw up in the middle of the night.

He knew if he hadn't done it she'd have rejected him, his furniture and his job—even if it meant having no money, no place to go—and he wasn't any good at lying. He'd barely been able to look her in the face as he'd fed her all those half-truths this morning.

'I'm here! You ready to go?'

Sylvie sounded like a girl given her first credit card, ready to head to the mall; she couldn't hide her excitement.

'Coming!' he called, and left his room taking the stairs two at a time.

He nearly tripped down five at once when he saw her.

He dated women who dressed in expensive silks, who tossed on jewels worth thousands, wore four-inch heels and glossy chignons that came of spending hours in a salon.

Sylvie wore a green floral print cotton dress with spaghetti straps, old brown sandals with heels maybe two inches high. Her hair was loose, the shine in her curls from simple generic shampoo. She'd probably bought her watch and hoop earrings for ten dollars at the markets. Her face was almost free of cosmetics, but her eyes were enormous with the application of mascara, and her lips shone with pale pink gloss. Her freckles glowed in her pale skin and rosy cheeks. But when she smiled at him like that, so excited to be going *shopping*, he felt fifteen again—gauche as a kid on a date with the girl he'd been moping over for months, hoping for his first kiss. He felt tongue-tied and scared and dizzy—and *scared*.

'Mark? Are you okay?'

He shook himself. 'Sorry. I spaced out for a minute.' He loped down the rest of the stairs. 'I'm ready. Let's go out the back way.'

She snuggled into leather seating with a luxurious sigh. 'Oh…this is so nice. It beats the bus and the train any day.'

He glanced sideways at her. 'You've never owned a car?'

She lifted a brow at him as if he was crazy. 'Duh. Of course I haven't.'

He didn't know what he could say to that—he knew what he wanted to say would be wrong. *Let me buy you a car.*

He could hand her a cheque for the ten thousand dollars—a number he'd plucked out of the air this morning—but she wouldn't buy a car; and if he bought her one she'd probably sell it, pay her debts and buy presents for everyone. It was her way. Three calls to her brothers today had confirmed his suspicions: her brothers had everything they needed. The family debts hadn't been paid with *their* trust funds.

They'd been shocked by what their sister had done for them. And they'd agreed to keep silence over his plans.

As he pulled out of the garage, he said, 'I haven't caught a bus or a train since before I graduated from uni.'

Her brows lifted. 'Since you were twenty-one?'

'I graduated at twenty-two,' he replied. 'But after I invented the Howlcat air filtration system at nineteen I could actually afford a car.' He grinned at her, hoping she wouldn't ask why he'd been a year behind. When and why he'd fallen a year behind...the stupid mistakes he'd made after Chloe's death.

Mistakes? What he'd done had almost taken a child's life.

Knowing it had happened was bad enough. Talking about it made it worse. What he'd done—the *stupid* decisions he'd made—the drinking and still more drinking when driving—was his private shame, the reason why he'd never have a serious relationship—why this...*wonderful* thing with Sylvie would never go anywhere. That year, his time in rehab and his marriage, were the only things he'd managed to keep from the press. And he had to keep it that way. It could destroy his family and any woman associated with him. And to have Sylvie in his life, his heart and bed, only to lose her—

'Did you go for the obvious and get a convertible?'

Relieved by the teasing note in her voice, he laughed. 'I was a teenage guy who suddenly had more money than he knew what to do with. What do you reckon?'

'I reckon you paid off all the debts for your family, bought them houses and stuff, then helped my family. You took care of everyone else first,' she said softly. 'I reckon you kept living with your parents until everyone was secure—and I reckon you caught a few buses and trains until then, or bought a cheap car first.'

He started at her perception. '*That* didn't make the tabloids. I'm sure of it.'

'I know you—remember?' She laughed, long and gentle, touched with as much affection as amusement. 'You *are* a family man, Mark, first and last. I always knew that. If you hadn't looked after them first, you wouldn't have thought of my family next.'

'You never believed the Heart of Ice stories? You never thought I might have changed with the money?' He gripped the wheel hard, wishing he could work out *what* he thought at this point. She had a way of turning him upside down and inside out without even trying.

'If you had, you wouldn't have remembered us—looked after the boys, as well.' Her voice was so tender it brought a lump to his throat. 'I always knew the person you are, Mark. You could never change to that degree.'

'I'm no saint.' He kept his voice light, hiding the inner darkness. 'A lot of those stories were true.'

Her silence hurt—but when she spoke it wasn't what he expected. 'We all do things we're not proud of to get through a day, to make it to another day, to keep body and soul and family together, to forget what's killing us inside. It doesn't mean we are what others paint us. It only makes us human.'

Her voice held the darkness he'd tried so hard to keep from her—because he couldn't stand to taint her sweet sunshine, to sully her innocence. But she understood desperation—hers to stay alive, to keep her family; his to forget.

Without thinking about their respective positions, he reached out to her, took a clenched hand from her lap and held it. 'At least you had a noble purpose, Sylvie. You can't have done anything to be ashamed of.'

'Don't be so certain.' She frowned out the window. 'Even little china dolls have to live, Mark. Appearances deceive—and once you've sold your soul to survive, you can't have it back. You know that.'

Then, in one of her lightning turnarounds, she pulled her hand from his and gave him a brilliant, glittering smile, thin as spun glass and just as brittle. 'How did we turn from Thrilled to be Shopping Street down Morbid Discussion Road? Let's get back on course. Any type of furniture you absolutely despise?'

'Minimalist,' he replied, wishing he'd made his millions before she'd done whatever it was that had filled her with such self-hate. He was burning with curiosity over what it was she'd done, but seeing the look in her eyes, hearing the repressed self-reproach in her voice, he knew he wouldn't ask. He knew what it was to want to outrun the pain, to leave it all behind, but he also knew it would forever haunt, like a murder victim in an unquiet grave.

No wonder she'd changed her name.

'Good—me, too,' she said with a cheerfulness that was still overdone. 'The cottage is—what?—a hundred years old?'

'About a hundred and thirty. I had it completely revamped when I bought the place, but in its original style. It had been pretty neglected by its former owners.'

'Why didn't you furnish it after that?'

He felt the suspicion lingering beneath the bright tone, and was glad he could tell her the truth. 'I did—I actually had it furnished before I moved into the house. But my first housekeeper had her own furniture and didn't like what I'd put in.'

'Free is good,' she said, with such emphasis he laughed and began to relax. 'What was wrong with it?'

He turned to her for a moment as he negotiated the Anzac Cove Bridge and smiled. 'Nothing, according to you. They were my grandparents' things—actually my great-grandparents' stuff that my grandparents inherited and then left to me. Since I moved it into the main house I've slowly given away the newer stuff I bought, and brought in things I've found at antique and maritime auctions. I like the way it all fits in—and I make sure to get matching wood when I buy a new piece.'

'I think your grandparents' things look perfect in the house.' She sighed dreamily. 'It's all oak and walnut and thick glass. It's lovely solid workmanship, too, and it will last. I'm so glad that your housekeeper didn't want it. If I'd inherited it all and found out it was your family heritage I'd be terri-fied to ruin it.'

She likes antiques.

If he bought her antiques now she'd reject them, but that didn't mean he couldn't buy her some good, solid furniture in antique style—and if he had to tell the store clerk to pretend it was on special offer and make the cost up later who did it hurt?

He hadn't felt so contented and yet so excited in years. To give Sylvie something of the life and things she deserved had given him a buzz all day. He'd even sung as he'd worked on the applications to his latest Howlcat design—something he hadn't done for so long he could barely remember. She was his friend, and—

Liar.

Okay, so he wanted her. So he'd almost swerved into oncoming traffic twice because he couldn't keep his eyes off her. His hands were itching to touch her silky skin, to kiss her and take in the sunshine and starlight happiness that flooded his entire being.

But while desire didn't last, the friendship they'd forged felt like his grandparents' furniture...built to last. She was as wholesome as the daisy he'd compared her to, as warm as firelight—and occasionally she burned him, both physically and emotionally, when he came too close. But that was what friends did. She was on a pit-stop in life, on the way to the career and home of her own she deserved, to the man and the family she—

'Mark? Are you all right?' Sylvie broke into his thoughts, lighting up his cold inner darkness with that sunshine voice.

He started and turned to smile at her. 'Sure. Why?'

'You're gripping the wheel so tight.'

He softened his grip, cursing the body language that called him on his delusions. Looking at her, hearing her say his name and feeling high on the cologne-and-pixie-woman smell, even thinking of another man touching her set off something cold, *primal* in him—made him want to pull the car over, haul her into his arms and kiss her into—

Stop it. Think of Sylvie!

He was nowhere near good enough for a woman like her. He didn't have enough of a heart left to give. But he could give her the best home she'd accept, dancing lessons and a friendship that hadn't faded in two decades and wouldn't fade in another ten. One day she'd bring her kids to visit—

'Mark?' She sounded really concerned. 'Mark, are you sure you're okay to drive?'

He frowned at her. 'Of course. Why?'

She pointed to the road ahead. 'You're in two lanes at once.'

Honking horns behind him put him in automatic rescue mode. He moved into the slow lane, and indignant drivers honked again as they passed.

In another few minutes he'd turned into the parking area of the furniture giant, and showed his invitation card to the parking attendant. He parked, and moved around the car to hand her out—normal practice for him. But she was already out, dancing from foot to foot in an excitement she couldn't hide. The thin veneer of the pretence of helping him choose furniture had been enough excuse for her to blind herself to the truth of his offer—because she'd lived with hand-me-downs and charity store furniture all her life.

He tucked her hand in his, determined to make this a fun-filled night she wouldn't forget—and her infectious, sparkling happiness soaked through their connected skin and streaked through his veins to his heart.

Not to mention other parts he wished would leave him alone. Head, heart and body—all entwined for the first time in half a lifetime. And because she was so *lovable* he couldn't shield himself with his usual wall of ice without her taking it on herself and hurting.

'Hey, Mark, wake up! Are we going?' she demanded, her eyes bubbling with joy like champagne.

Her sweet mirth went straight to his head. 'Come on, let's go.' Smiling with a crazy happiness that even though she was his employee she treated him as she would any other man, he swung her around and, their hands still linked, walked her through the car park.

Once they reached the outside of the megastore he released her hand in case he was recognised. He didn't want Sylvie embroiled in a tabloid situation any more than he thought she'd want to be famous—or infamous.

Uh-oh. This was bad, very bad, if simply unlinking hands made him feel so empty. What was it about Sylvie that made him feel everything twice as much?

Sylvie didn't look at him or comment on it, just kept walking beside him, singing softly in a sweet, slightly tinny voice—and it was all he could do to restrain himself from staring at her. She took his rejection with a respect no woman had ever shown before.

'So, where will we start?' she asked, as if nothing had happened…and maybe from her point of view it hadn't.

'Living, dining, bedroom, white goods—take your pick. I don't know much about furniture, so this is your show,' he replied, waving his hand around the entire place.

'Oh, *oh*!' she cried, veering off to the left.

Grinning, he followed in her wake.

That was how it was for the next hour: she chose, and he and the bemused saleswoman followed her in mingled amusement and admiration.

She promptly fell in love with a fat, comfy, old-fashioned brocade-style sofa, striped like the weird pants she loved, but far more pretty. 'How much is this?'

Mark didn't reach the saleswoman in time, and the woman told her.

Sylvie sighed and shook her head. 'I can't afford that much.' She didn't even look at Mark. She must have worked out a budget and she was sticking to it—even with his money.

Mark nodded meaningfully at the saleswoman. The woman hurried to say, 'Oh, silly me! I was quoting the pre-sale price. Of course it's forty-five percent off.'

Sylvie's piquant face lit and glowed. 'Is it? Oh, yes, I can afford it, then! Mark, I can afford it,' she cried, turning that megawatt smile of happiness on him.

'That's great.' Mark kept his sigh of relief to himself—and his other reactions.

Next she found a small round oak dining table and padded chairs that were within her range without discount, but she still bargained them down a bit. She did the same with a coffee table and with the desk and study chair Mark insisted on, saying housekeepers needed a place to plan the next week's work and menus.

She chose a solid antique-style dressing table, and bedside tables with lamps that would match her old wardrobe. She chose stuff somewhere between average and expensive, but always whittled the saleswoman down to the lowest price she could get.

The woman dropped as low as she could. When Sylvie danced ahead to the next section, the saleswoman whispered, 'I could be fired for this.'

'You won't lose a cent,' he murmured, and she beamed at him. 'I'll pay the right price for anything she wants, but it's all contingent on absolute discretion—both with her and with anyone else.'

'Of course, Mr Hannaford.'

He waved her on to where Sylvie was staring wide-eyed at the latest style of TVs, DVD players and cabinets to hold both. She accepted the woman's explanation that there were special prices for invited customers tonight, and that there was on extra forty to fifty percent off almost everything in her price range.

She picked small things that would suit the cottage, and bargained everything she chose down to the lowest dollar possible. Sylvie was a natural bargainer, used to saving what pennies she could. It didn't matter a bit to her that he had millions and millions of pennies; she was so adorably proud of her bargains he'd never tell her the truth.

She surprised him with her choice of bed. He'd somehow thought she'd choose a four-poster or a white-painted princess-style, but she chose a solid double mattress and base, and bargained for and received free pillows and sheets, a quilt and a cover.

'Thank you for everything, Mr Hannaford. I really appreciate your thoughtfulness at coming with me to fulfil the contract,' she said earnestly, shaking his hand after he put his wallet away. 'The housekeeper's cottage will be perfect now.'

He blanked out for a second before he realised: of course she had to protect herself in front of the saleswoman. A man of his reputation, buying a house full of furniture for a woman could bring unwanted attention on her. His admiration at her cleverness mingled with strong disappointment that she needed to protect herself. That she thought of him that way instead of as a friend— she'd obviously forgotten she'd called him by name earlier.

But he played along, shaking her hand. 'You're welcome, Sylvie. I'm sorry I left it so late. The furniture should have been in the cottage ready when you started work.'

He arranged for delivery and installation with a heavy feeling in his gut. But how could he blame her? It was her integrity even more than her delicate, pretty face that made her so—

Irresistible. It was the only word for her—and with the admission he knew he was in trouble. He'd known the danger from the first minute—seen it from the moment she'd walked into his office that first day and he'd caught his breath at her freckled, pretty face and auburn curls.

Right from the first handshake, he'd known he was in trouble. For the first time, he'd touched a woman and didn't *ache* with a loss so unending he reached out in blind desperation, taking them to a hotel in the need to feel something, anything…

But when he touched Sylvie his whole body smiled. A stupid analogy, but that was how it felt to him. He felt the old feeling take over—one he hadn't felt since he'd heard the word *osteosarcoma*: simple everyday happiness.

Funny how people said that. Strange how people took for granted the fact that they could walk into their house at night, call for the person who belonged to them and they'd be there. They could walk into those arms and give a pecking kiss and say *How was your day?* without ever thinking it could end. Funny how damn *terrifying* it was to begin to believe he could have it.

At least he wasn't beginning to believe he deserved it.

CHAPTER EIGHT

'So NOW I know what paella tastes like,' Sylvie said on a sigh, taking another forkful. 'My stomach hurts, but I can't stop eating. It's wonderful.'

Mark grinned. 'It's worth the forty-five minute wait for it to come fresh to you. I still love paella, but I branch out now when I come here, and try new items on the menu.'

She nodded with undimmed enthusiasm, not looking at the rabbit concoction he was eating. She'd never been allowed to have a pet—it was a cost they hadn't been able to afford—but the rabbit reminded her of her best friend Scott's pet, Big Ears. She'd loved him so much when she was twelve.

'This place is so…wonderful,' she finished on a lame note, switching from *'romantic'* in a heartbeat, in case he thought she was thinking…

What she *was* thinking. What she wanted so much her pulse pounded until she could feel it all over her body. She had ever since that kiss on *Harbour Girl*.

'I've been coming here for ten years and I still love it. The atmosphere's amazing—it feels authentic. The owners came from Castile thirty years ago and opened it. I come here when I want authentic Spanish cooking and a private atmosphere.'

He spoke as normal. The soft candlelight, the exotic scent

and scene wasn't putting sensuous thoughts in *his* head, obviously. But then why would it when he was used to dating such beautiful women and was only here from obligation and perhaps pity?

So stop thinking about it. Stop wishing for the moon....

She had more than she'd dreamed of even a month ago: a dream job, a wonderful boss, and a growing friendship that blended past and present so seamlessly it was as if they'd always been friends. So why did she keep wishing, hoping?

Poor little Cinderella still wanted her prince to see her, to give her that perfect midnight kiss, to give her a happily-ever-after...

She watched his face in the warm, flickering light, smiling at her, and she caught her breath, knew she was blushing.

Seeming oblivious to her aching desire for him to touch her, he dipped his fork into the edge of her paella, closing his eyes in culinary rapture as he ate. 'Mmm...I never tire of the flavour.'

An ordinary act, but sharing plates seemed so intimate—and it emboldened her. Carefully avoiding the remains of the rabbit, she tried the spiced potatoes on his plate, and groaned with pleasure as the taste exploded on her tongue. 'Oh....oh, that's *superb*.' And if part of her pleasure was the intimacy of the moment, she never needed to tell him.

The waiter came to refill their glasses, but as before Mark covered his, claiming he was fine with water as he was driving. He nodded at Sylvie's glass. The waiter filled it with Castilian red.

Needing an excuse for her flushed cheeks, she sipped at it. 'Am I very pink? Drinking wine always makes me hot...'

She wanted to sink through the floor when he looked up, an arrested expression in his eyes, and lurking amusement.

'Oh...oh! I meant *physically* hot—not that I become sexier...um. *Oh.*' Somebody please call the fire brigade! Her face was on fire by this time. 'I think I'll stop talking now,' she whispered in agony. 'This is why I don't like to drink.'

His voice sounded rougher, colder than normal as he said, 'Say what you like. I won't take it the wrong way. I told you— I don't seduce employees.'

Thunk. So that was the sound of your heart hitting your feet… Suddenly the gentleness of all his kisses made horrible sense. He didn't want her; he was trying to *heal* her.

'You've been so kind to me, and I repay you by embarrassing you,' she whispered, her throat tight and her breathing constricted. 'Maybe we should forget dancing and go home. You've given me more than enough for one day.'

'How do you *do* it?' he demanded, his tone as strangled as hers. 'Every single time I act like a jerk, you make me feel even more of one.'

She squirmed in her seat, on the edge of foolish tears. 'I'm sorry—I'm sorry.'

'No, I'm sorry, Sylvie. I'm ruining your nice night.' His voice was warm again. She looked up in anguish and hope, and almost melted when she saw his smile lighting those golden-brown eyes in the firelight, his hair like streaky gold. 'Come on, let's dance.'

He stood and held his hand out to her. Lost in his swift turnaround, mesmerised by him in any mode, she put her hand in his.

A thrill ran through her like quicksilver—intense, almost painful. He was so *wonderful*, and the night, warm and shadowed in this redbrick Castilian cellar, with soft classical guitar music playing, was the stuff of dreams. It wasn't lessened by her plain dress and sandals, his jeans and shirt. They could be wearing sacks or the rags of a fairytale for all she cared or noticed. All she saw was him….

On the floor, he drew her into his arms, and showed her by example how to Salsa. He didn't speak of *dance space* or tell her to straighten her back. He held her and smiled at her, pulled her close and flung her away in Latin-American style. Sylvie felt the drama and excitement of the dance. She revelled in the hot pounding beat of the music, of her blood, loving being so close to him, aching to kiss him one more time—this time to kiss him thoroughly, woman to man.

Did she dare to tell him how she felt?

The music faded out, and a laughing voice sounded around the room. 'All you lovers out there, you have come on the perfect night. Tonight we want to teach all the women the Jaleo—a Romany dance of love and passion, guaranteed to make your man your slave!'

'Oh…oh,' she breathed. A *free* lesson in sensuous dancing…and Mark would see her dance. Her eyes wide, her heart pounding, Sylvie took a half-step.

'We should go. It's getting late.'

The abruptness of his words dashed cold water on her dreams, her budding courage; she turned her back on the stage and the dance he didn't want her to do for him.

'All right,' she said quietly.

It wasn't as if they were lovers, after all. It wasn't as if they were truly anything but boss and employee with a weird and painful history.

He frowned down at her, and she knew the intensity of her disappointment must be showing in her eyes. 'It's late, and we both have a lot to do tomorrow. I arranged for delivery of your furniture and the installation of the TV and DVD all at once. They'll come soon after five, so you need to be there to tell them where you want everything.'

Sylvie's heart, already splintering from the rejection he'd given without putting it into exact words, dropped to the floor and shattered in silence. 'It doesn't give me much time to re-move what I already have, does it?' Her face was white and her head high, jaw tight. 'But you knew it wasn't necessary, didn't you? Because you've been inside.'

He stilled completely. 'We'll talk at home.' He stalked over to the table, threw some bills down, waved at his friends and left the restaurant with a promise to be back soon.

He didn't speak as he handed her into the car, driving straight to Balmain and the house. Sylvie sat huddled in the seat, wanting to shiver in the warmth of the late summer night. What a *sap* she'd been to believe his lies....

He'd been looking after her for years, and he was doing the same now.

She hopped out of the car before he could touch her again and headed for the cottage, more than ready to be alone and cry out her humiliation in peace.

'Would you come in, please? We need to talk.'

'I'd rather not,' she replied, tight and hard.

'I'm not leaving you to think the worst of me. Come inside, please.'

His voice was still taut. She turned on her heel and headed for the house.

It was only when they were inside and safe from prying eyes that Mark softened. He sounded diffident as he picked his way over the shards of her independence. 'I know it must hurt your pride to take what you see as charity, but it isn't. I did give furniture to my first housekeeper—and it has been standard in my contracts with live-in housekeepers.'

'Was the contract I read this morning my original contract, or did you sneak in the cottage—*my home*—to replace it while I slept?' she demanded.

He sighed. 'It should have been in the original. I don't know why my lawyer neglected the clause this time.'

'But he did—you did—until you invaded my privacy and felt sorry for me.' She turned on him in a flash. 'Yes, I'm poor. I have nothing but a lumpy mattress and a rug. But I have my pride, my integrity. I kept that throughout the years when I lost everything else. You can't trample on my pride and then soothe it with your money! *I don't want it*,' she yelled, losing it as hot tears pricked at her eyes, filled and fell. To her surprise, she saw she was barefoot. She'd kicked off her sandals some time during the argument, and now she couldn't see them. 'Where are my sandals?' She had to get out of here before he hurt her more with his charity.

'Hypocrite.'

She gasped and whirled back to face him at the single cool word. 'What?'

He lifted a brow and said, still cool and in control, 'I said you're a hypocrite. So I trampled on your pride and independence?'

Confused, she nodded.

'Tell me how I did that.' He folded his arms and looked down at her from his full six feet to her five-one.

She blinked. 'You know how—with your false contracts and your furniture, splashing your money at me.'

'Right.' He took a step closer, and it was all she could do not to move back. 'I offended your pride by buying you a few pieces of furniture?'

'And by going into my home, my private place, and seeing what I didn't have. What did you do? Make a list of everything I needed?'

'Did *you*?' he shot back, taking another step.

Her hand gripped the arm of the sofa. 'Wh-what?'

He moved right in front of her, so close she could feel the heat of his anger coming from his skin. 'Did you make a list?' he asked with icy precision. 'That first day when you came into my house, did you check my cupboards, my windowsills and my walls and see what I didn't have, make a list of the things you thought I needed?'

She frowned. 'Of course—it's my job…' She faltered, remembering all the things she'd done that weren't in her job description.

'It's your job to clean my house and make breakfast. Anything else is optional and has been from day one.' He went on remorselessly. 'You bought things for me—things you felt my home was missing, the food you found out I liked but didn't have at the time, yes?'

Her eyes widened. 'Well…yes…'

'Did you intend to give me the receipts so I could reimburse you, since you haven't touched the grocery money I left for you?'

Her toe began scuffing on the living room rug. 'They were *gifts*, Mark.'

'As were mine to you—but whereas I accepted graciously—' he ignored her as she snorted, remembering his 2:00 a.m. wake-up call '—I knew you wouldn't.'

'I spent a measly hundred or two!' she cried. Well, four hundred. But she wasn't going to tell him that, either.

'How much do you have in the bank, Sylvie?'

The furious demand left her sinking deeper in the mire of confusion. 'Why would you want to know—?'

'How much do you have left after buying those gifts for me?' he repeated, with a quiet cold control that enraged her over again.

'One hundred and forty-seven dollars and something cents,' she shouted. 'Happy now? Knowing how far apart we are?'

'This isn't about who has what,' he said quietly. 'It's about why you feel you can give to me, but why it's *offensive* for me to give to you. Why it's okay for you to break the contract by making dinners, spending almost everything you have on decorating my house and buying me food I like, but you find it *offensive* for me to spend a far lower percentage of what I have on your happiness because I consider you a friend. You're allowed to care about me and give to me, but you won't allow me the same joy of giving because you have pride?'

Put like that, there was nothing to say… But…

'I wanted you to be *happy*,' she cried wretchedly.

'Well, I was happy today—until you threw it in my face. I thought we were more than boss and employee, Sylvie. I thought we were friends—both all those years ago and now.'

'We are,' she cried. 'But—but it's always been you giving to me.'

'Has it?' He reached out and took her hands in his. 'Leaving money aside, which isn't the most important thing a person can give, has it *always* been me doing the giving?'

His touch soothed and aroused her at the same time, put her mind in a whirl—forcing her to think harder. 'A wet flannel, a few hugs…some food. That's all.'

'A friend who sat with me when I was so alone and scared I could scream. An overburdened girl who stayed beside me and gave me a hug when no one else saw how badly I needed it. A child who showed me how to make and keep a promise even if it hurt.' He released her hands to cup her face in his palms. His beautiful eyes looked so deeply into hers she wanted to cry all over again. 'A woman who came back into my life, saw through my façade and told it like it is—who won't let me eat or live alone…who tells me off, risks her job for my sake. You forced me out of hiding, Sylvie. The things you want from me are for me. They have nothing to do with my money or fame.' He drew her into his arms and held her with a gentle affection that made the lump in her throat unbearable. 'Any rich person can throw money at a problem—but the gifts you give are far more priceless than money. Don't despise them, Sylvie.'

With a few simple sentences he'd done more than show her what she meant to him—he'd given her pride back, so precious to her. Giving in to her own need, she wrapped her arms around his waist, her cheek against his heart. 'You didn't keep your promise to her,' she whispered.

'I know.' He laid his chin on her hair. He didn't explain; he didn't have to.

'She'd be so sad, seeing you like this.'

He shook his head, messing her curls. 'Not like this, not tonight. She'd be glad you came back into my life. I've been alone too long, lived too many years without the kind of friendship we have.' He hesitated; she could feel the indecision in him before he said it. 'I don't want to break that friendship, Sylvie. I don't want you to feel pressured to leave your position. One day, when it's time for you to move on, just tell me and we'll still be friends.'

She fought the urge to turn her face, kiss the cotton and skin covering his heart, the loyal heart whose ice only existed because it still hadn't mended, because it still loved a girl long gone. She wanted to dash at the tears slipping down her face, but let them go. 'All right, then, I'll take the stupid furniture. I'll even *like* the stuff. Happy?'

He chuckled and ruffled her hair further with the underside of his chin. 'Yeah.'

'I should go,' she murmured, as the craving to kiss him became intolerable. 'It's late, and I have exams tomorrow. Today,' she amended, as she checked the grandfather clock slowly ticking with its copper pendulum.

'Bring your notes in in the morning and I'll quiz you.'

'Thanks.' The word was husky as she fought against saying the words that would break his sweet delusion that *one day* would ever come and she would move on.

'I'll bring home dinner for us tomorrow. You study when you come home from college.'

Home, he'd said. *For us*. As if there was an 'us' for them, or as if their shared meals were more than a boss being kind. Her heart soared with hope; her eyes twinkled. 'You really want fish and chips, don't you? Isn't my cooking good enough for you?'

He laughed. 'Most of the time—but this place does the best fish and chips in town.'

'All *right*,' she groaned. 'We'll have a picnic then.'

'Good.' He moved out of her arms, his mouth smiling a little, his eyes intense. 'Goodnight, Sylvie. Sleep well.' He was looking at her mouth—and she caught her breath. She almost believed he wanted to kiss her as much as she ached for it….

But it was too late now. The moment had come and gone on the dance floor.

So she smiled back and waved, as if she hadn't laid her heart all but bare for him to see, and his blinkered eyes had only seen half the truth. 'Thanks. You too.'

She left her discarded sandals somewhere, like Cinderella's glass slipper—but she wore a dress from the markets, her shoes were factory seconds and her beautiful lost prince had already fitted the right shoe to the perfect princess.

She'd find them tomorrow—when she returned to real life, when she was back where she belonged, cooking and cleaning for him.

CHAPTER NINE

WHAT was he *doing*?

He berated himself all the way home, with the scent of fresh fish and chips rising from the paper on the passenger seat making his stomach growl. This was stupid—worse, it was irresponsible. He'd known it from the start. Hadn't he argued with himself before dancing with her that first time?

Touching her had been the mistake of his life—

No, not quite, he thought wryly, *but it's the third*.

And still he couldn't wait to do it again…

'Well, about time, Hannaford. Talk about keeping a lady waiting. I was going to start the picnic without you.' She waved a near-empty wineglass at him.

She was sitting on the grass in the backyard, with a blanket, a bottle and two glasses when he emerged from the garage. In a simple sundress the colour of autumn leaves with crossover straps, her hair loose and her feet bare, she turned around from contemplating the dancing lights on the harbour at night and smiled at him—she didn't have a scrap of make-up on, and her clean-scrubbed freckled face was just so *adorable*— and every one of his fears and arguments was sucked down a drain called happiness.

'Without the food?' he teased her as he sat down.

She sighed. 'That was the part I couldn't work out.'

He grinned and laid the paper-wrapped food in the centre of the blanket. 'The feast awaits, my lady, with my deepest regrets for keeping you waiting.'

'You're not eating like that—all trussed up in a monkey suit. Up you go.' She picked up the food and carried it inside, putting it in the oven. 'A picnic isn't a picnic until you're barefoot and no fancy threads.'

When he returned in surf shorts and a T-shirt, feet bare, she nodded in beaming approval, said in mock-admiration, 'You look hot,' and handed him a glass.

He threw a brief glance at the bottle: non-alcoholic. And though it meant she knew part of his secret, he relaxed and lifted the glass. 'To howling cats and Ginger wannabes.'

'Done.' She sipped at her drink. 'I'm so glad you prefer non-alcoholic. I become pretty silly after one glass. Could never handle alcohol at all.'

No way was he taking that less-than-subtle opening and telling her the real reason why he never drank. He'd rather she thought him a recovered alcoholic than knew about Robbie Allsopp, a kid having a good time on his bike until a binge-drunk seventeen-year-old, wild with grief and loss, trying to forget the past, sped around a corner...

So he asked, 'So...you think I look hot?' Teasing her again, inhaling the sweet scent of talcum powder or some similar perfume. 'Did you mean physically, as in from the heat, or dare I hope you no longer consider me downright ugly?'

She gave an exaggerated sigh as she laid the feast open. 'I told you you're good-looking once, Hannaford. Stop fishing for compliments.' She helped herself to food without a plate, and closed her eyes.

'Another hungry person's prayer?' he asked when she began to eat.

She sighed again and rolled her eyes. 'My faith might be simple, but don't knock it because you're an infidel.'

He shook his head and picked up some fish, smearing it with lemon and tartare sauce. 'A big judgement call for someone who's never asked me what I believe.'

'Are we turning theological now?' she complained. 'I'm too hungry to discuss the mysteries of life.' She turned and lay on her tummy on the blanket, her body facing the harbour, her face ecstatic as she ate. 'A clear summer night, wine, ocean views and marvellous food. Where else would you find this luxury?'

He almost laughed, thinking of any of his usual dates' reactions to a barefoot fish-and-chips picnic in his backyard; but then no other woman he'd met was quite like Sylvie, revelling in every experience that came her way. 'No idea.'

'The fish is perfect—not overcooked or soggy. Where did you buy it?'

He was deriving more enjoyment from watching her eat than he was from his own food. 'The fish markets beneath the Anzac Bridge. They batter and fry it while you wait. It's from a fresh catch.'

'Ah.' She nodded. 'Far better than Greasy Joe's down the road from our house. He half-cooks the battered fish and leaves it there for hours until some poor sap gets hungry enough to order it. And don't get me started on the potato scallops.' She shuddered.

'Is it really called Greasy Joe's?' he asked, since that was an Aussie euphemism for most fish and chip/hamburger stores.

She frowned and pursed her mouth. 'Yeah, right,' she snorted. 'How far from your roots have you come, Hannaford? All those five-star restaurants and fancy charity dos have made you forget the important things.'

'Like Greasy Joe's?' he retorted, holding in a grin. 'That's important?'

Her chin on one palm as she ate, she nodded, with an adorable seriousness that made him want to laugh at her. 'It's the little things—like fast food and picnicking in the backyard…tinkering with improvements to go-carts and bike wheels instead of working on things that will sell around the world…having fun in a workshop here instead of the big fancy one with shiny doodads you've no doubt got in Howlcat Industries—they're the things that make life meaningful. Success and wealth can't make you happy if you forget who you are.'

'And who am I?' he asked coldly.

'A guy who likes fish and chips in the backyard but probably hasn't done it in years,' she said softly. 'A guy who probably remembers the best times of his life as inventing stuff that would never work in the smelly, dusty old workshop his mum and dad let him have.' She looked away, frowning over the harbour, and he knew she was going to say something that would rip out his guts before she said it. 'A guy who held his girlfriend's vomit bowl and changed her sheets and pyjamas because she felt humiliated when the staff did it.'

'How the *hell*—?' Then he stared at her with narrowed eyes. Though not shocked, he was more appalled than he'd expected to be. He scrambled to his feet. 'You talked to her?'

She nodded without apology. 'I used to read to her sometimes, when you were all gone, and we'd talk. Or she would.' With a frown and a sigh she said, 'I think it was a relief to her to talk to me. She didn't have to pretend she wasn't scared with me, or act strong and say it was okay. Sometimes we lashed out, or cried together. Neither of our lives was fair…what was happening to us.'

Air whooshed from his lungs; he sat down before he fell down. 'She sent you here, didn't she? She foisted one of her impossible promises on you—*a thirteen-year-old kid.*'

Her eyes shimmering with tears, she nodded.

For the first time in many years he felt simmering anger at

Chloe. How could she have done that—and to a girl who'd had more than enough burdens to cope with? 'What was it?' he asked with grim foreboding. 'What did she make you promise?'

After a visible hesitation she said it—with a simplicity that told him it was a relief for her to tell him. 'If, by the time I was grown up and free from my obligations, you still hadn't fulfilled your promise to her, she wanted me to come back into your life, and—and be your friend, make you smile again.' She smiled mistily with a love for his dead wife undimmed through the years. 'She said I had a knack for that.'

'In general, or with me?' he asked, unable to let the subject go although he knew they were straying into dangerous waters.

She sighed. 'Both, I guess, since I could always make her smile, too.'

Fury filled him and overflowed, despite knowing Chloe had been right—maybe he was so furious *because* she was right. Gratitude and guilt mingled with the horror of what Chloe had done to Sylvie. 'She had no right to ask it of you. A girl already overburdened!'

'She knew you, didn't she? She knew if you ended up giving your promise you'd be lying.' Her gaze rested on him. In the night lights sending soft light down from the garage roof and the flood of summer moonlight her eyes took on a glow from within, looked darker, like mulled wine through firelight. 'It's not a crime to love someone so much you want them to be happy. I don't think she should have forced you into your promise, and I'm sure she thought I was too young to remember what I said I'd do, or remember you, either, by the time I was grown up. But it eased her fears for you—it made her passing easier.'

'You were only thirteen. It's been fifteen years.'

She shrugged. 'There are some people you just can't forget. Some promises stay with you through the years.'

Mark felt differently, but said nothing. Sylvie had been unlike any kid he'd known, with a compassion and maturity few adults ever achieved. He couldn't imagine anyone but her remembering a promise—even one of this magnitude.

'She was…unforgettable.' He heard the jerking of his voice. Yeah, he was mad at Chloe and she deserved it, but still he missed her.

'So were you,' Sylvie said softly.

He started and stared at her. 'Only because you saw me in the tabloids.'

'That was it in part, and the money you gave us,' she admitted without shame. 'But you underrate yourself,' she went on, in that tender, dreaming voice. 'I was a lonely, romantic kid with too much to do physically, but my mind was free. So I dreamed a lot.' She smiled at him. 'I'd see your picture somewhere and I'd dream of you. You became the prince of my fairytales—and Chloe was the princess. I wanted to be the princess—as girls do—but I never could see myself that way. I was always the one cleaning up after Prince Mark and Princess Chloe. And here I am, still doing it. It's my fate, I tell you,' she said in a mock-melodramatic tone, and laughed.

She didn't sound in the least self-pitying, yet Mark forgot his anger, his feeling of being overwhelmed by the intrusions into his personal life—he forgot about himself altogether. He ached for the overworked child she'd been, dreaming dreams of becoming his *housemaid*—and that was what she'd become. She'd come down from being the princess of fairy stories to being a real maid. Her dreams had narrowed to a life of servitude.

So he was going to make her feel like a princess….

'I have a charity event I need to attend Friday night—' he began, but her laughter had stilled, and she was shaking her head with a frantic kind of determination. 'Why?' he asked, curt with the sting of rejection. 'Surely there's no point in denying this thing between us?'

'Maybe, but not in public. I won't do it.' She jumped to her feet and began scrabbling around to clean up.

He laid a hand on her arm. 'Stop it, Sylvie, and talk to me. Being famous is part of my life, and if you're going to be any part of it—'

'I'm not,' she shot back, so bluntly it took him aback. 'I'm your housekeeper, Mark. *Your employee*. I belong *here*—this is where I stay.'

His eyes narrowed. He needed no clarification on what she meant. 'Then why did you start something you had no intention of finishing by kissing me? You always knew I had a public profile. It's part of who I am.'

'You kissed me, actually—and we played house for a couple of days. I always knew that was all we'd ever have.' She picked up the paper again. 'This is who *I* am, Mark—the cleaner. What we are is worlds apart.'

With a lightning movement he brought his arms down on the wrappers in her hands, scattering them. 'Don't you *ever* demean yourself that way again,' he snarled, grabbing her hands in his to stop her from bolting—but she didn't struggle, just looked up at him with those big eyes of hers, and he felt a hard thrill run through him. She did trust him, as she'd claimed this morning. 'You're worth so much more than you set yourself!'

The look in her eyes was pure puzzlement as she stared at him. Her chest heaved. 'I'm fine with who and what I am.'

'Are you?' he said, eyes narrowed. 'Then why do you lower what you do? It's *just* home-baked muesli. It's *just* lasagne. I'm *just* the cleaner. You do it all the time. What you are as a person isn't defined by the work you do!'

'Isn't it?' she panted, facing him down, all five-one of her, looking up at him unintimidated. 'It's how the world defines

people. *I'm a doctor. I'm a lawyer. I'm an inventor.*' Her jaw
tightened as she said again, 'I'm a cleaner.'

'And why is that?' Hands tightening on her arms, but
without force, he glared at her. 'Why did you start cleaning
in the first place?'

The confusion grew in her eyes. 'You know why. My family…'

'Exactly. You did it to take care of your family. You kept
them together. You paid the bills. Your father died in peace at
home, and your brothers are all respected professional men
because of your sacrifices.'

She was shaking her head before he finished. 'No. That was
you. Without the trust funds you set up—'

He had to struggle now to hold on to his anger and allow
himself to say what she needed most to hear. 'Your brothers are
all highly intelligent men who'd have found a scholarship
somewhere. All I did was give them a leg up. It was *you* who
saved them. They had time to study and get the marks they did
because you did everything for them. From the time your
mother became sick—when you were only *eight*—you began
your adulthood. By the time you were thirteen you were already
everything to your family: mother, nurse, cheer squad, cook
and, yes, cleaner. *You* kept your family together. You gave your
brothers a normal life at the expense of your own.'

She closed her eyes. 'It wasn't like that.…'

'Wasn't it?' he asked softly, the urge to touch her becoming
unbearable. 'Funny, that's what they tell me.'

Her eyes flew open. 'You've seen the boys?'

'I called them all today.'

She stiffened. 'What did you want? What did they say?'

'I didn't ask about *that*, though it was pretty hard holding
back,' he said, knowing what she feared most. 'I could tell
Simon knew.'

'What did they tell you?'

'Apart from what I just said, you mean?' He shrugged. 'They're your brothers and totally loyal to you. What do you think they said? They said I'd have to hear it from you.'

She relaxed visibly. 'Why?' she whispered, and he knew what she wanted to ask.

'Because you fascinate me. I don't know why you set such low labels on yourself and what you do for others,' he said quietly. 'You won't tell me. I want to know why you break your back trying to make others' lives work for them, and why, though you smile and laugh, there's so much sadness beneath the mask. You'll do anything to make people happy, but you seem to think *you* don't deserve the kind of happiness you give to others. You even brought a lone-wolf inventor out of living a lie with your wisdom and courage, your unfailing optimism in a life that would have made so many people hard and bitter,' he added, wanting to touch her so badly it felt like a fist squeezing his heart.

She shrugged again. 'A few things I bought. Some home-made meals. It's no big deal.'

'You're doing it again—demeaning yourself and what you do,' he said quietly. 'Don't you see that cleaning is the least of what you do, who you are? You're the best friend I've had since she died. You make me look forward to getting up every day. You're so beautiful you make me ache, yet you turn your back on personal happiness, only seeing what you can do for others.' He drank in the warmth of her cheek against his palms, only realising he'd cupped her face after the coldness in him diminished. 'You're a woman of extraordinary strength and compassion, Sylvie Browning,' he murmured as he bent to her. She lifted her face, waiting. 'You're exactly the sort of woman I knew you'd become. That's why I never forgot you. You were amazing at eight, incredible by ten, unforgettable at thirteen, and you're even more amazing now.'

And then, finally, he kissed her.

For a moment she didn't respond. Then with a tiny moan she moved into his arms, kissing him back, warm and sweet as marshmallows toasted over a fire, soft as his garden on a spring night, like daisies when they'd begun to bloom. Even her kiss made him think of sunshine and smiles and laughter. He was addicted to the way she made him feel.

Here in her arms, held in thrall by the ordinary everyday happiness of touching her, he knew the truth: he was falling for her, bungee-jumping at breakneck speed into love with an adorable, wonderful woman who refused to come into his world...and he could no longer go into hers.

'Is what happened to you the reason you won't go public with me?' he murmured against her mouth, and held her against him as she stiffened. 'It's not what's between us—we both know this is too strong to walk away from—and it's not that you're not good enough for me. If anything, it's the other way around. So tell me, Sylvie. I deserve to know.'

He felt the shuddering exhaled breath come from the deepest part of her, felt it against his shirt, warming his skin, and he felt absurd hope.

Then she said softly, 'I can't. I *can't.*'

For a moment the streaking pain of her rejection felt like crash-cart paddles on his chest, stopping his heart. Then, too late, he remembered the reason he *didn't* deserve to know— the reason he had to walk away from this, from her—and he nodded. 'All right.'

She looked up at him. 'All right? Just like that?'

She was so pretty, looking up at him in wonder, as if he'd pulled her from a burning car wreck. Keeping her secret from him meant that much to her—and though it hurt he couldn't make himself do the noble thing and walk away.

And too late he understood why. Though part of him still

loved Chloe, there was another person who'd always been snuggled inside his heart. The girl Mary had walked inside his soul years ago, claiming her share of his love by being who she was. As a woman Sylvie had walked back into his life with that same brave, defiant smile, the same courageous outspokenness and unstinting giving, and his ice—had melted. Just like that.

Falling for Sylvie? Nah, he was all the way gone—completely and utterly in love. And though he knew it couldn't last for them, he had some work to do before she left his life. He'd do whatever it took to make her see her worth, to show her what an extraordinary, *wonderful* person she was.

'Yeah, just like that,' he said huskily. 'So, Miss Browning, would you care to dance?'

She blinked, drew in a slow breath; her eyes lit and sparkled. Her hands, still around his neck, drew him down for a long kiss, her fingers caressing his hair. The sparkling joy that was Sylvie wrapped around him and filled him to overflowing.

'Why, yes, Mr Hannaford, I'd be honoured,' she replied when they finally, reluctantly, let go.

Then she shoved the papers from dinner in the recycling bin, shoved the glasses in his hand and snatched up the wine bottle. She took his free hand and led him into the house, put the remnants of their picnic on the counter, and led him on into the ballroom.

Throwing open the wide French doors, she ran past him with a sweet, naughty smile and put on some music. 'We're shifting gear tonight.'

Rhythmic clapping filled the room; an eighties classic boomed out. Sylvie did a little shimmy and pointed at him. She pulled him to her by his shirt; laughing, he came, and they jumped around. She sang to him in her pretty, slightly tinny voice.

If he'd never forgotten her before, he knew he'd spend the rest of his life regretting the months of stupidity that made him forever unworthy of this strong, beautiful woman who'd over-

come the tragedy and drudgery of her past to reach for every
particle of happiness she could find and share that shimmering
joy in living with him. She'd brought him back to life, taught
him to let go of the past, to seek happiness and hold on to it
while it was there.

As they danced for the next half-hour to all her favourite
songs, he faced the truth: he didn't deserve a woman as *wonderful* as Sylvie, and though it made his guts twist and his heart
scream with denial he had to accept it.

So he'd take what he could get with her, heal her of her hurts
if he could and then let her go with a smile.

But, dear God in heaven, what would become of him then?

CHAPTER TEN

'So HOW do I look?'

On the sofa, scribbling down notes for an assignment due next week, Sylvie tossed an angry glance at the stairwell—and lost the ability to speak. In a tux he was breathtaking. She couldn't *breathe*....

She squashed the unreasonable resentment that he was still going—taking one of his usual women. He'd told her this charity event was vital; he'd asked her first. She had no right to be jealous or to wonder if he'd be home tonight.

But she was, and she did.

She gulped down the screaming need to say something to keep him here with her and gave him a smile that felt brittle on her lips. 'Hot, boss. Totally hot. Your date's got no hope of competing.'

He came down the stairs and stood in front of her. 'There's no contest,' he said with soft meaning. 'I needed someone to sit with, Sylvie.'

Her stomach clenched hard; it was all she could do not to press her lips together. 'I know. It's cool.' *Don't ask...don't say it...* 'Cinderella doesn't have a dress to match that tux, boss, and no fairy godmother, either. You're better off with what's-her-name.' She wheeled away from him. 'Anyway, I have a hot-ter date than yours could ever be,' she announced, with a gaiety that sounded as much of a lie as the smile she'd given him. 'I should head out.'

'What?' He turned her back round, his eyes boring into hers. 'Who is he?'

She stared up at him and panted. 'Have I asked who *your* date is?'

He growled, 'Amie's an old friend in a long-term relationship. She agreed to sit with me because her boyfriend's running this gig. It's the only reason I'm going—to support a friend's pet cause. It's for Medicin Sans Frontiers.'

She almost melted on the spot. 'And my date is an adorable seven-month-old called Nicky Browning. Drew and Shelley need a night out. The baby's just over croup.'

Mark laughed and pulled her up into his arms. 'Have I ever told you you're a brat?' He looked down at her for an intense moment, then he kissed her with a lingering sweetness that *did* make her melt. 'Keep tomorrow free… Oh, and Sunday, as well. Tell your brothers you'll be out of town until Sunday night.'

Delight flooded her. A full weekend with Mark?

Where?

Aiming for a careless tone, she asked, 'Oh? Why and wherefore? And where?'

'It's a secret…but you can stop worrying. It's nothing that puts us in the public eye. In fact, it's very private—and we have separate rooms,' he said softly, and shivers of arousal, disappointment and relief raced through her. 'I'm not asking you, Sylvie, I'm telling you. You're coming with me.'

She had no intention of denying him—or herself. 'I'd bow in submission, my lord, but it's rather difficult at this present moment,' she retorted with a laugh, wiggling against him.

'If you move like that much longer I won't be going anywhere tonight but here with you,' he growled.

She felt a frisson of panic run through her. Immediately he let her down to the floor and released her.

'It's getting better, isn't it—the fear?' he asked softly, smiling down at her.

Startled to realise he was right, she nodded. The fear, a constant companion since she was fifteen, was receding so fast she couldn't see where it had gone. When Mark touched her, she felt not merely cherished and safe…she felt *beautiful*.

'Are you ready? I'll drop you to Drew's on the way.'

Relieved that he didn't probe her when she didn't know what to say—how could she tell him, *I'm only better when the man touching me is you?*—her brow lifted. 'Are you serious? You'll drop me to Ermington on your way to Darling Harbour?'

He grinned. 'Trust you to argue with me even if it saves you a train and a bus ride. It's only fifteen minutes out of the way. Come on.'

'You'll be late.'

He shrugged. 'I'm stag tonight anyway, so who'll care?'

A vision flashed into her brain: a stunningly attired Mark making a late entrance, all the single women taking note that he was alone…

She almost said she'd change and go with him, or told him to forget going away for the weekend. Pride and jealousy were a self-destructive combination—one she never knew she'd feel for any man—but this wasn't any man; this was Mark. After swallowing the hard ball in her throat, she summoned up a bright false smile. 'Let's go, then.'

And while he did his thing—out in a tux with all the beautiful people—she did what she did best: cooked and cleaned and changed dirty nappies…and wondered when he'd be home.

When she came home, after eleven-thirty, the big house was in darkness. And though she knew it was stupid she sat in the cottage, studying again—or trying to—knowing she was waiting for a light to come on.

It was almost one before the lights came on in the garage, and she felt pure bliss flooding her soul. He didn't bring women home. Rita, his mother, had assured her of that. And though it was ridiculous, she had the sense that he'd come home to *her*.

She switched off her lights before he saw a foolish, needy woman waiting for her man to come home…because he wasn't and never could be hers for long.

'Oh. *Oh*,' she breathed, at Mark's latest surprise of the morning.

He'd already made breakfast for her: her favourite Sunday pancakes but on a Saturday, with strawberries and maple syrup and fresh coffee. And now he wouldn't let her clean the mess, but said he'd hired a cleaning woman for the day.

'And don't pack a thing—you won't need it,' he said with a mysterious air. 'This weekend you don't do a thing but enjoy yourself.'

Her brows lifted in wonder, but the gentleness in his eyes, the acceptance that she was far from ready for the next step in a strange half-relationship with too many secrets, helped her trust in him to overcome the panic. She felt absurdly shy as she nodded.

'Good. Now, take this.' He held out a long embossed box to her, with the name of a famous designer on it.

She gasped and took it, her fingers trembling. She retreated to the cottage for a few minutes, and came out wearing a deceptively simple dress. It was pure linen, a soft leaf-green, with a light autumn-coloured jacket. There was also a pair of matching sandals, by a label she'd only dared peek at in store windows now and then, for they cost a month's mortgage payments. She came back to the house, intensely shy and a little proud of herself—and a woman was waiting with a mobile hairdressing unit. She washed and treated Sylvie's hair, and dried it so the curls bounced and shone.

'You have such lovely natural highlights in your hair I don't need to add any—and I'd rather leave it curling like this,' the woman said, smiling at Sylvie. 'You have hair women pay hundreds for.'

She'd never thought of her hair that way before. She flicked a glance at Mark, who was working on some kind of drawing design at his desk. He turned and smiled at her, nodding in agreement. 'I love her hair as it is,' was all he said, and her insides turned to jelly.

After the woman was gone he smiled again, a more intimate, private look in his eyes. 'You look beautiful.'

Then he led her out—not the back way to the car, but to the front door...

She blinked hard, winking away the silly tears forming in her eyes, and turned to him, feeling the radiance shining from her pores. 'This day has been—been...'

He touched her face with an expression approaching tenderness. 'This is just the start.' He opened the door of a big white stretch limousine with a flourishing bow. 'My lady.'

As if she truly was a lady he handed her inside—and she saw the champagne glasses, the bottle and the crushed strawberries.

'It's non-alcoholic, of course,' he said as he slid in beside her. 'As we both prefer.' His eyes twinkled.

Unable to hold back anymore, she cupped his face in her hands and kissed him, soaking herself in the joy of being in his arms as he drew her closer with a soft groan. With no words to say how she felt, she let her lips speak to him in silence.

When they finally parted, he whispered, 'You're welcome.' He reached for the strawberries and filled the base of the glasses.

By the time she'd finished her first strawberry champagne in a limousine, the driver had pulled up at Kingsford-Smith Airport.

With her mouth falling open, she turned to Mark. 'Um, where are we going? I don't have a passport....'

He leaned over and whispered in her ear, 'Ever heard of Turtle Island?'

Her eyes wide, she shook her head. 'Is that in the Great Barrier Reef?'

He kissed the ear he spoke into. 'It certainly is. It's the most exclusive island in the chain north of Cairns. It's where people go when they don't want gossip or the press.'

Touched to the deepest part of her heart by his thoughtfulness—and at this weekend that must be taking a massive bite out of even such a rich man's wallet—she laid her head on his shoulder. 'I don't know what to say.'

'What you said before, and the way you said it, was pretty well perfect,' he replied, alluding to her kiss with a teasing tone. 'But we should wait until we're on the jet.'

She blinked. 'We're going on a jet?'

His brows lifted. 'I promised you privacy. Big-name journalists quite often get paid first- or business-class flights to their assignments—and while they may not care what I do and who with, they might pass on the info to a contact with lower journalistic principles.'

He'd thought of everything.

Feeling like a true VIP, she enjoyed being ushered through an area reserved only for those taking private charters. Mark generously tipped those who expedited their travel. Then they were on a small jet, with wide seats and luxurious appointments.

Sylvie clung tight to Mark's hand all the way through her first take-off, squealing with the losing-her-tummy feeling. 'The boys and I went to Australia's Wonderland once, with the people from Stewart House, and the Bush Beast felt just like that!'

She could have bitten out her tongue at the thoughtless words. *Stewart House?* Why didn't she just take a permanent marker and write *'charity child'* on her forehead? They'd only ever asked for help once, when she'd become too sick to care for the family, and a neighbour, concerned, had called the famous charity. For a year they'd offered housekeeping help, free trips to the doctor for her father and fun outings for all four kids.

Her father had tried to call an end to it after that year, saying there must be thousands of people who truly needed help and they didn't. For once Sylvie, only fourteen at the time, had bucked against him, saying *she* didn't need the help, but the boys needed it. Drew and Simon in particular were doing nothing but work and study, and would have rebelled if those treats had been taken away from them.

Dad had been in a wheelchair by then, with the scleroderma that would eventually take his life, helpless against her angry demand. He'd capitulated with a bitterness that still rang in her heart. *'If you're willing to lower yourself enough to take charity, I'm not!'*

After a pregnant silence Mark said, 'So, I remember mentioning the way you speak to me the best…?'

He drew her into his arms, and as they kissed the churning confusion in her heart became lost in the haunting beauty of his touch, in the joy of all he'd done to make this weekend perfection.

The only question was: what could she ever give him in return?

'So, which of the dresses would you like to wear tonight?' asked the beaming saleswoman at the resort boutique.

Still unable to believe this was her life, even if only for a day or two, Sylvie said, 'Which do you think, Beverley?'

Beverley's smile grew even wider, more maternal, though she was barely forty. 'I definitely think the ivory-gold. Soft autumn tones bring out the highlights in your hair and make your eyes look incredible. And we have the perfect shoes—some gorgeous russet two-inch-heeled courts—' She shook her finger as Sylvie tried to turn down the offer. 'Mr Hannaford was very specific. *"Spoil her completely,"* were his exact words. *"Show her everything, give her anything she wants."'*

If she hadn't already been totally crazy about the man, those words would have done it. All her life she'd dreamed of one fairytale night, and he was giving it to her… 'I know—he would say that. But—'

Beverley interrupted, laughing. 'But nothing. This is my weekly quota you're denying! Just look at the shoes before you say another word, okay?'

She was vacillating already, and Beverley's quota comment had weakened her; she allowed the saleswoman to bring out 'a few' boxes. And once she saw the russet shoes she was as big a sucker as any other woman. *Shoes…beautiful shoes.* Six pairs of them, one for each of her new outfits.

And then came the stunning jewellery, the exquisitely light make-up…

That night, when Mark knocked on the door of her deceptively simple beachfront cabin, she was in the shimmering ivory-gold silk dress and the russet shoes, make-up on, simple ruby studs in her ears and a pendant around her neck—she'd refused even to consider the diamonds.

'You're beautiful,' he said simply when she opened the door to him. He held out a single amber rose with a deep golden heart, matching the colours she liked best.

He'd noticed.

The moonlight on the soft-lapping waves framed him like a halo. She caught her breath, wondering anew that this was her life even for a day; that this man—this incredible, giving man could want her. The glow in her heart had to be reflected on her face.

'Thank you.' He was more beautiful than she could ever be—with or without the classic tuxedo he wore.

'What, no comments about me being hot?' He tipped up

her face, smiling with his eyes, as well as his mouth. Smiling with his heart.

'You said the words I wanted to. You're a word thief, Hannaford,' she murmured, wrinkling her nose at him in an effort to be playful when all she wanted was—

'Then I take them back.' As she glared at him in indignation, he added, 'You look perfect. Well, almost perfect.' He pulled a handkerchief and dusted it over her nose and cheeks, removing the covering powder. 'I like your freckles.'

She had to close her mouth somehow or she'd blurt it out. *I love you.* No way would she put *that* burden on him. He was fond of her; he wanted to help her; he desired her—and that was enough of a miracle in itself. His love belonged to Chloe. If that hadn't changed in all these years he wasn't going to fall for someone like her.

There you go, demeaning yourself again. But if he knew her secret he wouldn't look at her as if she was wonderful to him. He'd leave her life at a million miles a minute.

The time was coming; she knew she couldn't stop it. Keeping her secret had begun to feel as if she was lying to him. Something died inside her every time he was so gentle and compassionate when she didn't deserve it. So she'd take all the joy she could with him, then tell him the truth and leave with only the same regrets she'd had when she came.

'I want to kiss you,' she whispered, as intense as a summer day before storm.

'Then do it. Kiss me, Sylvie.' He came into the room, closed the door behind him and stood before her, giving her choice and power.

She only hesitated for a moment. Then she moved her hands to his shoulders and up, winding her fingers through his hair. She breathed in his scent, felt the heat and need in his skin, and the now-familiar pulse of excitement and desire took over.

'Mark, oh, *Mark*…' She lifted up on her toes, brought him down to her and kissed him.

When he stayed still, using only his mouth to arouse her, she gave an impatient moan and put his hands on her waist, coming closer, deepening the kiss. Moving against his hard, ready body only made her crave more of him. Her hands grew feverish, needing to touch him, all of him; her lips wandered down his throat. She was aching to open his shirt and press her lips to his heated skin. She pulled at his tie.

He put his hand over hers. 'Sylvie.' The way he said her name—so gravelly with rough desire—sent hurtling thrills though her. 'You know where this is heading?'

'Yes, yes…' She drew him down for another kiss. 'I need you, Mark. I'm aching, burning inside. I need to touch you, to kiss your skin. I want you now…'

He groaned and kissed her, his hands moving over her through the silky dress until she writhed against him, making soft noises of feminine arousal; he slowed the pace, nuzzling her mouth and whispering between brushing kisses: 'To-night, sweetheart, if you're still ready, we'll make love all night.'

Disappointment jack-knifed through her. 'Not now?'

He bent until their foreheads touched. His smiling eyes still held the same frustration she felt. 'We can if you really want to—but it will wreck my surprise for you.'

Despite her body's screaming need, her eyes lit up. 'Another one? What is it?'

He chuckled. 'If I told you it wouldn't be a surprise—and I think I've been answered. Let's go down for dinner.'

Her gaze searched his face. 'Mark…I didn't mean to…'

A finger touched her mouth, silencing her. 'I'm the one who stopped, not you.'

'Did—did I…?'

A rueful grin touched his mouth. 'Yes, sweetheart, you did. More than any woman I've known since Chloe.'

She held in a gasp. It was the first time he'd said Chloe's name to her—and another thrill, almost painful in its intensity, shivered through her body. 'Are you all right?'

'I'll survive.' He kissed her nose. 'Whether we make love tonight or not.' He must have seen the doubt in her eyes, for his face turned serious. 'Men only say they can't control their re-actions so they rouse a woman's guilt, Sylvie, make her give in—or they blame her for what they've done. A real man—one who truly cares about the woman he's with—can wait for her to be ready. Even if it's painful at times.' His grin became more rueful, laughing. 'Like now, in my current predicament. But I can wait for you,' he finished, soft with meaning.

A lump filled her throat and wouldn't be swallowed down. 'I care about you, too,' she whispered. *I love you. I adore you.*

Then tell him the truth, her conscience murmured persistently.

Soon... But I can't tell him now and ruin our night. Please let me hold it back another day. Just one more memory with him...

Mark held out his arm to her. 'Shall we go?'

Trying to tamp down the love shimmering in her eyes and heart, she put her arm through his and they headed out into the soft, heady tropical night.

After an indescribably delicious meal, and a 'torte from heaven' which they'd shared—one plate, two forks—Mark stood and held out his hand to her. 'No lesson tonight,' was all he said. 'No waltzing. Just you and me.'

She rose and moved into his arms, and they swayed together on the shining parquet dance floor with barely a whisper of air between them.

She'd spent so many years working out the one perfect moment for them, and the rare times she'd found herself this close to Mark in her dreams it *had* been perfect. And here they were: Mark in the tuxedo of a prince, she in a golden-ivory dress fit for a princess, and they were on the dance floor.

It wasn't quite perfect. This wasn't a ball, they weren't waltzing, and the crown of her girlish fantasies was missing. But she was locked in his arms, and he was looking at her as if she was beautiful and special—all the things she knew she'd never be…but he believed it.

This was a moment in her life that reached higher than even the most perfect dream.

'This has been the happiest day of my life,' she whispered in his ear. 'It only needs one final thing to be perfect.' *Seeing the sun rise in your arms, knowing we're lovers*.

She was ready. Fear, her constant companion, still stalked her steps—but she knew that in Mark's arms desire and love would conquer the ancient enemy.

'There's still one surprise to go, remember?' he murmured, with a definite teasing twinkle in his eyes. 'You wanted something last week, but I took it away from you.'

She blinked. Right now she couldn't think of a single thing…

At that moment Mark nodded—and the emcee said quietly, 'At the special request of one of our clients, we have a real treat for you tonight, ladies and gentlemen—especially the gentlemen. Please welcome, from Castile via Sydney, the Colchero Dancers!'

Amid muted but polite applause from the startled guests, the soft clicking whirr of castanets and the muted strains of a flamenco guitar filled the air, and the dancers came on stage. With a confident smile a Spanish woman stepped forward. 'Good evening, ladies and gentlemen. I am Isabella,' she crooned into the microphone. 'Tonight the Colchero Dancers will not Flamenco, Salsa or Sarabande. Tonight we'll teach the ladies here the true roots of the Merengue—the dance of passion and excitement. The Jaleo is a traditional Romany-Spanish dance of desire unfulfilled, danced by a woman to entice her man. Tonight we'll teach you women how to make your man your slave!' Isabella beckoned. 'I call all the ladies to the stage!'

Sylvie gasped, and Mark stepped away from her with a wink. 'Go for it, sweetheart.'

'I c-can't!' she stammered, her eyes clinging to him for re-assurance. 'I'll ruin this beautiful dress, and the shoes…'

'As the rock you gave me says, "Believe". And I do, Sylvie—at last, after all these years, I believe. I believe in *you*.' His eyes shone with faith. 'The dress and the shoes are replaceable—the girls will look after you.'

Her mouth fell open and she stared at him in wonder. He'd done all this for her?

'You're making me cry,' she whispered in a choked voice.

'Not now, Ginger,' he said softly. 'Go and dance for me.'

In a daze, she headed towards the stage and walked up the stairs.

'So we have you here at last,' a laughing female voice, heavily accented, whispered to her. 'We saw it last week—our old friend Marco has finally found the one to melt the ice in his soul—but your passion still only simmers; we can show you how to bring it to fruition. He flew us here first-class last night, with a week's accommodation, so he could make his woman happy. So, come—you will dance for your man!'

Within moments she was transformed. They wound a red scarf in her hair, put hoops in her ears and red lipstick on her mouth; they sprayed her with rose scent. They hitched up the skirt of her dress, holding it up with another sash. 'Instruments of torture,' the woman who'd introduced herself as Isabella said in disgust as she pulled off Sylvie's beautiful shoes. 'You will dance barefoot.'

'But…but…' Sylvie stammered. *My shoes, my shoes*!

Isabella covered Sylvie's lips with a finger. 'I have watched you—both last week and here. You glow when you are in his arms. Your eyes ache. You want this man, yes? You want to be his lover?'

Sylvie gulped, bit her lip. 'Yes,' she finally whispered.

'Then learn from the best. Seduction begins with the foot. Come, you are ready to learn.' Isabella drew her to the front of the stage and the other women surrounded her. She clicked her fingers and the sensuous melody of Spanish guitar filled the air again.

'Follow us,' Isabella whispered to Sylvie as she took her place, shoving two castanets in her hands.

The music changed, became dark and throbbing with abandoned sensuality. The women lifted their arms to the sky, throwing their heads back, making a low, throaty growl as one.

If she ran off now she'd look like a frightened rabbit—but dancing beside these women, so effortlessly fluid and lovely, she'd probably look like a send-up. She shot a helpless glance at Mark, weighing her choices in a moment.

Then she saw the heated flash in his eyes as he looked at her, and it made the decision for her. She followed Isabella's movements.

Then she was too entranced to care if she looked foolish. Enthralled by the beat, by the beauty of the movements, she let herself be swept away into doing what her heart screamed at her to do. She swivelled her hips, pointed her bare feet and clicked the castanets, lifted her head and threw sleepy-eyed looks at Mark, hoping she looked somewhere near as enticing as the other women.

'Beautiful, beautiful,' Isabella murmured with a smile as the dance progressed. 'You are a natural dancer, and your movements are very sensual.'

After that she no longer worried about being silly or clumsy. She felt fluid, sensuous and *confident*. A woman at last....

The rose scent filled her head; the promise of the beat made her feel bold—a woman who knew what to do for the first time. It was as if she'd been stumbling around half-asleep all her life, and with the music and dance came an awakening of her spirit in time with the pulses and the clicks, and the clapping and *olés* of the men, who'd been transformed from rich, polite gentlemen to raw, primitive males from the moment the women began moving.

Tonight Sylvie was truly *alive*. Tonight she was bold and sensual, in thrall to the music, in ecstasy for the only man she'd ever dreamed of. And he was here, *here* with her at last, watching her dance with deep, abiding desire....

'Go dance around your table,' Isabella said softly as she danced past her. 'Your man looks only at you. He is ready for his woman.'

Without even pausing, she turned and danced her way down the stairs, towards the table. She paused as Mark rose to his feet, his gaze fixed on her, then she moved one final step, lifting her arms again to click the castanets. She reached him, standing at their shadowed corner table, stood before him, and clicked one final time. And she looked at him, hurting with desire and need.

His eyes were dark with restrained passion. 'Let's go,' he muttered, his voice taut. 'Leave the shoes. Someone will bring them back to your room.' Holding her hand, he led her to the secluded cove in front of their cottages, took off his shoes and said, 'Let's walk.' His voice sounded strangled.

Having expected to be in her cottage with a closed door by now, she had to swallow her sick disappointment. But he'd made her day perfect. All she could do was nod. If he wanted to walk, she would.

The islands of the Great Barrier Reef rarely had waves, protected by the massive coral shelf that cut the waters from the Tasman Sea, but tiny eddies came in, with soft *whoosh* sounds, and moonlight danced on the little white bubbles of their peaks.

Palm trees hung over the sand. Little hermit crabs flipped over and dug frantic holes to hide as they approached.

It was a magical scene—but right now there was only one kind of magic she wanted…

After a few minutes, desperation overcame scruples, fear and even pride, and she swung around in front of him. 'Did I do it wrong, Mark?'

'Hell, no.' As if her words had released some coiled tension in him, he dragged her against him and buried his face in her hair.

'Then what is it?'

'You know what I said about men and control? I think I lied. Because I'm way past that point now,' he rasped.

Her fears evaporated in pure tenderness. 'And that's a problem because…?'

He pulled back and stared into her eyes, his wild. 'Because you deserve your first real time to be slow, beautiful and perfect. And right now I want to bury myself in you over and over until I can't breathe.'

Sylvie drank him in, masculine and strong and beautiful, and out of control because of her…and she wrapped her arms around his waist. 'You just made this day perfect,' she whispered. 'I couldn't believe I'd drive any man wild with desire, let alone you. But—' she pulled back an inch, and lifted her gaze to him '—tonight, I believe.'

'Ah, sweetheart, you'd better believe.' He leaned in to her until their bodies touched. 'Do you want me?' he murmured in her ear, rough and hot.

Her palms and fingers and every nerve in her body were in pain, straining towards him. 'Yes, *yes*,' she whispered, aching to touch naked skin, to kiss his body.

'Then seduce me, Sylvie.' His voice was deep and taut, dark and lush, hot as a summer night before a storm. The heated current of want moved from his body to hers, and back again.

'I don't know how—that dance was all I had,' she blurted, feeling like the world's biggest fool. Stupid, infatuated girl–fighting for love without any weapons.

He laughed then, low and sensual, and he moved against her, showing her how aroused he was. 'If you don't know how, sweetheart, I can't wait to see you armed with full knowledge. That dance hit me like a bomb. I've wanted you since you first smiled at me—in your pyjamas, your shorts, when you waltz, when you were swimming, in your dress tonight. I love the way you never back down with me—and that dance… In a few weeks you've woken me up from this living death. You turn me inside out and upside down, and you make me want to live. I've been fighting it, but what you do to me all the time… Ah, you've turned me incoherent.' His lips brushed her ear as he spoke, and she shuddered with so many years of waiting for this moment. 'Just say, *I want you, Mark. Make love to me.* That's all it takes.'

'Oh…' It was a soft cry of passion, an admission of every-thing she'd felt for him for more than two-thirds of her life—for a lonely child's romantic prince, a woman's first and only love. And at last—oh, thank heaven—*at last* they were here, at this moment. 'I want you, I want you.' She touched her fingers to his neck, drew him to her as she went up on tiptoe, whis-pered, 'Make love to me, Mark,' and kissed him.

As he pulled her up against him, up into his arms, and carried her into the cottage, kissing her with a smiling tenderness that left her melted with desire, happiness, need and love, echoes of past warnings came to her: *Stop wishing for the moon, Sylvie. He's way out of your league now…and you'd probably be dis-appointed anyway. He's just another man.*

But here I am with the moon in my hands, she thought, thrill-ing to every touch.

And then Mark laid her down on the bed and lay beside her,

deepening his kiss to the passion she'd feared and craved for so long. He touched her face, tumbled her hair with his fingers, caressed her throat as he kissed her, wild and hot and deep. Weeks of gentle kisses turned primal, and because it was Mark she was with him all the way. Her body arched up to his; she moaned, her hands pulling at his tie, tugging at his shirt buttons, pulling his shirt off to kiss his shoulders. Every rational thought had long since fled. Everything was *him*—every thought and movement of her body, every wildly pulsing beat of her heart. *Mark, Mark...*

Then urgent hands pulled her dress up over her hips—and without warning she felt another pair of hands, eager and rough, yanking her school uniform over her stunned, trembling body, grabbing at her untouched breasts with greedy hands older than her father's. Her next-door neighbour, a trusted friend who'd saved them from being thrown out of their house, who'd paid the rent when she'd run out of money, had asked her to clean his house while his wife visited her mother. It would be such a nice surprise for her, wouldn't it?

'You knew what you were doing when you took that five hundred from me. You knew what I wanted when I asked you here today!'

Pain like a knife, splitting her in two. She was going to die...

The next thing she knew she was hitting back, flailing with clenched fists. Screaming incoherent cries of denial, writhing against him in the most elemental instinct to self-protect, to survive.

'Sylvie, it's me. It's Mark. It's all right. We won't do anything you don't want to do,' a beloved voice gasped. And as if a red mist had cleared, she came back to here and now.

To her horror she was kneeling over Mark on the luxurious king-sized bed, hitting him in the chest and stomach. He wasn't holding her fists or pinning her down, but letting her punch him.

'Mark!' she cried, and burst into tears against his chest. 'I'm sorry. *I'm sorry.*'

His arms came around her, fiercely tender, utterly protective, and he let her cry it out. 'You have nothing to apologise for, sweetheart. I think you've needed to let that out for a very long time.' His hands brushed the hair from her face; sombre eyes looked into hers. 'You didn't fight him, did you? What was it he held over you?'

She shuddered. *'I'll call the police and tell them you stole the money. Can you tell them where that five hundred magically came from? Your sick father and those little brothers of yours will be out on the street by tomorrow.'*

'Please,' she whispered, shaking against him, burrowing in for warmth in a world gone suddenly dark and cold.

He held her still in that protective tenderness. 'You've never spoken of this to anyone, have you?'

No, her lips mouthed, but she couldn't say it.

'Simon found you—after?' he guessed, his voice bleak.

She nodded, shuddering with the memory of *how* her brother had found her.

'It's time, sweetheart. The weight of your pain is burying you. *He's* burying you. Don't let him keep holding this power over your life. You have to talk to someone. I'm here, Sylvie,' he said quietly, brushing her tears away with his thumbs.

He's burying you.

With those words, something happened to her: she saw that by her silence, by never letting any man close, her attacker kept on winning the same victory. She'd keep on moving from place to place, looking after others but never meeting her own needs because she didn't deserve it.

'I'm here,' Mark said, kissing her forehead with so much tenderness that more tears rushed to her eyes.

Not for much longer. She closed her eyes, letting the tears fall, and said it—in the same blunt, hard way Mr Landsedge had said it to her all those years ago. 'It wasn't rape.' Was that her voice, croaking like a magpie? 'I sold my virginity for five hundred dollars.'

CHAPTER ELEVEN

ONCE you've sold your soul to survive, you can never have it back.

Finally he understood.

Mark looked at the white face, the make-up streaked with her tears, her eyes nearly black with self-loathing, and he saw the unbearable burden carried on those delicate shoulders for far too long. His heart almost burst with tenderness, but his love wouldn't help her now. She needed catharsis.

'Tell me,' he said quietly.

Her lashes dropped down over her eyes; she laced and un-laced her fingers. 'He was our neighbour. Mr Landsedge. He'd always been—kind. Offered to help out when things got hard for us.'

I just bet he did, Mark thought in blood-red fury, thinking thoughts of vengeance that wouldn't help her.

'What happened?' he asked, refusing to let her dwell on the 'kindness' of the dirty jerk. Child abusers were often very kind and helpful—until they reached their target. Then threats and lies became their stock-in-trade to avoid prosecution.

'One month, when Dad had been really sick, we needed money desperately or we'd be tossed out of the house. Welfare would split us up. He—he came to me and offered to pay a full month's rent to help us out of the hole.'

Noting the creep hadn't approached her father, who probably would have guessed what was going on, Mark said again, 'Tell me.'

She gave a shuddering sigh. 'He asked me to clean their house as—as a surprise for his wife when she came home from visiting her mother. Of course I did it. Of course,' she repeated, with a weary sadness more heartbreaking than any bitterness could be. 'And—and then he said he needed the money back. I didn't have it.' Pleading eyes lifted to his, begging in silence for him to understand, holding an underlying hopelessness—and he knew what she was thinking. How could he understand what she'd done when she still didn't? 'I—I offered to pay it by the week. I offered to clean the house every week for a year. But—but…' She shuddered and buried her face in her hands. 'He caught me in the spare bedroom. He tore my school uniform—the only—only one I had,' she mumbled, her voice lifting by octaves to a half-wail as she cried through her fingers. 'He said I'd known what he wanted when I took the money. He said my coming over was agreeing to—to…selling my virginity. He said it was obvious I'd *enjoyed* it.' She shuddered again. 'I thought I was going to tear in two, and—and then he tried to make a date to do it again the next week!'

A red mist covered his eyes, blood-red and pulsing with fury against the unnameable piece of filth who'd hurt his beautiful little Mary so badly she'd stopped being Mary.

I'm going to find the creep and—

'I'm sorry. I'll go now.'

The pathetic little whisper, her scramble to get off his bed, snapped him out of his wrath. How long had he been sitting there thinking about Landsedge while Sylvie waited for his reaction in growing hopelessness?

'Sweetheart?'

The word, soaked in all the love he felt bursting from his heart, stopped her clumsy flight. But she didn't look at him. Her back was stiff and straight, as it had been the day her mother died—when she'd faced a future filled with burdens all on her own.

She expected him to walk away.

'What happened next?'

A long, slow quiver ran through her, but still she stood straight and proud. 'I…I was sick. I couldn't get out of bed for two weeks. I couldn't even help the boys. He—he tried to be helpful again. He came in my room.' She sniffed, and said simply, 'I whacked him in the face with Drew's baseball bat.'

A startled laugh burst from him before he could smother it. 'That's my girl.'

She half twisted towards him, but then turned back again. 'I broke his nose,' she said, flat and hard. 'I told him if he came near me again I'd tell his wife. He said I knew where to come the next time I needed "financial help", and that he knew I'd come.' She stood trembling, and his gut twisted with a cocktail of murderous fury, compassion, love and a fierce pride in her. 'Then, two weeks later, *you* came to our rescue. I took five hundred out as soon as I could. I saw him in his garden and threw it in his face. Then I grabbed his shears and hacked off all his prize roses. The neighbours were watching. He didn't know what to do. I yelled that if he ever came near me again I'd go to the police.'

'What else happened, sweetheart?' he asked quietly, sensing the story wasn't over.

She sighed. 'Simon found me trying to get in the house with rips in my uniform without anyone seeing. After…'

He shot to his feet, crossed to her and pulled her close. 'Sylvie. Oh, sweetheart.'

She didn't move or react to his touch, stood stiff and cold. 'Simon told Mrs Landsedge, who believed it because of the broken nose and the way Simon and I refused to talk to him or look at him. She kicked him out. All the money was hers.'

A very neat revenge—as long as a probably still furious, vengeful but currently powerless Mr Landsedge never discovered she was now dating a very rich man and made his grubby version of the story public. *Mark Hannaford's girlfriend sold me her virginity for five hundred dollars*.

Now he knew why Sylvie refused to go anywhere where they might be noticed by the press. She was protecting him, protecting her family—and herself, of course. But he knew she'd put herself last, as usual. He'd never met anyone as loving and giving as Sylvie, and she set such a low value on herself.

Thinking quickly, he knew what he had to do. Sylvie would never tell this story to an outsider; it was her way. He was pretty well certain even Simon didn't know the whole story, either. He was so protective of his sister—if he knew what she'd done to save them…

It was up to him, then—and he racked his brain for the research he'd done on the subject when a female employee had recovered memories of childhood abuse and been too traumatised to work for months.

'Do you remember what I said about men and control?' He caressed those shining tumbled curls.

She looked up, a small light of laughter in her eyes. 'Duh. You said it three hours ago.'

He chuckled and kissed her forehead, so proud of her ability to laugh—she was a survivor, his Sylvie. 'Men who have no respect for women also lie about their reasons for forcing a woman—or a child—to make it appear to be her fault.' He lifted her chin with a finger, then cupped her face in his hands. 'He set you up, sweetheart. He chose you because you were vulnerable in your love for your family—and he manipulated events to get what he wanted. And when he knew you might go to the police he found a way to make you feel ashamed and scared. He made you feel like a prostitute so you wouldn't tell.'

After a long silence, he added, 'You didn't sell a thing, Sylvie. You were a child. All the responsibility for this *crime* belongs to him. He hurt you, lied to you and manipulated you so you wouldn't do the one thing he feared—go to the police.'

She gave a shuddering sigh, looking at him in pure wonder. 'You don't despise me?'

Gently he kissed her mouth. 'Never, sweetheart. Even if you'd been forced to become what you feared most I couldn't hate you.' He sighed. 'If anything, you should despise *me*. I've treated women badly for too many years. Until you came back to me women were a way to put another Band-Aid on a wound that wouldn't heal, to forget what I'd become. I didn't pay them, but in every other way I treated them with less respect than they deserved.' He looked in her eyes with total seriousness. 'It's not my forgiveness you need, Sylvie. You don't even need to forgive yourself. You need to see that you never did anything wrong.'

'Not—not even when I broke his nose?'

He nuzzled her hair with his mouth. 'Especially not that.'

With a tiny muffled sound she buried her face in his chest. 'I was so scared you'd hate me. I couldn't bear it if you hated me.'

And at last he knew the time had come to speak. 'I have no right to despise you. You're innocent of everything but trusting the wrong person.' He dropped his hands as the shutters fell away from his soul. 'It's me who's never had the right to be with *you*.' He refused to turn away, looking into her eyes with all the self-condemnation he deserved. 'You think I'm an alcoholic, don't you?'

With confusion in her eyes, she nodded.

'I'm not—well, not in the traditional sense.' He took her hand and led her to the two seats near the sliding-glass doors overlooking the ocean. 'After Chloe died,' he said deliberately, 'I went nuts. I skipped school. I got drunk to forget. My parents could barely find me to stop me. I only came home to sleep, or to take more money out of the bank. I wasted years of careful saving for university on drink and a cheap car. I lived in the car, and I kept playing chicken with red lights, screeching around corners. I wanted to die and join her.'

She said nothing, her gaze fixed on his face, waiting for the rest. Her beautiful old-sherry eyes were full of compassion, love and faith.

It was the worst possible moment to realise she was in love with him, that *he* was the prince she'd spoken of…

He went on in a hard voice, refusing to hide a single part of the missing year of his life. 'My family and Chloe's tried so hard to help me. They tried everything—from taking me to a counselor, to locking me in to saying she'd be ashamed of me. I didn't care. She shouldn't have left me, but since she had, all I wanted was to be with her. Eventually they closed my bank account. I got a job delivering pizzas and used the money to drink. The wonder of it is I never used drugs—but maybe I knew Chloe would really despise me for that. And yet something in me kept saying, *If Mary can keep going, why can't you?* Somehow your memory kept me from killing myself. Either with drugs or any other way.'

'I'm glad,' she said softly, her whole face alight with love, and he ached to touch her, to tell her he loved her, adored her…

So he told her the worst thing—blurting it out to stop himself from ruining her life with his need for her. 'Then I turned the wrong corner at the wrong time—too fast, too drunk. I hit a kid on a bike.'

She gasped. 'Was he all right?'

The distancing had already begun, and he couldn't blame her. 'Robbie spent the next five months in hospital, with multiple fractures in his legs and hip, arm and skull.'

'Robbie?'

'Allsopp,' he added with a nod.

'So…you stayed at the accident scene? You didn't run?'

'Of course not,' he snarled, but he knew she was right to ask. After all he'd done, why wouldn't he have played the coward's part and run?

Deflated, he said quietly, 'It woke me up. I wanted to kill *me*, not someone else. Then in the hospital—I fractured my arm—my family rallied around me, doing what they could for the Allsopps, too. I finally saw what I was doing—not just to me, but to everyone around me.' He sighed. 'I called the Allsopps every day, asking how Robbie was, begging forgiveness. They—were kind.' He dropped his head onto his hand. 'I couldn't believe it, but they forgave me. Robbie forgave me. The only thing they asked was that I get help.'

'And you did.' It wasn't a question. She knew he had.

He nodded. 'I went into rehab even before the case came to court. Because I'd gone in voluntarily and the counsellors said I was truly repentant, and when even the Allsopps came to testify for me, as well as against me, the judge was compassionate. He said my history showed I wasn't a delinquent and I was already in a rehabilitation facility. He recommended I never drink again. When I swore I wouldn't, he only took my driver's licence for two years. I didn't care about that. I'd already used the insurance on the car to pay for a little of Robbie's health needs. My parents sold their house to pay for the rest, and for my rehab.' He said simply, 'I was six months off turning eighteen. Being a minor, the files on me are sealed. It's the only reason the story never made the tabloids.'

'Where's Robbie now?' she asked gently. 'Don't tell me you don't know. I won't believe you. I *know* you've paid your debt there. In fact, I'm willing to bet you did that before you bought your parents their new house, or bought that second-hand car for yourself when you patented Howlcat.'

He looked up with a half-grin; how well she knew him. 'He's a physiotherapist. He says the accident showed him what he wanted to do—to help others through what happened to him. Maggie and Sean, his parents, say the accident gave him empathy for others' suffering.'

'As it did you,' she murmured, laying her hand on his.

He withdrew his hand. 'Don't be kind to me, Sylvie. I don't deserve your praise. I only did what I had to do.'

'At *seventeen*,' she said with soft emphasis. 'If I was a child, so were you. You'd lost the love of your life too young. You became a widower *at seventeen*. After five years of being strong, giving and responsible, doing everything right, suddenly you had nothing to do, nowhere to be. School was empty, because she wasn't there. Inventing just reminded you of her. You were like a spring held down too long, released to nothing—you just bounced all over the place. You became a teenage boy for the first time, doing stupid things without thinking of the consequences to others—and it's a time you obviously regret and will never repeat.' She came around the table between them and squatted before him. 'You've become a strong, fine, giving man who doesn't blow his trumpet. You have the forgiveness of those who matter. It's not *my* forgiveness you need,' she said, repeating what he'd told her only ten minutes ago. 'You need to forgive yourself.'

Unable to stand any more of her tender reassurance—it was too *tempting* to believe her—he jerked to his feet. 'I *can't*.' He pulled open the door. Without looking at her, he snarled, 'I know what you want to say. Don't do it. Don't love me, Sylvie. It's not worth it. *I'm* not worth it.'

As he headed for his cottage to change, desperately needing time out, he heard her murmur, soft and sad, 'It's years too late to tell me that.'

CHAPTER TWELVE

A week later

IN a beautiful bridesmaid's dress of soft apricot-pink that made her look more than ever like the hated china doll, smiling for friends and family, Sylvie walked down the aisle of the old church in the neighbourhood where they'd all grown up.

It was Scott and Sarah's big day, and she wasn't about to ruin it for them.

Even if she couldn't stop thinking of Mark the whole time, wondering where he'd been since they came home from Turtle Island. He hadn't come home, hadn't gone to work. He'd dropped her off in the limo and said he needed to get away. 'It's not you, it's me,' he'd said, in the time-worn phrase that always made women feel unloved and inadequate. He'd never left Chloe for a minute—no matter how much he'd needed to get away...

On the way home in the jet, she'd asked him to be her partner for the wedding. He'd said, 'I'd be honoured,' sounding anything but happy about it.

Then she'd made the monumental mistake of saying she loved him. His silence had filled her with terror. She'd added hastily that she expected nothing from him—yet still he'd disappeared.

He hadn't shown up for the wedding. He wasn't coming.

She heard the words of love, commitment and shared faith between her two dearest friends with a lump in her throat. She hugged and kissed them and said she was so happy—and she *was*—but she felt like a liar. She took Angelo's arm on the way down the aisle, posed for the obligatory photos and rode to the reception hall with him, applauded the bride and groom's entrance. She ate almost nothing of her dinner, pretending it was because she was smiling and laughing too much.

The tears of a clown beneath.

Then came the time for the bridal waltz. Without thinking about it, Sylvie left her seat and walked down the stairs from the high table, waiting for Angelo on the dance floor.

She waited—and waited. She turned to the table—he'd disappeared. She threw a frantic look at Sandi, his fiancée, who lifted her hands in the air in awkward apology.

Angelo had done a runner.

She stood in the middle of the dance floor as Scott and Sarah twirled gracefully around her, her cheeks scorched with humiliation, knowing a dozen video cameras were rolling and this would be a 'funniest home video' moment worth putting on the TV.

She looked around for Simon, Drew and Joel, who were always ready to rescue her…but her brothers just sat there grinning. Why weren't they coming to help her? Surely they could see she was writhing in her public embarrassment?

Then a deep voice said from behind her, 'I believe this is our dance, Miss Browning.'

She swivelled around in astonished joy. *'Mark,'* she whispered, her heart pounding as he took her in his arms in the traditional dance hold. He'd come for her. He'd rescued her again…

She took in the full tuxedo he wore, as if he was one of the bridal party. Careful not to say anything to drive him away again, she could only whisper, 'Thank you—thank you.'

He smiled down at her. 'After what you told me I thought Angelo might bolt, so I came prepared.' He stepped forward and she moved back in the waltz, and he twirled her, making her feel graceful and pretty. 'I tried to make it on time, but there was traffic on the bridge after an accident.'

'I thought you weren't coming.'

His mouth quirked up. 'You should know me better than that. I've always been there for you. Okay, so sometimes I've been a bit late, but I'm always there.' He took in her outfit. 'You look beautiful.'

She sighed. 'I look like a china doll again.'

'So did Chloe, if you remember,' he said, smiling at her. 'I've always been a sucker for china dolls.'

They danced in silence for a few minutes. Mark seemed content to be quiet. Sylvie had no idea what to say to his comparison of her to Chloe. He'd brought up her name with a smile on his face…

As the floor began to fill up with other wedding guests, he said, 'I guess you're wondering where I've been this week. I know Mum and the girls didn't tell you.'

Hearing the note in his voice—of a *peace* she hadn't heard in it either as a child or a man—she looked up. 'I'm sorry. I shouldn't have called your mother, but I was worried.'

'You can call my family any time, sweetheart.' He tipped her face up and brushed his mouth over hers. 'They all adore you, and they know you only want the best for me.'

At that, she lost control over her aching heart and runaway mouth. Shaking her head, she looked down and away. 'No. I want a lot of things—not only what's best for you.' She gulped and went on, feeling totally hopeless. 'I'm sorry, Mark. You're so good to me, so *kind,* and I know that I'm not her and I'll never be her, but I can't help it.'

'Can't help what?' he whispered in her ear.

She couldn't look up as she murmured in an anguished voice, 'Loving you so much.'

He dropped his hand from hers and her heart lurched—but then he wrapped his arm around her waist, drawing her tight against him. 'You don't hate me for what I did?'

She sighed. 'Nothing will change the way I feel, Mark. I've loved you since the day I first saw you. I know you don't want it—'

'Who says I don't want it?' he asked softly.

'Don't be kind to me,' she said with a gritted-teeth smile, remembering she was maid of honour, and they were surrounded by a crowd of happy dancers and photographers. 'Don't call me sweetheart. It makes me hope for things I can't have with you.'

'Why can't you have them? Why can't you have me?'

'Stop it!' she cried, forgetting everything but her pain. She tried to move out of his arms, but he held her in a deadlock. 'Please stop. I know you're *fond* of me—of little Shirley Temple. I know you want my friendship, want to take care of me just like you always have. You know I love you and you want me to be happy—'

'Correction,' he interrupted in a gentle voice. 'I want *us* to be happy. Yes, I want to take care of you. Yes, I know you love me. And, yes, I'm *fond* of Shirley Temple. I always have been. But that's in the past.'

'So's Chloe, and you still love *her*!'

'True,' he admitted without hesitation. 'I'm a faithful kind of man. Once I love, I can't change.'

'Then think how *painful* it would be for you if she was here now but she didn't love you the way you want her to!'

For the third time in as many minutes, he bent to her ear. 'Who says I don't love you the way you want me to?'

She stilled so suddenly he tripped over her motionless feet, almost taking her down onto the floor. He righted himself with her quick hands.

'That's my girl—always helping me up when I'm down,' he murmured, and took her back in his arms, dancing with a slow sensuality that made her insides feel like melted chocolate, liquid, hot and sweet, and so filled with love she could barely breathe.

'What did you say?' she asked in an anguished whisper.

He didn't pretend to misunderstand or tease her. 'I said I love you, Mary Brown/Sylvie Browning—exactly the way you want me to. There's just one thing wrong with your name-change,' he said softly. 'It should be Hannaford. But it will be when you marry me.'

The words she'd waited a lifetime to hear. Again, it wasn't the stuff of her dreams—not the long, romantic declaration she'd wanted. But when she looked in his eyes she saw not a fairytale prince but a man in love....

And she began hyperventilating, wheezing with each laboured breath.

Concerned friends and family began crowding around. Simon, Drew and Joel, all dancing nearby, shouldered their way through to where they stood.

'What did you do to her?' Simon demanded of Mark, with the fierceness he always used to protect her from the world, covering his anxieties with anger the way she did with a smile. 'You said to trust you with her, and now she's—'

'No need to worry, Simon.' Mark broke into Simon's tirade with a calm smile. 'It's marriage-proposal shock, that's all. She'll be fine in a minute.'

Her brothers were silent for about three seconds, then all three burst out laughing. 'She did it,' Drew said in a dazed voice. 'I can't believe she did it!'

'You should have known she would,' Mark said, doing the palm thing on her back she'd done with his hiccups. 'You can welcome me to the family when she's coherent enough to say yes. Excuse us now. We need some privacy.'

Amid her brothers' amazed chuckles and the understanding smiles of her friends, he lifted her up in his arms and carried her out into the warm, late-summer night to the garden surrounding the reception building. He sat on a bench amid a section of roses and held her with that cherishing tenderness she could never resist. 'So, are you going to keep me hanging? Or are you going to say *Yes, Mark, I'll marry you and I love you*?'

She felt the familiar stinging of her eyes. How he could bring her to tears so fast she'd never know. 'You love Chloe. You said it.'

'Yes, I do. I always will. Part of me will always miss her— she was my best friend, my inventing partner, the love of the boy I was. But she's been gone half a lifetime, and I'm not *in* love with her any more. I'm in love with you.' He trailed his lips over her cheek, her hair, her mouth. 'I think that was the reason I was so cold and uncaring all those years. I didn't realise that as I was losing Chloe you'd already come into my life and filled my heart. I spent all those years waiting for you to come back to me.'

She blinked, but found no words to say.

He smiled down at her and caressed her cheek. 'I think that's why Chloe foisted that impossible promise on us both, you know.'

Her brow crinkled. 'Why?'

'To bring us back together. She knew what we didn't.' He bent and kissed her again. 'All the things I loved about her she saw in you: the adorable stubbornness, the refusal to give up on me, always seeing the best in me, loving me no matter what. I think she knew what would happen to me without her—so she sent you to me. I thought I'd gone so cold because I'd lost Chloe, but it started months, even years before she died. It began when she was first diagnosed with cancer. Because I was going to lose her, to be alone, I became cold with every person outside the family circle. Holding off from the world was my protection against the pain. But with you I couldn't be hard or cold. You were too special to me.' His fingers trailed along her jaw, and she shivered with the power of it, the beauty. 'When she died and you left my life the sunshine disappeared. Even after I came out of rehab life felt bleak. The coldness never left me—no matter what I invented, what I could do for others, what woman I was with, or what level of success I reached.' He added softly, 'Then you came back to me. I felt the change at my first sight of you. I'm not the Heart of Ice now because of you. You melted me, Sylvie. You *melted* me.'

And *that* was why she could never wear make-up around him. 'You melt me, too—obviously,' she wailed, and hic-cupped, tears streaking paths through her professionally done face. 'What about the press—the story about me?'

'I found Landsedge this week,' he said grimly. 'He's not worth it, sweetheart. Since his wife kicked him out he's become a pathetic old man in a nursing home. He's got early-onset dementia. If he sells his story—which I doubt, because when I saw him he didn't know what day it was or remember your name—we'll survive it together.'

She nodded, touched that he'd gone to such lengths to re-assure her. 'I—might have other problems,' she whispered. 'When we—'

'I know, sweetheart.' He kissed her with sweet lingering. 'If you want to know where I went this week, I went to see Robbie, his parents—and I saw my old counsellor. She runs her own private clinic. She'd like to meet you. She's been where you are,' he added, when she made an instinctive movement of withdrawal. 'Amanda knows the shame and the fear. She doesn't think you need her help, sweetheart—and she says you did for me what she couldn't, because our trust in each other is absolute.' After a moment in which she had no idea what to say, he added, 'You were right, Sylvie. I told Amanda what you said about learning to forgive myself.' He brushed his mouth over hers once, twice. 'She said if I didn't marry you I'd be making the biggest mistake of my life, whether I believe I'm worthy of you or not. She said you're obviously a very intelligent and strong woman, and perfect for me.'

The indecision and fear receded. If Mark could face his worst nightmares, if he could see a counsellor for her sake and be willing to go with her, couldn't she be strong enough to go with him?

'Did you make an appointment?'

'Monday at 4:00 p.m.' He hugged her. 'Thank you, sweetheart. I knew you could do it.'

'Kiss me,' she said, lifting her face to his.

'You still haven't answered me. *Yes, I'll marry you, Mark. I love you, Mark,*' he parroted in soft insistence. 'No kisses until we're engaged.'

'You've been kissing me this whole time,' she pointed out, feeling her entire body shining with happiness.

He rolled his eyes, laughing. 'Okay, then, no *more* kisses until we're engaged. Now, say it, woman—or I swear I'll make you so crazy for me—'

She already was. Insanely in love… She whispered, 'Yes, Mark, I'll marry you. I love you so much. You were my first crush and you became my only love—the only man I've ever wanted or will ever want.' She smiled up at him. 'I've gone a whole week without touching you. Now, *please* kiss me—and you couldn't make me any crazier for you. You do that to me just by being alive,' she said softly.

'One more thing first.' He smiled, and pulled out a tiny box from his jacket pocket. He flipped it open and lifted the antique rose-gold ring out. It was studded with one sweet ruby, flanked by two little diamonds each side. 'It was my Grandma Hannaford's,' he said softly. 'Grandad said when he gave it to her that it was his reminder that he had a woman worth more than rubies. When she died twelve years ago he gave up. He gave the ring to me before he died; Grandma wanted me to have it. He said when I found a woman as priceless as Grandma, one worth spending every day of my life with, I'd know what to do.'

'Oh, *look* what you've made me do,' she wailed, as more tears ruined her make-up. She held out her left hand while swiping at her face with the right.

'I love you,' he whispered, and slid the ring on her finger. Then, at last, he kissed her—deep and slow and filled with love.

Much later, they heard loud voices complaining that first the best man disappeared for the bridal waltz, and now the maid of honour hadn't shown up for photos. They smiled at each other, and Mark pulled out a handkerchief, wiping off the mess of tear-streaked make-up.

'You're far prettier without it, anyway.' Then he lifted her to her feet. 'Go on in there, wife. You're needed.'

Wife… She promptly melted again. 'This is our engagement night. Come with me. We need a photo or three for our grand-children to smile at one day.'

As they walked hand in hand up the stairs he asked, 'So, when do we want the wedding, and where?'

She squeezed his hand. 'You know where. There's only one place for us, Mark, if Chloe's memory is to be part of our day. And she deserves that tribute.'

He turned to her, eyes dark with emotion. 'Perfect.' His voice cracked on the word, and he led her inside to raucous congratulations as he became part of her family.

The garden, St Agatha's Hospice, two months later

The stereo began playing the beautiful romantic thirties music they both loved, and Mark, flanked by Pete, Glenn, Drew and Joel, turned to see his bride.

Sylvie's friend Sarah led the procession, followed by Bren, Becky and Katie, down past the few standing guests that would fit in this little garden where they'd first met.

Then Sylvie came out on Simon's arm, wearing her mother's wedding dress, Mark's mother's silk wedding slippers, Mark's grandmother's ring and Bren's veil.

The dress was a plain slip of silk with an old-fashioned ivory lace overdress, falling straight to her feet in a hippie style; her hair was loose, shining through the gossamer veil. And her face was so radiant with joy and love it shone through the dainty lace covering her. Her gaze never wavered from him.

You may not feel worthy of her love, but she's given her heart and trust to you—only you, his heart whispered. *So make yourself worthy of her. Don't let her down.*

Mark almost couldn't breathe because he felt so choked up with love. She was walking down the aisle to him, the embodiment of everything he'd never believed he could have—and she loved him, with all his faults and private and public baggage. She trusted him with her future.

She reached his side; Simon lifted her veil and kissed her. Drew and Joel came around Mark and followed suit, not in rehearsed symphony, but as brothers who adored her, sharing in the joy of her day. She hugged them and said, 'I love you,' and they said it back.

Sylvie turned to Mark and took his hands in hers. 'Smile,' she said softly.

The light and warmth of her presence and touch filled him again; the shining happiness that was Sylvie streaked through his body.

'That's better.' She winked at him and they turned to the celebrant, his cousin Ryan, who married them with the same deep, abiding delight of the entire Hannaford clan.

Even Chloe's parents were here, so happy for Mark…

As Sylvie made her vows Mark drank in every word—and yet he heard a soft, feminine echo from the past. *'Promise me you'll be happy, Mark. Find a girl to love.'*

'They say you can't find lasting love as a child, that you'll forget,' Sylvie said, her hands in his. 'But "they" aren't always right. I've loved you since I was eight years old, and it's only deepened through the years. You were my prince, my hero, my reason to keep living—and now you're my love, my dearest friend, the other half of me. I make you my vow that it will never change, in good times or in bad, in sickness or in health, rich or poor, because it never has.' She smiled up at him, misty with love. 'It's built to last a lifetime.'

He choked up again, marvelling at the devoted love he'd found a second time in his life—and in silence he thanked its source. *You told me to find love again, but you'd already found her for me, hadn't you, Chloe? You always knew me better than I knew myself*, he thought with a smile as Sylvie slid the wedding ring on his finger.

Ryan pronounced them husband and wife, his smile going a fair way to splitting his face. 'Go ahead and kiss her,' he said with a wink.

'Alone at last,' Sylvie said on a contented sigh.

They'd chosen to stay home for their wedding night; Sylvie wanted the familiarity of beloved surroundings for their first time, and Mark felt exactly the same.

Tomorrow they'd fly to the Greek islands and spend their time on a yacht, finding B and Bs to stay in. Tonight was just Mark and Sylvie, in the home they loved.

Mark didn't carry her over the threshold; she didn't want to start their lives together with superstition.

'I don't need to worry about bad luck, Mark. I've been given enough miracles to know where to put my trust,' she said softly as they walked in the back door hand in hand. 'I think we could both use a cup of tea,' she murmured, when Mark had closed the door.

He could see her hands trembling. 'Just what we both need,' he agreed, aching with love and desire—but the imperative thing was to give Sylvie control, to make her feel safe.

So here they were on their wedding night, husband and wife, drinking tea…

She started talking about the utter joy of their day, uninterrupted by any media hype or circus. 'The photos should be beautiful,' she said, her fingers tapping on the cup.

Mark nodded, letting her babble out her nerves, caressing the hand he held in loving reassurance. They'd contacted and made an exclusive deal with a magazine, donating all funds to his favourite charity, Medicin Sans Frontiers, with the proviso that there would be no announcement made until they went to press, when they would be on their way to Greece. Their photographer was sending the shots tonight, with comments given by the guests and family.

Waiting was becoming an agony now. He'd been patient through the past two months as she'd explored her newfound sensuality and her power over him, knowing he'd always stop when she said, or when she trembled too hard. But she was his wife, he adored her, and—

'So—are we going to bed now?'

The question was a compound of timidity and eagerness. He drank in those beautiful eyes, huge with uncertainty. 'Only if you want to, sweetheart.'

'I do,' she burst out. 'I've wanted to for weeks, but…' She chewed on her thumbnail.

Mark leaned into her, touching his forehead to hers. 'I can wait if you're still not ready, Sylvie. We have a lifetime.' His voice was hard with the strain of saying it.

'What's *wrong* with me?' she cried wretchedly. 'Why am I so scared? I love you so much, Mark. When you touch me I feel so beautiful. I want to be with you.'

He groaned at the words. 'I love you, too. Enough to wait.' His body screamed protest at the words, but he said them for her sake.

She talked over him, as if she hadn't heard. 'But I'm scared of what I'll feel. I couldn't *stand* it if I freaked out and hit you again!'

In all the weeks he'd waited for her she'd never said that— and he almost laughed in the exquisite relief. So ridiculous, so beautiful and so Sylvie—she'd been raped and she still worried about hurting him, putting his welfare above her own, as ever… That was his girl. 'Is that what's been bothering you? Why you've always stopped at that point?'

Her face pale, she nodded, chewing fiercely on the poor abused thumb.

Gently he took her hand from her mouth. 'I can show you ways around that.'

Her mouth fell open. 'Really?'

'Really,' he repeated, thinking tenderly of this girl raised by a man, who'd run a house but had no time to play; whose only personal experience was violent. She was a virgin in all the ways that counted. 'I can show you how to make love to me, Sylvie. You'll be in control all the way.'

He waited for her reaction.

Not for long… Within moments her eyes took fire, she lifted their linked hands and kissed his palm, slow and lingering. 'I want you, Mark. I want to make love.'

Remembering the words from their fateful night at Turtle

Island, and the mistakes he'd made in his frantic need for her, he said softly, 'Then take me to bed.'

With a wide smile of delight, she stood and led him up the stairs. 'We can wash up later—after you teach me this new dance,' she said softly, and he chuckled. Tonight they'd dance with the oldest and most beautiful moves known to a man and woman in love.

When they reached the bedroom, he said, 'It starts with a kiss. Kiss me, sweetheart.'

With a half-smile and a full blush, she drew him down for a long, slow kiss. He allowed her to set the pace.

'What now?' she asked breathlessly, when they were both shaking with need.

'You undress me.' If he was the one vulnerable first, naked on the bed, maybe it would give her strength and courage, would arouse and reassure her.

With wide eyes and uncertain hands she worked at his shirt buttons—he'd already discarded the jacket and tie. But before the shirt was off, she whispered, *'Oh...'* in a tone of sensuous wonder and discovery. She peeled the shirt off, her hands caressing his skin, her lips trailing his chest and stomach, growing hotter, fevered. 'Oh, Mark, darling...'

He held on to his ragged threads of self-control. She'd come this far before, become totally aroused and then panicked. 'If you're ready, sweetheart, you can take off my pants.'

Too soon. Stupid, *stupid*! She closed her eyes, looking like a prisoner before a firing squad as she pulled off his belt and undid the button on his pants.

'You might need to take off my shoes first, or I'll fall over when the pants drop,' he whispered, angling for a laugh—and the lovely silver and gold gurgle of her mirth came. Her eyes alight, she bent to his feet and pulled off his shoes and socks.

He looked down at her curly head in anguish. He didn't know how much longer he could hold on.

But then she stood and looked in his eyes, and hers were filled with love and trust. 'Now the pants?' Her voice came out as a squeak, but she said it.

'If you're ready,' he said quietly. 'And put me on the bed.'

As he'd hoped, the sight of him on the bed, in a position of vulnerability and trust, aroused Sylvie so much she fell on him. 'Darling, *darling*,' she murmured, kissing and caressing his body with fevered lips and hands. 'I love you. I want you.'

'I love you, too. Always.' He closed his eyes as her touch drove him to the point of madness. 'If you're ready, take your dress off.' The final power and determination: if she took her dress off, which she'd never allowed him to do without giving in to terror—

'Mark?' she said softly.

He opened his eyes to see Sylvie in her underwear—silky, lacy pieces over tiny curves, exquisite. 'Ah, sweetheart, sweetheart—you're so beautiful,' he croaked. *Reassure her all the way that she's beautiful, loved and in control*, he chanted in his mind. 'My bride, my wife,' he went on, aware he was babbling, sick with nerves that she'd back out.

But he'd stumbled into saying the perfect thing. 'Yes.' She sounded fiercely proud. 'I'm Sylvie Hannaford...and you're my husband, my man.'

'For a lifetime,' he agreed, his voice aching with the desire that was half killing him.

With a sweet, mysterious woman smile, she reached behind her to unhook her bra...

Instinct and love took over; he showed her what to do, and she was too aroused, too soaked in newfound bliss and pleasure, to think of the past. And for the first time in half a lifetime Mark treasured the experience of what it was to truly make love with the woman he'd committed his life to: a woman who adored him, who'd never want to touch any other man.

He was a man doubly blessed in the women he'd loved.

As she lay on him after, he played with her hair while she kissed his damp chest, murmuring words of love and faith, and *for ever*. Of loving, making babies and being a family… They had a lifetime together.

Then she moved against him in unmistakable meaning. 'Can we do that again?'

It wasn't really a question, and as they touched and loved each other's bodies Mark knew that, though they had a way to go, everything would be all right for them from now on.

EPILOGUE

Five years later

MARK let himself in the door of his parents' house to hear the laughter and teasing of a family get-together. 'Hey, I'm back,' he called down the hall.

'Mark!' The voice was Sylvie's, filled with joy. He heard a chair scrape back and awkward steps running to him.

'Don't run, sweetheart,' he said as she burst into the hall, her face alight with love and welcome. 'You know you're not supposed to.' He moved to her with quick strides.

A heavily pregnant Sylvie snuggled into his arms with a deep sigh of contentment. 'Oh, I've missed you. Don't go anywhere without me again.'

'I've only been gone three days.' But he'd missed her, too— so much he'd caught a flight home from Singapore two hours earlier, on a different carrier. At thirty-four weeks pregnant, Sylvie couldn't fly with him, and the trip had been unavoidable, but as far as he was concerned it was the last trip he'd take without his family. A day without Sylvie's smile and touch was a day too long. Even after five years he didn't take her love for granted. Every day was still a miracle to him, her love a gift he didn't deserve but thanked God for.

Her brow lifted. 'You won't think it's *only* three days when it comes to bedtime. Katie slept in Chloe's room while she stayed, and now Madam Princess doesn't see why she can't sleep with *us* every night.'

Mark groaned. 'Oh, great. More bedtime re-education. Thanks, Katie.'

'And that's Daddy's department,' she said, with clear smugness in her tone. 'You're the only one who can get through to her.'

'Stubborn little puss. Her mother's daughter,' he teased with a grin.

'Kiss me,' she whispered fiercely, wrapping her arms around his neck and drawing him down to her. After a long kiss filled with heat, she whispered, 'When can we go home?'

'Can I at least say hi to the family and see my daughter before you make use of my body?' he mock-complained, loving that even after five years, and only six weeks away from her giving birth, he could arouse her with a touch. Sometimes the past came back to haunt her, but rarely when they made love; it was more on sad anniversaries.

She grumbled, 'Oh, I suppose so.' Her eyes twinkled. 'One more kiss.'

'When are you two gonna get *over* it?' Pete demanded from the door to the dining room. 'Everyone's waiting for dinner.'

Sylvie turned her head and grinned at Pete. 'Never,' she vowed fervently. 'You wouldn't, either, if you had a husband like mine.'

'*Eeew*. I've shared a room with him, remember? I'm definitely over it.'

They chuckled.

'Daddy-Daddy-Daddy-Daddy!'

Mark's grin widened at the frantic call; two-and-a-half-year-old Chloe always said *Daddy* in a blur of 'd's. 'I'm here, princess,' he called to her.

'Here comes the express,' Pete groaned with a grin, and stepped out of the way.

'Daddy-Daddy-Daddy-Daddy-Daddy!' A chubby-limbed blonde with a Pebbles hairdo came flying at him, much as Sylvie had done, and crashed into his legs. 'Daddy, I hab *missed* you,' she cried, trying to jump up into his arms.

He chuckled again, and picked her up. She wrapped her little arms tight around his neck, slobbering kisses on his cheek. With her blonde hair and golden-brown eyes Chloe was the image of him, but her personality was all Sylvie. And because he worked from home two days a week, caring for Chloe while Sylvie worked at the hospice, he was close to his daughter. 'I missed you, too, princess.'

'Chloe sleep with Daddy tonight?' she asked hopefully.

Pete sniggered as Mark made a face of helplessness at him. 'Yeah, good luck with that.' And he disappeared back into the dining room.

Sylvie laughed, but said firmly, 'No, pumpkin. Mummy sleeps with Daddy. You can sleep in the same room with the baby when she comes.'

'Baby come now?' Chloe asked, without missing a beat.

Mark hugged her, feeling unequal for this discussion after a tiring day and a long flight. 'Tell you what, why doesn't Aunty Katie come home again tonight and sleep with you?' Katie had started this problem; she could at least help out for another night. It might take her mind off her five-year hopeless quest to make Simon look at her—for a night, anyway.

Chloe promptly wiggled down to the ground and bolted for the dining room. 'Aunty Katie, Aunty Katie—you come sleep with Chloe again!'

'You're only putting off the inevitable,' Sylvie admonished him as she took his hand. 'But we can put off this discussion until you've eaten and slept.'

He looked at the upturned face of his beloved wife, and once again felt deep thankfulness for adorable stubbornness and impossible promises. 'Thanks, sweetheart.'

And they walked hand in hand into the dining room of his parents' house, to the teasing laughter and greetings of his loving family.

What's a
Housekeeper To Do?

JENNIE
ADAMS

Dear Reader,

Lally Douglas is a beautiful girl who made a bad choice in her past and, while she's been getting on with her life and is happy within her large, diverse family, she is keeping her heart very carefully to herself in other ways. Lally has lost some of her trust, and she doesn't know how to forgive herself for the results of her past actions. But she loves helping people, so when she sees Cameron Travers' ad for a temporary housekeeper she applies for the job and is determined to do it well.

Cameron Travers is a workaholic insomniac who develops properties and writes crime thriller books. He has nowhere near enough to offer in a committed relationship. He can't even sleep at night! When Lally starts to work for him, she makes her way deeper and deeper into his affections, and eventually his love, but what does Cam have to give to a special girl like Lally? Even if she does make him feel relaxed and at peace every time she is near him, just by being herself!

This story is about acceptance, forgiveness, hope and reaching out. It's about a man who is perfect in the midst of his unusualness and differences, and a girl who is loving and giving and good, despite the bad things in her past. Most of all it's about the promise of happiness between two special people I believe in with all of my heart.

I hope you'll enjoy the journey of Lally and Cam as they walk their path towards that happiness.

With love from Australia,

Jennie

Australian author **Jennie Adams** grew up in a rambling farmhouse surrounded by books, and by people who loved reading them. She decided at a young age to be a writer, but it took many years and a lot of scenic detours before she sat down to pen her first romance novel. Jennie has worked in a number of careers and voluntary positions, including transcription typist and pre-school assistant. She is the proud mother of three fabulous adult children and makes her home in a small inland city in New South Wales. In her leisure time Jennie loves long, rambling walks, discovering new music, starting knitting projects that she rarely finishes, chatting with friends, trips to the movies, and new dining experiences.

Jennie loves to hear from her readers and can be contacted via her website at www.jennieadams. net

For the girls in my bunker.
For cheeky lunch-time topics and midnight IMs.
For the Toby addiction (yes, you L), for the
Rwoooarhhh! (yes, you, C).
For talking me down on the phone
(yes, you V). For hugs in person and hugs
long distance.
For being my cheer squad. For sharing the
path with me with grace. For understanding
about the boots.
For my editor Joanne Grant and my senior
editor, Kim Young. I am blessed.
Thank you.
For my precious ones, and for you.

CHAPTER ONE

'I REALISE it's a little unusual, conducting this kind of business in the middle of a lake.' Cameron Travers' mouth turned up with a hint of self-directed humour before he shrugged broad shoulders in the misty Adelaide morning air. 'When I started wondering about this scene idea, and I knew I'd need a second pair of hands to test it out, I decided to combine our interview with some research. I hope you don't mind too much.'

'It's a nice setting for a job interview, Mr Travers, even if it is unusual. I'm more than happy to oblige.' If the man needed to row a boat around a lake at dawn to research for his crime-thriller writing, then Lally Douglas could work with that. She offered what she hoped appeared to be a completely relaxed smile because, yes, she did have a little bout of nerves going on. After all, she'd never had a 'real' job-interview before, let alone with a millionaire property-developer and world-famous crime-thriller author!

Cameron's attractive mouth curved. 'I appreciate your willing attitude. I could really do with some help for a while with the basics of day to day life so I can focus my energy on the property development I'm undertaking here in Adelaide, and to crack the challenges I'm having with writing my current book.'

The words somehow let her in. His smile let her in further. How could a simple, wry grin all but stop a girl's breath? Lally searched for the answer in deep-green eyes fringed with curly black lashes, in a lean face that was all interesting angles and planes in the early-morning light. In the charming sense of welcome and acceptance that seemed to radiate from him.

She'd sensed he was a nice man when they'd spoken on the phone to arrange this interview. They'd both approached a local job-agency and got an almost immediate match. And now again when they met up here in this leafy Adelaide suburban park to conduct his research experiment, and her job interview.

He was quiet, thoughtful even, and, from the depths Lally discerned in his eyes, he seemed to be a man who kept his share of things to himself. He also had a lovely way of making others feel somehow welcomed by him. 'I'd love to be able to help you so you could concentrate more of your efforts on your work.'

'Having someone to handle housekeeping and some general secretarial work for me—very basic stuff— will free up enough of my time so I can really do that.' Cameron Travers continued to row their small boat out towards the middle of the lake.

Not with muscle-bound arms, Lally. You're not even noticing the muscles in his arms. You're focused on this interview.

Eight weeks of employment as his temporary housekeeper with a little secretarial work thrown in as and when needed: that was what was on offer if she landed the job. Such a period of time in her life would be a mere blip, really.

'Did the agency explain what I'd want from you?'

Cameron asked the question as he rowed. 'I gave them a list of specifics when I lodged my request.'

'I'd have the option of living in or arriving each morning. I'd cook, clean, take phone messages, maybe do a little clerical work, and generally keep things in order for you.'

Lally had no trouble parroting the work conditions. And, feeling that openness was the best policy from the start, she said, 'I would prefer to live in. It would be cheaper than staying with Mum and Dad and travelling across the city each day to get to work.' Well, if she had to take a job outside the family, the least she could do was choose something she felt would be interesting and make herself comfortable in it.

'You have a good understanding of my requirements. I've always done everything for myself.' His brows drew together. 'But time is ticking away. My agent is getting twitchy. I need to hone my focus on the book and the property development and nothing else. I'm sure taking this step will be all I need to get past the writer's block that's been plaguing me.'

Lally didn't know how long it took to write a top-selling novel in a crime-thriller series, but she imagined it would be quite stressful not to be able to get the story moving while the days rushed by towards a deadline.

And, for Lally, she needed to work to put some money in the coffers. When the job ended she would dig back into her usual place among her relatives and continue to look after them through a variety of gainful employment opportunities.

For their sake. Lally worked for their sake. And it didn't mean there was anything wrong just because she'd been obliged to get out into the real workforce at this

time either. No one in the entire mix-and-match brood
happened to need her just at the moment. That was all.

Lally tipped her chin up into the air, drew a deep breath
and forced her attention to their surroundings; South
Australia in November. It was cool and misty over the
lake this morning, but that was only because the park was
shaded, leafy, the lake substantial and the hour still early.
Later it would get quite warm.

'It is certainly mood-inducing weather,' Lally said.
'For this kind of research.'

'Yes, and the burst of rain last night has resulted in
a nice mist effect here this morning.' He glanced about
them.

Lally was too interested in the man, not the scenery.
She admitted this, though she rather wished she hadn't
noticed him quite so particularly. She usually worked very
hard to avoid noticing men. She'd been there and made a
mess of it. She still carried the guilt of the fallout. What
had happened had been so awful—

Lally pushed the thoughts away and turned her attention to the dip of the oars through the water, turned her
attention back to Cameron Travers, which was where it
needed to be. Just not with quite so much consciousness
of him as a man. She trailed her fingers through the water
for a moment and quickly withdrew them.

'You said on the phone yesterday that you have plenty
of experience in housekeeping?' The corners of Cameron's
eyes crinkled as he studied her.

Lally nodded. 'I've worked in a housekeeping role
more than once. I'm a confident cook, and I know how
to efficiently organise my time and my surroundings. I'm
a quick learner, and used to being thrown in the deep
end to deal with an array of tasks. I see new challenges
as fun.'

'That sounds like what I need.' His voice held approval, and for some silly reason her heart pattered once again as she registered this fact.

'I hope so.' Lally glanced away and blabbed out the first thing that came to her mind. 'Well, it may be November, but trailing my fingers through that water made it clear it's still quite chilly. I wouldn't want to fall in.'

'Or dip your hand into water that might be hiding a submerged crocodile.' Cameron eased back on the oars a little. 'Wrong end of Australia for that, of course.'

'I've spent time in the Northern Territory and the Torres Strait islands. I have relatives up that way, on my mother's side of the family, but I've never seen a crocodile close up.' Lally suppressed a shudder. 'I don't want to.'

Lally didn't want to fall into awareness of her potential new boss, either—not that she was comparing him to a dangerous crocodile. And not that she was falling into awareness.

Cameron gave a thoughtful look as he continued to ply the oars until they reached the centre of the lake. Once there, he let the boat drift. 'It looks quite deep out here. I suspect the water would stay cold even in mid-summer.'

In keeping with the cool of the morning, he wore a cream sweater and blue jeans. The casual clothes accentuated his musculature and highlighted the green of his eyes.

Lally glanced at her own clothing of tan trousers and black turtleneck top. She needed to take a leaf out of her dress-mode book and be sensible about this interview, instead of being distracted by the instigator of it. She drew a steadying breath and gestured to the package in the bottom of the boat. 'You said we'd be tossing that overboard?'

He'd told her that much about his morning's mission

when they'd met where the boat had been moored, at a very small-scale jetty at the edge of the lake.

'Yes. It's only a bundle of sand in a bio-friendly wrapping. I'll be using my imagination for the rest.' His gaze narrowed as he took careful note of their surroundings. 'I need to get the combination of atmosphere and mechanics properly balanced in my mind. How much of a splash would there be? How much sound? How far out would the water ripple? The dumping would need to build tension without the reader figuring out what's going on, so I'm after atmosphere as well.'

'Ooh. You could throw a body over.' Lally paused to think. 'Well, no, the sand isn't heavy enough for that. What are you throwing in the story—a weapon? Part of a body?'

'Do I detect a hint of blood-thirsty imagination there?' He laughed, perhaps at the caught-out expression that must have crossed her face.

'Oh, no. Well, I guess maybe I was being blood-thirsty…a little.' Lally drew a breath and returned his smile. 'You must have a lot of fun writing your stories.'

'Usually I do.' His gaze stilled on her mouth and he appeared arrested for a very brief moment before he blinked. Whatever expression she'd glimpsed in his eyes disappeared.

'If you take me on as your housekeeper, I'll do everything I can to help you.' When she'd applied for this job Lally had only had two criteria in her mind: it had to be temporary, and she had to feel she could do the required work. Now she realised this truly could be interesting as well, even perhaps a little exciting; there was also plenty of room for a sense of achievement and to know that she had truly helped someone.

She might only be the housekeeper, but she'd be house-keeping for a crime writer on a deadline!

If it occurred to Lally that she had been a little short on excitement for a while, she immediately pushed that thought aside.

Lally shifted on her bench seat and quickly stilled the motion. She didn't want to rock the boat—literally. 'I haven't read anything suspenseful for a while. I usually save that for watching movies, but a good crime novel, curled up on a sofa...' She drew a breath. 'I'll try not to badger you with questions while you're plotting and writing. Well, that is, if you end up employing me.'

'I doubt it would bother me if you asked questions.' He smiled. 'Provided they don't start or end with the words "How many pages have you written today?"'

'I think I could manage not to ask that.' That would be like her mum painting, or Auntie Edie working with her pottery, and Lally demanding an account of the time they'd spent.

Lally cast another glance at Cameron Travers. He shared her dark hair, though his was short and didn't grow in waves, unlike her own corkscrew curls that flowed half-way down her back.

He had lightly tanned skin, and 'come lose yourself in me' eyes; now that she looked closely she saw very per-manent-looking smudges beneath those beautiful eyes.

So, the man had a flaw in his appeal. He wasn't totally stunning and irresistible to look at.

If you could call looking weary a flaw. 'Will I be help-ing you to get more rest?' That hadn't exactly come out as she'd intended. 'That is, I don't mean to suggest I'll be boring you to sleep at the dinner table or something.' He probably had a girlfriend to fuss over him anyway. Or maybe one tucked in every port, just like Sam had.

Well, Sam had had a wife.

And Lally.

She was not going there.

Sam was a topic Lally rarely allowed to climb all the way to the surface of her thoughts. It annoyed her that it had happened now—twice, really, if she counted that earlier memory of the mess she'd made of her life, and several others in the process.

Lally stiffened her spine and firmed her full lips into what she hoped was a very businesslike expression. 'I'll help you in any way that I can. It's just that you look a bit exhausted. That's why I asked the question.'

'Your help would allow me to focus my energy where I need to.' His gaze searched hers. 'That would be as good as helping me to get more rest. I don't sleep much.

'Now, are you ready to toss the sand-bundle overboard for me? It's quite a few kilos in weight. I do need a woman to throw it, as the "passenger" in the boat, but I hadn't stopped to think…' He hesitated and his gaze took in Lally's slender frame.

'I can manage it.' Lally flicked her hair over her shoulder where it wouldn't get in her way.

She might be slender but she was five-foot-seven inches in height and she had plenty of strength. If she could lift her nieces, nephews and little cousins of various sizes and ages, she could toss a packet of sand. 'Any time you're ready. Shall I stand and drop it like a bomb—hurl it from a sitting position? Do you want a plop or a splash, water spraying back into the boat?'

'Hurling would be fine, thank you. Preferably far enough out that we don't get drenched in the process.' Did Cameron's lips go from a twitch to a half-concealed grin? 'I think you should be able to throw the packet from a standing position, if we're careful. I do want to try that.'

He clasped her hand to help her come upright, and there went her resolve not to notice him in the slide of warm, dry skin over her palm, in the clasp of strong fingers curled around her hand.

Lally braced her feet and gave a slight cough. 'I'm, eh, I'm fine now, thanks. I have my balance. You can let go.'

He did so and she stifled a reaction that felt as much like disappointment as relief. It was neither, of course, because she wasn't fazed one way or the other by his touch.

Really, how could the clasp of a hand for a couple of seconds, a down-bent gaze as he helped her up, a curve of a male cheek and the view of a dark-haired head, make her heart beat faster?

How could his gaze looking right into her eyes, and his expression focusing with utter totality on her for one brief blink in time, make her feel attractive to him, for Pete's sake?

Trust me, Lally, you are not necessary to his very ability to breathe. You're looking like a solid possibility as a temporary employee, maybe, but the rest?

'Ready?' Cameron met her gaze with raised brows.

Lally uttered, 'Yes.'

He put the packet into her hands. It was heavy, but she invested all her effort into tossing it.

It landed several feet away with a satisfying splash and she eased back into her seat while Cameron's eyes narrowed. He mentally catalogued the impact—the upward splash of water droplets, water rippling out, the way the mist seemed to swallow everything just moments after it happened.

Lally watched Cameron, then realised what she was doing and abruptly looked away.

'Thank you. At least I know now that with two in the boat, even if he's otherwise occupied, she can toss the package over without drawing too much attention.' He stopped and smiled. 'Now that we've taken care of my research, tell me about your previous work-experience.' Cameron's words drew her gaze back to his face.

And put everything back in to perspective as an interview, which was of course exactly what Lally wanted.

'You don't need to make notes?' Well, obviously he didn't, or he would be doing so. She waved away the silly question. 'I've worked for the past six years for my extended family, doing all kinds of things: housekeeping, bookkeeping and cooking. I've been a waitress at my father's restaurant, *Due per*. It's small, but the place is always packed with diners.

'I've worked at my uncle's fresh-produce store, and another relative's fishing-tackle shop. My mother, several of her sisters and a couple of brothers are all Aboriginal and Torres Strait artists of one description or another. I've helped them at times, too, plus I've done nanny duties for my three sisters, and my brother and his wife.'

Lally drew a breath. 'I've travelled with Mum on painting expeditions. Anything the family's needed from me, I've done.' Except she had avoided Mum and Auntie Edie's attempts to get her to paint. Lally somehow hadn't felt ready for that, but that wasn't the point.

She fished in the deep orange, crushed-velour shoulder-bag she'd tucked beneath her seat and pulled out her references. Lally fingered the three-inch thick wad of assorted papers. 'I gave the employment agency three, but these are the rest. I have everything here that you might want to see in relation to my work experience.'

A hint of warmth crept into Lally's high cheeks. 'I probably didn't need to bring all of them.' But how could she have cut it down to just a few, chosen just some of them over the others?

'Better too many than not enough. May I see?' He held out one lean hand and Lally placed the papers into it.

Their fingers brushed as they made the exchange. One part of her wanted to prolong the contact, another worried that he'd know the impact his touch had on her. The same thing had happened when he'd helped her into the boat this morning.

Cameron flicked through the pages, stopping here and there to read right through. Aunt Judith had written her reference on an indigenous-art letterhead and added a postscript: *Latitia needs to pursue art in her personal time before she gets a lot older.* At least Aunt Judith hadn't labelled the reference with 'B-'. That was what Lally got for having an aunt who'd been a schoolteacher before she left work to paint full-time.

Cameron's mouth definitely quirked at one corner as he read Aunt Judith's admonishment.

Her uncle's reference was on a fruit-shop order form. Well, it was the content that counted.

'I don't know how you manage with so many relatives.' The concept seemed utterly alien to Cameron.

'Is your family…?' *Small? Non-existent?* Lally cut off the question; not her business, not her place to ask.

And just because she needed her family the way she did didn't mean everyone felt like that.

'There's only ever been my mother.' His gaze lifted to her face and he gave her a thoughtful look. He cleared his throat and returned his attention to the references. As his expression eased into repose, the sense of weariness about him returned.

How did he survive in life with only one relative? His expression had been hard to read when he'd mentioned his mother. Lally imagined they must be extremely close.

'I'm more than happy with the references.' Cameron said this decisively as he watched a grey-teal duck glide across the water beside them. 'Do you have computer skills?'

'I can type at about fifty words a minute in a basic word-processing programme, and I've spent plenty of time on the Internet.' Lally would do her best. She always gave one-hundred-and-fifty percent. 'You said on the phone that you're refurbishing the old Keisling building. I looked it up on Google. The place looks quite large; it must be a substantial project to undertake.'

Adelaide had a lot of old buildings. Lally loved the atmosphere of the city; it combined a big, flat sprawliness with all mod cons.

'The Keisling building was initially a huge home. I'll be converting it to apartments.' He nodded. 'Once the work is done, I'll either sell it or put tenants in.'

'There are a lot of old buildings in Adelaide that I haven't seen.' Lally made the comment as he began to row them back towards shore. 'I've seen a reasonable amount of Australia generally, though.' She paused as she realised the interview appeared to be over. 'Am I rambling?'

'Slightly, but I don't mind. You have a soothing voice.' Cameron continued to row. 'I've travelled a lot myself. Sydney is where I keep a permanent apartment, and I'm in the same boat with that.' He glanced at the oars in his hands and humour warmed his eyes. 'I know a lot of Australia, but there are parts of Sydney that I don't know at all. There's a tendency to stick to what you need to know on local turf sometimes, isn't there?'

'Indeed there is.' Now Lally could add 'empathy'

and 'able to laugh at himself' to his list of attributes. Employer's attributes. 'Do you often travel and incorporate your writing research or settings with your property-development projects?'

'Yes. I work long hours and need to keep occupied, so I actively seek ways to keep my mind fresh and to keep busy.' A slight sound that could have been a sigh escaped him before he returned his attention to his rowing. 'Property development came first for me. I got into that straight out of school, and was fortunate enough to make money and be able to expand and make a strong, successful business of it. When I needed more to keep me occupied, I hit on the idea of writing a book. I mostly started that for my own amusement because I enjoyed reading. I was quite surprised when my first book was picked up by an agent, and from there a publisher. Making a second career out of writing was an unexpected bonus.'

And now he entertained and fascinated readers around the world.

I'm not fascinated by him, Lally told herself.

But her other side wanted to know why she couldn't be a little fascinated within reason, provided the fascination was focused on his work. 'And you became a famous author.'

'An author with a looming deadline and an unwelcome bout of writer's block.' Cameron brushed off her reference to his fame.

But he was famous. His series had gained a lot of popularity over the past few years. He had become at least somewhat a household name.

Cameron seemed to hesitate before he went on. 'Usually I'd thrive on my deadlines, but lately? There's the development of this property to get in motion, the rest of the business to keep an eye on via remote control and I'm

more tired than usual—maybe because I've been pushing harder with the writing, trying to get somewhere with
it.'

He didn't just want an assistant, he *needed* one.

The knowledge went straight to the part of Lally that
had given herself to her family so exclusively for the past
six years. The part that yes, had felt just a little threatened
when they hadn't needed her at the end of her last job.
Even her sisters had said no to child minding, and they
were always asking if Lally could find blocks of time for
that.

'Oh, no thanks, Lally. I've put them all into after-school
care and a sports programme for the next few months.'

'Actually, Ray's parents are going to have the girls after
school for a while.'

And so it had gone on.

Who'd heard of Douglas children going to after-school
care? The family did that! And Ray's parents never had
them.

It had felt like a conspiracy, but that thought was silly.
Lally shoved it aside accordingly.

'You need to be looked after a little, to have someone to
take the stress off you so you can focus on what you most
need to get done.' Lally could care for this man for two
months, and then she would go back to where she wanted
and needed to be—to the heart of the family who had all
been there for her through thick and thin. 'I'll be the best
housekeeper and assistant I possibly can, Mr Travers, if
you choose to employ me.'

Cameron eased the boat in towards the makeshift dock.
'I do want to employ you.' He named a generous salary.
'We'll need to figure out what days you'll be having off,
that sort of thing.'

'I have the job? Oh, thank you!' The wash of happiness Lally experienced had to be relief that she would be financially secure for the next two months, she decided. Her family would have helped her out, of course, they'd all offered that. But she couldn't accept that kind of support and then just sit around and twiddle her thumbs.

So this was good. Very good. 'Thank you, Mr Travers. I'll do everything I can to be a valuable employee to you.'

For some reason he looked quite taken aback for a moment. Cameron let the small craft bump into the dock. 'How soon can you start?'

'Later today, or first thing tomorrow. Which would suit you best?' Lally said—judiciously, she hoped, though excitement was bubbling all through her.

'Let's go with first thing tomorrow.' Cameron left the boat with an agility that made it look easy. He extended his hand and offered a smile that seemed to wash right through her. 'It will be nice to have someone else in charge of some of these things while I try...'

He didn't complete the sentence, but Lally assured herself that that was not because he was distracted by the touch of her hand in his.

More likely he had to focus on not letting her plop into the water like that packet of sand, because she wasn't paying as much attention to proceedings as she should have been as she wobbled her way out of the boat and onto the dock.

Pay attention, Lally, to getting your feet on solid ground—or planks as the case may be—not to the feel of warm skin against your hand!

'Um, thank you.' Lally detached her hand from where it had somehow managed to wrap very securely around his. She could feel the pink tingeing her cheeks again; yes, it was possible to *feel* pink.

'You were about to say, while you try…?'

'To manage two key areas of my life so they both get, and stay, under control.' Cameron pushed his hands into the pockets of his trousers.

He appeared quite unaware of the way that the action shifted the cream jumper across his chest so Lally could enjoy an unimpeded view of the movement of the muscles that ran beneath the layer of cloth.

She was not noticing!

To make up for her consciousness, Lally gifted Cameron Travers with a full-wattage, 'thank you for employing me' smile. 'Your property work and your writing. I understand. So, seven tomorrow morning at your development site, bags packed and ready to leap straight in to whatever is on your agenda for the day? Me, not the bags, I mean.'

Cameron blinked once, and the dark green of his eyes darkened further. 'Yes. That will be fine. We'll eat breakfast while I give you a list of duties to start you off.'

'Excellent.' Lally considered shaking his hand again, and rejected the idea.

Better to keep her hands to herself. Instead, she tucked a long brown curl behind her ear and turned towards the exit of the park. 'I'll see you tomorrow, Mr Travers.'

'Cam,' he offered mildly, and took her elbow in a gentle grip. 'Cameron, if you really must. I'll walk you back to your car.'

'And I'm Latitia. Well, you'd have seen that on my job application and some of the references. But I prefer Lally. Um, will your boat be safe?' Lally's words ran together in a breathless rush.

'I hired the boat. The owner should be along to collect it soon.' Cameron didn't seem worried one way or the other.

He could probably simply buy a replacement. The man no doubt had the money to do that if he wanted.

Lally hot-footed it at his side to the exit as quickly as she could, where she immediately made her way to her elderly, fuel-inefficient station wagon, and bade him an equally swift farewell. The car seated six people, and that was important when a girl had a really big family. She needed to regroup and get her thoughts sorted between now and tomorrow, so she could approach this new work from the right perspective. From a completely efficient, professionally detached, businesslike perspective.

'See you tomorrow.' He turned to walk towards his own car, parked some distance beyond them.

The last thing Lally saw as she drove away was Cameron getting into a sky-blue convertible and putting the top down.

Her final thought was of how much she would love a drive through the countryside in that vehicle with him.

Even if it would only fit the two of them.

Not that she was thinking of them as 'two'.

That would be just plain silly, and dangerous into the bargain.

Lally hadn't protected her emotions and avoided men for the past six years to now get herself into trouble again in that respect!

CHAPTER TWO

'HERE I am, suitcases in tow as promised.' Lally spoke the words in a tone that was determinedly cheerful and didn't quite cover a hint of nerves.

She pulled the suitcases in question behind her along the courtyard pathway. 'I have more things in my car, but I can get those later. I pretty much take my whole world with me to every new job among the family; it's a habit I've formed over the years. I like to surround myself with my belongings. That way I can feel at "home" wherever I am. I'm sure I'll feel at home here, too, once I've settled in.'

Perhaps she'd formed the habit of chattering sometimes to try to hide things such as nerves.

Cam felt an odd need, that seemed to start in the middle of his chest, to reassure her and set her at her ease. He rose from where he'd been seated at the outdoor dining-table, and started towards her.

'I take a few regular things along when I travel.' Those things were mostly to do with both aspects of his work commitments: laptops, business files, his coffee machine and research materials for his writing. The coffee machine was definitely work related! 'Let me help you with that lot; your load looks ten times heavier than you. And I'm looking forward to you getting settled here too.'

It was ages since he'd spent any significant amount of time in close company with a woman. The last effort had been a disaster, but this was different, a working relationship. Cam wanted his housekeeper to feel welcome and comfortable.

She drew in a deep breath and let it out slowly, and he watched much of the tension ease out of her.

Lally Douglas was a beautiful woman. It would be a very novel experience for him, to have a woman living in as his housekeeper, and to have this woman specifically. He'd anticipated someone older, perhaps in semi-retirement.

Maybe he would learn some things through contact with Lally Douglas that would help him to pin down the quirks and foibles of the female character for his book.

He did wonder why his new housekeeper carried that edge of reserve that seemed contrary to the vibrancy of her imagination, and the sparkle in her deep-brown eyes when something interested her. Cam put this curiosity down to his writer's mind, and studied Lally for a moment from beneath lowered lashes.

She was a slender girl with skin the colour of milky coffee, and curly almost-black hair; she had thick lashes, high cheekbones and a heart-melting smile that revealed perfect white teeth when it broke over her face. Today she wore a tan skirt that reached to her knees, sandals with a low heel, a simple white blouse and a light camel-coloured cardigan thrown over her shoulders.

'I can manage the suitcases.' Lally gestured behind her. 'As you can see, they stack, and the whole lot is on wheels.'

'Yes, I can see.' But he took the handle from her anyway. Their hands brushed and he tried, really tried, not to notice the smoothness of her skin or the long, slender fingers with perfectly trimmed, unadorned nails. Cam wanted to stroke that soft skin, wrap those fingers in his.

And do what? Bring her hand to his lips and kiss her fingertips? *Not happening, Travers.* He'd had this same reaction to her yesterday, and had done his utmost then to stifle it. Mixing business with awareness to a woman really wasn't a smart idea.

Cam didn't have time to worry about an attraction anyway right now. He saved that for when he felt like socialising, and chose companions who were not looking for a long-term involvement. Past experiences in his life hadn't exactly helped him to trust in the concept of women in deeper, personal relationships, between the way his mother had raised him and the one relationship he'd tried to build in his early twenties that had failed abysmally.

Cam towed the load of suitcases to the doorway of the complex's large apartment and pushed them inside before he turned back to Lally.

She had dropped her hand to her side almost awkwardly. Now she gave a small smile. 'Thank you for that.'

'You're welcome.' He gestured behind him. 'That's the apartment we'll share while you're with me. It's the only one in the building that's been kept in half-decent order and fully furnished, as caretakers have come and gone prior to my purchase of the place. I've claimed one of the bedrooms for office space, but there are two more, as well as all the other necessary amenities.'

'That will be fine. Dad checked with the agency and confirmed your character references.' She bit her lip.

'It's best to feel certain that you're safe.' Cam led the way to the outdoor-dining setting and indicated she should take her seat. It was a large table, with half a dozen wrought-iron chairs padded with cushions facing each other around it. Lally and Cam sat at one end.

'Thank you; I appreciate that you understand.' Lally's gaze went to the covered food-dishes and settled on the silver coffee-pot. 'If all that's as good as it smells, I think I'm being very spoiled on my first morning at work.'

Cam shrugged, though her words had pleased him. 'It took less than half an hour to put together. I cooked while I tried to brainstorm some more ideas for my story.' 'Tried' being the operative word.

'I'll make sure I have a good breakfast ready for you each morning from now on.' As Lally spoke the words, the noise level at the far end of the site increased as two of the workers began to throw tiles off the roof into a steel transport-bin below.

Lally tipped her head to one side and her big, brown eyes filled with good-natured awareness. 'Has the noise been interfering with your writing?'

'No. I can usually work through any amount of noise.' He wished he *could* blame his lack of productivity on that. Cam didn't know what to blame it on, or how to fix it, other than sticking at the writing until he got a break-through with this tricky character, and using Lally's help to allow him to really hone his focus on that. 'But they only actually started the work this morning. I've been here less than a week myself, and most of that time's been spent organising a work crew, working with the site boss to get our orders in for materials, that sort of thing.'

Cam liked a good work challenge. He just wasn't enjoying it quite as much as usual this time, thanks to his problems with the book. He'd always managed both aspects of his life—the property development and the writing—and kept both in order. He didn't like feeling out of control at one end of the spectrum.

'It's good that noise isn't a problem to you.' Lally
glanced around her, taking in the large pool that looked
more like a duck pond at the moment. 'Oh, look at the
swimming pool. It's a nice shape, isn't it? A kind of curvy-
edged, squished-in-the-middle rectangle. Very mellow.'
Her gaze moved around the large courtyard area, and
encompassed the building that surrounded it in a U-shape
on three sides, before returning to meet his eyes.

'I can see why you wanted this place. It will be wonderful when the work is done.' An expression that seemed to
combine interest in her new job and a measure of banked-
down hurt came over her face. 'At least I'll have plenty
to do here while my family don't need me.' She drew a
breath.

'Ah—your family?'

'I'll be back in the thick of it with them straight after
this.' She rushed the words out as though maybe she
needed to do so, to fully believe in them herself. 'I help
out in all sorts of ways.'

'I'm lucky to have you to look after me for a while.' It
was true. His body was exhausted, pushed by even more
hard work beyond the usual state of tolerable weariness
induced by him being an insomniac-workaholic. 'It'll be
nice to have someone to take care of some of the very
ordinary everyday tasks.'

Heaven knew, he could afford to pay for the help; he'd
just never sought it before. Doing the cooking and cleaning for himself burned up time, and time was something
he usually had oodles of on his hands. He still had lots of
time, but, thanks to a female character who simply refused
to come to life on the page for him, that time wasn't productive enough.

Cam lifted the coffee pot, glanced at the cup in front
of Lally and raised his eyebrows in a silent question.

'Yes please.' The colour of her eyes changed from dark brown to clear sherry and a dimple broke out in her cheek. 'I'm ready for my first dose of caffeine for the day.'

They sipped in silence for a moment. Cam let the rich brew hit the back of his throat and give his body a boost. He'd tried leaving coffee out of his diet for a while, hoping it might have a positive impact on his sleep issues, but it hadn't made any difference.

Lally laced her fingers together in front of her on the table and looked about her again. 'This property would make a great base for a character in your book.'

She cast a sheepish glance his way. 'I bought the first book in your series yesterday after our interview. It said in the back that you sometimes use your development projects as settings for your stories.'

'I hope you're enjoying the read.' It made Cam happy to know he was providing entertainment for readers, but Lally had said she didn't usually read crime novels. 'My kind of books aren't to everyone's taste.'

Lally said earnestly, 'Oh, I finished it! I was on the edge of my seat the whole time. I'm looking forward to reading the rest of the books in the series so far. The only thing that could have made the story better would have been a love interest for your hero.' She clapped a hand over her mouth. 'I'm so sorry. What would I know about it?'

Cam gave a wry grimace. 'The need for a love interest is an opinion shared by my editor and agent. I'm quite prepared to add her in, but I'm having trouble cracking her characterisation.

'Let's eat, anyway.' Cam lifted the covers off the hot food and invited her to help herself. He'd prepared bacon, eggs, sausages and grilled tomatoes, and had added fresh bread-rolls from the small bakery two blocks away. 'I

hope there's something here that's to your taste, but if not
I have cereal, fruit and yoghurt inside as well.'

'This will be fine. Thank you.' She helped herself to an
egg, two grilled tomatoes and a warmed bread roll. 'I'm
truly sorry for what I said about your book. It's none of
my business.' Lally still looked stricken. 'I shouldn't have
told you that I wished there was a female counterpart in
that book.'

Cam said gently, 'It's all right. My ego can take some
constructive criticism of my work. Who knows? I might
bounce some of my ideas off you. In fact, I'll almost certainly ask you to help with research, as you know your
way around a computer and the Internet.' That was a
bonus Cam hadn't expected to get in his temporary housekeeper.

'Ooh. Helping will be fun.' Lally's eyes gleamed. 'I
can look up all sorts of interesting things for you.'

Cam smiled. 'Perhaps I should just be grateful that my
editor and agent waited until my sixth book to talk to me
about the need to include this new character.'

'Yes. You escaped it until now.' Her grin started in the
depths of chocolate eyes, crinkled the skin at their corners
and spread across her lips like sunshine.

Teasing; she was teasing him.

And Cam was enjoying being teased. A corresponding
smile spread across his face and they stared at each other;
the atmosphere changed and suddenly he was looking
deep into her eyes and the humour was gone. His hand
lifted towards her.

He dropped it back to his side. They broke eye contact
at the same time.

Cam reminded himself that this awareness he felt towards her, and that she perhaps felt towards him, wasn't a
good thing. Cam lived a chronically busy lifestyle. It had

been that way for years. He pushed himself to survive, survived to push himself more. By doing both, he filled the endless hours in which he could never manage to sleep properly.

There was no breaking that cycle. He had to live with it. It was the only way he could live. It certainly wasn't a cycle that lent itself to him getting into any kind of meaningful relationship with a woman. He'd proved that fact in the past.

Yet, you're thirty-two now. What if you get hit with one of those biological urges and need to settle down, produce children or something?

Like his mother had produced and settled. Well, she'd produced.

Cam shoved the conjecture aside. It was quite pointless.

Lally took another sip of coffee and looked at him over the rim of the cup. 'This is very nice. Thank you. I have to admit, I hang out for my first dose of coffee each morning.' She gestured towards the far side of the building. 'The work crew seem to know what they're doing. If they keep on at that cracking pace, the work will be done quickly.'

'That's my goal.' Cam glanced towards the crew and then let his gaze trail slowly back over the courtyard area; a small frown formed between his brows. 'I'm not quite sure what to do out here. It needs something.' He didn't know what; surely getting the place organised into apartments was enough anyway?

He was only going to rent or sell them, so what did it matter if he thought the courtyard lacked soul? 'I want to have the pool converted so it's heated for year-round use. The courtyard and surrounding gardens need to be brought up to scratch as well.'

'The place will be a hive of activity for the next while.'

They ate in silence for a few moments. Cam watched Lally's delicate movements, observed the straightness of her back in the wrought-iron chair.

Her fingers were lovely. If Cam had to create a female love-interest for his book, she would have hands like Lally's, he decided. They'd look good wrapped around a gun, a champagne glass or an assassin's throat while his heroine resisted the threat with all her worth, or the woman could even be an assassin.

Cam had lots of ideas. He just couldn't seem to hone them into something coherent. He cleared his throat. 'The duties list…'

'Do you have a written list for me?' Lally asked her question at the same time.

They stopped and each took a sip of their coffee. Lally drew a breath that lifted her small breasts beneath the cowl-neck top. Her hair was loose about her shoulders, as it had been yesterday.

Her top was sleeveless, and Cam wanted to stroke his fingers over the soft smoothness of her skin. She had strength in those slender arms, despite her small size. So much for deciding he wasn't going to notice her appeal.

While Lally nibbled on a bite of tomato, Cam fished a piece of paper from his shirt pocket. 'I've jotted down a few basics for now.' He handed it across the table to her.

While she read, he got on with his meal.

Lally finished the last of her tomato and egg while she read through the duties list. Though his gaze wasn't on her, she felt his consciousness of her, and had to force herself to concentrate on the words in front of her.

The list included taking care of his laundry, cleaning the apartment, meals and changing the linens. She would be in charge of his mobile phone during the hours he was writing, take messages and make the decision as to whether to interrupt him or not depending on what messages came through from his Sydney business.

There were a few lines about how to deal with the work crew, but he mostly wanted to handle that for himself.

'That all seems very reasonable.' Lally glanced up.

'I may ask for other duties as time progresses. Once the crew begins to get the apartments up to speed, I may send you in to clean them ready for occupation.'

'I'll be glad to do that.' Lally wanted to work hard for him. 'I like to keep busy. The task doesn't matter, just so long as I'm occupied.'

Had she made herself sound boring?

Why would it matter if you had, Latitia? You're his housekeeper. You don't have to be interesting, just productive and helpful.

'I'm good at multi-tasking through phone calls.' Lally's phone usually ran hot with calls and text messages. Yet, in the beaded bag at her feet, her phone was still and silent. The contact from her family had all but stopped since Lally had realised she was going to have to go outside normal channels to look for a job.

A man in a hard hat strode across the courtyard towards them. He stopped just short of their table. 'Morning, Mr Travers. Sorry to interrupt, but I'm ready to discuss these plans any time you are.' He gestured to the clipboard in his other hand. 'The crew should be in this morning to start the work to get that swimming pool up to speed too. They'll have to drain it, to do the work to turn it into a heated pool, but the water's too far gone to fix by shocking it with chlorine and balancing agents, so you're not losing anything on that score.'

Cam glanced towards the building. 'What other plans are on for today?'

'Makes the most sense to strip all the apartments at once, so that's what we'll be doing.' The man's gaze shifted to Lally and lingered. 'We, eh, you don't need any of the other apartments until all the work is done, so this'll streamline the process.'

'Thank you.' The words emerged in a deeper than usual cadence. Cam frowned and then said, 'Let me introduce you. Jordan Hayes, this is my housekeeper, Lally Douglas. Lally, meet my site manager.'

The man stuck out a hand. 'Nice to meet you.'

Lally shook his hand, reclaimed her own, and got to her feet. 'I'll leave you both to your discussion. I'd like to get started on my workload.' Her gaze shifted to the breakfast table. 'I'll clear this away once I've settled my belongings inside.'

Lally slipped away before Cam could think of anything to say in response, and then the site manager spoke and Cam forced his thoughts onto the work here.

Cam didn't want to examine the tight feeling that had invaded his chest when Lally had slipped her hand into the other man's grip. If that reaction had been possessive, Cam had no right to it. His mouth tightened. He did his best to relax his expression as he spoke to the manager. 'We'll go into my office and talk there. It will be a bit quieter.'

Perhaps if he tucked himself away in there after this talk—focused on the property development, checked in with his Sydney office for the morning and then attacked his writing—he would get his thoughts off fixating on a certain brand-new, temporarily employed housekeeper.

For the truth was she had looked far too good when she'd arrived this morning, pulling a bunch of suitcases along behind her while her hips swayed and her legs ate up the ground beneath her feet in long strides. Cam had noticed how good she looked, far too much.

It was one thing to do such minor and insignificant things as notice the shape of her hands, he told himself, but that noticing had to stop.

Cam led the way into his office, the site manager behind him.

He would put Lally Douglas right out of his mind and not think about her again until lunchtime.

It wasn't as though he couldn't control his mild attraction to her. How ridiculous would that be?

CHAPTER THREE

'YOU'RE quite sure you're okay, Aunt Edie?' Lally had her mobile phone jammed between her shoulder and her ear. It felt right there, and so it should. Usually she spent a lot of her day with a phone in that exact position, talking with one relative or another while she went about her work and various family members checked in with her.

Today she'd had to phone Auntie herself; she had only received a couple of text messages all morning, mostly from two of her teenage cousins who'd recently got their first-ever mobile phones.

Of course, she'd been kept busy with calls and a few text messages coming in to Cam's mobile. It felt a little intimate to take all his calls and messages. What if a woman phoned?

And what if the phone he gave her was purely for business and he had another one for his social life? Lots of people did that.

Right. Why was Lally fixating on Cam's social life, anyway? She should be fixating on her family's silence. Lally had kept so close to all her family in the past. It felt unsettling now not to hear from them much.

'You're working an outside job,' she muttered. 'They probably don't want to call and disturb that.'

'Beg pardon, dear?'

'Oh, sorry, Auntie. It was nothing; I was just talking to myself.' She was talking to Auntie, who seemed quite happy to talk, so what was Lally worrying about anyway?

Lally whisked eggs in a bowl and quickly poured the results over a selection of cooked vegetables in a heated pan on the stove. 'Promise me you're well, Auntie. You're taking all your meds? You've got Nova coming over to sort them out for you for the start of each day? Because I could drive over at night during my time off.'

'I'm fine, Lally. Nova comes every day, but even if she didn't I could cope. You just enjoy your work out there in the world where you might meet—' Her aunt coughed. 'We all think you'll do a very good job, just as you always do, dear.'

'Thank you. I appreciate that.' And Lally did. She was being quite silly to feel displaced. For heaven's sake, she'd only been at the new job for half a day. By the end of the week she might be getting so many calls and messages from her family that her new boss would be quite angry with her, if he didn't see that she always kept working throughout those calls and messages, hard and at speed.

And, of course, she would put answering his mobile first.

Lally had learned a long time ago to multi-task. Cameron seemed to live that way too. It was something they had in common.

What you have in common is that he's the boss and you're the employee, Lally. Try to remember that!

'Shouldn't you be focusing on your new job this morning, Lally?' Auntie asked the words into the silence, almost as though she'd read Lally's mind.

'I am.' Lally glanced around the kitchen. Cam had left no mess, so it had been easy to give the whole area a deep

clean. Now Lally sprinkled fresh, chopped herbs into the
frittata and turned it down to heat through.

With a light salad, that would take care of their lunch,
and this afternoon she'd see about their dinner. So far
she'd cleaned most of the rooms, settled her things into
the room across the small hall from Cameron's bedroom,
looked over the pantry supplies, made a list of things she
would need to buy soon and organised this meal.

And had taken Cameron's messages. None of them had
sounded unbearably urgent, though the content of many
of them from his Sydney office had brought it home to
Lally that Cameron truly dealt in big dollars.

Lally prepared the salad with cherry tomatoes, lettuce,
mushroom slices and slivers of avocado mixed with a
tangy dressing; that job was done. She checked on the
frittata; it was almost cooked.

Sam had liked tangy dressing on his salad.

The thought slid sideways into Lally's mind; it wasn't
welcome. She so rarely thought about Sam. If getting out
and working with a man would make that a common occurrence, Lally was not going to be pleased. 'I'm working
and talking at once, Auntie. I can talk. Tell everyone else
they can call me too. Even if just early in the mornings,
or in the evenings, if they're worried that much about my
job. I'm sure I can fit in some calls—'

But her aunt had already rushed out a, 'Love you,' and
disconnected the call at her end.

Well!

Lally drew a deep breath. 'It might have been nice to
get to say "I love you" back—'

'Whatever that is, it smells wonderful.' The deep words
sounded over the top of hers and cut them off abruptly.
'Sorry, were you on the phone?'

'Oh. I didn't realise you were there.' She'd been talking

out loud like a loon. 'Um, no, I'm all finished with my phone call. It was my phone that time, but I have a heap of messages from yours.'

'On the phone to the boyfriend?' Cam's words were unruffled, and yet something in his tone made Lally seek his gaze.

His eyes were shielded by those long, silky lashes.

'I should have brought this up at our interview. I apologise that I didn't, but I'll cover it now.' She did feel guilty, even though there was no need. 'I like to speak with family members when I have a moment. I'll do it discreetly, I won't disrupt you in any way, and I always keep working. I can assure you I don't lose any work time or concentration over the calls I make, and of course I'll always use my own phone.'

'Family.' Cameron's expression was complex. He ran his fingers through his short hair. 'Of course that's not a problem. You're welcome to keep whatever contact you need.'

'Thank you.' Lally considered telling him there was no boyfriend, but he'd probably figured that out anyway. In any case, it wasn't important. 'I appreciate you being understanding about my need for contact with my family.'

Now, if Lally could just get her *family* to come back on board with that contact.

'I can see you've been busy.' Cameron's glance roved the kitchen, dining room and lounge areas, before it came back to rest on her, and his expression softened. 'Thank you for what you've done already to help make me comfortable.'

'That's what I'm here for.' But his praise and appreciation wrapped around her just the same.

Being needed: it was an issue for Lally. She knew it;

she would even admit it. Until now she'd thought it was all just about family relationships for her.

And it was. This just felt sort of similar because she was helping him, too, and that was what she did for them. Her happiness certainly had nothing to do with that softening of his expression when his gaze rested on her. She wasn't looking for tenderness from him, for goodness' sake; that would be ridiculous.

Lally was too wary to consider something like that with a man again anyway. And she was still young, she justified to herself. She had plenty of time to think about getting back into the dating game. And she'd been really busy with family commitments.

Busy enough that they might have pushed her out so she'd find time for a social life again?

Her family had been known to stick their noses into each other's lives at times. Lally had been guilty of it too. In a big, loving family that would always happen, and she'd had her share of them hinting that she could do with getting out more.

But they wouldn't take it this far, would they? Of course they wouldn't…

'Lunch is almost ready now, if you want to take a seat in the dining room.' Lally would far rather eat lunch than go on thinking about that topic. She gestured to the freshly polished dining-table. 'Or we can eat outside, if you'd prefer? It's frittata. I hope that's okay.'

'Inside will be fine, and I eat most things.' He paused and the hint of a smile lifted the edges of his mouth. 'No artichoke. Other than that, I'm very agreeable about food.'

'That will make cooking for you a dream. I'd like to take advantage of the fresh markets for produce for a lot of our meals.' She wanted to feed him on the freshest items available, because she thought it might help with whatever had been exhausting him—lack of sleep, long hours, book stress, whatever the problem. Even if it didn't, it would put his body in a good place, health-wise.

Yes, fine, she was acting like a little mother. Why not, when she'd had a hundred or so relatives to practice those skills on? They all deserved to be loved to bits and looked after as much as possible, especially considering how much they'd had to put up with from her.

Not that she felt the need to earn their love. Well, that would be just silly, wouldn't it? And she didn't feel like a little mother; she felt like a determined housekeeper.

Lally turned the frittata onto a serving plate, carried it and the salad to the table she'd set, and took her seat. 'I hope you'll eat while the food is hot and at its best, and have as much as you want. I made plenty. I do have a bunch of messages from your phone, but I think they can all wait until after you've eaten.'

Now she sounded as though she was very generously allowing him to eat his own food, and making his work-related choices for him while she was at it. 'What if your editor rings?' Lally asked suddenly. 'Or your agent?'

'You'll be able to tell if they need to speak to me urgently, otherwise they can wait.' He gave a wry smile. 'I'm too professional to ask you to dodge them on my behalf if they phone and then ask for a progress update—though there might be certain days when I'll be tempted to do that if things keep going the way they have for the past few weeks.'

'You can't help it if you're in the middle of a sticky patch with your muse,' Lally declared. 'These things happen. It must be quite amazing to be internationally famous too. You probably have fans chasing after you and everything. Lots of women—'

The words burst out of her and Lally's face flooded with heat.

'I can't say I've been particularly *chased*, at least not to my knowledge.' Cam drawled the words. He felt far too pleased that Lally's words—when she'd got to the 'women' part of her statement—had sounded as though she was quite jealous at the thought of such a thing happening.

Two seconds later he realised that wasn't exactly the response he should have to her. And he didn't *want* women chasing him; he'd rather go and find them when he felt the need.

Cam helped himself to a piece of the frittata and some salad and took a first bite. The frittata was perfect, the accompanying salad the exact counterpoint for it; the zing of tangy dressing hit Cam's tongue, completing the experience. 'Did you make the dressing yourself? Where did you learn your cooking skills?'

'I did make the dressing. I learned to cook from two parents who both love it, and do it very differently but equally as well.' Lally's smile softened at whatever memories were in her head. 'What they didn't actively teach me, I guess I've learned by observation anyway.'

She seemed to take her skill level as nothing out of the ordinary.

'Your father runs a restaurant; I momentarily forgot that.' She'd told him that at their interview, and Cam had spent a few moments piecing together her family history in his mind. Torres-Strait Aboriginal mother, Italian father; the surname of 'Douglas' suggested that her father might not be fully Italian.

'Dad's mother married a Scotsman, just to keep things interesting.' Lally's lovely smile lit her face again.

'You have a diverse family tree.' Cam returned the

smile, and gestured to his plate. 'The food is delicious, thank you. I think I've struck it lucky with you, Lally, if this meal and the work you've got through already are any indication.'

'You're welcome for all of it.' Her skin didn't show a blush. Yet somehow he suspected one had just happened—by the change to the sparkle in her eyes, perhaps?

What would she be like in the middle of passion?

Cam cut the thought off. The answer to that question was that it was not his business to wonder.

'I've done as much work as I could this morning.' Lally seemed flustered as she pulled the duties list from her pocket and flattened it on the table beside her plate. She glanced at it and raised her gaze to his face. 'I'll do all that I can to look after you, help you start to feel more rested and focus on what you need to do with your time.'

'I appreciate that.' Surely in another week or two he would get back to sleeping at least the four to four-and-a-half hours a night he usually got? Cam didn't expect Lally to be able to do a thing about that. Why would she? All the experts had failed to give him any long-term solutions that didn't involve knocking himself out at night with medications he didn't want to let become a habit in his life.

'I haven't forgotten about book research.' Her finger rested on a point on the list. 'I'm ready to help you with that in any way required.'

'I have a research project for you for after lunch, actually.' Cam went on to explain what he needed. 'I have two laptop computers. What I'd like you to do is use the second laptop and get the prohibition laws about using these substances in this state...' He jotted the names of several chemical compounds onto the bottom of her list.

'I'll do the rest of the research myself. Some of it has to be handled carefully; I don't want you dealing with anything that could be potentially dangerous to you.' He paused. 'At least I can still make forward progress with my lead character's investigations and activities to some degree, even if other aspects of the story are being difficult.'

Lally's eyes widened and her soft lips parted. '*You* take care with your research? You keep yourself safe?' Her words were so genuine, filled with concern for him.

Cam got that strange feeling in his chest again. 'Always. I always take care.' He was even more determined to take care of *her* in this admittedly small way.

As their gazes met and held, Cam was very conscious of her.

She was conscious of him. It was there in her guarded expression, the rejection and the self-protectiveness in every line of her body, and didn't fully manage to conceal the interest beneath.

They threw sparks off each other, and Lally didn't want to feel those sparks.

Were they for him? Or for any man at the moment?

And, either way, *why?*

But he didn't need to know why; Cam told himself this. He needed to develop a three-dimensional book character, not know every aspect of his new housekeeper's make-up.

They both dropped their gazes at the same time and Cam rubbed his face wearily.

'Are you okay, Cam? You mentioned you don't sleep well—I assumed that was due to stress or work pressures.' Lally's soft words impinged on his thoughts. 'If there's anything else I need to know…'

'I'm a long-term insomniac. It's annoying sometimes but it's nothing to worry about.'

Though he didn't care who knew about it one way or another, this wasn't something he discussed often. Cam wouldn't have held the answer back from her, though, not when her face had filled with such concern.

Lally gave a nod of acknowledgement. 'It's no wonder you felt like being spoiled a little. Maybe you can enjoy some more rest than usual, even if it doesn't come in the form of sleep.'

'Maybe I will. I've got my eye on the pool.' He shrugged his shoulders. 'A swim now and then would be relaxing.' He hesitated. 'If you hear me up and about in the middle of the night...'

'Do you like company at those times, or to be by yourself?' Lally's expression had softened so much, it was almost as though she needed to find a chink in his armour and felt somehow reassured by finding it. 'I'd be happy to heat you some warm milk or sit up and talk.'

Cam pictured them sitting at this table at midnight. Somehow he doubted that drinking milk or talking would be the first things on his mind. He'd be thinking about kissing his way up the slender column of her neck until he reached those luscious lips and closed his own over them.

The urge to kiss her now, right in this blink of time, silenced him for a moment. It was one thing to imagine, even to want, but this urge felt somehow to be more than that.

Maybe you should just ask her if she'd curl up on the sofa with you, with your head in her lap, and stroke your face with her fingers until you fall asleep, you big baby.

Or you could admit you find her more than a little

intriguing and that you're not doing a very good job of pushing back that interest.

All right, he did find her intriguing, but he wasn't about to act on it. Theirs was a working relationship and that was exactly how Cam wanted it to be.

And that left how he wanted to deal with the rest of the day. And the next.

Cam cleared his throat and side-stepped the question. 'I'll take you to the market tomorrow morning and we can buy fresh produce together. I'll be awake anyway, so it makes sense that I go with you the first time at least.'

He could tell her what foods he liked the most, could carry her basket for her.

Or throw down his cloak for her to step on if she came across a puddle in her path!

'Excuse me.' He got to his feet and assured himself the only thought on his mind was getting back to business.

He was not running; he was planning and retreating so he could focus on his book. A totally different thing.

Cam took Lally's written list of phone messages and the phone itself from the table. 'I'll see to these and drop the phone out to you before I start writing, if that's okay?'

'Thanks.' Lally glanced down at the notes he'd written for her to research. 'And I'll bring my research results to you as soon as I have them.'

Cam looked at the sweep of her long black lashes. 'Other than that, perhaps you can just keep going with your housekeeping jobs.' If Cam stayed clear for a few hours, maybe he would get these strange reactions to her sorted out a little better.

Lally rose and started to gather dishes into capable hands. 'Good luck with the writing.'

'Thanks.'

Cam nodded and left.

CHAPTER FOUR

'I MEANT to unpack all this as soon as we got home.' It was the next afternoon. Lally reached into one of the string bags sitting on the kitchen counter in the apartment and pulled out several canned goods.

Her voice was raised a little to be heard over the outside noise of the refurbishing crew. Cam had to admit that right now they sounded more like a destruction mob. 'Are you okay with that noise? It's not driving you crazy?'

'Oh, no,' she said. 'I'm fine with it. If anything would get to me, I think it would be too much quiet.'

Cam understood that only too well. Maybe noise was what he needed at night.

You've tried that, remember? You've tried every trick there is. Noise or no noise; light or dark; quiet or loud; whatever, you don't sleep beyond what your body has to have to survive. That's all there is to it.

He returned his gaze to his housekeeper. 'You got busy when we got back here.' Lally had called it 'home' and hadn't seemed to notice the word. But in truth where did Lally Douglas call 'home'? She'd told him she had a room at her parents' home; was that it? At twenty-four, didn't she want her freedom at some point?

And why did it even matter to Cam? 'Home,' he'd

never had. A faceless, nameless apartment in the centre of
Sydney that he visited now and then hardly counted.

Yet wouldn't it be nice to have a home? A real one?
With a permanent housekeeper like Lally to look after
him?

Dumb thought, Travers. This was a temporary measure, nothing more. Cam drew a breath. 'There's nothing
in the foodstuffs that will have spoiled.'

'No. I put the perishables away straight off, at least.'
Lally removed the remaining articles from the bags and
started to pack them into the larder.

Cam resisted the urge to help. He'd crossed the line
enough by insisting they shop together at the market first
thing this morning. When they'd got back, he'd eaten
breakfast with her—then had taken himself off to his
office and proceeded to give his hero's love-interest so
many of Lally Douglas's traits and characteristics that
he'd had to delete half the work he'd written.

So he'd deleted, and he'd wrestled with his story some
more, and he'd come up with what he knew was a great
scene-idea—but then he couldn't get that to work either.
Without realising he did it, Cam heaved a sigh.

'Is the writing not going well?' Lally's words were
empathetic.

He shook his head. 'I've got a scene planned in my
mind, but when I try to write it I can't visualise it properly.
I can't "see" the heroine in my mind's eye. I'm not sure
how to use their surroundings. It's a scene that I know will
work, but I can't seem to *get* it to work. I think as long as
the heroine remains shadowy in my mind, this problem
is going to continue.'

'What would bring her to life for you?' Lally's eyebrows

drew together as she considered the matter. 'Could you "interview" her? Ask her questions to get to know her?'

'Stream-of-consciousness interviewing? I did try that about a week ago, but I didn't get anywhere with it.' Cam forced himself not to scowl his irritation over this. 'I feel as though I need to somehow throw her into the middle of this scene, really get in deep there with her. Once I see how she reacts, the pieces will all come together. Maybe.'

'Hmm.' Lally was silent for a long moment. She tipped her head to the side and tapped her finger on her chin before her eyes lit up. 'When Mum gets stuck on a painting, she tells my aunt the concept. Auntie takes a sheet of paper and whips out her interpretation of how she'd do the painting. Mum invariably says that's *not* how the idea should be executed! Rejecting one idea helps Mum to figure out how *she* wants to execute it.'

'That's an interesting concept.' It was Cam's turn to frown. 'I'd try that, if there was a chance it would rattle loose *my* interpretation. But how?'

'You need a "volunteer from the audience".' The smile deepened on Lally's lovely mouth. 'Someone, or more than one person, to act out the scene for you. You don't have to like how they do it, but it might help you figure out what you *do* want for the scene.'

Cam gave a surprised laugh. 'That could just work. I'd have to find an acting society or a theatre group willing to act it.'

'Or you and I could do it.' The words came out in a little rush and she immediately bit her lip. 'Not if you didn't want us to, but if you didn't want the hassle of trying to find real actors—if you only needed to play-act it to help you figure it out—we could do that, couldn't we?'

'We could.' Her enthusiasm started to spread through

him too. 'My idea is a wheels-within-wheels kind of situation, where he's pretending interest in her but he suspects her of being a double agent or spy or assassin. He thinks if he disarms her with food, wine and attention he'll figure out what she's up to.' He went on. 'She's got an equal number of suspicions about him. She pretends to be "buyable" for the night, to gain access to his hotel room to search it later, and then she's going to disappear—but he lures her to the roof top of the building after dinner when he suspects her motives are as duplicitous as his are.'

Cam drew a breath. 'Before dinner he spends money on her, buying her a dress and other gifts.'

'It really is wheels within wheels.' Lally's eyes were like stars. 'Oh, but that sounds so exciting. We could role-play the whole evening from beginning to end. It wouldn't have to be an exact match, but it could be a lot of fun!'

'Let's do it.' Cam's smile spread until it was as wide as hers. 'It'll have to be late in the day. If we're going to do this I want the right atmosphere, time of night, all of it.'

Happiness filled her face. 'Tonight?'

Cam couldn't seem to look away from that happiness. 'Yes, we'll do it tonight. We'll leave here at seven p.m. I'd better get on the computer and figure out where we can go that will provide the kind of backdrop I want.' He started to turn away; he *had* to turn away. 'Can you manage that?'

'Of course.' She did a little bounce on the balls of her feet. 'I'll go on with other work until you're ready for us to leave.'

He looked at her and tried not to think about the curve of the side of her face, her cheek, her chin and her lush lips that looked soft and kissable. 'We'll be out until around midnight, so feel free to take some time off this afternoon before we leave. I don't want to over-tire you.'

'I'll take a nap for an hour if I can get to sleep,' Lally conceded, but with a glow of anticipation still all over her face.

Somehow Cam doubted she would relax into sleep in this mood, but he wasn't a good one to gauge her chances. Just because he wouldn't have been able to sleep in the afternoon didn't mean she might not be able to nod off any time she decided she wanted to.

'I'll see you at seven.' He glanced at her clothes. 'You can come dressed as you are now, or in something similar; it doesn't really matter. Choosing clothes in the same way the female character would do that tonight will be part of our role-play. I'll need to locate a big hotel that has boutique stores. We'll shop there, enact the time in the dining room, and then go up on the rooftop for that part.'

Her eyes widened. 'It—it won't cost you a lot, will it? I didn't mean to suggest...'

'Something that might get my writing back on track after weeks of it driving me crazy because I haven't been able to get there?' He felt lighter than he had in all those weeks. 'If it costs me a little to organise this evening and I get a result, I will be more than happy, so don't give that another thought. Whatever I spend I'll be able to tax-deduct, anyway.'

'Well, I guess.' Lally frowned. 'Make sure it's a hotel that does clothing hire, or has cheap stores. We can go through the motions, buy or hire what we have to, I guess, but keep the expense right down.'

Cam smiled at the earnest face looking at him. 'You need to think of it as a cross between Cinderella and—I don't know—winning a shopping spree or something.'

'Oh, well, okay. I guess.'

'Good.' Cam turned away. 'I'll see you when it's time to go.'

'This is it. The boutique shops inside should provide what we need.' Cam spoke to Lally as he handed his car keys to a parking valet. He paused on the footpath that led into the hotel itself.

Lally drew a big breath. 'So we're all set for our night's acting. Oh, I hope it'll be fun, and you'll go back later and your story will just pour out of your fingertips because your imagination will have worked out what you want to do. The hotel looks awfully fancy.'

Her anticipation was so sweet that Cam just had to smile. Lally might enjoy wearing some different clothes, too, he thought with a hint of fondness that crept up on him. She dressed nicely already, but sometimes he felt she dressed to try not to be noticed. 'I haven't fully explained the final part of the evening when we'll go up on the rooftop: you'll be entirely safe, but I need an unanticipated reaction out of you. If you don't mind.'

'Your mysteriousness is making my imagination run wild.' Lally admitted this with a smile as she met Cam's gaze. 'I don't mind. You can surprise me. That can be part of the fun too.'

Cam cleared his throat. 'Thanks for being a good sport about it. You truly won't mind being dressed up and having your hair and make-up done?'

'Hair and make-up too?' Her eyes widened. 'I imagine I'll feel as though I'm being thoroughly spoiled.'

Lally gave her answer to Cameron and tried to gather her concentration. Cinderella; he'd said to think of it as that.

Her boss in a dinner suit; that was a big part of the

reason for her distraction. In truth, Lally did feel like Cinderella—well, Cinderella with a slightly weary but anticipation-filled prince at her side.

A prince who looked divine clothed this way, and wore his exhaustion more attractively than should be legal.

When she'd first emerged from her room and seen Cameron waiting for her, Lally's pulse had raced.

'Thank you for agreeing to this,' he'd said, and clasped her hand briefly before leading the way outside to his car. Beautiful car, gorgeous driver. Cameron had relaxed her with easy conversation during the trip, and even now as they walked through the hotel he somehow made her feel special whether he was looking all about him to research his book or not.

A night out of time, that was what this would be for Lally. She could do it, of course she could, and have a whole lot of fun in the process!

Cam led her straight to the grouping of boutique clothing-stores with fashionably sparse window-displays. Lally glanced around the opulent hotel's interior; that opulence tied in with what she saw here. A qualm struck; she leaned towards Cam and whispered urgently, 'That looks like a *designer original* dress in the window.'

'It is, but from my research there are plenty of non-designer dresses in the shop as well.' Cam stepped inside without giving Lally a chance to argue it one way or another. 'And here's our shop assistant ready to help us.'

'But the money,' Lally whispered, and tugged on his arm. 'It *all* looks expensive. You can't…'

He turned and gave a reassuring smile. 'These purchases are a legitimate business expense. I'll claim them against tax, and I get to give a great housekeeper the gift of a few things after we've used them for my research—if you'd like them. You'll let me do that rather than throwing them out, won't you?'

'Throw?' Lally bit back a gasp. He wanted her to let him buy the things and then give them to her, but she'd thought if that happened it would be in a very inexpensive way.

'It's not hurting anything, Lally.' He said it in such a businesslike way. 'I need this kind of setting. You understand?'

Lally calmed down a little. This was just work, when all was said and done. Unusual, maybe, but still work.

If her awareness of him suggested differently, well, she would get that sorted out. She would. She'd just watch very carefully to make sure they didn't end up buying a dress that cost a ridiculous amount of money.

'Good evening. How may I help you?' The saleswoman was already sizing Lally up.

'We need a dress. Something bright, flattering and elegant; a handbag; earrings, and I think...' Cam's gaze shifted to Lally's neck and lingered there. 'Yes, a necklace. I'll know what I want for that once we choose the dress. Hmm...' He turned to the saleswoman.

'I don't know much about this, but something that will suit her colouring, bring out the brown of her eyes and make the most of her hair. That's what I want.'

You should be in colours, Latitia. You were born for them on all sides of your family tree!

Mum had said that to her—recently, actually, now Lally thought of it. She had given Lally an almost disappointed look when Lally had shrugged her shoulders and said she preferred plain colours, and shades that blended rather than stood out. Mum had looked away and muttered something about 'long-term hibernation behaviour.'

A week later Lally had finished working at the fishing-tackle-and-bait store, and she'd no longer been needed in the next job she'd had lined up in the family. The whole family had been just fine getting along without her, and she'd ended up with Cam.

Now they were shopping, and he had his arm loosely against her shoulders; when had that happened?

Lally looked away in case she was gaping over the list he'd just given the saleswoman. Lally's glance fell on a mirror on the shop-wall that showed their reflections. Cam had a spark of enjoyment in his eyes.

Worse was the corresponding sparkle in her eyes.

More dangerous still was how much she liked the look of those two reflections; side by side.

Lally could count on one hand the number of times she'd been out on a date since the disaster of Sam six years ago. The last time must have been over a year ago. Those dates had been pleasant enough, she supposed, but in a very controlled way for her, and she'd never looked for a repeat.

Her reaction just now hadn't felt controlled. Plus, this was *not* a date!

'Nothing designer,' Lally said with about as much spine in her tone as an overcooked noodle. She cleared her throat and tried again. 'Maybe you have a sale rack?'

'Perish *that* thought.' The sales lady said it with good humour, disappeared for a moment and returned with a garment over her arm. 'Perhaps you'd like to try this? It's middle range, though it's an odd thing to be told *not* to include designer choices!' She held up a flow of deep-red silk.

'Oh, it's…gorgeous.' The words poured out of Lally's mouth before she could stop them; to her credit she tried to back-pedal as soon as it happened. 'That is, I'm not sure. It's awfully noticeable—the colour and style…' Lally broke off and turned to Cam. 'I guess that doesn't matter. It's only to help you to figure out what you want.'

'That's right. It seems…as good a choice as any.' He nodded. 'I'm having fun, Lally, and that's got to be good for my muse. So, go and try the dress on, please.'

'It will make you look absolutely radiant, dear.' Somehow the woman had her hustled through the store and into a changing room with the dress pushed into her hands before Lally quite realised what had happened. Her last glimpse before the dressing room door closed was of Cam turning to examine a shelf of evening bags with a purposeful and cheerful glint in his eyes.

Lally locked the dressing-room door, turned to the mirror, and saw a bright-eyed girl with red silk clutched in her hands.

'It won't fit,' she muttered, not sure if she was being hopeful, practical, hedging her bets or trying to talk herself out of a love affair that had already taken wings the moment the saleswoman held up the dress.

'You're such a predictable female, Lally.' She muttered the words beneath her breath. 'The first time someone throws a pretty dress at you, and all your past decisions about fashion choices and colours go out the window.'

Oh, but this was different. This wasn't for *her,* not really. This was for research so Cam could look at Lally and choose a whole different look for his book character.

It was reverse psychology, and it would work; Lally just knew it would. Lally was just the human mannequin for the evening, as cardboard and one-dimensional as could be.

She was filled with a lot of excitement for someone who was one dimensional, though.

'Are you done?' Cam's voice sounded from outside the cubicle. 'May I see the dress on you?'

Lally was done. She'd simply been standing there staring mutely at the transformation that had appeared in the mirror. She didn't feel much like a mannequin; she felt like a girl in a gorgeous dress.

'I'm not sure if this…' Lally put her hand on the door latch, unlocked it and pulled it open.

'You…' The single word trailed away as Cam's gaze slowly travelled from her head to her toes and back again.

'It seems to be the right size.' Lally resisted the urge to fidget with the hem or twitch the fabric over her hips. The dress fitted like a glove and flowed over her curves in all the right ways.

'It's perf— That is, I'm sure it'll be fine for our purpose, to help me figure out what the heroine in the story would wear.' Cam gave one slow blink and his voice deepened as he held out his hand. 'Put these on with it, please.'

A drop-necklace and set of dangling earrings were settled into the palm of her hand, and her fingers were curled closed over them. 'I slipped out to the jewellery store beside this one while you changed into the dress.'

'Okay, well, I'll put them on.' Their fingers brushed as Lally made sure she had a proper grip on the items.

Her heart was pounding. It was so stupid, but she fell silent as she withdrew her hand. Had Cam's hand moved away quite slowly, as though he might have been almost reluctant to lose the contact?

'There's a bag too.' His voice was deep and he cleared his throat before he went on. 'I'll give that to you when you come out.'

Lally could have put the necklace and earrings on in

front of him, but she was rather glad for a moment to herself. She had to pull herself together.

The earrings were simple gold with a pearl drop that bumped against her neck when she moved her head. The matching pearl-drop necklace nestled between her breasts. It would have been difficult to find a set to create a better foil for the dress.

No, Lally, it suits you and *the dress perfectly.*

Lally tucked her hair behind her ears to showcase the earrings. They really needed an upswept hairstyle; so did the dress. Lally took another proper look in the mirror.

The dress was deep red with a crossover V-neckline that cupped her breasts. It was deceptively simple, clinging in beautifully cut lines until it fell in loose folds to just below her knees. The hem was handkerchief-cut and swirled as she moved.

Cameron had dressed her the way she would have dressed herself six years ago. No; he'd dressed her the way that eighteen-year-old would have dressed six years on if she hadn't hidden herself in bland colours.

She hadn't *hidden* herself. She'd outgrown colours.

Have you, Lally? Because you look great in this, vibrant and alive and ready to take on the world. Ready to participate *in the world, not avoid it from within the heart of your family.*

Oh, this was silly! Lally was helping Cam; they were doing research. She wanted to get on with that and leave these other thoughts behind her. He'd look at all this, and it might look good on her, but it would help him see how he wanted to dress his heroine. He might put his character in faux fur, or shiny pink plastic, or dress her in blue velvet.

Lally gathered her other clothes into her hands, flung the door open and stepped out. She joined Cam at the service counter where he'd just finished paying for his transaction. 'I'm ready to get on with the rest of our research.'

And *that* was what this was truly all about.

CHAPTER FIVE

'THE hairdresser is next.' Cam made this announcement and led Lally towards the hotel salon. He pressed a small sparkly bag into her hands as they walked. His other hand held a bag the saleswoman had kindly supplied for Lally's day clothes. 'In the scene, the female character would make out that she wanted to be showered with as much "spoiling" as she could get.'

'And your male lead would be determined to do that, to keep her suspicions at bay about his real motives. They'll be deep in their false roles.' Lally took the small bag; she couldn't take her eyes from his face. The grooves at the sides of his mouth were deep. His face had the kind of stillness that concealed attraction and awareness.

Though she knew she shouldn't, though there were a thousand reasons why it would be better if she failed to react to this at all, Lally's gaze locked with his. Her fingers closed about the short strap of the bag, she drew a deep, deep breath and admitted, to herself at least, that she was equally attracted to Cam. That had to stop right now. They had to get the fun back and avoid these other inappropriate responses to each other. It was probably just the atmosphere getting to both of them, anyway.

Somehow Lally got through the appointment with the

hair stylist. It helped that Cam sat on a lounge in the waiting area and buried his nose in a magazine.

Half an hour later Lally got up from the chair with her curls artfully drawn away from her face in a high pony-tail with just a few tendrils trailing down her back.

'Shoes.' Cameron murmured the single word as his gaze tracked over her hair and the vulnerable nape of her neck.

'You'll have to decide about your heroine's hair,' Lally said, and hoped the desperate edge couldn't be heard in her tone. 'It's probably ice-blonde, straight and swept up in a bun away from her model-gorgeous face.'

'Uh, yes. Perhaps.' Cam drew her to a shoe shop.

Lally's transformation to Cinderella-dressed-for-the-ball reached its final moment as they stepped through the door. She spotted the sandals immediately. They were third row down on an elegant stand, they had their own name—Grace After Midnight—and she had to have them.

Six inch stiletto gold-and-black heels; tiny criss-cross gold-and-black strips across the instep. Elegant ankle straps. All of Lally's sensible thoughts and cautions disintegrated for that moment of time. She forgot the purpose of the night, forgot everything—well, not Cam, but he did take second place to the shoes for a minute.

'I'll pay for these myself.' They were in her hands before she finished speaking the words, on her feet moments later. They fit like a dream; these shoes were meant to be.

Lally had her credit card and there were fifty dollars in the pocket of the skirt that had gone into the dress shop bag with her other clothes. She held her hand out to Cam. He came back into focus, and so did his grin that held outright amusement—was that a hint of enchantment?

Of course it isn't, Lally. It so totally isn't! 'I need the bag, please.'

'No. I've got this.' Cam paid for the shoes and hustled her out of the store.

'You don't understand. I had to have them, you see.' How did she explain the compulsion that took a pair of shoes from stage prop to girl's best friend? And how that meant she couldn't let him pay for her pure indulgence.

'And I'd have paid that much or more for any choice that you made.' With those few words, Cam dismissed the matter.

And he truly did dismiss it. The glint in his eyes was a good-humoured one, but it also warned her that arguing would be futile. He tucked her arm through his and led her towards the hotel's restaurant. 'You look great, Lally. You're made for bright colours.'

'That's what Mum says.' *Business, Lally!* She must remember tonight was about his work, no matter how he'd been looking at her or how it felt to walk at his side and feel as though she were made to belong there.

'Over dinner we'll discuss where this has put you in terms of figuring out your heroine,' Lally declared, and led the way with determination towards their dining table.

Lally looked amazing; the thought washed through Cam yet again as he escorted his housekeeper into the restaurant. She looked amazing, was dressed amazingly and walked incredibly in heels that would have stopped a lot of women in their tracks.

He'd told Lally she was made for colours. What he hadn't said was that she was made for all of this—the dress, the shoes, the lovely hair, the sparkle in her eyes...

Yes, he had needed this research for his story. Seeing Lally in the clothes had somehow made her more vibrant and real to him, and that had, indeed, already helped him to start seeing his book's heroine.

Not an ice-blonde, but a woman in her late thirties with elegant looks and straight brunette hair in a cap-cut to her head. A woman who wore classic black. Lally's reverse-psychology theory was working. Her quirky approach to the problem had got him well on the way to resolving it.

He'd thought that to fix his writer's block he needed a housekeeper to free up his time so he could concentrate better.

What he'd needed was tonight's insights.

'This way, please.' The waiter seated them with a flourish at the table Cam had booked earlier. The man's gaze rested for a long moment on Lally's beauty.

Cam could only silently agree.

'I feel quite transformed.' Lally's fingers toyed with the clasp of the small bag in her lap after the waiter walked away. 'Cinderella ready for the ball, except the shoes aren't glass.' Her lips pressed together. 'Well, this isn't about me. What would your book character be wearing? What would she have bought in the shop?'

'The shoes are better than glass.' They revealed the beauty of Lally's calf muscles, the delicate shape of her feet, the slender ankles. But that wasn't something Cam should tell his housekeeper. 'My heroine would be in a black dress. Full length and fitted. She's in black stiletto-shoes with a closed toe and heel—what do you call those?'

'Pumps?'

'Yes.' Cam nodded. 'She's wearing diamonds, a choker around her throat, a thick tennis-bracelet style of cuff on her right wrist. Earrings that are a carat apiece.'

'You're working her out! That's great.' Lally glanced down at the bag in her lap. 'The diamanté on this is amazing. It looks so real.'

Cam thought about avoiding her gaze when she raised it, but in the end he simply returned it and hoped he didn't look too guilty. Or too sheepish. 'They are real, but there aren't many, and they're very small. The bags with fake stones cost nearly as much.'

He added somewhat craftily, 'It's the perfect size for a small ladies' handgun.'

'Ooh.' Lally's eyes lit up and she leaned forward in her chair, her whole face alight with interest and excitement. 'Is she an assassin? A double agent?'

'Close to that.' He knew he was being mysterious, but the desire to tease her just a little had got hold of him. Cam's gaze tracked over her hair and the sweep of her neck, the soft nape, and he forgot about his characters.

Instead, Cam wanted to kiss Lally right there at the base of her neck, to inhale the scent of her skin and brush his lips over the side of her neck and across her face. He felt ridiculously proud that he'd been able to distract her about the cost of the bag. 'Don't tell anyone what ideas I have in mind for the heroine.' He winked. 'I have to keep the book's secrets until it hits the shelves, otherwise my career as a writer is over.'

'I won't tell a soul.' She crossed her heart with her fingers, joining in the fun. 'I guess it's all right to confess I'm enjoying the dress, and I love the shoes. I had a pair that were similar when I was fresh out of high school.' Lally made this admission almost guiltily. 'They were cheaper, and not quite as pretty, but they made me feel…'

'Beautiful? You are.'

Maybe he shouldn't have said it—*probably* he shouldn't have said it—but the words were out.

'Thank you.' Lally registered Cam's words and tried not to let her feelings melt. If she simply felt complimented, that would be okay, still manageable. The charming man tells the girl she looks great, the girl appreciates his words of admiration and takes them for what they are: a compliment. The same as he might give to any other woman while they were working on an unusual project together.

But she didn't feel only complimented; she felt Cam's awareness of her, and hers of him. She felt the consciousness that flowed back and forth between them that had been beneath the surface from the start of the night, but hidden under the excitement and fun factor of their research and role-playing.

That consciousness *was* there. Even now as they sat here, Cam's upper body leaned forward as though he'd like to close the distance of the table that separated them and press a soft kiss to her lips.

Lally's body leaned in too, until she forcibly stopped herself and straightened her spine.

She had to remember that Cameron Travers was her employer, not a man she would like to melt into, to kiss and be kissed by.

'We should choose something to eat.' Lally dropped her gaze to the menu; she flipped it open and stared blindly at the *entrées*. 'Do you need us to choose anything specific for research purposes?'

'No. Just choose what you'd like to eat.' Cam, too, turned his attention to his menu.

You see? They were being perfectly sensible.

Eventually the list of dishes unscrambled itself enough that Lally could read it: tuscan prawns; artichoke and sweet-potato soup—Cam would avoid that one—lamb, leek and bread broth; baked cheese bites in puff pastry with a dark-plum dipping sauce.

'I think I'll have the broth.' Lally rejected the appeal of spicy prawns, of sensually melted cheese in pastry. 'Yes, the broth. Something healthy and ordinary. It seems exactly what I'd like.'

She was a sensible, ordinary girl, after all, even if she had allowed herself to be swept up in the purchase of a lovely dress and a pair of stunning shoes.

Over all, Lally had progressed past being influenced by emotions, sudden whims or anything else uncontrolled.

Sam had taught her that lesson—well, in truth, the pain she had caused out of knowing him had taught her. Lally's good cheer wobbled.

In that moment Cam glanced at her, smiled and said softly, 'Thank you, Lally, for being such a good sport tonight. I've really enjoyed myself, enjoyed the research. I've got ideas coming into focus in my mind. You've helped me to get the muse back on track.'

'You're welcome. It's been my pleasure to help you.' Lally pushed those other unhappy thoughts far away.

Cameron's eyes moved over his menu, but a smile lingered on his face. After that he led the conversation onto the topic of his property development; maybe he knew she needed that easing of tension.

He talked about the challenge of obtaining good workers in locations all around Australia wherever he purchased properties to develop, and the properties themselves. Lally relaxed and her happiness came back.

'You've certainly developed some interesting projects over the years. Several of my family members might be interested in the art gallery you mentioned in the tourist township on the Queensland coast.' Some of them might like to have work exhibited there, if the gallery manager was interested.

Their *entrées* arrived and Lally dipped her spoon into the broth. It was thick with chunks of lamb, loaded with fresh colourful vegetables, and the aroma was spicy. She took the first taste onto her tongue and closed her eyes while the flavours exploded on her palate.

Cameron cut a piece from a Tuscan prawn, popped it into his mouth and chewed. He gestured towards her soup bowl. 'How is it?'

'Fabulously interesting and totally yummy.' Lally smiled in wry acceptance. She was wearing a beautiful red dress and killer heels—would it really hurt for her to eat exciting food too?

They talked about nothing much. It should have been totally unthreatening; instead, a rising consciousness seemed to fill the air between them once again until every breath she took held the essence of that consciousness, whether Lally felt ready to feel like that or not.

When Cam picked up his fork and knife, Lally realised they'd both been sitting there staring at each other in un-moving silence.

At what point had they put down their implements and simply sat in quiet stillness?

Almost…like lovers.

The way you used to stare at Sam across a dinner table, totally besotted, and with no thought for anything beyond the smooth words, smoother smiles and the looks he used to send your way?

'How, um, how would your heroine behave at this point of the evening?' They'd finished the *entrées;* Lally sipped her water and told herself she had to do better than this.

'Here we are.' A waiter deftly reordered their table setting and offered Cam a choice of wines to go with their main course. Cam had chosen flame-grilled steak; Lally, Barramundi fillets with a creamy herbed-lemon dressing.

'I'd like Chardonnay, please.' Lally felt pleased that her voice sounded normal. They'd opted out of the wine to start with, and she'd appreciated that too.

Cameron examined the labels of the wines the waiter had brought and approved a Chardonnay for Lally and a red for himself. The waiter poured and left, and they started their meals.

Cam answered her question then. 'The heroine would be doing her best to distract the hero and keep his mind jumping so he doesn't have time to wonder what she's up to.' He glanced at his plate and then hers. 'For us, for now, I'd like descriptions of the food so I can use the dishes in the book, I think. I can see the characters eating these meals.'

'Oh—okay. The fish is moist and flaky; the sauce is tart enough to balance the creaminess.' Lally did her best to describe the combination of textures and tastes.

She could see Cam making mental notes, and she tried to feel that they'd left behind their consciousness of each other, but it felt as though it still simmered beneath the surface.

There had to be some way to stop that simmering. It was inappropriate for her to simmer in this setting.

And if your boss is simmering?

Well, Lally didn't know—and what were they anyway, a matching set of human saucepans?

'Do you think you'll take on other property-development projects in Adelaide?' Yes, that was the way to express an everyday, businesslike interest and nothing more—ask a question that made her sound as though she wanted to be assured he wouldn't be leaving after a few short weeks!

'Tell me about your family. You mentioned art and restaurants.'

Cam spoke at the same time. They both stopped. He brushed his hand over the back of his neck.

If Lally got started on family, they would still be here when the place closed for the night. And she did want to know what his future plans might be, even if that made her nosy.

'I may take on further projects here.' Cam didn't seem to make too much of her question. He started to talk about other buildings in various parts of Adelaide. 'There's a block of apartments, dilapidated but in an area that I know would resell really well. I put an offer in on those earlier today.'

As though there was nothing exciting or fascinating about buying up another building; perhaps to him there wasn't. He bought and sold in dollar figures she could only dream about. She found his ability to write stories fascinating, too, his imagination and his interest in hands-on research. The dimple in his chin, the groove on his forehead...

Are not fascinating, Lally!

All right, fine; as a person, Cameron Travers was inter-esting—complex, busy, bordering on workaholic. And an insomniac. And, for whatever reason, Lally found all of this a little too intriguing for her own calm and controlled state of mind.

They made their way through the remainder of the meal. Cameron occasionally jotted notes on a small note-pad he drew from his trouser pocket, but Lally felt as though his attention never left her, never left *them*. Which was quite silly, because this wasn't about her or *them*.

Finally, they finished the last sip of their coffee. Lally pushed away her half-eaten dessert of a profiterole filled with *crème* custard and coated in crunchy strands of caramelised sugar. 'That's delicious, but I can't fit it all in.'

Cam patted his flat stomach and pushed the platter of cheese and crackers into the middle of the table. 'I'm done there too.' He glanced at his watch and met her gaze with eyes that were piercing and interested, weary, alert and conscious of her all at once. 'It's after eleven. Will you come and do the final step of tonight's adventure with me now?'

Deep tone. Words meant to be about his work. Expression that was somewhat about that. Yet…

'That's what we're here for.' Lally agreed while her senses were in a muddle reacting to him.

She agreed before her brain engaged at all, really. That was dangerous, as was the feel of his arm holding her fingers tucked against his side as they left the restaurant after he paid for their meal. She could feel the muscles over his ribs moving as he walked; his skin beneath his shirt was warm against the back of her fingers.

He felt lean and fit—he *was* lean and fit—and gorgeous and appealing into the bargain. Lally shouldn't be feeling these responses to him because she needed to protect herself. She was not ready to tackle another relationship with a man, and, even if she was, that man wasn't going to be a millionaire, incredibly focused, fabulous and famous temporary boss: Cam was way out of her league.

So, what was she about, leaning against his side this way?

They climbed into a service lift that took them to the top of the hotel.

'It's only five storeys high, but I do want to go all the

way to the roof for this.' Cameron said it almost as though he felt he should apologise for this fact.

'Whatever works best for your story.' Lally told herself she had overcome her momentary lapse, that she had herself well in hand now.

That theory lasted until she looked into Cameron's eyes and her pulse started to throb at her wrists and at the base of her neck. And—oh, it was silly—she suddenly she felt a bit…nervous too.

'That's exactly what I wanted to see, Lally—the edge of caution, even though at this stage you don't believe you're in any true danger.' His words were a glide of consonants and cadence that crossed her senses like the brush of velvet over her skin. 'That's a look I can describe for my heroine to good effect in the book.'

The lift stopped and they stepped out onto the flat rooftop area of the building. Cam glanced around and led her towards the edge with a firm grip on her arm. 'You don't suffer from vertigo or anything like that?'

'No. I don't.' Even so, Lally made no bones about leaning into his firm hold now; it was a long drop to ground level. Too bad if that made her look clingy just at the moment. 'What?'

'Look at the drop for me. Then we're going to act out…' He led her close enough that she could look over.

As Lally truly registered that they stood five storeys up on a deserted rooftop late at night, her imagination kicked in. What did Cam plan to write about this setting? What did he want her to do?

Lally glanced at her boss, and adrenalin and excitement coursed through her veins. It seemed necessary to speak in a hushed tone, and she whispered, 'This is going to be a real rush, isn't it? Like skydiving or something. My instincts are telling me it will be exciting. My heart's in my throat already and I don't even know yet.'

'I don't know what you'll think.' His fingers tightened their hold around her arm. 'But we're going to find out.'

CHAPTER SIX

'YOU'LL be completely safe, Lally, but you may not feel safe for a moment or two.' Cam's gaze searched her face.

'Whatever it is, I'm ready.' Lally ignored the breathless edge to her voice and the nervous tension that went with it.

Cam clasped his fingers loosely about her elbows. 'This would all happen very fast. She wouldn't have time to think, but for the point of this exercise I'll talk you through some of it. I want your thoughts on what her reactions would be.'

It was automatic for Lally's hands to come up and splay against his chest through the cloth of his dinner jacket. The evening bag was over one of her wrists. 'I think your heroine would feel her heart-rate speed up, and she would tell herself to be careful. Be very careful.'

Cameron's glance rested briefly on her mouth. 'She doesn't know whether he intends to kiss her, attack her, accuse her, hold her at gunpoint, try to overpower her or throw her over the edge. Is he on to her secrets?'

'And is she on to his?'

No sooner had Lally got the question out than Cam drew her back a little from the edge. He swept her up in his arms in a lightning-fast move. One hand came under the back of her thighs, the other cupped behind her shoulders. Her handbag was jammed between their bodies. His face was inches from hers.

They were a safe distance from the edge but, oh, it didn't feel safe in those first moments. Lally caught her breath and a soft gasp of sound left her parted lips. Her free hand locked around the back of his neck.

'Easy.' Cam felt Lally's arm lock around the muscles in his neck, and he took two long steps, not towards the edge but parallel to it. 'Sorry. I need to know how my male lead would feel carrying her.'

'If he's doing it to get closer to the edge, she'd be fighting him.' Lally's words brushed against his temple and cheek. 'She'd struggle to get free.'

Lally was tense, but not struggling.

Cam had to think about his characters. The research. He could see the characters clearly in his mind.

That was great; his instincts told him he would be able to write this scene. He had his female character fixed now, defined, he knew who she was and that she would work well for his story. That issue was resolved for Cam.

What wasn't resolved was his desire for the woman in his arms. That had been getting further and further away from his control since they'd first schemed this idea up earlier today. Maybe the excitement of it, the sheer fun of planning and executing it, was why Cam hadn't controlled his other responses to Lally very well.

'Yes, she would struggle to get free, but I'll deal with working that out for myself or we can role-play it elsewhere. Even though we're away from the edge, I don't want to risk losing my balance or anything while we're up here.' He tried to sound focused and interested in the research. Not distracted…

'If he does intend to throw her, the best thing she could

do is refuse to release her hold on him, unless he was prepared to go over with her.' Lally made this observation with what judiciousness she could find in the face of her distraction. Being held this way, held close to Cam's broad chest, made thinking difficult. 'Or unless he had the capacity to subdue her some other way before he tossed her over.'

In tandem with her words, Lally's hand locked harder about his neck.

Cam moved his body enough to allow her to get her other hand free. 'In the scene, she would struggle to get that hand loose.'

Lally added it to her hold about his neck. 'So she'd hold on like this?'

'At this stage, yes.' God, his voice was way too deep, and his entire body seemed utterly focused on what he held.

And what he held was Lally Douglas in a flowing, beautiful dress that made her look both sultry and alluring. He felt the brush of the soft fabric over his hand where he held her in his arms; the hem wrapped around his trouser legs. He held Lally, her face upturned towards his, excitement and an edge of uncertainty stamped on that face.

It was not because she didn't feel safe with him. There was apprehension of another kind, the sort a person felt when they entered uncharted territory with someone they found attractive.

Are you cataloguing her reactions now, Travers, or your reactions to her?

Cam stopped walking and murmured, 'She would quite probably try to reach for the gun in her purse.'

'Yes.' Her words whispered into the stillness. She didn't move.

Cam's focus was on her face, his gaze touching on each feature—eyes, cheeks, nose, finally lingering on her mouth. His look, filled with want, desire and something perhaps deeper than both of those things, drew Lally's gaze to his eyes and locked it there. Her breath stilled all over again. All around them was darkness and city silence, which was no silence at all, but it still shrouded them in isolation here while the world went by below.

Darkness and aloneness and consciousness.

Cam's gaze met hers once more in the dimness, and everything slid into a different place for Lally. The evening; the slow meal and their talk about his writing and work projects; her determination not to look too deeply into herself: it had all mixed in together and blurred into this one moment that was so much more than the compilation of those parts. That really had nothing at all to do with those parts.

'I shouldn't have picked you up like this.' He murmured the words, but he didn't let her go.

Instead his hand wrapped more firmly behind her shoulders and he shifted to stand with his legs splayed apart.

His head lowered towards her. 'Tell me not to...'

'Not to...?' But Lally knew. She looked into his eyes and she couldn't say the words. How could she say those words to Cam when his gaze was on her this way, desire stamped across his cheekbones, burned into the shadows beneath his eyes, etched over lips that softened and dipped towards hers?

She should say no. She needed to protect her emotions and not take risks, but Lally could only wait while her lips softened in anticipation.

And then he was there. The kiss she had secretly longed for was happening.

His lips tasted faintly of coffee, and were both firm and gentle as he softly kissed her, oh, so softly, as though they had all the time in the world and all he wanted to do was this.

She'd thought she was holding her own, that she had control over this evening with him. That she had at least held on to a little of what it was all about, remembered they were doing this for his research and no other reason.

Well, this didn't feel like research. Her lips softened beneath his and when he slid her slowly down his body until her feet touched concrete it felt natural and right to let his arms close around her, to step fully into his embrace and let the kiss take them where it would.

Cam made a soft sound in the back of his throat. He deepened their kiss, his lips caressing hers, moulding to hers, tasting and giving and taking. One hand splayed against the small of her back; the long, lean fingers of the other wrapped around her jaw.

Lally responded with a deepening of desire for him, but she also softened for him. Her emotions melted into a puddle inside her; if he'd wanted, he could have walked straight in and…

Well, she wasn't sure. Taken whatever he wanted? Hurt her because she wasn't ready to trust a man again, wasn't sure she could ever do that again? She wasn't sure she could trust herself.

Lally became conscious of just how intimately they were pressed together; their bodies were flush against each other from chest to knee. Cam's fingers were stroking up and down her bare shoulders and back. Hers—were in his hair, clasping his shoulder while her entire body seemed to strain for closeness with his.

Oh, Lally. What are you thinking?

Lally forced her mouth to leave his, her body to draw

back. Each action felt as though it took an aeon to execute. She shouldn't feel *anything* towards Cam, not in this way. He was her boss; she was his employee. Lally felt panicked.

Think how Cam kissed you, Lally. How he drew a response from you so easily and so thoroughly, made you feel as though you were receiving your first ever real kiss.

Sam had made her feel that way. With Sam, it *had* been her first ever kiss. First kiss, first everything.

That was hardly the point here.

Well, what was the point? She couldn't let herself be affected by what they had shared in these moments. She couldn't let herself care again—

Lally forced herself to meet Cam's gaze and opened her mouth to speak, to play this down, to say something about work or characterisation or research.

Anything.

But her lips still tingled from the press of his. Even now her body begged her to step back into his embrace, to take their kiss even further, prolong the closeness and connection.

Finally Lally found words. 'I'm not looking for an involvement. Not that I'm suggesting you are. This… We forgot ourselves for a moment. There's no need to make a fuss about it, but it mustn't happen again; it's not wise. You're a busy man with loads on your plate, and your struggle to sleep to deal with, let alone a recalcitrant muse and a highly demanding business in Sydney. And I work for you!'

'I know.' He swallowed hard. Regret etched lines into his face that hadn't been there before. 'I understand all of that, Lally. It was wrong of me to kiss you. I'm not looking for a relationship. I don't—that's not in my agenda, and it's not smart to mix work with that anyway. And you're quite right. You wouldn't want...'

Whatever he'd been about to say, he cut the words off, but the message was there anyway. He agreed with her. This kiss shouldn't have happened. They had to respect the boundaries of their working relationship. He didn't want her, not really. Not like that.

Lally drew a breath and blurted, 'I didn't mean to set up this night to lead to this.'

'I know.' His words were deep and genuine. 'I had a problem with my writing, you thought of a great solution. We both got excited about it and in that excitement, for a few moments, we forgot ourselves.'

His summary of events left out a few things—such as the way they'd both become more aware of each other as the evening had worn on—but Lally nodded. 'That's right. I'm glad we got that sorted out.' She forced a relieved smile. 'Phew. Well, are we finished here? Do you have what you need for your research? Maybe we should head home—I mean, back to your property development.'

'I have everything I need.' Cam watched emotions flit across Lally's face and felt them churn inside him. Kissing her had been amazing. Yes, he'd made all sorts of comments on how that had come about and why it shouldn't have and everything else. Those comments were real and true; they just weren't all of it. And they didn't even begin to touch on how he'd felt inside himself as a result of these shared moments. Cam didn't want to examine those feelings, but the thoughts came anyway.

He'd kissed her softly in a way he had never kissed any other woman. He'd kissed Lally after trying to ignore the need to do it all night. He'd kissed her to pay homage to her beauty and how lovely she looked in that dress. He'd done it because something inside him had needed to.

He couldn't tell her any of that. Because Lally didn't want this. She'd made that clear and she'd looked scared when she said it. Scared from somewhere inside that Cam shouldn't mess with because she could end up getting hurt, and the last thing he wanted was to hurt her.

He wanted to know *what* had hurt her, but he mustn't mess with that either. He had no right, no claim on her, aside from being her very temporary employer, nor would he ever seek to change that. Cam didn't want this either; he couldn't pursue it. He'd only end up disappointing her, not being what she needed. He'd proved that about himself already.

He was an insomniac, workaholic, novel-writing businessman who couldn't stay in one place, couldn't rest, had no idea how to be a family. He and his mother might have been linked during his childhood but she hadn't wanted him. And Cam had learned not to be wanted.

He'd tried to break out of that once, in his mid-twenties. Gillian...

Cam had built up Gillian's expectations, and when she'd realised just how much of him would never be hers, when she had come to understand just how much his past history and his insomnia impacted on his daily life, she'd been let down, disappointed and ultimately hurt. She'd wanted and needed more than he'd been able to give her. She'd been right to want that, and right to walk away.

They'd gone their separate ways and Cam had learned a lesson. He didn't want to hurt a woman like that again. He didn't want to set himself up for that kind of loss again either. He knew what he could and couldn't have.

Yet tonight Cam had forgotten all that past history, that painful learning-curve that he'd sworn not to repeat. He'd kissed a slip of a girl on a rooftop, had found all this tenderness and all these other responses to her inside him. He hadn't simply wanted to give them to her, he'd felt *driven* to bring them to her. That wasn't something he'd experienced with Gillian; it wasn't something he'd ever experienced with any woman.

That fact perhaps had driven him to kiss Lally. It had certainly made his reactions to her even more dangerous. He forced his arms to drop away from her, forced himself to take a step back. Every fibre of his body and mind seemed to object at once. If he drew her close again, he knew he wouldn't want to let go at all. He'd take her hand, lead her back through this hotel, take her home and make her his completely.

Not happening, Travers.

'We should go.' He led Lally back the way they had come and ushered her into the service lift.

As the doors closed, Lally turned to him and said quietly, 'Your book—did we achieve what you needed?'

It was a ploy to get the focus off them and back to the reason for this evening. Cam acknowledged this and did his best to further it. 'I've decided the female character will be an undercover special-services officer, but she's a double agent with marksman skills and a history as a hired assassin as well...' Cam talked about his story until he had Lally out of the hotel and safely ensconced beside him in the car.

In the car's dim interior, Cam could hear every breath Lally took, smell the soft scent of her skin and whatever lotion she'd rubbed into it after her shower tonight. He tried not to notice any of it.

'I'm glad the research was successful and that you have a good understanding of this new character you're bringing into your story.' Her fingers fidgeted with the small bag in her lap. 'You know, I really shouldn't keep any of these things.'

'Please. Maybe you'll wear them some place again one day.' *And think of me.* Was that what Cam wanted? His eyebrows drew together.

As they passed beneath a streetlight, Cam glanced towards her. The breeze had whipped at her hair, dishevelled it just enough to make him want to bury his hands in it, caress his fingers over her scalp and use that touch to tilt her head so he could kiss her neck, kiss her chin and find his way back to soft lips.

You're not thinking about kissing her, remember?

They'd researched; that research had led to a kiss that shouldn't have happened. A kiss that had blown him away, because she'd been so giving and he'd loved that and had wanted to give back in equal measure. Cam drew the convertible to a halt in an allotted space inside the property-development site. No matter how tempting, no matter how much she soothed him—no matter anything—he had to take due care that nothing like this happened again.

A woman like Lally deserved better than an insomniac workaholic who had no sense of family or ability to meet a woman's deep needs.

There was no other way for Cam. No other way that he knew.

CHAPTER SEVEN

'HE PUSHES himself so hard, Auntie. I really want to help him find a way to get more sleep. It's the one thing I think I might be able to do for him, beyond the work I'm already doing.'

A week had passed since the night Lally and Cam had role-played, when he had tried to 'toss her over' the top of the hotel.

Lally had revisited those moments more often than she wanted to admit—not the pretend tossing, but the kissing that hadn't been about role-playing at all.

Cam had placed his lips over hers and it had felt like the sweetest kiss of all time, sweet and gentle and tender, and Lally needed to forget it. She must have built it way up in her mind, anyway, mustn't she? For how could she feel such a depth of reaction and response to something that, for him, must only have been the result of place, time and circumstance, nothing more?

She couldn't start to have feelings about Cam, or towards Cam, not like those.

Lally bit back a sigh. 'He's my *employer*.' She put a certain emphasis on the word 'employer'; yes, that drew even more attention to her need to hold him to that role in her thinking.

If she thought of him in that light, spoke of him in that

light, then eventually she would accept he *was* only in that light for her.

Lally glanced about her. It was only just past dawn, but already the markets were teeming with life. Mum stood with her arm linked through Aunt Edie's. Well, that was family; you all looked after each other.

Lally felt a sudden tug of emotion as she acknowledged that thought. For six years she'd built her life around looking after everyone as best she could, and then they hadn't needed her.

'I've missed everyone. You didn't mention how Jodie is getting along. How could I not ask about one of my sisters? Thanks for meeting me here this morning for coffee and talking about so many of them.' She'd asked them to come and had used wanting to help her boss as her reason. And that *had* been the reason. Mostly.

They'd talked. Mum and Auntie had brought her up to speed on all the gossip about the family—well, almost all. Lally reiterated that she could take calls and text messages at work, that her boss wouldn't mind.

Mum and Auntie seemed fine about that, but Lally still came away from that part of the conversation wondering if there was more under the surface. Maybe she should have just asked, but a part of her was scared of the possible answer.

Perhaps the issues with her employer were behind her general sense of unease. He'd done an exemplary job of avoiding her in the past week, aside from meal times, handing over work-lists and asking her to do various specific jobs for him. Another research trip had needed two sets of hands, not one.

He hasn't avoided you at all, Latitia. You've seen loads of him.

Lally frowned. That was right, she had seen loads of

him, so why did she almost feel as though she was missing him?

'Jodie's fine,' Mum said.

Lally bit her lip. 'Good. I'm glad.' She was. And, if the answer to her other question was that she wanted Cam all over her with gentle feelings, and maybe the need to kiss her again, then she needed to stop longing for things that were completely out of the question. She was better off without them, because she really wasn't ready to face that kind of emotional gymnastics again.

You don't deserve ever to have a meaningful fulfilling relationship. Not after all the harm you've caused in the past.

The thought sent a shaft of pain through Lally's chest. 'What were we talking about?'

'You were telling us about your hunky new employer,' Auntie declared, and a grin split her weathered brown face.

'My boss has insomnia,' Lally said primly, and in a depressing tone focused on stopping Auntie's speculations. 'I woke three times last night, and every time I could see a strip of light beneath his office door and knew he was in there, working.'

Lally had been restless; she'd been restless ever since the night he'd kissed her, to be honest. 'I wanted to know about bush foods and remedies for Cam in case there might be something that would help him sleep better.'

Her voice softened when she said his name; it went completely to mush just like that. And, because that was such a give away, Lally felt a blush build beneath her skin. She needed to put Auntie and Mum off the scent, not encourage more speculation.

'Fresh food is a good start, of course.' Auntie spoke as she examined Lally's face.

'For Cam, yes.' Mum chipped in with her opinion, and a gleam in her eyes that definitely seemed to hold a hint of satisfaction.

Could the family have conspired to get Lally out into the world, as she'd wondered, with a view to her meeting a man, maybe?

Lally glanced at her watch and found a sudden need to become highly time-efficient. 'I should get on with my shopping while we finish this talk.' Lally strode to the nearest fruit stall and lifted a ripe pawpaw. If this also happened to mean that she wasn't quite so obviously the centre of their speculation, well, that was purely happenstance.

Mum and Auntie quickly caught up with her, and Lally decided, if they were talking, she might as well spit out something else that she'd avoided once already this morning. It was bothering her. She was better off dealing with it so it could stop doing so.

Lally turned. 'This job is the first one I've had where I wasn't working for family. I want to do well at this, but I also need to know I'll be coming back to the family the minute my work is done for Cameron Travers. Someone will need me, won't they?'

'Oh, well, I'm sure they will, but haven't you found spreading your wings to be fun? It sounds as though it has been.' Mum went on, 'You say your employer bought you a dress and a handbag, and you helped him with research on the roof of a hotel at midnight?'

Well, not at midnight, but Lally supposed that was near enough. And, yes, it had been exciting. It just had also become somewhat complicated by the end of the night. 'Yes, we did some research for his current book.' Lally paid for the pawpaw and set it gently into the bottom of her shopping basket. 'But, truly, the only reason I brought up his name this morning is because I want to try to help him sleep better. He looks so exhausted.' She turned to her aunt. 'Do you have any ideas?'

Auntie's wrinkled face creased into even deeper lines. 'There *are* bush foods and remedies; it depends on why he's that way in the first place. Has he seen a doctor?'

'I asked him about that the other day. He's visited doctors and sleep specialists, done all the sleep studies. I think he's tried everything he's been told to try and come to the end of the line with no real solutions.' Lally hesitated. 'It's not that he's not alert, because he always is—he's sharp as a whip—it's just that...'

'He's sharp while he's pushing himself, can't relax, only sleeps until the edge is off his exhaustion, then he wakes and it's on again for another day for him.' Auntie nodded.

She transferred her hold from Mum's arm to Lally's and they made their way through the remaining market-stalls. Lally worked through her shopping list while Auntie talked.

'You remember the tribal elder I took you to visit when you were a girl?' Auntie named the elder. 'He has a store. He and his wife know just about all there is to know about this kind of thing. It might be worth giving them a call.'

Lally did remember, and wished she'd thought of this earlier. 'Thanks. That's exactly what I need.'

They completed the shopping. 'Thanks for meeting me this morning. I should get back to work.'

Mum laid her hand on Lally's arm. 'If you're interested in your boss...'

Yes, there was definitely a gleam in Mum's eyes that said 'the plan is working.' Auntie's too.

Lally's mouth formed words before she could stop

them. 'You all ganged together to say there was no work so I'd get out more, didn't you?'

She wanted to be angry, to say 'how could you?'

But Mum gave a sheepish nod and came right out and admitted it. 'We wanted you to have some fun, Lally. Maybe this boss...'

'He kissed me and I kissed him back, but it was a bad idea on both our parts and neither of us wants it.' Lally drew a breath. Apparently her mother still possessed the ability to get her to confess, even when it should have been Mum doing the confessing. 'I just care about his insomnia issues. It's in my nature to care. I've always cared about the family.'

Lally gave Mum a stern stare. 'Even when they've tossed me out on some made-up pretext without so much as a by your leave.'

'The family cares about you, Lally.' Mum sighed. 'Please don't be angry. Maybe we shouldn't have done that, but it's only for two months. We wanted to help, to see you enjoy yourself, maybe just make some nice friends.'

'Or meet a man friend?' Lally shook her head. 'I wish you hadn't. You don't understand.' But she wasn't mad, and she gave Mum a hug to make that clear. 'It's too late to change anything now, but I'd appreciate it if you all didn't do this again.'

'We interfered too much. I'm sorry, Lally.' Mum looked guilt-ridden.

Lally let it go. 'It's okay.' She gave a wry smile. 'In a family the size of ours, interfering happens. I know that.' Lally couldn't explain why she didn't want a man in her life again. She bit her lip.

Auntie had wandered a little distance while Lally and

Mum talked. She returned now and glanced at her watch. 'Are you ready to go, Susan?'

'Indeed I am.' Mum gave Lally another hug.

Auntie gave Lally a hug.

Lally hugged both of them back, and then there were more quick words and waves. There was no need to say anything to Auntie about the rest of it.

They disappeared, and Lally walked towards the exit of the market. It was only a few blocks back to her boss's development; maybe the walk would help her to clear her mind. At least she knew what her family had been up to now. They'd better all start contacting her again, or she *would* have something to say about that!

Lally glanced into her basket, checked the contents one last time and realised she'd forgotten the baby-spinach leaves she'd wanted to use in a warm chicken salad for lunch. She turned around and strode back into the heart of the market again.

'Lally, wait up, I'll carry the basket for you.' It was Cam's voice, morning-roughened and deep.

He'd called from behind her; Lally turned her head and looked over her shoulder and there he was, his gaze fixed on her as he strode forward through the crowd.

Her heart did a ridiculous lift. The world seemed suddenly brighter simply because she'd caught a glance of his face, a glimpse of a smile and softened expression directed her way.

Oh, Lally, can't you do better than that at resisting how he makes you feel? Do you want *to end up out of your depth again? He's already made it clear he isn't interested.*

Lally just couldn't trust again. The risks were too big. So she had to focus on the ways she could be a good employee to him.

As he joined her, Lally examined his face for signs of weariness—she found them. 'You couldn't sleep again this morning?'

'No, and I'm sorry if I disturbed you last night.' He scrubbed a hand over his jaw; it bore a day's beard-growth. That combined with a pair of jeans, black T-shirt, and shades pushed up on his head, looked just a little disreputable. Appealingly so.

Not noticing, Lally!

She said quickly, 'You didn't disturb me. I was already awake. I'm just sorry you haven't been managing to sleep more.'

'That's how it is.' He took her arm and raised his eyebrows. 'Where are you headed? When I first spotted you, I thought you'd finished and were ready to go home.'

He'd walked here just to meet her, to carry the basket for her; Lally handed it over and Cam held it easily in one hand.

She drew a breath. 'I forgot to get baby spinach. I want it for our lunch.' Healthy foods, healthy ingredients; she would try to help Cam eat well and sleep better. She had to try. 'Have you had a check-up lately for your insomnia? There might be new treatments. I meant to ask that when we discussed this the other day.'

'I have check-ups a couple of times a year.' He shrugged his shoulders. 'So far, permanently fixing it for me hasn't worked out. I know it's not something people can put up with.'

Now, what did he mean by that?

'Let's get the spinach. Over there?' He waited while she made her purchase, and then walked with her back to the exit. They walked through and started back home along the suburban streets.

Lally had to stop thinking of it as home. It wasn't even

particularly home-like; the project was going to be full of
rental apartments, for goodness' sake, and Cam wouldn't
even be staying here once the work was done. Just because
she'd become used to thinking of all sorts of places among
her family as home didn't mean she could add Cam's
property-development project to that list.

Lally didn't know what he'd meant about people not
putting up with his insomnia, but was the answer all that
relevant? She could try to help him, that was all.

'I met my mother and aunt here this morning and asked
Auntie about folklore. Changes in diet and some bush
remedies may help—they won't harm you, and I'd like
to try.'

'You're welcome to do that.' It was clear he meant it.
'It's thoughtful of you.'

Lally's heart did an odd little stutter. 'I'm happy to do
that.' *Don't let yourself be too happy with him, Lally. It's
dangerous.*

But she turned her face up to the sun and felt happiness
get her anyway. 'I think it's going to be quite hot later
today.'

'Yes, help yourself to a swim in the pool if you want
to. It's safe to swim in now.' He led her around a child's
tricycle that had been left abandoned on the footpath. 'I
swam in it myself this morning before I came out to find
you. The water's the perfect temperature, thanks to the
pool's heating.'

'I brought a swimsuit; I might take a dip some time. We
could—I mean *I*...' Lally cut herself off quickly before
she could say more. What she definitely must not do was
let her mind wander to swimming in that pool with her
employer.

At midnight, when it was quiet and silent and they had

complete privacy to bathe by moonlight, or at least by city light. Either way would be quite romantic.

Which ruled the idea out entirely!

As for her happiness, that stemmed from no longer feeling uneasy about her work future, or her family.

Yes. It was all about that.

Cameron watched the changes of expression cross Lally's face, watched interest and attraction to him war with good sense.

Lally had met with her mother and aunt at least in some part for his sake. Cam couldn't remember the last time anyone had done something to try to care for him. He couldn't remember that ever happening. His mother hadn't exactly been the type, and he'd gone out on his own the first chance he'd got anyway.

Nowadays his mother just gave in to her wandering gene completely and went wherever the mood took her without ever making even a half-hearted effort to convince herself to try to settle anywhere.

Most of the time he wouldn't have been able to track her down if he'd wanted to. The thing was he pretty much didn't want to any more.

Whatever missing gene his mother lacked when it came to family had passed squarely down to Cam. He'd got over trying to connect with her.

Yet he would have liked to meet some of Lally's family.

'I'm sorry I missed meeting your mother and aunt.' Cam tucked her hand more securely against his side. 'And thank you for wanting to help with my sleep issues. Having you around to do some of the day-to-day things is a help all by itself, whether I'm sleeping more as a result or not.'

He turned his head to smile down into her upturned face. Had he gone about with blinkers on until now to stop himself from truly noticing loveliness? Because Lally was lovely in ways he hadn't seen before in anyone else. Beautiful, oh yes, she was that—but her beauty came from inside her as well as from her looks. He'd wanted—no, needed—to dress her in that vibrant outfit last week to pay homage to that beauty, to see it shine, and let all the world see it shine.

The night might have started out as an attempt at trying to rattle his muse loose, and Cam was grateful that that had indeed happened and he'd made good progress with his book since then. But he'd taken pleasure in Lally from the outset that evening. He forced himself to admit this.

Lally had shone. Her eyes had glowed, and she'd chosen the sexiest pair of high heels and worn them as though she'd been made to wear such things. Cam had wanted to sweep her up and kiss her senseless.

He'd done exactly that, and come out of it feeling as if he'd been the one swept off his feet at the top of that building. He hadn't been able to get their kiss out of his mind since. For the first time in his life, Cam was faced with a particular dilemma that he hadn't faced before: he wanted something that he knew he couldn't have, and he couldn't seem to get past the depth of that wanting. He wanted that closeness with Lally again, wanted to be able to take it forward, but he wasn't capable of successfully doing that, and he knew it.

'Auntie knows a lot of bush lore, remedies from our people that might help you.' Lally's eyes had softened and mellowed into warm, sherry pools.

Cam noted that, noted the sting of deeper colour across her cheekbones, and felt the skin of his face tighten in response. Did she know he could see her awareness, her interest, even as she did all she could to fight it? She was trying to stick to the topic of helping him somehow, and even that was way too sweet of her. But her expression also gave away other feelings.

Cam shouldn't want to see that…

Lally's gaze locked with Cam's and for a long moment she didn't breathe. Her body distilled into consciousness of Cam even as they walked the final stretch of footpath and began to hear the sounds of construction, men calling to each other, hammers, drills and pieces of timber being lifted and dropped.

Her gaze shifted to a point just below Cam's chin. 'I won't try any quack remedies on you, in case you're worried. Auntie would never recommend anything dangerous, or suggest I consult with anyone who would. I know I can trust her judgement with that.'

'What does your aunt do for a living? Or is she retirement age?' Cam asked the question to force his thoughts away from wanting to take her into his arms, but he realised he was truly interested. In fact, he admitted he had been intrigued and interested in Lally's history from the day they'd met. He'd put that down to the curiosity of his writer's mind, but he had to admit this felt more personal. He wanted to *know* Lally, know her deeply, understand what made her tick.

Cam had needed to figure out the female character for his book. Lally had helped him with that.

But the need to know *Lally,* to understand her, that was something that still burned in Cam.

'My aunt is an artist and a potter.' A hint of pride crept into Lally's voice. 'Her pottery and clay sculptures are truly unique and very beautiful. She's fifty-five but I don't think she has any plans to stop working on her art any time soon.'

'Your family seems to have a lot of talent between them.' Cam's words held admiration.

'I think so. I'm very proud of them.' Lally waited while Cam walked them through the courtyard area and into his apartment.

And then she did what she needed to do, and had to keep doing until it became her habit, her 'this is how it is and will go on being' self.

'Thank you for carrying the produce for me. If you have anything new for my duties list, please jot it down and leave it on the kitchen bench for me. I'm going to start some laundry and then I'll be back to prepare breakfast. I'm sure you'll be very busy, so I'll make sure I keep out of your way.'

Without looking at Cam's face, Lally removed herself to the laundry and buried her thoughts in the process of sorting the fluffies from the non-fluffies.

That was what housekeepers did—and her work was *all* Lally should focus on doing!

CHAPTER EIGHT

'I WISH I could figure out what's missing from the court-yard area.' Cam had just come from a phone call that Lally had asked him to take and had walked into the kitchen to return the mobile phone to her.

The call had been about an issue happening at his Sydney firm, and he'd resolved it easily enough. When he rejoined Lally in the kitchen, his gaze had shifted to the courtyard, and he'd again been struck by the thought that something was missing out there. 'I've already dis-cussed with the site boss making the courtyard a feature area in the complex. He's advised against it. He feels that smaller, separate outdoor-areas would be the way to go. But people might want to be able to mingle.'

'It could turn into a real little community, almost like a family,' Lally said.

'Can you spare a minute, Mr Travers?' The site boss spoke as he knocked on the open apartment-door. 'Those door panels we ordered have arrived. I think they'll do as a substitute for the ones you originally wanted that were out of stock, but I figured you'd want to see for yourself.'

Cam did want to see. Lally was already turning away to start her lunch preparations.

'I'll come now.' Cam stepped outside and told himself it was perhaps best that they'd been interrupted. What was the point of plying Lally with personal questions that couldn't make any difference to their relationship anyway?

That would be the relationship you're not having with her—the one that involves not thinking about kissing her, not wanting to kiss her again and not needing to know everything about her and understand her even more?

Lally Douglas was his housekeeper and assistant. He didn't need to know her past and her history and what made her tick. *He didn't.*

Cam's mobile phone beeped in his pocket and he made a mental note to check his text messages straight after this. Somehow, multitasking every moment of his day didn't feel quite as appealing any more.

When had that happened to him?

'Right. Let's look at these panels.' He strode purposefully forward with the site boss. At least his writing and the development were going well.

Two evenings later, Cam and Lally stood in the swimming pool with their arms resting on the edge. It was Friday, around eight p.m. The day had been unseasonably hot, and they'd both made their way to the pool to cool off. Cam had already been in the water doing laps when Lally had joined him.

They'd swum, and Cam had told himself not to think about long, bare limbs and a flow of wet hair down the graceful curve of her back. Now they were side by side in the water at the edge of the pool, looking out over the courtyard. Lally wore a one-piece teal swimsuit. It was modest, not that Cam should be giving more than a cursory glance anyway.

'I'd put a pebble mosaic there.' Lally raised one wet arm to point her finger at the centre of the courtyard. 'One with a water feature in the middle so it made the area feel cool and restful all year round. I'd do it in earth tones and use a style similar to a dot-work motif.'

'Symbolic of a traditional Aboriginal painting?' Cam forced his thoughts to that idea. 'That would look good. The colours would work with the existing pavers. The fact that they're weathered would work really well with it. Do you know much about that kind of work?'

Cam turned his head to look at her, and came very close to totally losing his train of thought.

Lally was in the process of wringing the excess water out of her hair. The swimsuit *was* modest—one-piece, cut to her thighs, criss-crossing over her breasts and coming up into a halter tie at the back of her neck—but the outfit also left rather a lot of her back bare to his gaze. Her shoulders were gently sloped, fine-boned and sun-kissed. Cam wanted to follow where the sun had been, kissing his way to where she'd lifted her hair to wring it out and tie it in a loose knot at the back of her head.

Sleek, touchable hair that looked different with some of the curl soaked out of it.

No touching, no thinking about touching, and definitely no memory of kissing or wanting to do it again.

'I've done mosaics myself.' Lally uttered the words in a voice that held an edge of breathlessness, but not because of the topic of conversation. Her gaze dipped to his bare chest and skittered away again. That simply, that easily, they were back to where they'd been all those nights ago when he'd held her in his arms at the top of that building.

Cam had tried not to let his thoughts return there. He tried now, but he couldn't tear his eyes from her—from every feature, every curve and dip, and all the loveliness from her soft, brown eyes to the lips that he had tasted and dreamed of tasting again. 'Lally?'

'I'd make a circular theme for the mosaic.' Lally pushed the words out as Cam leaned towards her, and she leaned towards him.

'That sounds good.' It did, but looking into her eyes felt better. Stupid, maybe, but better.

'With…' Lally stopped and drew a deep breath. 'With a pathway leading to the water feature and leading away from it. The feature itself would be at the centre of the circles.'

Cam's hand rose; his fingers just brushed across her damp shoulder. He wanted to pull her against his chest and kiss her until he was satisfied by the taste of her, the velvet of her mouth, the press of her softness against him. Instead, he nodded. 'With the right colours and design, that could be really striking. Restful and interesting at the same time.'

Cam cleared his throat and discovered his hand had come to rest on the pool-edging beside her. Though he wasn't touching her at all, his body formed a half-cradle around hers. She could shift away in an instant, or she could take that one movement forward, all the way into his arms.

'That's what I thought.' Her words were as distracted and breathless as his had been deep. She seemed to force herself to stick to the topic. 'There's a lot of garden edging the courtyard area—predominantly green most of the year, I'm guessing, with a few assorted colours of flowers? I think a mosaic in traditional colours from white sand through to ochre and dark browns would work really well.'

'Yes.' Cam inhaled and didn't think about her mouth.

Not at all. 'And the mosaic itself could tell a story, couldn't it?'

'It could. The stones in the centre, surrounding the water feature, could represent a lake or the sea.' She drew a shaky breath. 'Coming in and going out of the feature could be rivers surrounded by their sandy banks.'

'Right.' Cam's mind worked through the idea slowly at first, but he liked it. 'Will you do it for me, Lally?'

Before she lowered her gaze, he thought that she had murmured she would do anything for him.

When she lifted her head, her shoulders were thrown back and she had a glint of determination in her eyes, a businesslike determination. 'You should know I've only done a couple of smaller mosaics in the past, but I do have confidence that—with the help of the site boss to guide me with the water-feature part of it—I could do a good job of this.'

If Lally said she could do it, she could do it. 'We'd need to make some trips to beaches to gather the colours of pebbles you want.'

'I'd thought to perhaps source the pebbles industrially, but gathering them straight off beaches would mean more interesting stones.' Lally nodded. 'They would definitely give the mosaic a more natural look and feel.'

'You didn't tell me you're an artist like some of the others in your family.' One of her referees had noted that Lally should be painting—was she capable of that too?

Lally moved away from him finally and made her way to the steps. She grasped the railing with one hand and looked at him over her shoulder. He could almost believe that those earlier moments hadn't happened. Almost.

'I haven't done much painting.' Lally went on. 'More than one family member has encouraged me to really take it on, and I would like to learn. It's a privilege to be handed down painting traditions and stories within the family. I don't know why I've put it off.' Yet shadows filled her eyes as she admitted she'd stalled on pursuing this part of her life.

'What's in your past, Lally Douglas?' What was there to make her feel she couldn't let herself have that privilege she'd just described? Had she held herself back from painting, just as she'd held back from allowing herself to bloom with all the vibrancy and colour she should embrace in other ways? What would make her feel that way?

'Nothing. There's nothing,' she uttered.

Cam wrapped a towel around his waist while she dried off in jerky movements and tied her towel sarong-style with a knot between her breasts. The words had come out too quickly, too defensively.

Their eyes met and locked, and Cam sensed so much hurt.

'I didn't mean to pry.' His gaze softened on her taut face, the tight shoulders and defensive posture. He wanted to cuddle her, to pull her gently into his arms, to wrap his hold right around her and encourage her to feel completely safe, unthreatened and secure.

Cam wanted to protect Lally, because there *was* something. That fact was now abundantly clear. Cam thought it might have been a man.

The thought of some nameless male hurting Lally was hard for Cam to take. He didn't want to think of anyone doing that to her.

So don't you mess with her, Travers. You can't give her those gentle, kind things you just thought about. You might have had a random thought about them, but they're not for you to give to her. Don't hurt her by pulling her into anything when you can't follow it through.

If Cam drew Lally close, he would end up hurting her. So he looked away, and Lally looked away.

She said with a great attempt at brightness, 'The garden would play its part to make a pebble mosaic look great. The two things would complement each other. There's already potential in the garden; it's overgrown and untended but the basics are there.'

She stepped across the courtyard to the nearest part of the garden and tugged a leaf from a mint plant. When she rubbed the leaf between her fingers, the pungent smell of the mint released into the air. 'The mosaic would boost the garden, and the garden would enhance the mosaic.'

'You're completely right. I wanted a solution for this area, and what you've suggested works.'

Lally had said it would make the area feel welcoming, and she'd mentioned giving a sense of community, like a family. If Cam wanted that…

He wanted it for his prospective tenants, even if the site boss recommended otherwise.

And when it came to his responses to Lally, his consciousness of her, yes, Cam still felt the tug of desire, the war of emotions he didn't understand. He also felt the ongoing impact of gut-deep weariness.

He didn't notice that as often when he was in her company. And he felt Lally's secrets, whatever they were. He had his, too, and these facts just underlined the importance of keeping an employer-employee line in the metaphorical sand between them.

For both their sakes, for so many reasons.

'My mother asked me to travel to a place on the coast to see her.' Cam's text messages had told him this; now he put it together with the thought of Lally creating this mosaic. 'She's going to be there tomorrow and invited me to have dinner with her. The town she'll be in is out of the way, slow roads for some of it, but there are a lot of good beaches around that area.'

Cam kept his mother informed of his whereabouts. She usually failed to respond to any of that information, but now and again they managed a meeting. It was usually Cam who went looking for those, though he didn't look all that often.

'That'll be nice for you, but perhaps a bit of a strain with the trip itself.' Lally made this comment as she absorbed her employer's statement that he planned to see his mother. 'You'll take care on the roads? Not drive if you're too tired?'

Lally wanted the meeting to be great for Cam. She'd thought he and his mum would be close, but he'd said they didn't see each other often. And his tone of voice as he'd said that…?

'Would you like to make a combined trip of it? We can scour up and down some beaches in that area for pebbles.' Cam's words interrupted her thoughts. 'I wouldn't anticipate us being with my mother for more than a couple of hours. We could squeeze in scouring one beach, maybe, before we meet her tomorrow. Stay overnight somewhere, look at some more beaches the following day, early, then head back here? I'd really like you to do this work, Lally. If you're willing.'

'I would like to do it.' Oh, Lally would like it very much. But an overnight stay away with him?

She told herself this was about practicalities, about getting materials, and it *was* about that. He'd asked about her past, but that wasn't relevant to this. It didn't come into making a mosaic, or attending dinner with he and his mother. Or anything.

'I think I'd really like you to meet my mother.' Cam murmured the words and then seemed surprised by them.

Lally was, too, and then it hit her that she would be meeting her boss's only relative. Whether it turned out they were close or not, what would his mother think of her? Lally wanted to make a good impression.

'I have to figure out what to wear,' she blurted, and blushed with fiery heat beneath her skin. Yes, she needed to make a good impression, but only as his employee. 'Um, I mean, I'd like to know where we'll be meeting her. Will it be a casual sort of place, or more formal? Because I can do either, but not in that dress we bought for your research. That would be way too much.'

As was her mega-blabbing!

Lally closed her teeth together with a snap so no other words could rush out.

But Cam just smiled. 'If I know my mother, it won't be a formal style of restaurant. Whatever we wear for wandering around on the beach will do.'

Lally appreciated the way he said 'we', as though both of them had been stressing over this topic. Cameron Travers truly was a kind and generous man, one whose smile disappeared when his mother's name was mentioned. That knowledge made Lally concerned, and a little sad, because she didn't think she was imagining this.

Cam said quietly, 'It will be nice to have company while I visit Mum.'

And just like that, he made Lally feel wanted, needed and let in; the idea of going away with him seemed totally appropriate despite anything she'd just been thinking, even while they were standing here in their bathing suits discussing it. Yes, they were covered in beach towels, too, but that was hardly the point.

Lally wasn't sure if she wanted to understand the point any more, to be honest. Because she had a suspicion it would end up being something to do with still being way too aware of her gorgeous boss, and now having far too many emotional connections towards him as well.

A genuine interest in him had developed—an appreciation for his cleverness and imagination, a need to look after him. Concern about his relationship with his mother.

But she didn't want to let him into her personal life. Not the history part of it, anyway. *Do you, Lally?*

Cameron touched her arm with his fingers, the lightest of touches. 'So, do we have a plan? Leave first thing tomorrow morning with a couple of days' clothes, some buckets and strong plastic bags for the pebbles?'

'Yes. We have a plan.' Lally's skin tingled where his fingers rested against her.

Well, tomorrow she would be stronger.

Tomorrow she would be totally strong.

'I'd best go see about what I need to pack.' She excused herself and went inside. She wasn't removing herself from the way of temptation—that wasn't necessary, because Lally Douglas had her world, her attitudes, her thoughts and her feelings completely under control.

Oh, yes, she did!

CHAPTER NINE

'I MEANT to check the forecast for the next two days for this area.' Cam made the statement as they climbed from his convertible onto an isolated stretch of beach. It was mid-afternoon.

After the long trip, it was good to step out into such beautiful surrounds. The beach was not ideal for swimming; the sea looked too rough for that, but there was sand, the smell of salt water, gorgeous sky and sea extending until they melded their shades of blue together on the horizon.

Lally seemed happy, anyway. She breathed in a deep breath as they got out of the car and her face had relaxed into an expression of pleasure.

Cam told himself not to dwell too much on that look, to think rather about the business end of this trip, such as making sure it would work for Lally. For that reason he couldn't quite keep the self-directed disapproval from his tone as he went on, 'I usually think of those sorts of things, but, even though I spent hours working on business and writing and that should have meant I was totally focused on all the different things on my agenda, I didn't consider the weather.'

He'd focused on his business matters, had prepared instructions to leave for the site boss in case he and

Lally weren't back to speak to the guy by mid-afternoon Monday and had worked on his writing. He was well on track for his deadline now.

Perhaps Cam had overlooked the weather because he'd been trying to avoid some of his thoughts. Thoughts that had to do with whether it was wise to take Lally on this trip. He'd touched her arm after they'd been swimming last night, just touched her, and all of his senses had gone on alert again. Cam couldn't—one hundred percent could not—allow himself to be so overwhelmed by her. He had to resist desiring her.

Cam needed to focus on professionalism where Lally was concerned. Wanting to understand her, know all about her, know her secrets—he couldn't pursue that.

'The weather looks fine. I don't think we'll have any problems in that respect.' Lally spoke after casting a brief glance at the sky.

'Here's hoping you're right. But I'm leaving the top up on the car anyway. I don't trust coastal weather, it can change very quickly.' Cam took two buckets from the trunk, lined them with thick plastic bags and led the way onto the beach. If he treated this time as perfectly ordinary, that was what it would become eventually—wouldn't it?

And he might do better if he didn't touch her. At all. 'Let's see if we can find some nice, coloured pebbles and stones for your mosaic. I'm not sure if I'll be able to help or just be the "carry person" for you. I guess that'll depend on how specific you need your choices to be.'

'At first I'll only know what I want when I spot it, but, once I know, I don't see why you won't be able to find similar pebbles and stones and help gather them.'

Lally wanted to create the mosaic for Cam, and perhaps a little for herself. Maybe her relatives were right and it was past time for her to explore her artistic ability. She shouldn't feel that. She had no right to feel that.

She did feel happy and full of anticipation. About the work; it had nothing to do with the idea of strolling along beaches with a gorgeous man. A man who had the ability to turn her senses and her emotions to mush just by letting her see into the depths of his eyes.

Oh, Lally. That's not a helpful thought to have!

'You're quite sure you're happy with the style and design I want to use for the mosaic?' She'd been up later than she should have been last night working on the fine-tuning of that design. Cam had been restless too. Lally had heard that, but only because she'd been awake anyway. He always tried hard not to disturb her sleep.

With ideas buzzing in her mind, Lally had sketched out her plan for the mosaic and had noted what colours she'd use for the various parts of it. She'd shown those plans to Cam this morning before they'd left the apartment. She thought about them again now to try to help her control her wayward thoughts.

'I'm totally fine with it. You're the artist at work in this situation, Lally. What you say about it goes.'

Cam had been very supportive of her ideas earlier too.

Lally rubbed her hands together. 'Let's see if we can find some suitable pebbles.'

Lally strolled the first part of the beach. She looked at pebbles scattered here and there, bent to examine a shiny, flat rock weathered into smoothness by time and tide. Truly she didn't think once about how good Cam looked in his jeans-shorts that reached just below his knees, running shoes and T-shirt. Not once.

Lally wore white capri-pants, runners and a red, short-sleeved blouse. Lately she'd been reaching more often for the few brighter clothes she had in her wardrobe.

You've been reaching for bright clothes, like the dress Cam purchased for you that night.

Well, it wasn't as though she couldn't give herself permission to wear whatever colours she wanted to wear.

Really? You don't think that's just one indication that you're attracted to Cam and you want to attract his attention right back the same way you worked to attract Sam's attention six years ago?

What did one have to do with the other? Lally suppressed a frown.

'Is that stone a yes as a keeper, or a no?' Cam held the two empty pails in his hands. He gestured to the stone she was turning over and over in her hand.

'Oh, um...' Lally glanced at the stone blankly and back up into Cam's face. He hadn't shaved this morning, and her fingers itched to run through the light covering of beard growth. The texture would be prickly and silky at once.

If he kissed her, she would feel that silky prickliness against her mouth, brushing over the sensitive nerve-endings beneath her lower lip. It might not be smart, but Lally wanted Cam to give her that kiss. She glanced into his eyes and caught an equally aware, desire-filled expression there.

So why not just give in and kiss him, get a second taste of something that had felt rather like paradise?

How could one girl, who didn't even want to be involved in such a way, miss a man's kiss after having it just once? How could she miss it enough to think such thoughts when they were dangerous to her emotional well-being? She searched Cam's eyes for the answer. But she wasn't sure if she wanted to find it.

Then she remembered a different question. 'The stone is smooth, beautifully rounded and a good colour. It's definitely a keeper.' She dropped it into the pail. She was supposed to be shopping for mosaic materials, not wishing she could kiss her boss.

Cam steered her in the direction of a ridge of pebbles that had been thrown up by the tide.

Lally bent to look and forced her mind to focus on the task of examining them and picking up the ones she thought had the best colours. She didn't want to think about any of the rest of it.

For the first while, Lally was uneasy as they gathered their pebbles. But Cam was a good help, standing patiently while she chose stones, picking out others that complemented the colours and shapes she'd chosen, and eventually she began to relax.

'Did you have any painting lessons at all? Non-traditional ones, I mean?' Cam asked as she sifted a handful of pebbles through her fingers.

'I painted a little during high school. Art classes, how to paint fruit in a bowl, that sort of thing. But I stopped after that.' Lally dropped a few pebbles into the bucket and bent to scoop up more.

Cam reached down at the same time and their fingers brushed. The sound of the sea ebbing and flowing on the shoreline seemed louder as Lally's breath stopped. Her gaze turned to Cam's face and got caught in the deep green of his eyes.

'Sorry. I wasn't looking.'

'I should let you check them first.'

They both went to get up, and Lally's sneaker sank into the damp sand. It made a squishing sound, and she couldn't hold back a slight smile. 'Do you know? I wish

I could feel the sand beneath my toes. I haven't walked barefoot on a beach in ages.'

'So take your shoes off and get the full experience.' Cam said it in a teasing tone. His lips quirked and he bent to remove first one shoe, then the other.

His encouragement could have stabbed right through her. For wasn't that exactly what she'd done to get herself in trouble in the past—been a hedonist? Indulged in what she wanted while blindly ignoring all warning signs that she might be headed for trouble?

That wasn't the same, Lally. You're just walking on the beach. Lally removed her shoes.

They abandoned both pairs right there, just like that. Well, Cam seemed more than comfortable. And what was the harm, really?

'No one will take them.' Cam glanced about. 'It's totally deserted here.'

He was right about that. When he set the bucket down and held out his hand to her, a little thrill went through Lally before she placed her hand in his and let him lead her to the water's edge.

Cool sea-foam washed over her feet and splashed against her ankles. Cam's hand felt warm and firm in comparison with the skin of her palm. As the water rolled out again, the sand sucked away beneath Lally's feet.

'I do love that sensation.' She glanced up at Cam and smiled. 'It's sort of icky and wonderfully good all at once.'

Cam laughed and his gaze softened as he looked into her eyes. There was such tenderness in that one glimpse of time. His hand tightened on hers; Lally realised they were still holding hands and told herself that should stop—but she didn't want to stop it. Particularly not when he looked at her this way.

Oh, but she needed to stop it, most of all because of that look; Lally broke away. 'We'd better get back to looking for pebbles. It's what we're here for—the mosaic. I want to do a good job of it for you.'

So they searched for pebbles and gathered quite a few. Lally loved the texture, the smoothness rounded into the stones by the constant movement, time smoothing off the edges. She glanced at Cam and thought, if only life could be that simple. Her six-year-old edges were still way too sharp.

Cam crouched down to sift through some pale-white stones. He played them through his fingers. From where she stood nearby, Lally had a view of the top of his head, the way his hair grew, the strength of the back and side of his neck and all of his face in profile.

'What do you think of these ones?' He looked up, caught her gaze on him and the green of his eyes darkened.

Lally's breath caught as her pulse sped up and her emotions responded to the expression in his eyes. He smiled then, and his smile was everything a woman could dream about. She wanted to melt into a puddle at his feet. She could have done that easily.

'The pebbles look good. Yes, I'd like to keep those ones, and I have some more.' Her fist closed about the ones she had gathered. She stepped forward and dropped them into the bucket beside him. 'I, um, I'll look further afield. Over there.' She gestured randomly and forced herself to strike out away from him.

He let her go. That was good because they couldn't be like this. *She* couldn't be like this. When had she become emotionally involved to the degree that she couldn't look at him in profile without wanting to step forward, wrap her arms around him, hold him and not let go?

'We'd better think about going if we're to meet my mother at the allotted time,' Cam said decisively as he stepped across the beach towards her about an hour later. He'd kept her supplied with buckets, but otherwise had left her alone.

Lally glanced up and her heart did it again—leapt, opened up, melted. She came forward with her current bucket brimming with stones; a mantra played in her head that she should play this cool, not let him see how he impacted on her.

'That was good timing. I think I have enough of any colours I can get from this beach.' She glanced down at her bucket and as she did failed to look where she was putting her foot. 'Ouch!'

A sharp sensation spread through her heel.

'Let me see.' Cam set his bucket down in the sand and had his fingers shackled firmly about her upper arm before she could even think.

It was natural to wrap her fingers around his strong forearm and use him for balance while she held her foot off the ground.

Cam looked at her foot, gently taking it in his other hand and turning it until he could see the bottom. Then he looked down into the sand. 'You've cut it on a rock. It doesn't look too deep, but it should be cleaned and dressed. Let's get you to the car so we can take care of it properly.'

'I might need your arm so I can hop along—' Lally got that much out before he swept her up into his arms and her thoughts fractured.

Consciousness of the sting in her foot faded as Cam's warm chest pressed against her arm and shoulder and his arms held her securely.

She'd been held by him like this before, at night at the top of the small, Adelaide-style skyscraper.

The whimsical thought brushed through her mind as her hands tightened together behind his neck. Lally told herself under no circumstances was she to stroke that neck, or in any other way reveal how being held by him made her feel.

You don't think that melting into him like a boneless blob might give him a hint?

'Okay. Let's sit you here and I'll take a proper look.' Cam eased her into the passenger seat of the convertible and seemed to release his hold on her reluctantly. He knelt at her feet and checked the wound. 'I've got a first aid kit. I think I can take care of this with cleaning solution and a couple of butterfly strips.'

'It probably only needs a plaster. Really, most of the sting has gone already.' Lally felt silly with her foot clasped in his hand and with him fussing over her. Silly and conscious of him all at once. 'It's just a cut. I'm sure if we clean it...' She leaned forward to try to take a look.

Cam tightened his fingers on her foot. '*I'll* clean it. You just sit tight and look beautiful.' He reached past her to open the glove compartment and pulled out the first-aid kit. He rummaged through it for the items he wanted. 'I've got a bandage too, so I can wrap that around it to make sure it all stays together when you put your shoe back on over the top.'

Lally sat back and let him take care of her, and he did, handling her foot gently and making sure he cleaned the wound thoroughly before he put on the steri-strips and covered it all in a bandage. He jogged back to the beach and retrieved both their pairs of shoes and the collection of stones, and helped her put her shoes on.

He was once again on his knees at her feet, a strong

man who seemed completely comfortable kneeling before her, looking after her.

When he glanced up and caught her studying him, his gaze darkened as it had back on the beach—except now there was nowhere for Lally to go, nothing to do but acknowledge the way he made her feel.

His hands bracketed the seat on either side of her legs as he leaned closer. 'I don't like that you got hurt.' His gaze was locked on her lips.

'It wasn't hurt badly, and you looked after me.' He'd told her to sit back and look beautiful. His eyes had taken in the wildness of her hair and Lally had *felt* beautiful, lovely, appealing and desirable. She realised she hadn't let herself feel that way for a long time.

His expression made her feel that way now. Lally caught her breath and a reserve inside her that had held together for six years frayed rather noticeably around its edges.

'Lally.' He murmured her name and leaned closer.

Lally heard her name and the warning in his tone as he spoke it.

Don't let me, his tone seemed to say.

But she was too busy reacting, and that reaction was to lean towards him while he leaned towards her until they were almost nose-to-nose. She could smell the blunted, woodsy scent of his aftershave lotion where it had blended with his skin.

He smelled good. Lally wanted to press her nose to his neck and just inhale him.

'God, Lally, when you look like that…' Cam broke off and closed the remaining distance between them.

CHAPTER TEN

CAM's lips drew closer. Every pore of Lally's being wanted and needed his kiss. He kissed the side of her face in the shallow spot beneath her cheekbone. He kissed where her cheek creased when she smiled.

He kissed the edge of her lips with a teasing press; Lally turned her head and blindly sought the second full press of his lips to hers. She got it, and her eyelids felt way too heavy to hold open, so she let them flutter closed as he pressed more soft kisses to her lips, and she kissed him back just as softly.

The ocean rolled against the beach down on the shore. A seagull cried; Lally breathed Cam deep into her lungs and held him there.

His hands came up to clasp her shoulders, to brush gently over them and rub against her back. His fingertips worshipped the softness of her skin, and he made a sighing sound as though he'd found exactly what he'd been looking for and just wanted to enjoy it.

That slow, detailed attention swept Lally away more effectively than anything else would have. It was as though Cam took time in his hands and stilled it so they could have this, indulge in it and experience it in its fullest measure.

His lips pressed to hers.

Her mouth opened to him because he made what they were sharing feel so completely safe, so utterly right.

Lally forced her eyes open to seek his; slumberous green looked at her. He seemed so at ease, restful to the point almost of being sleepy. Lally didn't know why that response in him made her feel powerful, but it did.

'Lally.' His fingers sifted through her hair, caught the long strands and played with them, before he pressed those fingers with just the right amount of pressure against the base of her skull and drew her forward so he could deepen their kiss.

Their tongues met, stroked.

Lally didn't know how he did it, but somehow in his gentleness and focus Cam encouraged her to take whatever she wanted of him. He offered his tongue. She drew it into her mouth and explored the taste and texture. She felt her back arch as he gave a soft sound of pleasure and his arms drew her closer still.

His fingers pressed against her shoulders until their bodies were chest to chest. It felt good, it felt right, and Lally relaxed even more.

She didn't know when the kiss changed, when slow became deep, when sultry became focused, when restful became hungry and desperate became need-filled; it just happened. Cam was kissing her utterly then, his mouth locked over hers. All of his focus and all of hers was fixed on this exchange, these sensations.

Even as her hands rose to his chest, to his shoulders, Lally knew this kiss was different. This kiss was not Sam kissing her, relying on his charm to lead her to do whatever he wanted, to overwhelm her so she didn't think about his motives, so she didn't suspect them.

This kiss wasn't like Cam's last kiss either. That had been wonderful. This was more, so much more that Lally could not remember why she shouldn't do this. She needed this, *had* to do this. Lally *liked* Cam, admired him, was attracted to him not only physically but to his thought processes, his creativity, his business acumen, drive, ambition, attention to detail, enthusiasm for his work, imagination...

How could she fight this kind of attraction? It was more than she had ever felt for any other man, Sam included.

That fact got through to Lally as nothing else had. If she let herself follow this path, where would it end? How capable would she be of getting hurt? How could anything be *more* than Sam had been in her life? Sam had irrevocably changed it.

Lally had to stop this. Even now her instincts fought her mind. Her lips remained right where they were, pressed to Cam's. Her hands slid to Cam's upper arms, a precursor to letting go, but her fingers clasped those arms. Lally dropped her hands but they slid away from him slowly.

It was Cam who broke the kiss itself, his gaze already searching hers. What Lally imagined he saw there was echoed in his own expression.

Desire and caution, want and the need to stop.

'Lally, we have to—'

'We have to stop—' Lally lost the words in the depths of his eyes, found them again in the drive inside her that insisted she keep herself safe, that she not get hurt again, not yield to feelings for a man who wouldn't value them, not make a mess, create guilt—oh, so many things.

Cam was her boss, he was wealthy, famous and amazing, and Lally was the temporary housekeeper and assistant. Cam was very much out of her league. In the end he was as much out of her reach, as Sam *should* have been, if for other reasons. And Sam was part of Lally's reason now, that tainted history.

The resignation in Cam's eyes told her he felt the same way about this, at least to the extent that he knew this had to stop, that it wouldn't be wise for them. What were his reasons?

'We should get going. Your foot's okay? It's not hurting you?' Cam put his shoes on while she settled herself properly in her seat.

'It's fine now that it's cleaned and wrapped. And we don't want to be late for dinner with your mother.' Lally spoke the words through kiss-swollen lips, over the taste of him that was still on her tongue, trying to make sense when she couldn't think straight.

Cam searched her eyes for a moment before he closed her car door, crossed in front and got into the driver's seat. Just a few moments with those broad shoulders in motion, his long legs eating up the ground until he slid behind the wheel, and Lally couldn't concentrate again.

'Would you like the top down again?' Cam glanced her way.

Lally quickly nodded. 'The breeze is nice.'

She didn't care about her hair getting whipped about; that could be fixed when they arrived. Maybe the wind would blow this lapse of control away.

Cam got things organised. Then he sat there with the engine idling and finally turned his gaze her way. 'Lally…'

'Don't.' She shook her head. 'Please. We have to see your mother. Can we just…do that?'

So they went.

'Here we are.' Cam drew the car to a halt in a restaurant's small parking-lot. 'Hopefully Mum will be here and won't have changed her plans without letting me know.'

'Does she do that often?' Lally asked as they made the short walk to the restaurant's entrance.

'It happens.' Cam's mother did a lot of things he didn't always like. 'How's the foot? If it's hurting, I can help you.'

'Oh, no, it's okay—and I wouldn't want your mother to think—' Lally broke off.

But not before Cam saw the memory of their kisses cross her face. Lally might have set out to say she didn't want his mother to think she was anything other than able to look after herself, or something like that, but her words had quickly led her thoughts elsewhere.

Cam could identify with that, because all his thoughts seemed to lead elsewhere at the moment.

And all those 'elsewhere' roads led to one place: the kissing Lally place. His lack of control around her was substantial, it seemed. Cam wasn't exactly proud of that and yet he couldn't regret what they'd shared.

'Then I guess I won't carry you inside.' He said it with a smile that took effort at first. But he thought his mother might actually do a double take if she saw him walk into the restaurant carrying Lally clutched to his chest like a prize, and his smile became more natural.

He turned to her as they made their way inside. 'There's about an eighty-percent chance we'll be meeting someone else as well as my mother for dinner.'

'I'm not sure what you mean.' Lally seemed to be just on the edge of nervous.

Or maybe that was left over from what had passed between them back at the beach. Cam glanced at her. Even hobbling a little, she still managed to look graceful. He looked again. He realised his mother might be likely to bring 'a friend' yet again to meet him, but Cam wanted to show Lally off to his mother. That was very much a first.

As your employee. You want to show her off as your employee.

Yeah.

Right. That was what he wanted. That was no doubt what had driven him to kiss her again back there at the beach, lose complete sight of where they were. It was what he'd told himself he would and wouldn't do when it came to Lally.

Cam wasn't sure he wanted to think about his motives for that. Somehow they appeared to be linked to something far too deep inside him that he'd thought he had worked out. He *did* have it all worked out!

'I guess you'd say Mum's a free spirit. She's not someone who will pin down to anything for long, but when it comes to relationships that's not a lesson she's been able to acknowledge within herself. She keeps leaping in and backing out again just as quickly.'

'Oh.' Lally gave a calm nod. 'I have an older cousin who's like that—revolving-door relationships. I don't know how she deals with the stress, although, now that I think about it, she manages to walk away apparently unscathed each time. I couldn't do it.' She fell abruptly silent.

Cam had a feeling it had occurred to both of them at once that they weren't really in the best position to discuss this as uninvolved observers. 'We can't be—'

'Well, there you are. Cameron, come and meet Tom; he's such a darling. I don't know where I'd be without him.' His mother stepped forward as she spoke the flow of words, hugged him quickly and stepped back.

The obligatory hug was over for another year, and it had happened so quickly that Cam had almost missed it.

Men weren't supposed to feel the lack of that kind of thing, were they? Yet it occurred to Cam in this moment that he'd missed a lot of real, genuine hugs in his lifetime. Lally would never hug half-heartedly like that. Cam just knew this.

He'd felt it for himself when she'd held him, and everything inside him had relaxed and felt as though it could rest and be still.

That stillness wasn't something Cam understood, and he hadn't truly thought about it in relation to Lally until now. But she gave him that feeling. It was as though somehow being around her helped him to find peace or something.

And what are you now, Travers? Some kind of tortured soul? For crying out loud!

Cam turned his gaze to his mother. 'Hello, Mum. This is Lally. Lally, meet my mother, Dana.' He shook hands with—*John? No, that was the last one.* 'Hello, Tom.'

'What have you been doing, Cameron? Dull old business things, I suppose, with a bit of writing thrown in on the side?' His mother picked up her menu and started to scan it. 'You should rest more. Weariness isn't attractive, you know.'

'Insomnia isn't quite the same as weariness, Mum. And I always do try to rest.' Cam said it gently; he didn't expect Dana to really listen. He drew a breath to turn the conversation elsewhere.

'I think Cam deals really well with his insomnia.' Lally's words came softly into the conversation. 'It can't be easy to have all those long hours to get through, knowing you can't rest as much as you'd like to be able to.'

Cam hadn't expected her to speak. The support behind the words touched him. He stared into liquid brown eyes and felt much of the tension over seeing his mother again ease out of him.

With a few soft words, Lally had him in a better place with things. Cam needed to make sure his housekeeper and assistant was in a good place too, because beneath the surface of her cheerful attitude he could see a hint of unhappiness that he suspected might have been for his sake. His mother had turned her head to speak quietly to Tom for a moment.

Cam touched Lally's hand beneath the table. 'Thank you,' he murmured so only she could hear him. 'Mum doesn't mean any harm. We're not very close, you know? But I still like to see her occasionally. She's the only relative I've got.'

Could those words reassure a woman whose life to a large degree seemed to revolve around her love for her big extended family? It wasn't a topic Cam could cover further now, at any rate.

'You should just take sleeping pills, Cameron.' His mother tossed these words out. They were an easy solution, a fast solution; Dana was good at offering those and then forgetting all about whatever issue had arisen in the first place.

She just wasn't good at seeing that some things didn't *have* fast, easy solutions. 'I'm sure after a few days of those your body would retrain and you'd be fine.'

'Lally's trying some bush-food remedies to see if they'll help,' Cam offered with a determined smile. 'And I have felt more relaxed in the past while.' That was down to Lally herself, in Cam's opinion, but he kept that thought to himself.

And now he really wanted to change the topic.

'I see.' His mother looked back at her menu then glanced at her watch. 'We should make our selections. I'm sure the waiter will be along at any moment.'

Lally blinked just once before she lowered her gaze toher menu.

Cam had the odd urge to take her hand again beneath the table and this time keep it in his clasp.

Instead, he turned his attention to choosing a meal.

Tom spoke, bringing up an interest in fishing and four-wheel-driving. 'What do you drive, Cameron?'

Cam gave the older man the make and model of his convertible. 'I like—'

'The fresh air.' Lally glanced at him and smiled. 'It was nice this morning, wasn't it? Coastal roads, warm weather and a sea breeze.'

'What exactly is your relationship to Cameron, Lally?' his mother suddenly asked nosily.

Cam opened his mouth to answer, somewhat protectively. His mum's tendency to stomp all over people's privacy with her questions was something Cam hadn't taken into account when he'd invited Lally along for this. He should have thought about it.

But Lally beat him to it. 'I'm working as a temporary housekeeper to Cam while he's in Adelaide.' She smiled. 'And building him a pebble mosaic for the courtyard of his property development there, while he creates his latest crime story to keep readers on the edges of their seats.'

'Oh.' Mum seemed to be somewhat at a loss. 'So, you're a bit of a Jill of all trades? Stone masonry is an unusual career choice for a woman.'

'Well, pebble mosaics are a little different to stone masonry.' Lally quickly outlined her vision for the mosaic. 'I'm looking forward to doing the work, anyway.'

'And I'm looking forward to seeing the end result.'

Cam closed his menu. Because he didn't want his mum cross-questioning Lally for the rest of the meal, he really did change the subject now. 'Catch of the day for me. You can't beat fresh fish, isn't that right, Tom?'

They discussed fishing and real estate through the main course. When he'd first got enough money to do it, Cam had bought his mother a home in Sydney and had invited her to settle there. He'd hoped to have her nearer, to be able to see her more.

That had been a vain hope. His mother had taken the property, immediately rented it out, and gone on her way travelling, content so long as no one asked her to put down roots.

'Remember, the house is always there for you, Mum.' He didn't know what made him say it.

Dana gave him an uncomprehending look. 'Well, and so it should be. It was a pay-off for the years I sacrificed to raise you. I deserve that rental income to allow me to travel in my motor home wherever I want to go.'

'You could change for the right man—settle down in a real home,' Tom muttered beneath his breath. He followed it up with a teasing smile, but he frowned and pushed his dinner plate away at the same time.

Cam glanced at his watch. Only a little over half an hour had passed since they'd sat down; it felt like much longer.

'I have family in Queensland and the Torres Strait islands,' Lally said as she pushed a fat, golden chip around her plate with her fork. 'My mother tries to get up that way every couple of years. I've enjoyed making the trips with her a few times.'

Lally glanced briefly towards him.

Ah, Lally. Don't care about this. It just isn't worth it.

The conversation segued to a discussion of bush foods

and other cuisine. That took them through the rest of the meal. When it ended and Cam's mother mentioned coffee, Cam shook his head and stood.

'We need to push on, find a suitable place to stay this evening. It was…good to see you.' He nodded to Tom. He didn't bother trying to kiss Dana's cheek or hug her. She hadn't got up and clearly didn't intend to.

Instead, Cam took Lally's arm in a gentle clasp, nodded to his mum and Tom once again and led Lally out of the restaurant.

'Your mother seems very…autonomous,' Lally said as diplomatically as she could.

Cam saw her effort to avoid saying so much else, and he appreciated it for what it was. He shook off his mood because there was no point and he didn't want to spoil the rest of their evening. 'She always has been. I try.'

Cam *did* try. He kept a one-way stream of communication with Dana throughout the year, using whatever medium of contact she made available to him. The contact just didn't come back his way very often.

'Did your mother look into your insomnia when you were younger?' Lally asked with a frown.

'She didn't acknowledge it as anything more than a child being annoying about not wanting to sleep.' There'd been a lot of nights spent lying awake. The settings had changed all the time, but the end results had been the same.

Lally seemed to fight with herself for a moment before the need for expression finally got the better of her. 'Your insomnia probably started as a result of you being picked up and moved around all the time. If you'd received the right kind of attention back then…'

'That's a long way back. I don't think it was that.' Yet Cam had developed that problem as a child. He'd just assumed he got it from the gene pool of whoever had fathered him, that it was a genetic issue, not one that might have developed from his circumstances. 'I've lived away from that environment for a long time now.'

'And kept moving around, the way your mother always has.' Lally searched his eyes. 'I'm not saying you shouldn't travel if that's what keeps you happy, but maybe you haven't had a decent chance at finding that kind of peace to allow you to properly rest?'

Cam opened his mouth to say that moving around was as necessary to him as it was to his mother. Then he closed it again, because he wasn't quite sure if it *was* as necessary as he had always thought.

Yet, if it wasn't, why did he keep on the move all the time, constantly searching, looking for the next challenge, the next brick in the road, the next great book idea and property-development idea? 'I guess travelling has been a way to fill all the time that yawns in front of me.'

Cam just didn't know what else it meant. And he felt oddly uncertain about the whole topic. 'Let's go find a nice bed and breakfast for the night.'

'Yes. Let's.' Lally didn't push the topic. Instead, she drew a deep breath and smiled as they reached his car and climbed in.

They got on the road, and Cam slowly forgot about the visit with his mother.

Instead he took the opportunity to gently grill Lally about her family situation. Lally seemed to need them so much, and Cam wanted to try to understand where she stood in relation to all that.

He wanted to understand the why of her needs, and whether that somehow related to the occasional sadness he saw in her eyes.

'I'm looking forward to getting back to my usual work

among the family after this assignment is over.' Lally glanced his way. 'I'm happy with you as well. I just need to do that for my family. It's safe—' Lally cut the words off and frowned.

They passed through one small place, but the accommodation didn't look particularly inviting. Cam chose to move on. He'd researched a bed and breakfast on-line in the next town that had looked good in the photos.

Lally leaned her head back against the seat and became silent. A few minutes later, she fell asleep.

CHAPTER ELEVEN

CAM reached into the car, lifted his slumbering house-keeper into his arms, carried her inside the bed and break-fast, up the staircase and into the only room they had free.

The rain had just stopped. It had pelted down for the last hour as he made the slow trip here. Cam had sat the last few minutes out in the parked car, right outside the B&B, with Lally gently sleeping in the seat beside him. She slept so peacefully—Cam could envy that!

She must have been exhausted, and Cam felt at least partly to blame for that. He'd been disturbing her sleep since she'd first moved in with him. He knew it, even though he'd tried to be quiet at night when he moved around in their apartment.

He should put her out into one of the other apartments. How long would it take to gather up enough furniture to make her comfortable? He could order the lot over the phone in about twenty minutes.

Cam's arms tightened about his burden that felt like no burden at all. He'd be quieter, make sure he didn't disturb her in future. He didn't want to move her out.

'Are we there already?' Lally murmured in a sleepy voice and then seemed to realise she wasn't on her feet. Confusion filled her gaze and she blinked at him with wide eyes that quickly changed from slumberous to conscious and softened as they locked on his face.

One look from her, one glimpse into those unguarded eyes, and all Cam wanted…

Well, he couldn't have what he wanted. If he'd let himself wonder otherwise, spending time with his mother today had concreted the fact that he just couldn't go there with Lally.

She deserved more than someone who'd pack up and move around all the time, who would not want to settle down somewhere with her, not want babies and a picket fence. Not know how to give that even if he had wanted it.

You could have babies and a courtyard and a big, old family home that you're converting into apartments right now. You already know it would work quite well as a home.

Since when had Cam started to think about that big, old place as a potential home, rather than a sound business-investment? Let alone think about settling down. It was out of the question; totally and utterly out of the question for him.

Cam set Lally down in the small living area of the room and backed away. 'Eh, you fell asleep in the car. There's been a storm, so I drove us to this B&B. All they had was this room, and they told me all the other accommodation in the area is booked out. The bad weather took a few travellers by surprise, apparently.'

He rammed his hand through his hair upwards from the base at the back. 'So, eh, I can sleep in the car.'

'Oh.' Lally blinked, blinked again and glanced around them, taking in the surroundings, the double bed beside the bank of windows. 'Well, um…'

'Yeah. I'll go get our things. At least I can have a hot shower.' Cam swung about and left the room.

As Cam left, Lally drew a deep breath and tried to calm herself. She wasn't nervous, though maybe that feeling would catch up in a minute. She was just trying to come to terms with waking up in his arms like that. Had she melted into him before she woke up? What if she'd talked in her sleep? Snored? Kissed him? Dribbled?

Oh, for heaven's sake; she was just snoozing.

Snoozing right through a fierce storm, apparently. And Cam had sat with her in the car then carried her inside. He must have a lot of patience.

Well, the man couldn't sleep himself. He was probably used to needing a lot of patience to get through all those hours when he wanted to be asleep but wasn't. Maybe he'd got some vicarious satisfaction out of knowing she was sleeping.

And maybe Lally was letting her imagination run away with her so she wouldn't have to think about sharing a room with her boss tonight.

'Room service,' Cam quipped as he stepped into the room and dumped their bags. He glanced at her face, and shoved his hands in his pockets. 'I said it already, Lally—I'll sleep in the car.'

'Yes, well, you see, that's the problem—I can't let you do that. You'd be so uncomfortable. It's a great car, but it's not made for sleeping in.' She couldn't let him do that. 'There's really nowhere else we could go for the night?'

He was shaking his head before she even finished speaking. 'There's nowhere nearby, and they seem to think there'll be a second storm-front.'

'I don't know why I did that. Slept, I mean. It must have been all the fresh air and wandering on the beach earlier.'

'Fresh air and exercise has that effect on a lot of people.'
He set their bags against the wall out of the way. 'They're
offering winter warmers in the dining room: would you
like to come down, have a hot drink, at least?'

Lally nodded. 'That would be nice. I'd better tidy
up.'

At least they had their own bathroom tucked behind a
door. Lally picked up her handbag that Cam had kindly
brought in for her, stepped into the bathroom, shut the door
and splashed water over her face. Her hair was springy
from the weather. She knew better than to brush it. If she
did, it would just get springier.

So she twisted and tied it in a loose knot to keep it
half under control, applied some lipstick and a spritz of
perfume and called the job done. 'I'm ready.'

'You look lovely,' Cam murmured, then took her
arm and led her from the room. 'Let's go see what's on
offer.'

Lally hadn't been alert enough to think about the intimacy of the room. Now she tried to absorb his compliment and felt a glow come over her, because being told
by a man that she looked great would naturally give her
a glow, wouldn't it?

It was nothing to do with this specific man. Any man
saying that would have had the same impact.

Oh, she really wished her thoughts wouldn't step in
and question her like that. Sometimes ignorance, or at
the very least letting herself think whatever suited best,
truly could be bliss. It was better than delving too deeply
into the truth.

*Like the truth of knowing you need to share a room
with him tonight?*

Maybe she should offer to sleep in the car.

But he wouldn't allow it, and Lally knew that.

'It looks like that table is free.' Cam led the way to a small table in the corner and they took their seats. The table was beside a window and outside streaks of drizzling rain ran down the pane of glass.

'I'd thought we might have to sit at one large, long table and share our company with everyone else,' Lally observed.

Since when did you become a hermit, Lally Douglas? Usually you love big dinners with lots of people around.

That was when she was with her family. This was different. She didn't want to admit that she wanted Cam all to herself.

She must be still sleepy, not thinking straight. 'Not that I'd have minded,' Lally declared a little too loudly and with a little too much emphasis, and felt telling heat creep into her face. 'I'd have been quite happy to share. I'd have been quite happy to share news with the other guests, have a bit of a chat. Well, the table setting is nice, don't you think?'

Lally gestured at it and told herself the fat red candle in its old-fashioned brass holder didn't look at all romantic, nor did her boss look equally so with candlelight playing across the angles and shadows of his face.

He was grinning, just the slightest bit—as one was wont to do when a woman blabbered, Lally pointed out to herself with an inner frown.

The guesthouse manager came to their table and gave a friendly nod. 'We're not overly fancy here, but we've got a really nice soup on offer, cake or dessert, plus tea, coffee and hot chocolate.' He rattled off a description of each choice.

Lally was surprised to discover she actually felt a little hungry. 'I'd love to try the soup.'

They both opted for that to start off.

Lingering over the supper would use up some of the time until they could go to bed and hope to sleep.

Well, Lally would hope to sleep. Cam didn't at the best of times; she doubted he'd do better when he didn't even have the bed to himself.

Thinking about getting into bed with him was really not a good idea when she was sitting across a romantic table-setting from him.

'It's *not* a romantic table-setting,' she muttered, and fell silent.

'Water?' Cam judiciously ignored her comment and poured water for both of them from a carafe on the table. He passed her drink to her before taking a sip of his own.

Lally watched him drink and thought he even did that appealingly.

Do not let your thoughts start wandering where he's concerned. He's your boss. The boss and the house-keeper—got that? Good!

Maybe they could put a line of pillows down the middle of the bed or something. Or one of them could sleep rolled into a blanket so there was no chance that their bodies would touch. What did they call that in the old days—buffering? Bundling?

The soup arrived and Lally stirred her spoon through it. 'Mmm, I think it has some mushroom in it, beef and tomato, and I suspect some brown lentils. Basil, carrot; definitely parsnip. I'm not sure what else.'

Very good, Lally. Perhaps you could rabbit on about the soup some more, totally bore him under the table in the first five minutes.

'And some pasta whirls and green peas.' Cam dug his spoon around in his soup and glanced up at her through his lashes. 'There's also either sweet-potato or pumpkin. There's a reason they call some soups a meal in a bowl.'

In this case they were small, shallow bowls. Lally took the first mouth-watering sip of the soup and her respect for this tucked-out-of-the-way B&B rose even more. 'I wish I knew how they made this.'

'Would you like me to try to get the recipe for you?'

Lally wouldn't be surprised if he managed to charm the recipe out of the manager's chef or wife, or whoever did the cooking. 'Well, only if the opportunity comes up. My sister Tammy would love to cook this.'

They fell silent for a few minutes, simply enjoying the warming fare.

Lally thought about something else that was on her mind and said, 'I'm trying to imagine what it would be like to only have one relative and not see her very often.'

The manager removed the empty soup bowls and offered them a selection of desserts off a trolley. After they'd chosen, he left again with a murmur. Outside, the rain started to come down in thick sheets. It spattered against the window and made Lally glad to be inside. The memory of Cam's kiss earlier today rose in her mind, and she tried very hard to push it back out again. She was too vulnerable right now to let herself remember.

Cam glanced at the window and returned his gaze to her. The green of his eyes seemed particularly deep in the candlelight as he met her gaze. 'I see my mother when she's prepared to fit me into her schedule. Usually that's a couple of times a year. To be honest, though, I do try to keep a flow of text messages and things going her way; that amount of contact is enough for me.'

Because his mother didn't take much notice of him when they *did* meet. She didn't listen to the things he told her; she was a lot more interested in herself than she was in him. Lally suspected that Dana Travers might not bother even to respond to many of her son's communications at all.

The woman had acted as though having a home given to her as a reward for putting up with him as a child was more than her due. 'Was your mother always…?'

'Like what you saw today?' He shrugged his shoulders. 'I came up knowing she hadn't really wanted the responsibility of a child, but she did keep me with her. She just did it her way, I guess.'

'By travelling all the time.' Lally's eyebrows drew together. She was trying hard not to judge the other woman too harshly but it wasn't easy. 'You must have been very good academically to survive that kind of existence and still do well.'

'Books helped.' Cam took a spoonful of fluffy lemon mousse, let it slide over his tongue and swallowed it. 'Every town we went to, I read as many library books as I could before we moved on again. I guess that helped a lot with keeping me where I needed to be with schoolwork. That and a few understanding teachers here and there along the way. I spent a lot of time by myself while Mum…'

'Wasn't there?'

'Yeah. We lived and travelled in a camper van. I thought being left by myself was what happened to every kid.' He said it in a matter-of-fact tone, yet Lally felt certain he rarely if ever talked about this.

This amazing man had been more ignored into adulthood than raised. His mother had let him know he was an inconvenience to her. That was unkind, cruel, to a little boy. What had Dana been thinking?

She'd been thinking of herself, and not the impact that her attitude would have on her son.

And who are you to judge, Lally? You sent not one but three young boys away from their mother!

'You must have had a lot of nights when you went to sleep wondering where you'd be the next day.' Lally swallowed back her guilt.

'I did, but on the upside I got to see a lot of gum trees, caravan parks and bush campsites,' Cam quipped, and then fell silent. His eyebrows drew down and a thoughtful expression crossed his face before he sighed and shook his head. 'How's your dessert?'

'It's nice. I'm glad I chose the mousse too.' She dug her spoon into the dish and gave thanks that he hadn't discerned the tone of her thoughts. 'This tastes so good, I'm guessing there's got to be a gazillion calories in it. And that's just the portion I have on my spoon.'

Cam laughed, as she had hoped he would. They fell silent, finished their desserts, lingered over coffee and ended up talking about football teams, current affairs and whether it made sense to invest in gold bullion in today's economy.

It was relaxing and interesting. Relieved, Lally found herself looking into his eyes for the sheer pleasure of seeing the almost sleepy expression there.

But it was the slumberous look of a big, contented cat. There was leashed power behind it, an interest in her that was also leashed. Lally knew that, and sensual awareness built gently between them as they shared that exchange of glances, long, silent looks and casual conversation that was a cover for all that wasn't being said.

The dining room began to empty out, and Cam gestured to her cup. 'Would you like me to try to rustle up another drink for you?'

'I've had enough, I think. I hope that I'll get at least *some* sleep tonight.' She stopped and bit her lip, because even mentioning that made this intimacy feel even more intimate.

'We'll go up.' Did his voice hold the slightest hint of inevitability?

Or was that all inside her?

He rose from the table and took her arm to guide her out of the room.

They trod the staircase in silence. As they moved upstairs, the sound of the rain became louder. It sounded so lovely, the water hitting the corrugated-iron roof of the old building, sluicing into the gutters and running down the drainpipes.

'I'll enjoy listening to that tonight for however long it lasts,' Cam commented as he unlocked the door to their room.

Their room. For the whole night. With Cam awake while she slept. 'I, um, I hope I don't snore or talk in my sleep.' Or cuddle up to him without realising it…

'I think any of that will be the least of our worries,' Cam murmured. He closed his eyes for a moment and opened them with a question on his lips. 'Would you like to use the bathroom first, Lally, or will I go?'

He asked it so gently.

'I'll go first, if you don't mind.' She got her things, slipped into the bathroom and used the time under the shower to try to pull herself together.

When she came out in her nightwear—boy's shorts and a matching camisole top covered with the longer shirt she'd had on today—Cam glanced at her.

His gaze dropped to her bare legs for a split second and slid away again, and he scooped up his things and closed himself in the bathroom.

That hadn't been too bad. Really, she'd been worrying about nothing. Lally shrugged out of the shirt, lifted the covers of the bed on the side closest to the window and scooched under.

Cam stayed in the shower until he couldn't put off getting out any longer. He dried off, used his deodorant, tried not to think about the scent of Lally in the bathroom that had been tantalising him since he stepped in here and pulled on his boxers.

Though he considered getting back into his T-shirt, he pushed the thought away. Sleep was difficult enough, and he never slept in a shirt. Lally would already be in bed anyway, probably with the light out if his guess was on the mark. So it wasn't as though she'd be looking at him, and she'd seen him dressed in as little when they'd been in the swimming pool anyway.

Cam pushed the bathroom door open, oriented himself, clicked the light off and made his way to the bed.

The room was quite dark; that was probably a good thing. Cam lifted the covers, got into the bed, drew a slow, single breath and held it.

He could smell the sweet scent of Lally's deodorant, and the body gel she'd used in the shower. He could smell her, warm and soft and very, very close to him. Close enough that he could feel her body heat beside him in the bed.

'Goodnight, Cam. I hope you sleep at least a little. I don't want my presence to add to your trouble with that.'

She sounded concerned, and a little breathless.

Cam wanted to pull her into his arms and kiss her until she was breathless for other reasons.

Yeah, that would work well. He'd get her in his

arms, not want to let her go and it would go way beyond kissing.

Don't think about kissing her. Think of standing outside in that driving rain getting soaked and cold.

'Goodnight, Lally.' He doubted he would sleep a wink, but there was no need to tell her that. 'The main thing is for you to relax and sleep as much as you can. I'll be happy lying here listening to the rain. I can spend some time plotting the next part of my story in my head. I might write a scene where they stay in a B&B during a wild storm.'

'Story writing must be great that way.' She said it sleepily. 'You can utilise all your experiences.'

'I guess so, though I'm not about to claim that I've experienced any of the gory stuff I write in my books.' He accompanied his soft chuckle with a nod, and realised he could see the outline of her face and the soft glow of her eyes.

His vision had adjusted to the dark. The crack of light coming in beneath the door from the hallway was enough to allow him that much. That meant Lally had been able to see him from the moment he'd stepped out of the bathroom because she'd already been lying there, warm and soft.

Enough thinking about that!

'More pebble-collecting tomorrow? We've done well so far, don't you think?' It was an odd version of pillow talk, but it was better than wrapping his arms around her and kissing her until he went mad with need.

Need? Or desire, want? Well, of course it could only be desire and want. He wasn't capable of anything else.

'We have done well with the pebble collecting. I hope the rain stops before we get up tomorrow, otherwise we might not get anywhere with the rest of our search.' She yawned into her hand and tucked the covers more snugly about her chin. Beneath the blankets, her knee brushed against his leg as she shifted position.

'Oh, sorry.' She whipped her leg away and said breath-lessly, 'It's not a very big bed for a double.'

'Standard size, I think.' But he knew what she meant. All he'd need to do was reach for her, tangle his legs with hers…

'Goodnight.' He uttered that single word and rolled over so he was facing away from her. Amazing just how much a man could want to resist making that one, small move.

Cam lay in the darkness and kept his breathing deep and even. Lally first lay very still and barely breathed at all, then wriggled this way and that before finally relaxing until her breathing evened out to something close to the pace and cadence of his.

She was asleep about two minutes later, fully immersed in it within half an hour.

The rain continued to fall outside the window. Cam rolled over again and gave himself a moment of looking at her face in repose in the dimness. He drew a deep breath and yawned.

His body did a weird thing; it sort of relaxed, even though he was still utterly aware of her. Well, he was a man, they were in bed, she was beautiful, he liked her and he already knew what she tasted like.

Cam sent his thoughts outside into the driving rain again to get them off that particular trail. Obviously he wasn't going to be totally relaxed in these circumstances, but even so he felt calm. Content. He felt like he did when he finally got exhausted enough to sleep, but also differ-ent. He wasn't about to pass out but he felt like he could drift away on a cloud or something.

Maybe he would think about his story a bit later. He yawned again and all his muscles relaxed.

For now, he really was tempted to just close his eyes for a bit.

He did that…and slept.

CHAPTER TWELVE

LALLY woke to the sound of a cloudburst. In the moment that she opened her eyes, she realised it was pre-dawn—dim but not entirely dark; maybe about four in the morning.

Then Lally became aware of so much else: the press of a man's warm body against her soft curves. Cam. The scent of him mixed with her scent in the warmth of the bed they shared. A heartbeat registered through the tips of her fingers where they lay against his bare chest. Strong arms wrapped around her, skin on skin where the camisole top left so much of her back, arms and chest bare.

And a chin tucked over the top of her head so that she was cuddled into him, as though he'd reached for her, put her there and hadn't wanted to let go.

Lally's breath caught and her senses exploded with a surge of desire and need while her emotions clamoured with the torn feelings that came from being in his arms. So many conflicted feelings; she hadn't anticipated any of them, yet they washed all through her.

Lally tried to blame her rioting feelings on suddenly finding herself in this position. What if she'd ended up here because *she* had rolled into his arms, cuddled up to him quite shamelessly? What if she'd done that while he was wide awake and he'd put up with it rather than waking her? She wouldn't have said Sam's name in her sleep, would she?

But Lally knew she would not have done that, because it wasn't Sam who'd filled her thoughts since the day she'd met Cameron. Sam hadn't filled her thoughts for a long time, other than with guilt.

Cam made a contented, sensual sound in his sleep and his arms tightened their hold about her. Lally's worries gave way to more immediate responses, and not all of those responses came out of the fact of their physical closeness.

That set it all off. She wanted his kisses and to be loved by him; she wanted his body—but she also wanted him to want her soul. Lally wanted Cameron far too much to be safe in that wanting.

'Easy, Lally.' Cam stroked the backs of his knuckles gently over her back. His words were slurred and relaxed, more asleep than awake. 'It's just rain. We're safe. We know where we are.'

The mumbled words said so much about Cam's attitude to feeling misplaced.

'I wasn't...' *Worried about that.* She heaved in a breath. Given that brought them even more chest-to-chest, that didn't exactly help. His voice had been all raspy, as though he'd been in a deep, deep sleep. 'I know we're safe. We're at the B&B after our pebble collecting and dinner with your mother.'

She threw that in just in case he needed to be reminded, so he could completely orient himself.

Lally cleared her throat and whispered into the night, 'Did you sleep like that for long?'

There was a beat of silence and then a slow, surprised, 'Out like a light, and I must have slept for about six hours. I fell asleep listening to you sleeping. I'd still have been asleep if you hadn't started to wake.' His voice deepened again. 'Not that I minded.'

There was a great deal of 'not minding' along with the surprise that he'd slept so well in those few words, maybe more than he'd meant to let slip.

Lally felt thrilled because she'd helped him sleep. How silly was that? He'd probably slept due to some totally different reason. Maybe rain falling helped him to sleep. Didn't people listen to recordings of water falling and things like that, for that reason?

But he'd have tried that and be doing it all the time, if it worked for him. Cam's hand curved against her shoulder. He barely moved it, and yet all of Lally's body responded with a deep and demanding command to arch into his touch.

Was it the early hour of the morning and the dimmed intimacy of the room that made his words sound like the most sensual thing she had heard? His touch an invitation, a hope and a promise?

Lally tried desperately to pull herself together, but all that came out was, 'If I snored I'm going to die.' Her body arched into his despite herself. She stretched like a cat, right there in his arms. Lally stiffened with embarrassment and wished her emotions and responses would stop fritzing out on her.

Until Cam drew a deep, unsteady breath and went very, very still against her. 'You breathe like a kitten. You make purring sounds in your sleep. It's very…sexy.'

The words wrapped around her, made her feel desirable, gorgeous and lovely.

When had she stopped letting herself feel like that? Why had she stopped? The thoughts washed away as Lally registered the craving in his strong body, the desire mixed with gentleness in the fingers that stroked over her

shoulder blades. They slowed as her body melted despite
her, stroked to the back of her neck and oh, so softly drew
her forward until his lips were a breath away from hers.
'May I?'

Kiss her? Love her? Do whatever he wanted with her
and never, ever stop?

Her whispered, 'Yes,' ended in a sigh as his lips covered hers. Lally justified that it was only a kiss, one kiss,
while rain fell on the roof above them. Cam tugged the
sheet and blanket with his fist until it was wrapped around
them, then she was snuggled hard against his chest while
his mouth explored hers and their bodies pressed against
each other.

There was always a point when the choice was made,
a cut-off point, a chance to draw back; Lally and Cam
pushed straight through that barrier with this one single
kiss. He opened his mouth and offered her his tongue. She
claimed him, exploring his mouth, letting their tongues
brush, and to that claim she yielded herself.

'You're so beautiful.' Cam's hands skimmed over her
upper arms. His fingers splayed over the side of her neck
and speared into her hair. He buried his nose against her
scalp, closed his eyes and inhaled, and his body tightened.

He pressed fully against her, tangled his legs with
hers, and his muscles locked. 'I don't want to hurt you,
Lally—emotionally. There are things I can't give you. In
my past, I've proved that. This can't be…'

'I know.' And she did know. If Lally had thought about
anything, it was that neither of them wanted to get twisted
up in something that they couldn't walk away from.

If her heart hurt a little at that thought, it was probably
because she'd once had a lot more faith in her ability in
relationships.

But that was then, and this was now, and she liked to think that she and Cam were friends; in some ways, wasn't that far steadier and more special than a lot of other things might be? If they both had histories that held them back emotionally now, well, maybe that meant this was okay for her with him: no false expectations, no surprises.

Just this. Now.

'I don't want it to be anything other than this.' Not more than right now; she didn't want the complication. Lally told herself this and tried not to notice the thoughts in the back of her mind that clamoured for so much more. 'We're just two people reaching for each other out of friendship and mutual desire. That's all it is. And it's allowed to be that.'

It was safe to take that, and to give it. It wasn't the same as thinking she'd fallen deeply in love, only to discover the man of her dreams had deceived her and that a marriage had failed as a result of their association.

She'd thought she was in love back then, but it had got a lot worse than even that marriage failure.

Cam searched her eyes in the dimness. She searched his too, though she didn't know what she was looking for and didn't know what he would find.

After a long moment, he stroked his fingers over her jaw.

Then she didn't think any more because he was kissing her with slow kisses and touching her oh, so gently.

Lally eased into those kisses and touches. She couldn't have said when they built to need, and when need became more need, until it consumed her and her emotions flared and rushed through her, even though she'd thought she knew what they were all about; now she didn't.

Sensation crowded through her too. Her mouth melted beneath his, yielded parts of her that she hadn't known were shut inside, hadn't imagined she would give to him because this shouldn't have been about that.

In a few short words, they'd laid down their rules. Tangled feelings, overwhelming feelings, were not part of this, yet she felt them pushing from inside to try to come out.

Lally could have panicked then but she didn't get a chance. Cam brushed her hair away from her face. Their clothes had disappeared; now he brought her to a place of desperate neediness. He eased her closer still and kissed her mouth.

Though he smiled and his eyes were calm, they were also full of heat, and his heart was thundering against her chest. His body quaked against hers and his fingers trembled as he stroked her face and slowly entered her. 'Lally.' His mouth closed over hers, worshipping her lips with the sweetest of kisses.

Lally's eyes fell slowly shut, and opened again as her body adjusted to his presence. How could she explain the sense of rightness, the feeling that their bodies had been made for each other, for this moment together? She looked into his eyes and didn't know why she needed this the way she did. How could she think about that question when all she could do was feel with her body, her senses and her emotions?

'Are you all right?' He kissed her lips. His body rested against hers, stilled within hers, as he waited for her answer.

'Yes.' She drew a breath. 'Yes.' And she was. Lally just knew that; she accepted it and let her worries go.

He loved her gently, loved her thoroughly, until every sense and nerve ending was tuned to him and only him. With whispered encouragement he helped her climb towards completion. His gaze locked with hers and he gave her all his pleasure and tenderness.

At the last moment he splayed his hand across her shoulder blades and pressed them heart to heart; he kissed her as she shattered in his arms, and he shattered with her.

When Lally thought it was over, he kissed her neck and shoulders, and used his hands to massage the muscles in her back, waist and over her hips until her body arched. He whispered her name and they made love a second time.

Dawn came and went as she lay in his arms, drifting between contentment, completion, half-consciousness and sleep. Thoughts didn't exist. How could they when all she could feel was the soft stroke of his fingers on her skin? When all she could hear was the even tenor of his breath against her ear? Lally let go and allowed herself to sleep once again.

Cam held Lally while she drifted on the edges of consciousness, and eventually as he gentled her with his touch she drifted all the way over and gave way to sleep. He kissed the top of her head and let himself tuck her close, then come to terms with feeling as though he held the most incredible treasure in his hands, treasure that he didn't want to let go of.

Had he done the wrong thing by her with this? When he'd woken with her in his arms, it had been too easy to reach for what he'd known deep down they both wanted.

But had that been best for her? And for him? Cam sighed and tucked a strand of her hair behind her ear. He pressed his lips to her temple and gave her the softest butterfly kiss. Where did all this tenderness in him for her come from? Cam hadn't been tender in his life like this. He hadn't wanted to wrap a woman up gently in his arms, hold her softly, cuddle her for as long as she needed, and then cuddle her some more because *he* needed it.

He didn't understand such feelings and he couldn't begin to imagine where he should try to go with them. There was no place he could go with them. Lally was his employee, his temporary housekeeper. Even that wasn't going to last. And Cam wouldn't last in an ongoing relationship with her, would never be able to settle, stick with it and focus on it, be committed to it.

He spent most of his time warring with his inability to sleep, filling his life and his world with way too much work to make the long hours pass. Yes, he'd slept in Lally's arms, but that wasn't normal for him. It had probably happened for some random reason, or because he'd become so totally exhausted that his body had finally allowed him to take that rest that he'd so desperately needed.

Cam knew his limits. He shouldn't have allowed this to happen, but he had, and how would they deal with this now?

Cam sighed, forced himself to let her go, and then he climbed out of bed. He'd take a shower and get dressed, and maybe then he would think about all of this more clearly.

She'd said she didn't expect more than what they had shared. Cam had ended up feeling that they had shared a great deal more than he had expected. But exactly *what* had they shared? What made him feel this experience was different, deeper, so much more? And what did he do about any of that?

He had no answers.

CHAPTER THIRTEEN

'LALLY. About last night.'

'It was special; a gift. I'm choosing to see it as a gift and think of it as that.' Lally's rounded chin tipped up and her eyes glittered with determination.

She didn't quite meet Cam's eyes, not fully.

He couldn't blame her. Instead, he admired her so much for this show of strength when they both felt awkward and uncertain. Cam felt uncertain, and Lally *looked* uncertain beneath the façade of control and wilful good-cheer.

Cam should be thanking Lally for the gift. Nothing he'd experienced in his life had come close to what they'd shared last night. She'd brought him peace, sleep, rest and then the most moving intimacy he had ever experienced. 'I don't know what to say to you. It was—I've never; I can't explain.'

'You don't have to, Cam. You don't have to explain anything.' She kept her head facing forward.

They were in the convertible, headed for the first beach on their list for the day. A part of Cam had wanted to call the rest of their pebble-searching off and head straight back to Adelaide. But what would that solve? Nothing.

Yet Cam couldn't find the words to explain what was inside him. So he brought up one thing that should have been discussed last night—*before* they'd made love. 'Is there a chance you could end up…?'

'No.' She shook her head and warm heat flooded her face beneath the tan of her skin. 'I'm on the Pill—irregular periods.'

Right, well, that was good, then. No chance of a baby. Cam blew out a breath that had to be relief. He couldn't explain why the relief made his chest feel tight. His hands clenched around the steering wheel and he tried to relax them. 'Uh, this is the beach, just here.'

After stating the abundantly obvious, he pulled the car to a stop and they both climbed out.

It went like that all morning. They picked up pebbles, moved on to the next beach, picked up more pebbles. They were uncomfortable together, completely conscious of what had passed between them last night, silent about it, while unspoken further words screamed between them.

They finally finished finding pebbles and drove to the next town. They bought gourmet deli-sandwiches filled with prawns and other seafood on long rolls; they could eat them straight away, and they did, because it seemed the thing to do.

'We'll make good time back to Adelaide.' Lally got up from the park bench where they'd been sitting and brushed crumbs from her skirt.

Cam stood too, and his brow furrowed as he noted the shadows beneath her eyes. Those could have come from unhappiness or strain as easily as they could come from tiredness.

Lally stared at him as though willing him to just get them into the car so they could go. He returned her stare and dredged for words to say; he fought the need to hold her, and a wave of emotion rolled through him.

'Yes, we'll make good time,' Cam acknowledged, and

Lally drew a shaky breath and headed for the car with such relief that he couldn't say another word. Not now. Not when she seemed so fragile.

And not when he didn't know what to say.

Cam just…didn't know.

'I'll let the supplier know we won't take the pavers, then.' Jordan, the site boss, shrugged his shoulders. 'My opinion stands. I'm sure the pebble mosaic will look great, and I'll help out with anything that's needed for it. But I think for the commercial plans you have for this place leaving the existing pavers down is going to make it look a little too comfy—like a big home, rather than a newly refurbished apartment-complex, albeit one created within an old building. Over all I don't think that's going to best serve the place.'

'And I respect your opinion, but I'll stick with the plans that I have for the mosaic and the existing paving of the courtyard area.' Cam shoved a hand through his hair. 'I have to go with my instinct on this. It feels right to do the area this way.'

Lally stood at Cam's side. It was afternoon. They'd arrived back, stepped out of the car and Jordan had asked for a few minutes to go over various matters. The courtyard area and a chance to get new pavers for it at a bargain price had topped the list.

Cam went on now. 'Lally's going to put in her mosaic, and you'll go ahead with the plans to get the garden surrounds into good order, but that's all that needs doing.'

'Okay. It's your call.'

The two men ended their discussion and the site boss walked away with no hard feelings.

That left Lally, Cam, a car full of pebbles, a few things that had been said and some that hadn't. Such as all the thoughts inside her head that Lally wasn't sure she wanted to examine. And the emotions that wrapped around the time she had spent in Cam's arms, how special that had been for her.

She wanted to walk away and never come back, to run and not stop running. At the same time, she wanted to step forward into Cam's arms, hold him, be held tight by him and never, ever let go. She hadn't been able to talk any more about it.

Lally had done what she'd promised herself she wouldn't do: she had let her feelings get involved. Now she had to un-involve them—somehow. She didn't know how.

Lally didn't know how she would get through the rest of her time with him at all. There were things inside her, deep, emotional things to do with them making love and the surrender to him that had somehow happened deep within her. Lally couldn't let herself think about those things, not if she wanted to get through this. Not with her past. With Cam, she'd taken something she had no right to. That was what kept coming to her.

'Lally.' Cam cleared his throat.

'There's nothing to say, Cam. Please, can we just forget it?'

'I'm not sure if I can forget.' He hesitated, then said on a short burst, 'I fell asleep with you. I didn't believe I was capable of doing that. Maybe it was a one-off…' Doubt filled his words. 'I can't be settled. I'm a man who will never be able to stop in one place. I don't know how to be in a normal, loving relationship. I tried; I made a total wreck of it. And my mother…'

'It's not your fault that your mother can't settle down.' Lally did *not* believe that Cam was the same as his mother. 'And if you can't sleep, you can't sleep. Any person who knows you and love—*cares* about you, shouldn't ever feel anything about that other than empathy with your difficulties with that.'

Lally managed to stop her flow of words, but she couldn't stop what she'd almost said pouring through her heart. It rolled over her and consumed her.

She'd fallen in love with Cam. The knowledge was deep down inside her, true, total and absolute. She'd fallen for him before she'd ever made love with him, and of course she should have known that that was so.

Why else would she have needed that intimacy so much, if not to put into expression what was inside her heart for him?

Oh, Lally. How could you fall in love with him? How can you protect yourself now that you've done that?

She had never felt this way about another person. Not Sam, and that shocked her, because she thought she'd loved Sam so much. Only Cam had said he'd tried to love once before and failed. That was his past, his secret—that he'd loved.

And don't expect him to love you, Lally. Don't expect it.

'I just want to do the mosaic for you.' For him, for her, to leave her mark here on this piece of property that would make a great family home, for a very large family to come and go. But not for Cam, who had almost no family and didn't want one of his own, and had only bought this place to develop it.

But he could be happy as part of a family. He wouldn't have to settle into one place to do that. If he needed to travel, couldn't he do that with someone at his side?

Oh yes, Lally? And would he choose you to be that someone? A woman who broke up a marriage? Had an

affair with a married man? Sent a woman into a care
facility and her children into foster care?

Lally hadn't been able to do anything to help them.
Sam should have done that but instead he'd walked away.
Lally's thoughts put an end to any dream she might have
had. She'd lost her right to dream, and all she could see
that she had left to lean on in that moment was her professionalism. If she returned her focus to her work, maybe
she would manage to get through this without Cam realising that she had discovered she loved him.

She didn't want him to know. It wouldn't change
anything, would it? 'It shouldn't take me long to do the
mosaic and have the water-feature put in. I'm happy to
work with Jordan.'

'You're here for eight weeks.' Cam spoke as though he
felt he needed to be assured of that.

It was her chance to say, no, the moment she finished
the mosaic she would leave. Or turn around right now and
walk away.

Lally couldn't do it.

She couldn't find it inside herself to lose any of the
time she had left here, no matter what. Even though that
probably made her a masochist. 'Yes. I'm here to take
care of housekeeping duties, build the pebble mosaic and
anything else that's required for your book research or
your phone messages. You don't need to sacrifice time
to help me with the mosaic. I'll be fine on my own.' She
forced the words out. They had to be said. She would
finish here, leave her gift, but that was all. 'It will be…
better if I just do it.'

Cam's deep green gaze sought her eyes and locked.
Oh, she wanted simply to let all the emotions inside herself loose, throw herself into his arms and hope for some
miracle to make it all somehow work out.

But life wasn't that simple. Cam didn't want her with the kind of feelings she had for him, and if he did she'd have to explain her past—and Lally couldn't face seeing his reaction to that.

'Then I'll spend some time in my office now,' Cam said. 'Do some writing and catch up on my Sydney business interests.'

'That sounds like a good idea.' They'd had one special night. They'd made love. Lally had fallen *in* love with her boss, but that didn't mean he'd suddenly developed the same feelings towards her. Nothing had changed between them other than there was now the awkwardness of knowing what they had shared.

Well, Lally could finish out her time here without letting that history or her current feelings get in the way of doing a good job as his employee.

She could. She *would!* 'I need to get working too. I want to prepare a good meal for tonight, as well as do some preliminary work on the mosaic.' No matter how hard she wanted to work on the mosaic, or how quickly she hoped to get it finished, she did have to make sure that taking care of her boss still came first.

Because Lally was the housekeeper, with a side order of helping him with his book research if required.

And Cameron was the boss. He was a little unconventional in his requirements at times, perhaps, because of his career as an author, but still the boss.

There couldn't be more between them. He hadn't offered more, and she needed to convince herself she didn't want or need more. Life had limits. In the case of 'Lally and Cam,' the limits were that there couldn't *be* a 'them' outside working together for a very temporary amount of time.

* * *

Lally wasn't sure she could lose that much, not yet. She didn't know how she would at all. So for the next five days she focused solely on doing her work on the mosaic and on looking after Cam. Her boss spent long hours in his office in the apartment, working. Sometimes at night she heard him out swimming laps in the pool. She swam, too, but never again at the same time as him.

Lally pushed her emotions down inside her and worked. And, despite doing that, or maybe because of it, the mosaic came together beautifully. When Lally stood back from the work on Friday night and dusted her hands down her legs over the denim cut-offs, she tried to give the mosaic an objective examination. Was it truly good? Or did she just want it to be, and so that was what she saw?

Lally admitted she not only wanted this work to be good, but she *needed* that, as her gift to Cameron. This was the part of herself that she could give to him and that he was prepared to keep. That was how Lally felt.

Oh, God. How could she walk away and leave him? Lally's heart filled with so much love for him in that moment that she hurt.

'It's brilliant.' Cam's quiet words sounded from a few steps behind her, deep words in the most gentle tone of voice, and then he was there. Lally had to do what she could to seem normal to him, while she felt her heart must truly be breaking in two, because she loved him so much. Yes, she could give him this, but she felt as though her one true opportunity to deeply give her love to him had been and gone too quickly.

Words rushed around inside her, came from her heart, filled her mind and had to be stopped before they crossed her tongue.

I don't want to leave you.
I don't know if I can stop loving you.

Can't there be a chance for us? Can't I be someone that you want enough that you overcome your hesitations about commitment? Can I hide my past from you, keep that secret and love you?

Of course that couldn't happen.

Oh, she hated this!

Lally turned slowly and tried simply to appear happy about his compliment, and about a job that he seemed to feel was well done. 'Thank you. I only finished it minutes ago. I was looking at it, trying to be objective. You're truly satisfied with it?'

His gaze shifted from the mosaic to her face. 'You've done an amazing job. You have true artistic talent, Lally. I think, if you wanted, you could do mosaics for a living.'

'Thank you.' Lally prayed that all her feelings weren't written across her face and tried to give him a simple, ordinary smile. If it was a little wobbly around its edges, she couldn't help that. 'I think the results work. The water feature is great; your site boss really came through with sourcing that.'

Cam's face relaxed into something close to a smile. 'He's a good site boss. I'd use him again any time. I didn't have the successful bid on the other property here in the city, but if anything else came up...'

'I imagine he'd be very happy to hear you'd use him again.' What if Cam told her that was enough now and let her go?

Suddenly Lally had her family on her mind. All the aunts, uncles, cousins, her sisters, brothers and parents. She'd missed them, and had worried, had wanted to get back to working with them. Yet now...

'It's a weird thing to ask, but I'm hoping I can talk you into going out for a fast-food meal instead of making dinner tonight.' He hesitated. 'You've worked really hard.

We could go to a restaurant, of course, it's just—would you come out for a hamburger? If you're in the mood for that kind of food.'

'You don't have to reward me.' She didn't want him to feel that he needed to do that. 'I loved doing the mosaic. It made me happy to do that for you.'

Cam's face softened.

She wanted to believe it softened with love towards her, but he was just showing appreciation.

And yet, he pushed his hands into the pockets of his jeans and came close to shuffling his feet before he glanced up at her through the screen of his lashes. 'Will you come and eat salty junk-food with me—hamburger and fries? And maybe a completely nutrition-empty fizzy drink to go with them? Just…do that?' Not for a reward, just to do it.

'I will.' The words escaped her before she had any chance of recalling them.

Lally admitted she didn't want to take the words back.

If Cam wanted her company for an hour to go and eat fast food, she decided she would give herself that. There wouldn't be many more memories; maybe she should take them where she could find them.

'Good. That's good.' Cam took his hands out of his pockets and half-turned before he swung back to her. 'Half an hour? Time for you to shower off the dirt?'

'Yes.' She started towards their apartment.

His apartment, she corrected, in which she was a temporary, employed guest.

CHAPTER FOURTEEN

CAM stood in the centre of the living room, waiting for Lally. He didn't fully understand his edginess. No; that wasn't right. Cam knew the source of his inner upheaval. He'd been this way since he and Lally had returned from their trip to collect pebbles. He'd been edgy since they'd made love.

They'd both acknowledged they couldn't go there again, and Cam didn't need to know Lally's reasons for that. Yet in other things she was such an open girl. And Cam felt the need to understand her depths, even if his own weren't making a lot of sense to him right now.

Did he feel so affected by their love-making because it had followed *sleeping* beside her, sleeping whilst holding her? He'd never *slept* with a woman in his life. Sleep for him, solo, hadn't been a possibility for more than a certain amount of time. Sleeping with a *woman* in his bed? Yet with Lally he had slept, slept longer and better. He'd relaxed with her even in the face of wanting to make love to her.

Then he had made love to her. And now Cam had this urge to make sure she couldn't leave his employment, to find some way to keep her with him. Yet they couldn't remain lovers; it had been a mistake to let things go that way. If she stayed longer than the agreed time frame, was it even possible that they could relax into each other's company in a purely platonic way and be happy simply as boss and employee? As property developer–thriller writer and housekeeper?

Cam's mind told him that when the work on this complex was done—which would only be a few weeks away now—he had to let Lally go, say goodbye, move on with his life and forget her. That would be the smart thing to do.

So why ask her to go out to eat with him?

Because you've been here, and she's been here, and days have passed while you've both tried hard to get on with things, but you've missed her.

'I hope I didn't keep you waiting too long.' Lally spoke in a carefully neutral tone from behind him.

He turned and took her in. For an hour or so there'd be nothing to do but concentrate on each other, and Cam wanted to concentrate on her, and somehow without putting them in a worse place than they were now. He resisted the urge to jam his hand through his hair. Did he truly know what he wanted about anything any more? 'I really do like you in red.' His voice deepened despite himself. 'It's vibrant. It suits you.'

She'd dressed casually in a black skirt with splashes of tiny red flowers over it. The skirt flowed to mid-calf and swirled about her legs when she walked; sandals left her feet beautifully revealed. Her hair was up in a pony-tail, she had gold, dangly earrings in her ears, and she wore a fire-engine red, clingy, sleeveless blouse that showed her slender curves to perfection and accentuated the long lines of her arms and the narrowness of her waist.

Cam's body noted all these things, but it was something a lot deeper than awareness that locked his eyes to hers and made it impossible to look away. Something that came from way deep down inside him and gave him pleasure to see her dressing in a way that allowed all of her vibrancy to shine out.

'You look beautiful.' The words escaped without his control.

Lally's face glowed beneath her tan and she dropped her gaze. 'Thank you. I bought the blouse at a stall at the market a few days ago; I guess it just caught my eye.' She seemed almost surprised by this, or perhaps a little discomfited.

'Bright colours suit you.' He'd told her so before, but this time her gaze rose to his and there were a thousand questions in her eyes.

But she only said, 'Thank you,' and suggested they get going.

Cam took his cue from her and hustled her to his car, and they drove the twenty minutes' drive to the restaurant. 'One of the workers mentioned this place and said the food's good, a cut above the ordinary.' Cam told her the name of the restaurant. Yes, he was making small-talk, but that was a start. If they could relax...

'I've heard of it, but I haven't been there. I think it's a little more ritzy than an average fast-food outlet.' Lally seemed to be trying hard, too, and Cam hoped that she might want this time with him as much as he wanted it with her.

'So long as the food is salty, hot and at least a little bit fatty, I'll be happy.' He forced the words out and worked hard to produce a natural smile. 'There are just days—'

'When you want that kind of food.' Lally smiled a little, and then her smile became genuine.

Cam knew his had too.

Lally glanced again at Cam's face and some of her tension eased away. She didn't understand how she could relax in his company when her heart was aching so much. But she would rather be here with him than anywhere else in the world, and if she could have this, and they could enjoy themselves, well, she wanted it. She was glad he'd asked for this time.

Cam found a parking space and they walked the better part of a block to get to the restaurant.

The place was busy with a good cross-section of patrons; families, singles, people in business wear and tourists were all represented. Lally looked around and acknowledged she was happier in this moment than she'd been for days.

Just a little focused time with him, and she felt this way. Later she might feel twice as bad, but for now Lally was going to take what she could get.

A woman around Lally's age appeared and led them to a table tucked into a corner. She stared at Cam as they were seated, and then said, 'Oh, my God—aren't you Cameron Travers, the crime-thriller writer? I love your books. Oh, would you sign something for me?'

Cam signed the back of one of the paper menus for the woman and smiled her away. The back of his neck was red, and once they were alone he looked at Lally with a slightly trapped expression.

Delight washed through her, and she laughed. 'How often does that happen?'

'Not often, thankfully,' he growled. He lifted the other paper menu from the table and buried his nose in it. 'And we're short a menu now.' Cam lowered the one he held and laid it on the table so they could both look at it.

And, in the face of his discomfort at being recognised as a 'star', Lally relaxed the rest of the way into his company and just let herself enjoy their time together for what it was.

She was tired of trying to work things out in her head
and heart. She loved this man with all her heart; that was
fact. She couldn't avoid it or do anything about it, and
there would be pain when she left him, but she wanted
to try to enjoy her time with him until she had to leave.
Was that so dangerous or foolish or silly? *Probably*.

They ordered the house special of a gourmet hamburger on a sour-dough bread roll baked on the premises
and toasted to perfection, and a basket of fresh-cut chips.
Lally gave up any pretence at being ladylike, picked up
her hamburger in both hands and took a bite.

The tastes exploded on her tongue: the most divine,
melt-in-your-mouth meat patty, crisp, fresh salad greens,
spiced beetroot, succulent tomato, a barbecue sauce and
mayonnaise that were both to die for. She watched Cam's
face across the table as he, too, tried the hamburger.

His smile started in his beautiful green eyes and spread
until it turned up the corners of his mouth. 'Do you think
the trip was worth it?'

'Yes.' She'd have said so anyway for other reasons,
but Lally simply smiled and went on, 'And we haven't
even tried the chips yet.' She reached for the bowl in the
centre of the table at the same time Cam did. Their fingers
brushed, and his stilled where they touched hers.

He lifted his lashes and looked at her, and just for a
brief moment his fingers stroked over hers before he took
a chip, she took one too and they both ate.

'The, um, the chips are great too.' They were a perfect
counter-balance for the delicious hamburger.

Cam reached for another one. 'The menu says they're
oven baked, but they're so good I've decided to forgive
the lack of excess fat.'

Lally licked the taste of salt from her lips and laughed,
and a little silence fell as they paid attention to their food.

It wasn't a bad silence but rather a comfortable one. Lally soaked it up with all her heart, studied each nuance of expression as it crossed his face and refused to think about any moment but right now.

The end of their meal coincided with the people at the table beside theirs receiving their desserts. Lally cast one longing glance in that direction before she shook her head.

Her boss gestured to the menu. 'We can take a selection of desserts home for later, if you'd like?'

It was a small thing, but that thoughtfulness made Lally feel treasured. Or was it the soft expression in his eyes as he waited for her response? Oh, why couldn't they?

'I'm tempted, but I don't think I'll be able to eat a thing until tomorrow.' She pushed the thoughts away. 'Thanks for the offer, though.'

Cam settled their bill and minutes later they stepped out onto the busy street and strolled back towards his parked car.

He turned to her as they reached it. 'Thank you for doing that with me tonight.'

'Thank you for asking me to come along.' Lally sought for something light to say. 'Maybe you'll be able to use that in your book somehow too.'

Her boss thought for a moment. 'There are possibilities: the scent of fries leads my super sleuth to his answers…'

They were still laughing about it when Cam unlocked the car. Lally stepped towards the kerb and glanced up as a woman's voice penetrated her thoughts.

'We'll go to look at the sports store, Danny. We just don't want to walk that far. Going in the car will be best.'

A man's voice joined in. 'I'll buy us all an ice cream after the sports store, so don't hassle your mum, okay?'

'Sorry, Mum.' A teenaged voice went on with a hint of cheeky cheerfulness, 'You know I love ya, even when I whinge.'

General laughter followed this comment.

Lally knew that female voice. It wasn't one she would ever be able to forget. Memories and guilt, so many things, hit her at once; at the depths of them was remorse. She didn't want to look, but she had to see. Her head turned, and her gaze shifted over the small group of people preparing to get into the car behind Cam's convertible.

The man looked about forty. There were three boys ranging in age; Lally didn't know the exact ages, but the youngest had been under two years old back then. They all looked a lot like Sam; Lally noted that as she searched their young faces, searched all over each of them for signs.

And the woman was Julie Delahunty. Here. Right now. With all three of her sons. The group looked like a family, comfortable with each other. Happy.

In that moment, Julie looked up, recognised Lally, and her mouth pinched into a tight line while her face leached of every bit of colour. Her hands reached for the boys nearest to her, as though she needed to physically stop them from being taken from her side.

I am so sorry.

The thoughts were trapped inside Lally's mind, trapped deep in her heart. She'd written them to Julie long ago; her counsellor had helped her to get them sent to Julie at the care residence. There'd never been a reply; Lally hadn't expected one. But something in the expression on Julie's face now told her she'd received and read the words. So at least she did know of Lally's regret.

It doesn't change anything, Lally!

And it didn't.

Lally's hand rose, palm up, in a silent expression of supplication. Her mouth worked, though no words came out. Guilt and remorse ached in her heart.

Cam's voice impinged. 'Lally? Sweetheart? What is it?'

She felt the touch of his hand on her arm, his fingers closing around her wrist in a gentle clasp as his body turned to hers, as though he would shield her from whatever harm was trying to befall her.

In all that had happened between Lally and Cam, she'd managed to push this part of her history mostly away. She hadn't let herself look at this, admit this, acknowledge how it stood between her and certain possibilities in life. Happiness; she didn't deserve happiness. Lally didn't see how that could ever change.

The woman hustled her sons into the car. The man spoke to her in a low voice, glanced in Lally's direction, and his mouth tightened too.

Lally wanted to turn, hide her face in Cam's chest and just will it all away. Shame stopped that thought before it fully formed. Lally had longed to be able to love Cam and have him love her back—oh, she admitted this—but how could she ever have hoped for that?

If Cam knew.

The family drove off into traffic. At least they were gone. There were other impressions from these moments trying to register, but Lally couldn't see past Julie's stricken face, her hands reaching for her sons.

Lally let Cam put her into the passenger seat and they too headed into traffic in the other direction, heading for…

Not home. Heading for Cam's property development.

'Who were they, Lally?' Cam's words were stern in a way she'd never heard from him before. 'It's clear that seeing those people has hugely upset you. I want—I *need* to know why. If you're in trouble, I'll help you, protect you.'

'Her name is Julie Delahunty.' Lally did not want to speak of this, but she couldn't leave Cam worrying for her sake.

She would tell him the same part of this that she had told her family. Lally's voice was a flat monotone as she said, 'I had an affair with her husband six years ago. Julie's three sons were smaller then, still very dependent on their parents, obviously.'

Dependent. 'When Julie found out about the affair and became…unwell over it, Sam, he walked away. He didn't care about her or his sons.' Sam hadn't cared about Lally, either, but that paled in comparison. Lally clamped her lips together. She'd already said more than she had wanted to.

She'd put the words to Cam more revealingly than the cold, minimal facts she had told her family six years ago.

Cam's hands remained relaxed on the steering wheel and his gaze was clear and steady as he cast a quick glance her way before turning his attention back to the road.

Lally saw his compassion, but he took care not to show pity or judgement.

He asked quietly, 'And the gentlemen with her just now wasn't her husband?'

'No. I don't know who he was.' Lally dredged her mind for a way to end this conversation. 'Please, Cam.'

What did he think of her, now that he knew she'd had an affair?

It didn't matter to Lally. There was no hope for her

with him. This had just underlined that fact for her. The rest was irrelevant.

'I love my family.' The words were jerky; they exposed her, came out as long-buried guilt and pain forced their way past her control and reserve. Past six years of silence. 'I've been trying—'

'Ever since to make it up to them?'

Somehow they were inside the apartment, and with the door closed behind them Cam threw his car keys onto the entry table and led her to sit on the sofa in the living room. He clasped her hand in his. Lally didn't deserve his comfort but they were here and he wasn't letting go.

She wanted to run, but a part of her wanted to confess things she'd not confessed, except to that counsellor who hadn't been able to accept, or judge, or punish, or forgive, who had only been able to acknowledge and try to guide Lally so she could fix this for herself.

Fix a guilt and heartbreak that was unfixable. So Lally had buried it deep, and, yes, she had hidden out in her family. She had needed to feel safe.

'Won't you tell me? Maybe I can help somehow.' Cam looked into Lally's beautiful brown eyes, and thoughts and emotions he'd stifled in the days since he'd made love to her bubbled to the surface inside him. 'You've done so much to try to help me.'

This beautiful girl had been punishing herself for so long. That was so clear now. He had half known, had half guessed that already from her silent determination not to get involved with him. He'd guessed it was because of a man somehow, but he hadn't guessed all this guilt.

She'd punished herself by wearing dull coloured clothes. She'd sown herself into serving her family and hadn't wanted to step outside of working among them. Lally had hidden herself because of guilt.

Within her family, she had maybe even tried to work off what she perceived as her sin by giving, giving and giving to them. Was Lally seeing her past in a genuine light? Or was it coloured, *mis*-coloured, by a young girl's memories and guilt that had never been resolved?

'How old are you now, Lally?' He asked the question in a calm tone while his fingers stroked over the back of her hand.

She'd relaxed that hand into his clasp, though he wasn't sure if she realised she had done that, trusting him with that much of herself. Cam wanted to help her, but he also wanted her to trust him with so much more. The thought drew his eyebrows together but he didn't get a chance to examine it before Lally answered his question.

'I'm twenty-four.' Her brown eyes shimmered with regrets and hurt. 'It was in my CV.'

'Yes. So you're twenty-four now.' Cam pressed on, 'That means you were eighteen when you were seeing that woman's husband—Julie, was it? And how old was he?'

'He was ten years older.' Lally bit her lip. 'I knew it wasn't a good idea to see someone that much older.'

A part of Cam wanted to go and find the other man and make *him* take responsibility for hurting the young girl Lally must have been then. He bit back that impulse and went on, 'Did you know he was married?'

Brown eyes met his gaze. 'No. I didn't know he was married.' She bit her lip.

And Cam said softly, 'What happened?'

She drew a deep breath and the words slowly came out. 'He swept me off my feet. He flattered me, said he loved the way I dressed in my bright colours, loved my vibrancy. Sometimes, when I've thought about it...' She stopped and swallowed hard, shook her head.

'You were very young, and you were preyed on by a man who must have known better.'

That's not your fault, Lally. Let yourself accept these facts and find the forgiveness you've been dodging all this time.

Lally's fingers gripped his as she went on. 'My family said it wasn't my fault. But they didn't know—I talked to a counsellor after it happened. I didn't need to say more to the family. It wasn't necessary.' Lally fell abruptly silent.

'It wasn't your fault, Lally.' He squeezed her hand. 'I'm guessing you've blamed yourself, perhaps, for his marriage breaking down?' It wasn't hard to work that out. 'You shouldn't. It was *his* behaviour that caused the breakdown of his marriage.'

'You don't understand.' Lally shook her head. Her tone became tortured. 'When she found out, his wife had a breakdown. Sam just walked away from all of it. Julie got put into a care facility and her sons were placed into foster care.'

She drew a shaky breath. 'I couldn't help. I broke up an entire family, harmed innocent children, made Julie so unhappy that she lost her grip on...'

And there it was; all of Lally's guilt was finally out there. Cam felt absolutely ferocious in that moment, ferocious in his need to protect her, to reverse time, to take this pain away for her. He needed to heal her as she had tried so hard to help him heal his insomnia, and help him in so many other ways.

Tenderness welled up with that protectiveness, soft emotions he couldn't name but had to act on.

'She was with her sons today,' he said carefully. 'That looked like a permanent arrangement. They looked like well-adjusted, typical boys for their ages, and she looked happy in her role as their mother, with a man who appeared to be her current partner.'

'Yes.' Lally frowned. 'She looked well and happy...at least, until she noticed me.'

'You can't change the past.' Cam said it in acknowledgement. 'But you're not to blame for it, Lally. So be glad that you saw her today, that you know she is well now and has her children with her. Let it go now so you can move on with your life.'

Lally searched Cam's eyes and couldn't believe that she had told him all of this. She felt lighter, somehow. Not suddenly all better, but Cam had accepted it. He hadn't judged her. 'How can you not think badly of me?' That was what Lally couldn't understand. She was happy that Julie's life seemed better now, but that still didn't change the past.

And, whatever Cam thought about this, it didn't change the fact that he didn't *love* her. He was kind, thoughtful, accepting. But he didn't love her. So what had changed, really?

'I need to get an early night.' Lally hit the end of her ability to cope, to think. To do anything. She just needed to get away. 'Thank—thank you for tonight, for the meal and for...this. But will you excuse me?'

Somehow she was on her feet and her hand was back in her possession, and Lally didn't wait to see what would happen after that. There was nothing that could happen. Because she and Cam didn't exist. They just didn't, and that was that.

CHAPTER FIFTEEN

'THANK you again for meeting me here. I realise I'm stepping over a line, but I hope you can understand why. You
need to talk to your daughter, help her get this out so
she can stop punishing herself.' Cameron's voice came
to Lally clearly as she stepped around a corner stall at
the market.

Two days had passed since they'd come across Sam's
ex-wife and her new family, since Lally had admitted her
guilt to Cam. She'd been silent, withdrawn, thinking about
his words. But what difference did it make in the end?

'I should have guessed there might be more to this.'
Mum's voice choked up. 'I feel just awful. We all thought
Lally just needed a little push to get her to trust in life
again, so we pretended no one needed her help right now.'
Mum drew a sharp breath. 'All we did was take away the
sense of safety that she needed. When that affair happened, we wished we'd understood things sooner so we
could have protected her from Sam Delahunty. We all felt
we'd let her down. We didn't know about…the rest.'

Shock drove Lally forward. She stepped into their path.
There was Cam, and there was Mum; Mum saw her and
handed a bag of something to Cam. Lally was in Mum's
arms, throttling back emotion because she didn't want to
cry in front of him.

'Oh, Lally, I'm so sorry.' Mum's touch went straight into Lally's heart to wrap around a part of her that she hadn't realised was so broken. It didn't matter then that Cam appeared to have sought Mum out, or that they'd been discussing personal things about her.

Lally buried her face in Mum's neck and breathed in deep, and they stayed like that for a long minute.

Finally Mum stepped back and held her at arm's length so she could look deep into her eyes, brown eyes to brown eyes, filled with so much love. 'I should have talked to you about it more, Lally. I didn't realise…'

'I shouldn't have held onto the guilt the way I did.' Lally finally accepted that now. She hadn't meant any of Julie's hurt or the hurt of her sons. She had been tricked and she had made mistakes, but she hadn't done anything out of malice, lack of care or anything else like that. She could never have guessed what would happen.

'I can't regret that I spoke about this, Lally.' Cam's words were low and careful. 'I thought your mother needed to know.'

And she did. Lally's gaze shifted from Mum's face to Cam's, where he stood silently beside them.

Cam gripped the bag Mum had given him in tight fingers and used his other hand to rub at the back of his neck. 'Me meeting your Mum this morning—I got her phone number out of the book. She brought painting materials. One of your aunts is being pushy about you painting again, apparently.'

He shook his head. 'What am I talking about? That can wait.' Cam seemed at a loss as to how to go on.

Lally's heart melted all over the place because, whatever else there was, his care was so clear.

Lally looked deep into Cam's eyes and he looked just as deeply back. How did she respond to his kindness, to this thing he had done for her sake? How did she deal with all the feelings and emotions whirling about inside her right now? Feelings about Sam, Julie and the three boys, yes—but even more deeply about Cameron. Somehow, it was a big tangle. Lally had to figure out how to unravel it, if she could, or perhaps how to weave it together within herself. To weave her past in, and let it be part of her, but the right kind of part.

That wouldn't make a difference with Cameron; of course it couldn't. He didn't love her the way she loved him. He was wonderful and special, but she mustn't kid herself that his kindness meant he had very special feelings towards her.

But if she could convince him that he could commit? That his insomnia didn't need to get in the way of a relationship for him? That his past failure in a relationship didn't have to mean his next attempt would fail, that he, too, could address his past? That it was okay to acknowledge that his mother hadn't cared well for him and he wasn't obliged to feel close to her? If only Lally could help Cam see all his value purely for who he was. What was she thinking? None of it made any difference to *her* limitations.

'Lally, darling.' Mum touched her arm gently and released her. 'We do need to talk, but I'm guessing maybe that needs to wait a little.' Though she didn't glance in Cam's direction, Mum's eyes were full of far too much understanding, *Love* and understanding, that had always been there.

Mum started to turn away, and Lally uttered, 'We *will* talk, Mum. I'd like that. And I want to be taught painting.'

'I'm so glad, Lally. It's your tradition. It will be good for you to try it. I love you, Lally.' Emotion filled Mum's face. She gave a nod and a wobbly smile and disappeared, and Lally turned back to Cam. There were a thousand things she wanted to say; Lally couldn't find the words for any of them, and she said lamely, 'I saw your note that said you'd come to the market and would take care of the shopping.'

Lally had come to join him on the very thin pretext of helping. Even though she'd been withdrawn and hadn't wanted to talk about her past any further with him for the last couple of days, she had longed to be close to him, just *be* with him, in his company. Or something.

'I took care of the shopping.' He indicated the bag at his feet, and as he did so placed the bag her mother had handed to him inside it as well. 'Are you angry, Lally?' His gaze searched hers. 'That I interfered? After we talked, I…didn't feel that I'd fully helped you to let go of all that blame you'd been carrying. I thought maybe your mother could.'

Cam searched Lally's dear face as he waited for her answer, and he finally understood.

He had fallen in love with Lally. It was so simple, really; he didn't know how he could have missed it. He couldn't miss it now because it consumed him. He had a need that was all about her, all about needing to love her, care for her, help her resolve her problems and hurts, be there for her, protect her, encourage her.

Where could he go with these feelings?

'I'm not upset, not really. You wanted to help me.' Lally started to turn. In a moment she'd walk back to the property development.

'Please.' Cam didn't want to lose these quiet moments with her, not yet. He didn't know what he wanted to do, or say… 'Would you come to the park with me? It's not far from here, not far out of our way.'

'I guess that would be okay.' Lally didn't understand Cam's motivation.

She should give him her resignation and leave before this got any more complicated.

The smart, sensible, take-care-of-yourself part of her suggested that would be the thing to do.

But Lally had been running and backing away and not addressing things for long enough. If Cam wanted to go to the park, they would go to the park.

She walked silently at his side until they entered the park. Cam kept walking and Lally wondered if he would ever speak, and if he did what he would want to say. Lally had things to say. 'You said you'd had a failed relationship—in your past. That sounds as though *you* feel to blame for *that*.'

'I did. I'll explain.' Cam took Lally to the makeshift jetty. There was no little boat this morning, just the lake and quietness. He set down the bag. He'd taken the time during their walk here to try to marshal his thoughts into some kind of order; he wasn't sure if he'd achieved that. 'I'll come back to that.'

All he knew was he needed to express these feelings that were inside him. He needed Lally so much that he couldn't make himself step aside, not if there was any chance that they could find a way.

'I remember you interviewing me on the water. I was nervous that morning.'

'I'm nervous now.' He held her arm while she sat on the edge of the jetty. The jetty stuck out far enough over the water at the end that they could sit without their feet touching the water. Cam sat beside her and turned to face her. So much love welled up inside him. He didn't know what to do with all the feelings.

'Why would you be nervous?' Lally asked and shook

her head. 'I'm the one with the horrible past and six years of going around with my head in the sand not dealing with it. I'm glad Mum knows it all now. Somehow that's a weight off my mind. I didn't want to hide it from my family, but I did, and then it felt too hard to try to tell them.'

Lally loved him for his admission of nerves. 'When I talk to Mum, maybe she might be able to help me work out a…healing process.' She dipped her head before she forced it up again. 'You might think it's silly, but there are spiritual things Mum could help me do.'

'I think that's a great idea.' Cam didn't even blink, simply gave his support.

Her expression softened as she searched his gaze. '*Your* mother might be still on the face of the earth, but she doesn't keep contact and closeness with you the way she should. I'm sorry you've missed out on that all your life.'

'You said something a while back about us moving around so much that I must have not known where I'd wake up half the time.' Cam had pushed the comment aside at the time. Maybe it had been easier to go on blaming his insomnia just being how it was.

'It's so long ago, but I developed a fear of sleeping back then. I used to be afraid that I'd wake up and Mum would have abandoned me somewhere and gone on without me.' He shook his head. 'It sounds stupid now. I've been a grown man and in charge of myself for a long time. I never thought about it until after that night that I…slept with you.'

'You trained yourself into a habit of not sleeping, and until you figured that out about yourself…'

'I had no hope at all of sleeping and feeling relaxed unless I felt deeply happy and secure.' As he had felt the night he'd held Lally in his arms and had drifted to sleep to the kittenlike sounds she'd made while she slept. Was it any wonder he'd woken and needed to express all his feelings to her the way he had? 'You gave me that feeling, and so much more.'

The sleep didn't even matter, and Cam needed to tell her that. 'I'm not doing a very good job of expressing myself. I don't need to get some instant or fabulous fix for my sleep issues. If I can go back for some further professional guidance about that, get in a better place with that now that I've realised that childhood fears have most likely contributed to the problem, that will be great—but if not...'

He drew a breath. 'I don't think I have to let that issue, or the hours that I work, or the way I was raised and my lack of closeness with my mother, stop me from trying to make a success of a relationship that matters to me.' He swallowed. 'Where there's a deep enough love, can't most things be figured out?'

He searched her eyes, and he wasn't sure what he saw there. Was it kindness that made her eyes shine in that way? Cam wanted her to let him in to her heart.

He took Lally's hands in his and gently squeezed her fingers. 'I thought I couldn't be in a relationship. I blamed that on the insomnia, my workaholic tendencies. What would I have to offer a woman? That's what I asked myself. I failed once, but I've realised now that I didn't love Gillian.' He drew a breath. 'I doubt she really loved me.' That didn't matter anyway, now.

'I've fallen in love with you, Lally. You're so deep in my heart and I can't bear the thought of you leaving me. I'd been wracking my brains for ways to keep you with me. I thought of asking you to be my travelling housekeeper, to go everywhere with me. But I don't want only that. I want *all* of you.' That was Cam's admission, and what he needed to say.

'I don't understand.' Lally wanted to comprehend this—her heart begged for that—but how? 'You know about my past.'

'And you know about mine. I want a chance for both of us to reach out and be happy. Past histories—they are *in* the past, Lally. They can make us stronger and better. They don't have to hold us down or hold us back.'

Cam had realised this; he needed Lally to see it too.

Lally looked at Cam. He wanted her to be happy with him? He'd said he loved her? Lally took the wondrous thought deep inside herself. Could it be true? It could, because Cam wouldn't say that if he didn't mean it.

The knowledge finally penetrated all the way to Lally's heart. Hope rose there. She looked into Cam's eyes and knew she had to fully open her heart. 'I'm in love with you too. It happened the night we made love. I didn't understand then, but I realised later, and I didn't know how to deal with my feelings. I was certain you wouldn't be able to feel the same way towards me.'

'You love me?' Cam uttered, and his hands tightened, one around her hand, the other over her shoulder. The next moment she was snatched against his chest and his arms were against her back, his hands pressing into her shoulder blades before he reached very, very gently and raised her face so he could look into her eyes. 'Say that again.'

'I love you.' Lally did, and it felt so good to admit it and to realise that he loved her too.

'Do you truly believe we can have a future?' Dared she ask?

But, yes, Lally did dare ask because she longed for, wanted and *needed* a future with Cam. If there was any chance of that, she wanted to grasp it. For the first time in six years, she felt hope.

'Yes. Yes, Lally,' he uttered in the deepest, most sincere voice Lally had ever heard. 'I want for ever with you, and we can have it if we both try.'

Lally slowly nodded. 'If we love and accept. I would understand about your wakefulness, Cam, even if it never got any better. And your need to focus on your writing while your muse is willing to talk.'

Cam laughed and shook his head. 'I still have a deadline, but I must admit writing hasn't been my first priority since the night we made love. I've kept working, but all I've really wanted to think about is you.'

He drew a breath. 'Because that old relationship fell apart, and Gillian said she couldn't cope with my work focus and sleeplessness, I thought I didn't have enough to give. And I'm *not* close to Mum. You have a big family. I don't know if I could fit in.'

Lally searched Cam's face once more and knew his concerns were genuine. She smiled gently. 'You seem to get along okay with Mum.'

He nodded. 'Your mother is a kind, giving, lovely person…just like you.'

Oh, his words went straight to Lally's heart and found their way deep inside it. She let a teasing edge touch her smile as she responded, 'So just multiply Mum by about a hundred and you have my family. Since you're a rather great person to get along with yourself, I think you would be fine fitting in.'

It hit her then just how deep this conversation had gone. They were talking about 'for ever' kinds of things. Did Cam want…?

'I'd like to be part of your big family.' Cam's expression sobered into a deep, open love, into hope and need.

'And I would like to have babies with you, make our own special family, when we're ready for that step.'

In that moment, Lally gave herself utterly to this man who had been her boss, her lover, a friend and would now become everything to her. The thought of having his child overwhelmed her, filled her heart with a love she couldn't begin to comprehend.

Lally buried her face against Cam's chest and let her fingers rest over his heart. The brush of his mouth against her forehead made her lift her face, and he kissed her lips softly and drew back to look into her eyes.

'Will you marry me, Lally? Let me hold you in my arms at night, love you, be with you whether I sleep at your side or stay awake, and be happy because I'm with you?' He hesitated. 'I don't know if I can settle in one place. It's not something I've tried, but this property development—I thought from the day I met you that it would make a good family home, so maybe we could try...'

'Yes.' Yes to all of it, including trying. 'We can work those things out. We'll both need to adapt and understand what we want out of life together.' Lally would go anywhere with him. In her heart, she knew that, though it would be nice to be close to her family when possible.

'I won't take you from them, Lally.' He said it gently and she knew he'd read her emotions on her face.

Lally was just fine with Cam knowing her feelings so well. 'If we travel, we can still come home here to the family, if you don't need to be based in Sydney for your business.'

'I've become quite adroit at running that business from afar. There's no reason why I can't continue to do so.' Cam smiled and hugged her. 'I will love your family, but I'll love you most of all. We can have this, Lally. We can go forward.'

She nodded. 'Let our pasts be what have formed us to this point, but we'll form our futures with each other.'

'Yes.' Cam's voice deepened. 'Yes, Lally.'

And there, on a makeshift jetty at the edge of a small lake in a suburban park, Cam proceeded to tell Lally about all the hope that was in his heart for their 'for ever.'

And Lally soaked up every word while the sun rose over the lake and sent vibrant sparkles of colour shining through the mist.

After a long moment, Cam said, 'I can't wait to marry you, to see you walk towards me on that special day and know you're going to be truly and completely mine to love and care for always.'

'Oh, I can't wait for that either.' Lally's heart filled with love for him.

His arms closed about her, and he turned her face up and kissed her mouth gently. 'Our future starts right now. I want you in all of my life, Lally. Everything. I want you to learn to paint from your mother, or whoever else in your family will teach you. And I want to encourage you with more mosaic work.'

Lally's heart filled all over again with love for this wonderful man. 'We can travel all over Australia for a while leaving a trail of property developments with pebble mosaics in their courtyards if we want to.'

Cam's gaze met hers, with all his heart right there for her to see. 'So long as we keep coming home to *this* property, and settle here eventually. There'll be room for visits from all your relatives, and my mum, if I can ever convince her to stop by.'

'Maybe one day we will convince her.' In this moment, Lally believed that anything might be possible.

Home, happiness, family and a future. And, though they did travel, that was exactly how it turned out to be.

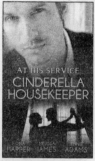

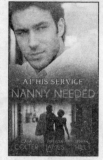

Special Offers

Every month we put together collections and longer reads written by your favourite authors.

Here are some of next month's highlights— and don't miss our fabulous discount online!

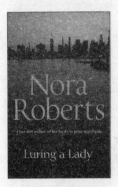

On sale 3rd August

On sale 3rd August

On sale 3rd August

Save 20% on all Special Releases

The World of Mills & Boon®

There's a Mills & Boon® series that's perfect for you. We publish ten series and, with new titles every month, you never have to wait long for your favourite to come along.

Blaze®

Scorching hot, sexy reads
4 new stories every month

By Request

Relive the romance with the best of the best
9 new stories every month

Cherish™

Romance to melt the heart every time
12 new stories every month

Desire™

Passionate and dramatic love stories
8 new stories every month

Have Your Say

You've just finished your book.
So what did you think?

We'd love to hear your thoughts on our
'Have your say' online panel
www.millsandboon.co.uk/haveyoursay

- 🌹 Easy to use
- 🌹 Short questionnaire
- 🌹 Chance to win Mills & Boon®
  goodies